CAPTIVE INNOCENCE

Fern Michaels

G.K.HALL & CO.
Boston, Massachusetts
1991

Published in Large Print by arrangement with
Ballantine Books, a division of
Random House, Inc.

G. K. Hall Large Print Book Series.

Set in 16 pt. Plantin.

Library of Congress Cataloging-in-Publication Data

Michaels, Fern.
Captive innocence / Fern Michaels.
    p. cm.
  ISBN 0-8161-5122-9 (large print)
  1. Large type books. I. Title.
[PS3563.I27C37 1991]
813'.54—dc20   90-45900

Prologue

He listened for the sound of her footsteps padding quietly across the Persian carpet. His senses were alert, sensitively attuned, every nerve in his body vibrating erotically with anticipation. Soon, he told himself, she would come to him. He would be aware of her heady perfume as she entered the room, he would feel the motion of air as it glided across her naked body before she slid into bed beside him. His arms ached to hold her, his mouth was greedy for hers.

The door on the far side of the room opened, allowing a brighter shaft of light to pierce the dimness inside. The gaslights had been turned low, the way she liked them, the way he liked them. She never wanted to make love in the dark. "I want to see you," she would complain, murmuring low, in the sensual voice he loved. "I want to look at you. . . ."

No more than he loved seeing her, looking at her, expecting and cherishing the pleasure he saw in her eyes and the slight tilt of satisfaction near the corners of her mouth.

She stood in the shaft of light, knowing it outlined her splendid body, allowing it to bathe her silhouette and lend its radiance to her every movement. Her dressing gown was of gossamer silk, red and vibrant, bringing out the soft gold tones of her skin, buffing it to the sleekness of satin. Her long wealth of golden hair hung about her shoulders and over one breast, making her appear virginal, innocently modest, belying the message he read in her eyes.

As she approached the high tester bed, moving toward him, his heart seemed to stop in his chest. She was beautiful, his little lioness, desirable and untamed. He was as attracted to her mind as he was to her body; the combined effect on his senses was devastating. Each curve, each line seemed edged in flame. She was his, this golden woman, only his. The perfection of her thrusting breasts, the full and glorious hips tapering into lean, strong thighs that protected the very center of her being were his alone for the taking.

With an elegant gesture that was far more sensual than innocent, she shrugged off the vibrant crimson dressing gown, standing silently still for a moment, allowing her eyes to follow his muscular torso upward to his magnificent panther's head. Love spoke from his eyes; desire pulsated through her body, communicating with his own hungers and needs. And when she threw back the blanket, uncovering him, her frank and guileless gaze was sassily directed to a place beneath his flat belly. Seeing the evidence of his desires, she smiled, brash and bold, confident of her effect on him, quivering in anticipation of the touch of his body to hers.

The bedding moved beneath her slight weight, and yet he knew her to be full bodied and not lacking any of the softness and alluring curves that bewitched a man, despite her petiteness and delicate frame.

The scent of her aroused his awareness, the sound of her skin sliding against the sheets, like silk on silk, brought a stab of barely controlled lust. He loved this woman, he wanted her, as he had for a thousand times in the past and would for uncountable times in their future. She was his golden girl, his woman of indefinable mystery, the perfect balance of mind and beauty.

With a tenderness born of love, he reached for her, bringing her hard against him, feeling the growing fever enflame him, cautiously placing a guarded check on his overpowering need to throw her on her back, to have her, to lose himself in her. His hands smoothed over her delicately skinned breasts, reveling in their weight and fullness, gliding down to her slim waist and her velvet haunches, permitting himself a long and sensual kiss on the fleecy triangle her nudity offered.

Hungry lips devoured her, satisfying his passion for her beauty, finding details and perfections that were like a potent wine to his sensibilities. The sleekness and length of her thighs, the flatness of her belly, the elegant length of her legs, and always he returned to her mouth, her wonderful, giving, yielding mouth, that spoke of its own greedy hungers and appetites. His attentions strayed and lingered on her breasts, delighting in the hard nubs of their rosy crests that offered their own silent provocative appeal.

Royall's body sang a siren's song, alluring, seductive, calling through the dimness to an answering need in him. She writhed beneath his touch, loving it, needing it, crazed with the desire to offer herself completely to the explorations of his fingers and lips.

Sebastian, loving this need and madness in her, advanced further in his caresses, spurred by his thirst for her endless beauty, teasing, stirring, touching, and at last offering the ultimate caress of his lips on the place that held such attraction for him.

Their passions were equal, joyously met.

Her fingers played in his hair, brushing it back from his brow, exposing it to her lips. She kissed him lightly on the lips, tasting herself there, straining toward him, her body rising and falling with the tides of passion that demanded obedience to the desire to culminate their love.

Determined hands pressed him against the pillows. His breath came in hard, short gasps of expectation. Her full breasts pressed against his chest, their tips burying themselves against the erotically crisp furring that marked its broad expanse. She knew her power over him and yielded to his mastery over her. Beneath her fingers his skin glistened moistly, and the long, masculinely hard length of him consoled her yearning need for him.

Her lips tasted every nuance of his physique,

and her fingers touched the familiar yet never less exciting ripples and muscular smoothness of his adored body. Licking and teasing kisses at the hollow in his throat evoked a low, throbbing groan of sheer pleasure and delight. She brought his face to the ripe plenitude of her firm breasts, feeling him inhale their fragrance, reveling in the teasing torments of his mouth, surrendering to the reach and height of desires that his kiss brought her.

The contact between them was smooth, artful, deliberately paced and yet abandoned. He came alive beneath her fingers and his desires throbbed between them, igniting her to a burning flame whose only purpose of existence was to bring warmth and comfort to the man she loved. And within the fires of her own passions, she knew she would be consumed and rekindled time and again, until her satisfactions became ashes from which a renewed desire would rise like the legendary phoenix to take her into flight and carry her beyond the limits of the flesh. And her flight was not a lonely one; beside her, a part of herself, he would be with her, touching, adoring, loving.

She cried out his name, arching her body to receive him, her fingers digging into his hard muscles as she held him fiercely. She tumbled skyward, bringing him with her, becoming a part of a rushing wind that scoured the heavens and purified lust into a sacrament of love. "Sebastian," she whispered, answering his response, and she knew that the only name she knew or would ever need to know was his.

He held her in his arms, cherishing the contact between them, soothing her into a blissful sleep. Tiny, barely perceived touches of her lips caressed his chest. Even in sleep she loved him, his golden girl. His arm tightened, bringing her closer. And he loved her. Always, he loved her. And he marveled at the fates that had brought her to him to soothe the aching within him, the loneliness that only she could fill.

Chapter One

Words and foreign phrases rioted through her head. Belém. Rio de Janeiro. Impressions of a world far from the one she knew. Sparkling opalescent waters of Guanabara Bay stretching across the Tropic of Capricorn. Names and places on a map—places she never dreamed she would see. Sun. Heat. Throngs of people, darker skinned, wearing brighter colors. A people of the tropics in this land south of the Equator where unfamiliar languages were spoken. This land called Brazil.

A thrill of anticipation tingled Royall Banner's spine as she watched the natives of Rio de Janeiro ready the streets for Mardi Gras. It seemed so strange to be here, on the other side of the world from her native New England, where dark skin was more familiar than white, where colorful dresses and bare feet were the norm. Royall's amber-gold gaze peered through sooty black lashes, preserving the memory of her first day in Brazil's seaport city.

"This must seem like a fairy story to you, Royall," her companion, Rosalie Quince, smiled. "Traveling by ship to a tropical city south of the Equator, seeing things that you'd only read about in books. I grant you, Rio is a far cry from Bos-

1

ton." The older woman's bright eyes took on a gleam as Royall's infectious excitement made her remember her own experiences at Mardi Gras. She sighed. That was so long ago—when she herself was a lovely young woman like Royall. When her own complexion would flush to pink, and her own eyes couldn't see enough. Where had those days gone? "It's a pity we can't stay for the celebrations, but we must leave on the boat that will take us to Belém and then by paddlewheeler up the Amazon to the plantations."

Royall nodded her bright golden head, her amber eyes never leaving the far side of the cobbled street where vendors were preparing their stalls and arranging their merchandise of huge paper flowers and glittering sequined masks. From the distance came the beat of drums and the sound of musicians tuning their instruments. Tonight there would be music, dancing, revelry, the last celebration before the start of Lent. Shrove Tuesday, Mrs. Quince had called it. Tomorrow would be Ash Wednesday, when the predominantly Catholic population would flock to church where a priest would smudge their foreheads with holy ashes and intone the message, "ashes to ashes, dust to dust"—a reminder of man's mortality.

A frown etched itself between Rosalie Quince's sparse brows. She sensed in Royall a desperate need to join the revelry, to tap her feet to the music and dance in the streets. Scandalous behavior, since Royall was still in her period of mourning—highly improper for a widow whose

2

husband had been buried less than a year before. And it was unheard of to wear a carrot-colored silk dress while still in mourning. The frown etched deeper. Royall said she had done her grieving at the gravesite and left it there in the clammy dampness. This was a new life, and she wouldn't be bogged down with heavy black bombazine. Rosalie Quince had never truly seen the imp of devilishness in anyone's eyes in all her fifty-two years, but the unmistakable gleam in Royall Banner's eyes clearly stated that she meant to get on with her life and enjoy it.

Royall whirled around suddenly and exuberantly threw her arms around Mrs. Quince. "This is an adventure, and I don't want to miss a minute of the excitement. I'll stay here and watch the preparations while you go back to the ship and take a nap."

Mrs. Quince was properly horrified at the suggestion. "You'll do no such thing. Whatever would Baron Newsome think of me leaving you to your own devices? Royall, you must come with me," she scolded as she hooked her arm through the younger woman's. "You can watch the activities from the deck of the clipper ship. I take my responsibilities very seriously. This country is a far cry from what you're familiar with in Boston. Now, come along. You'll positively wilt in this heat. We'll have a nice cool drink, and then I'll take my nap." The plump little woman gathered her old-fashioned voluminous skirts in hand and proceeded down the street that would lead them to the wharf.

Royall's back stiffened. It was no different here than back in Boston. Someone was always telling her what to do, how to behave. She was, after all, a responsible woman of twenty-three years, and a widow. She hadn't needed a nanny since she was a little girl and she didn't need one now. Especially a self-appointed nanny like Rosalie Quince, who was determined to perform her Christian duty by playing duenna. What had begun as an adventure to remove herself from the cloying overprotectiveness of friends and family in Boston had ended in her becoming a prisoner of propriety under Mrs. Quince's tutelage.

Matching her steps with Rosalie's, Royall craned her neck to see a group of women with wide, bright-banded skirts and white peasant blouses pulled low over their smooth brown shoulders, cooking chickens over an open fire. Children played nearby, and she saw one little boy get his hand slapped soundly when he attempted to steal a piece of delectably crisp, spicy meat. "Royall, I declare, must you see everything? Come along. This heat has just about done me in."

Royall obeyed, as she had always done. Obeying first her father and then her husband and, most recently, her husband's grown sons and daughters with their narrow-minded New England sensibilities. When, oh when, Royall silently cried, would she be allowed to follow her own instincts and seek her own adventures?

4

What in the name of all that was holy did Rosalie think would happen to her if Royall was out of her sight for a few hours? Was she afraid of Royall being robbed, her money taken? Impossible! The only funds she carried in the little reticule that swung from her arm were small amounts, for shopping and gratuities and perhaps for carriage fare.

A small giggle erupted in Royall's throat, making Rosalie turn and look at her askance. She could just imagine Rosalie having fears that her charge would be kidnapped, sold into slavery, carried off by a dashing dark-haired scoundrel who was intent on ravaging her slender, young body.

Ignoring Mrs. Quince's quizzical glance, Royall kept her eyes straight ahead, kept her feet in rhythm with the older woman's step. In spite of herself, moisture gathered at the corners of Royall's prettily pouting mouth at the silly thought. What *would* it be like to be ravaged, loved, desired by a handsome, hard-muscled man? A man who could fulfill those longings in her that her marriage to MacDavis Banner had only hinted but had never accomplished.

Guilty at such a disloyal thought, Royall felt her cheeks coloring. No! she thought sternly, what's fair is fair; and MacDavis, while a gentle, considerate man, had never imagined the fires that burned within his young wife, much less done anything to satisfy them. Older than Royall by almost thirty years, Mac had never been her choice for a husband. It was in deference to her father that Royall had agreed to accept his proposal.

MacDavis was a wealthy man, and he had promised Royall's father that he would always see to her needs. And he had, while he was alive, at least. Soon after his death, his four children, each of whom was years older than Royall herself, took control of the family fortune. Her allowance, once so generous, became a mere pittance. They became intent on selling their father's home, and there was nothing Royall could do to stop them. MacDavis's will read that his sons were to see to their stepmother. He had relied on the honesty and generosity of his children. How wrong he was. Royall had little more to show for her two years as MacDavis Banner's wife than her jewelry, her yearly stipend, and his name.

So it was with a clear conscience that Royall was able to put those two years behind her. She owed MacDavis nothing and owed his memory less. While he had provided her with a beautiful home and jewels and standing in the community, she had provided him with the comfort of a wife, tender care during his last days, and tolerance for his inept and impotent lovemaking.

A slow, rosy-hued flush crept up her slender neck. Actually, all things considered, she was almost a virgin. Almost. Her sexuality had been aroused but never fulfilled, her appetite whetted and left unfed. She was no longer an innocent, young girl, unaware of the ritual of the marriage bed. She was a woman, awakened and aware and needing. She wanted a man, someone who would make love to her, caress her body with strong, sensitive hands till she cried out with desire, not with frustration as she had done so many times with MacDavis and his Puritanical Scottish morals that preached a "good woman" saw the marriage bed as one of her duties, not one of her pleasures. But there had been times . . . times when a strange and forbidden pleasure was within her reach; as if sensing this, MacDavis would push her away, leaving her with needs and desires that had no name.

The sparkling blue waters of Guanabara Bay could be seen at the end of the wide thoroughfare they were walking. The wharves were straight ahead, where cargo ships and passenger ships alike were anchored in the deep harbor. Tall, ranging masts seemed to scrape the sky in stately parade. Although their sails were reefed, the majesty of the ships was still evident. Ships that had sailed the world, gathering goods for distant markets. Names and places that were unfamiliar to the tongue and held all the dark mystery of romance. Royall's house had had a spectacular view of Boston harbor, and she had never tired of looking through the brightly polished windows down to those wonderful ships that circled the world. A world she hungered to learn about, to experience. Coming to Rio de Janeiro was the farthest she had ever been away from Massachusetts. She had always envied the young men of her acquaintance who had been allowed to take the "grand tour" of Europe before settling into life and responsibilities. She remembered remarking upon it to her father, who was properly aghast at the idea that his daughter, his lovely feminine daughter, would dream of traveling abroad without proper chaperones.

"But, father," she could hear her own voice come down to her through the years, "what would be the sense of chaperones? I would not have any more freedom than I do right here in Boston!"

Freedom, it seemed to Royall, was something that women were denied. It was a right and privilege reserved only for the opposite sex.

Their ship was docked at *muelle doce*, pier twelve, reserved for passenger ships. Their own vessel was a sleek-lined clipper, boasting seven sails and fast as the wind. From Boston they had stopped in several ports before reaching their destination in Brazil's largest seaport. From here they would sail north again, to Belém, where they would board a paddle-wheeled steamship to take them up the Amazon to the wilds of the jungle, to plantations near the new city of Manaus. Traveling by one of the new steamers would have been quicker, but Mrs. Quince would have none of it. God gave us the wind to sail by, she told Royall indignantly when a steamer was suggested. If He had meant for us to travel by machine, it would say as much in the Bible. Royall didn't dare remind the lady that the paddlewheeler that would carry them up the Amazon River had no sails.

"Here we are, safe and sound," Rosalie Quince

chirped as she maneuvered her bulk up the gang plank.

"More's the pity," Royall grimaced as she daintily lifted the hem of her orange-gold skirt and followed behind. "I don't want to be safe. For once in my life I want to be free. If I have anything to be sorry about, I can worry about it later. I want to taste life. Here! Now!"

"And now for a nice, cool lemonade. Let's sit here on the deck and relax a bit."

"Mrs. Quince, that's all we do! Relax! That's all we've done since we boarded the ship in Boston that brought us here to Rio. I don't want lemonade. I'd like a nice glass of port wine."

"There is no such thing as a 'nice' glass of port. Now claret, that's something else. Port is too heavy, too potent. Why, in this heat it could go straight to your head and you could fall overboard! These roughnecks and dock workers would have the time of their lives hauling you out!" The older woman was obviously agitated, but Royall was feeling too restless to care.

"Not to fear," Royall snapped. "With these petticoats I'd go straight to the bottom, and this damnable bustle would keep me there. I'd like to take this dress off and strip down to bare skin . . . feel the sun on my body . . ."

"Child, child! You must not speak that way! Good Lord, what if you were overheard? Why, we could be raped in our beds!"

Royall smiled.

"Child, you must learn to curb your tongue.

9

Why, there are savages all about us, lusting after fair-skinned women. I can't believe my ears. You really do need someone to look after you, and I, for one, intend to do my duty until you're safely in the hands of the Baron."

Royall sighed wearily. How dreary this all was. All she wanted was a little harmless adventure before she settled down into her new life on one of Brazil's lucrative rubber plantations. Just a harmless little adventure—was that too much to ask?

Rosalie Quince tapped the tip of her parasol on the deck to gain the steward's attention. "Two lemonades," she said firmly, eyes daring Royall to contradict or defy her.

Leaning back, sipping the tart drink, Royall decided that she would give anything if she could walk down the streets of Rio, join the festivities tomorrow. She could pretend to be anyone other than who she was. She could throw caution to the winds and never once worry about her reputation. She would flirt with handsome men, and if there happened to be one in particular who caught her fancy, why she would just . . . she would. . . . Her eyes darted to Rosalie Quince, who was busily draining her glass. Why, I'd just take him to the bushes and I'd . . . kiss him soundly! A wicked gleam shone in her amber eyes. Maybe, just maybe, there was a way.

"Mrs. Quince, I know I've shocked you. I don't know whatever possessed me to say those things. I suppose MacDavis's death is still a shock. I apologize, sincerely. Perhaps you should nap here in the shade. I don't imagine there's the slightest breeze in our cabins. I'll sit here beside you."

"I knew you were just playing a game with me, Royall. Why, no lady of quality ever talks that way. But you're right, I am sleepy. I'll remember you when I do my God-blesses this evening." Within a few moments, she was asleep, low, rumbling snores coming from what Royall thought was the tip of Rosalie's toes.

The lusty snores, ricocheting off the deck, made Royall smile in spite of herself. Poor Mrs. Quince. She was always so worried about being the proper lady, and look at her now. Plump cheeks mushroomed out and then deflated as her lower jaw hung slack with each raucous snore. Royall was just about to inch herself gingerly from the deck chair when Mrs. Quince's triple set of chins quivered, making the poor lady gasp for breath. Royall resembled a bird poised for flight until once again the rumbling sounds wafted across the polished deck.

Holding her skirts in both hands, Royall raced along the companionway until she came to her cabin. Pell mell, she tossed the contents of one bag onto the hard bunk, followed quickly by another, till she found what she was searching for. A thin packet of white powder lay in the palm of her long, slender hand. Tilting her head to one side, she tried to recall how much of the feathery granules was required for a good twelve hours' sleep. Quickly, she multiplied in her head for the

11

time she felt she would need to elude the ever-vigilant Mrs. Quince. Recklessly, she decided two quick shakes would make the ponderous lady sleep for an entire day. Royall excused her actions by telling herself Rosalie needed a long, relaxing sleep tomorrow while she, Royall, went out to meet whatever Mardi Gras had to offer. Her decision to administer the sleeping draught to her traveling companion so exhilarated her, she felt decidedly weak in the knees. Mentally, she cursed Mrs. Quince for not permitting her to have the glass of wine. If ever there was a time for sampling the spirits, this was it. Throwing caution to the winds, she left the cabin in search of a steward. Briskly, in a no-nonsense voice, she ordered a glass of wine brought to her stateroom and then, at the last minute, changed her order and haughtily demanded an entire bottle.

The steward knocked and entered her cabin and deftly placed the small tray on a table next to the bunk. He refused to meet Royall's eyes as he backed out the door, closing it softly behind him.

"God only knows what rumor will be going around this ship tomorrow," Royall muttered aloud. With no wasted motion, she uncorked the decanter of port wine and then poured until the goblet was full to the brim. "To Mardi Gras and freedom," she said softly to herself. She held the glass high, marveling at the scarlet liquid. By this time tomorrow I will be tasting life in a new land, having a high adventure and enjoying every minute of it. "To freedom," she sang aloud as she once again held the glass high.

By the time the decanter was empty, Royall was twirling around the room, humming to herself. The decanter slipped from her hands and rolled under the bunk. Laughing delightedly, Royall tossed the goblet under the bunk, where it came to rest next to the sparkling bottle. Long, sooty lashes closed momentarily and then flicked open. Now, all the evidence was gone. Just like tomorrow. She would leave no telltale clues or evidence behind when she set off for Mardi Gras . . . alone.

Rosalie Quince poked her head around the half-open door. She had knocked softly, and when there had been no response, she opened the door. Seeing her charge sleeping peacefully, she quietly withdrew. Sleep was exactly what the poor child needed. Sleep would help her cope with her bereavement. Only in sleep could one forget. Yes, sleep was what the child needed. Even if she slept through the dinner hour, she wouldn't wake her. Later, if she was hungry, she could get a snack from the steward. Sleep was more important than nourishment.

An hour before dawn, Royall woke, uncertain of her surroundings. The ship rolled sickeningly against its moorings. Lordy, her head throbbed and her stomach felt sour and queasy. Then she remembered. She sighed heavily as she swung her legs over the side of the bunk. "Oh, no," she groaned aloud. Holding her hand over her mouth, she raced to the pail in the corner of the room.

Exhausted, Royall sat down on the hard bunk with her head bent, palms massaging her throbbing temples. She winced at the loud knock on the door. She wanted to snarl and spit at the cheerful countenance of Rosalie Quince.

"Dear child, didn't anyone tell you that the early bird gets the worm. Come along now, we don't want to be late for breakfast. You know what happens; all the breakfast buns are cold and the coffee gets flies in it."

"Well, if that happens, we'll just give the flies to that early bird you're so worried about. You go along without me, Mrs. Quince. I want to ring for the steward to have some warm water for a bath. I'm really not very hungry this morning. I think I. . . I think I may have slept too much. My head is throbbing unmercifully."

"Miss breakfast!" Rosalie Quince was aghast. "But, child, you had no dinner last evening. You should be starving. We don't want you wasting away to nothing. You realize, or you will soon, dear child, that nothing is going to bring back your dear, departed husband. This life is for the living. I know you must feel that you are being sorely tested, but there is really nothing else for you to do but make the best of your bereavement, and by that I mean not missing your meals. I'll let it go this time, but I expect to see you at the luncheon table. Here," she said fishing in her reticule, "eat this bit of sugared ginger. Ginger cures any and all ills. Join me when you've freshened up. I'll be on deck with my needlework."

"I'll do that, Mrs. Quince. Join you later, I mean. And, Mrs. Quince, thank you for being so concerned about me. I'll be fine, truly I will."

"I know you will, child. You're young and beautiful. Before you know it, the suitors will be lined up all around the Baron's plantation. I know you can't possibly be thinking of taking a new husband, but after all, we have to face life. A man needs a woman, and a woman, it doesn't matter who she is, needs a man. You just think on the matter while you're soaking in your warm tub." With a swish of her long skirts she was gone, leaving Royall feeling confused and slightly embarrassed.

The cabin was hot and airless as Royall stepped from the tepid bath. She toweled herself dry and lay down on the bunk unclothed. Her headache seemed to be abating. Perhaps it was the sugared ginger Mrs. Quince had given her, because her stomach had settled back to normal while she had relaxed in the warm, wet bath water. Her eyes took on a dreamy look as she contemplated the prospect of Mardi Gras. What to wear in the way of a costume? She had nothing that would be appropriate, but she did have a mask that she had bought the day before, telling Mrs. Quince it was a souvenir. It was a gay, scarlet half mask that had small wires to attach it to her hair. A new hair arrangement, and who would know who she was? For that matter, who would care except Rosalie Quince? She was feeling better by the minute with the anticipation of the coming afternoon. First

15

came the big parade where everyone walked in costume. Then there was the music pavilion, along with assorted food stalls. Contests and wine would be more than abundant for all the happy frolickers. Then, in the evening, after a large dinner in the center pavilion, would be the masked ball, and wine would flow and spirits would soar.

Royall's eye fell on the packet of sleeping powder, knowing a twinge of guilt. What in heavens was she thinking of? How could she give sweet, well-meaning Rosalie Quince a sleeping draught? What kind of person was she that she would contemplate such drastic methods? For all she knew the dear Rosalie might never wake up, and then she would have it on her conscience for the rest of her life. She shuddered—she would be a murderer! All for a day at Mardi Gras. There must be some other way to evade her ever-watchful guardian.

An hour passed and then another as Royall massaged her temples, her mind racing, negating one idea after the other. She was just about to get up and get dressed and tell Mrs. Quince the truth— that she was going to Mardi Gras with or without her—when a disturbance outside her door startled her from her thoughts. Quickly, she threw on a dressing gown and opened the cabin door a cautious crack. Two heavy-set stewards were escorting Mrs. Quince to her room. On closer examination, it appeared they were carrying the portly lady. Their breathing was labored, and Mrs. Quince made no effort to soften her moans of agony. Alarmed at the look of pain on Mrs. Quince's face, Royall hastily closed her door and raced after the struggling men. "In the name of God, what happened, Mrs. Quince?" she demanded.

"A very foolish thing on my part, Royall," Mrs. Quince said through clenched teeth.

"Is there anything I can do? What can I do to help you?" Royall cried wretchedly, her plans for thwarting the older woman forgotten.

Carefully, the two stewards laid Mrs. Quince on the bunk and then propped her leg on top of several hard pillows. "The captain has sent for a physician, Miss," one of the stewards gasped as he straightened his shoulders. "It would be best if you stayed with the lady until he arrives."

Royall's eyes were wide. "But of course I'll stay with her. I wouldn't think of leaving her." Her gaze shifted from the steward to Rosalie's tight, pain-racked features. "You must tell me, Mrs. Quince, what happened?"

Rosalie Quince leaned back against the pillows at the head of the bunk. Her plump, pink cheeks were white with strain as she struggled with her pain. "As I said, a very foolish thing. I keep forgetting I'm not as young as I used to be. I thought I saw a neighbor of mine and I got up from the table so I could call to him. In doing so, my foot caught in the rung of the opposite chair, and down I went for all members of the dining room to see. I feel such a fool. A clumsy fool."

"A sprain or a bad bruise, Mrs. Quince. A few

days of rest and you'll be as good as new," Royall said, trying to make her voice sound reassuring.

"I'm afraid not, Royall. I heard the bone crack as I fell. That's what happens when you get to be my age. Bones snap like twigs in a strong wind. No, my ankle is broken. Poor Alonzo, when he hears of this, he will say he told me so. Husbands are like that, Royall. He didn't really want me to make this trip, but I insisted and he went along with my idea after he saw how much it meant to me. Now look at me. I do so hate to be a burden to anyone. In Manaus when a horse gets old and limps, they shoot him. That's how I feel right now."

"Please, Mrs. Quince, just lie there and rest. Talking is too much of a strain. You're pale and exhausted. Perhaps a cool cloth on your forehead will help." Not waiting for a reply from the woman, Royall dipped a soft cloth in a basin of water that stood near the bunk. Tenderly, she placed it on the older woman's face. "Mrs. Quince, I'm going to my cabin to dress and I'll be right back. You must not move. Promise me."

"Child, where could I go and what could I do?" Her tone was tart, and she immediately apologized to the young woman. "The thing that bothers me the most about all of this is I still don't know if it was Sebastian or not that I saw down on the wharf. It must have been. There aren't two such handsome devils in the world. I'm just a foolish old woman. I thought if it was Sebastian Rivera he could perhaps take you to Mardi Gras, as I

18

know how badly you want to see the festivities. Sebastian would keep you safe." Tears of self-pity gathered in Mrs. Quince's eyes as she stared at Royall.

A lump of something she had no name for settled in the pit of Royall's stomach. And she had been about to administer a sleeping draught to this wonderful old woman. For shame, Royall Banner, she scolded herself on the way back to the cabin. God will punish you, she told herself as she hastily dressed. I deserve to be punished, she almost wept. The poor old lady was thinking of her all along, and here she was acting like some . . . some . . . some damn criminal. She dressed quickly in a light green morning gown, and after several quick swipes with her hairbrush, she was ready to return to Mrs. Quince's cabin.

Voices from within the adjoining cabin startled her. The physician must have arrived. Nervously, she paced the corridor for what seemed like hours. When the cabin door opened, Royall reached out to grasp the doctor's hand. "Tell me, did Mrs. Quince break her foot? You must tell me so I will know what to do. I want to take care of her."

"My dear young lady, please calm yourself," the tall, thin man said in a quiet voice. "The lady did indeed break her ankle. I've set the bone, and she'll mend when God is willing that she should walk again. There is nothing you can do for the lady now. I've administered a sleeping draught that will take effect soon. She'll sleep off and on for the rest of the day and into the night. When

19

she wakes, she'll have some mild discomfort, but that's about all. I've seen to it that there are biscuits and tea next to her bed. The captain will have one of the stewards bring it along any second now. If the lady awakens, they will be within her reach. She's not to have any heavy food for the rest of the day. So, you see, there is nothing for you to do or for you to concern yourself with. Go to Mardi Gras with all the other young people, and enjoy yourself."

Royall wanted to throw her arms around the doctor. He was giving her an order and at the same time absolving her of her guilt. She was used to obeying orders, and obey this one she would.

"If you're sure, doctor." Her voice was hesitant, almost pleading.

"Open the door and see for yourself," the doctor said jovially.

Moistening her lips with the tip of her tongue, Royall opened the cabin door a bit and peered into the dimness. Rosalie Quince lay on the bunk with her hands folded over her ample chest. There was a peaceful half smile on her face as strange sounds erupted from her throat.

"You see, the lady is sleeping quite peacefully. There's nothing you can do. If only all my cases were so simple. Close the door now and prepare yourself for the grand parade. I've told the captain I'm sending a woman to stay with her until the boat departs."

Royall was still unsure, her own guilt riding her shoulders like a devil imp. He was a doctor. After

20

all, he must know what he was talking about, and Mrs. Quince did look peaceful. "Very well, doctor, I think I will take your advice and do as you suggest. Thank you for taking such good and prompt care of my . . . of my friend."

"My reward will be that you enjoy yourself. That's what Mardi Gras is all about. I've had my day of revelry, as has the lady inside. It's your turn this year. Enjoy yourself, and store away your memories of this season."

Royall stared at the man. His face was bony, almost craggy, and his eyes were too deep set, as though he didn't get enough sleep. It was hard to believe that he had ever participated in Mardi Gras, or that he was ever young, for that matter. A pity, she thought. Now all he had was his memories. But he was right: revelry was for the young, and she was young. She deserved this brief respite from the pressures of her marriage and her sudden bereavement. A new land, new people to contend with, the plantation in the middle of the jungle, would soon enough occupy her mind and thoughts for the rest of her life. This was her day, doctor's orders, and she was going to enjoy it to the fullest. After all, Manaus was thousands of miles away and she was here. She nodded her head in the doctor's direction and then entered her own cabin.

Royall's cabin looked as though a disaster had struck by the time she decided she was ready to leave the confining quarters. Ribbons, shoes of all colors and shapes, along with a multitude of petticoats, were draped everywhere. Bangles and beads sparkled from a half-open chest on the bunk, winking and blinking in the filtered sunlight that came in through the porthole window. She was ready. At the moment she would have cheerfully parted with one of her back teeth to have a long looking glass. She knew she looked ravishing in the sapphire silk with the low-cut bodice. Perhaps *ravishing* was the wrong word; *daring* was more like it. Daring and regal. It was the sapphire necklace MacDavis had given her on their wedding day that lent queenly bearing. And the matching gems that dangled from her tiny earlobes. Her golden hair piled high on her head emphasized her long, graceful neck and accentuated the deep, revealing cut of her bodice.

Her mask was clutched tightly in her hand as she made her way down the dim corridor to the outer deck. She would put it on when she reached the street where the parade was to begin. The captain had made it clear that the sailing time of one hour after dawn was firm, and passengers who were not aboard would be left behind. All new passengers would board at the same time, providing their baggage and passage had been cleared beforehand.

Admiring looks and low-voiced murmurs greeted her as she made her way down the rickety wooden gangplank. A heavy sigh of relief escaped her as she picked her way through trash and debris that seemed to litter every wharf in the world. Casually, from time to time, she looked over her shoulder as she made her way to Odelony Street, where the parade was to start. Just the day before she had paid close attention as she and Mrs. Quince had taken their stroll. Remembered landmarks greeted her, making her feel confident that she knew exactly where she was going. The music seemed to be getting louder and louder. She must be close to Odelony Street. She stopped a moment to affix her mask, being careful that the tiny wires were securely fastened beneath her curls. She was ready.

Her heart thumped wildly as she was pushed and jostled by the masked participants of the parade. A peal of laughter to her left made her smile. A young woman dressed as a shepherdess was busy poking her feathered staff into a harlequin's ribs. From all appearances the harlequin was enjoying himself. He picked up the girl and whirled her through the air, her ruffled pantaloons showing for all the world to see. Crimson devils with long, swishing tails trailed behind their black-clad counterparts. Pitchforks waved in the air with gay abandonment. All manner of members of royalty were represented, with colorful brocade and satin. Crowns perched precariously on the revelers' heads were objects of much laughter. Royall edged her way between two devils and patiently waited for her turn to move up to the beginning formations.

Mandolins strummed continuously, making Royall's pulses throb with excitement. As she advanced a step, she became aware of the man standing beside her. Her breath caught in her throat.

23

A buccaneer was staring down into her eyes. Without a doubt, even in his half mask, he was the most handsome man she had ever seen. He was tall, towering over the other contestants by a good head. Raven black hair fell low over a sharply defined brow. His teeth, when he smiled, were as white as the shirt he wore, open to the waist, revealing a massive, sun-bronzed chest. Tight, black trousers and rich, gleaming, leather boots finished him off to perfection. Again, Royall's breath caught in her throat. Her eyes fell to the man's hands. Strong hands with short clipped nails that were clean and well-manicured. Hands, she knew, that could caress a woman with sensitivity; hands that knew work and had worked. Strong, capable hands. She swallowed hard as she saw the amused look in the man's eyes. What must he think of her staring at him like this? God almighty, he probably thought she was bold or, worse yet, a lady of the evening. Well, this was midday with the sun shining brightly. Evening was a long way off.

"Allow me," said a deep voice beside her. It was the buccaneer. "We both seem to be without a partner, and everyone must have a partner." He gallantly cupped her elbow in the palm of his hand, escorting her to a place in line. A man with an orange wig and dressed as a court jester handed them each a numbered card, which they hung around their necks.

Nervously, Royall glanced about her, and she could feel the buccaneer's insolent gaze upon her.

He'd spoken in Portuguese; Royall wanted to say something to relieve the tension, but she knew her Portuguese was stiff and hesitantly awkward. A feeling of dismay settled itself between her shoulder blades. This was foolhardy. She knew nothing about this man who was pressing closer to her, except that his dark eyes flashed when he smiled and his touch made her tingle. Turning back toward her, he smiled again, tilting his magnificent dark head to the side.

"Even behind the mask it is evident you are a beautiful woman." His words were soft, his tone hushed; unexpectedly, shock waves quivered up and down Royall's spine.

Even after she cleared her throat, her voice was something akin to a squeak. "Thank you. You're rather dashing yourself." Gaining confidence with her words, she continued, "You seem to be the only buccaneer among kings and princes." She suddenly realized she had spoken in English and hadn't expected him to understand. His eyes widened momentarily and then he threw back his head and laughed, a deep, melodious sound.

"Tell me, beautiful lady," he answered in her own language, "do you see anyone but myself who would dare to wear this costume?"

"Certainly none with your arrogance. You chose wisely. I suppose you had childhood dreams of riding the seas to pillage and plunder the Spanish galleons."

"Of course," he agreed, leaning closer, bending to place his lips near her ear. "But now that I'm

25

a man, Spanish galleons hold little allure. Beautiful women are my targets now."

Something in his voice, perhaps the bold expression in his eyes, made Royall's breath catch in her throat. She stepped backward and felt his hand close over her arm.

"Did you have fantasies of being a queen or perhaps a fairy princess? If so, you have outdone yourself for the role."

"Of course, every girl sees herself wearing a crown and long, flowing gowns of silk and ermine. Alas, you see, I am but a handmaiden," she quipped, offering a deep curtsy.

The buccaneer moved a step away, his piercing, jet black eyes holding hers. "You would never be a handmaiden. Only a queen would do. There is a certain bearing . . ." He stopped in midsentence and then continued his close scrutiny. "Yes, it is there . . . a royal bearing."

Royall burst out laughing, continuing with the charade. "Tell me, kind sir, are you spelling royal with one L or two?" Her tone was mocking, matching his own for insolence.

The buccaneer scowled, giving him a dark, forbidding look. His tone, however, was light when he spoke, "As every school child knows, with one L."

A river of alarm swept through Royall. She had gone too far, as his dark look was telling her. This man did not like insolent women who could turn his own game onto him. This was no fop who could be twirled around a woman's finger. This buccaneer was a man with no trace of the boy left in him. The thought excited her yet frightened her. She raised her head slightly, tilting her chin, putting her gaze on a level with his. "You shouldn't scowl so. It makes you appear ferocious."

His lips tightened into a thin line. He didn't care for women who teased and mocked. It was not something women usually practiced on him, and he didn't like those who enjoyed themselves at his own expense. The thought infuriated him. Through slitted eyes he watched her as they gradually moved with the crowds of revelers for their place at the start of the parade. He wished he could see behind the mask she was wearing, and was tempted to snatch it from her face. That she was lovely, there was no doubt. He looked down at her hand that was placed so casually on his arm. The skin was white, delicate, and the nails long and perfectly shaped. This was not a hand used to labor. Her golden hair shone with silver highlights, and the jewels in her ears were remarkably good reproductions of the real thing. Even her gown, pure silk, light and rustling, told him something about her. Again, his ebony eyes narrowed. She wasn't the ordinary *dama de noche*. There was a certain quality about her, but he couldn't quite place it. She made a wonderful masquerade of being well placed and well bred. Her voice was soft, naturally so, and her mouth, made for kissing, pouted prettily, invitingly. Behind the mask he could see that her eyes were amber, flecked with gold, with long, velvety lashes remarkably black for a woman with hair so light.

Boldly, his speculative glance settled on her deep cleavage, revealing full, round breasts that invited a man's hands or lips. He was eager to touch them, to experience their softness. It never occurred to him that she might not be willing to bestow her favors on him. When he wanted a woman, she was his for the taking. This one, with her bold, insolent tongue, would be no different. By midnight he would have her in his bed in his townhouse or his name wasn't Sebastian Rivera. A night of full, rich pleasure before he boarded the steamer that would take him to Belém and then on to his plantation near Manaus.

Royall could feel the buccaneer's eyes devouring her, and she became totally aware of him as she walked beside him, oblivious to the noise and music surrounding her. She could imagine what he was thinking: that she was a lonely, unattached woman eager for a night of revelry. A slow flush crept up her neck and stained her cheeks. No doubt he was contemplating how and where he could get her alone, take advantage of her. The look in his eyes promised more than just a daring kiss in the bushes. This man would demand much, much more. The flush was burning her cheeks, spreading to her throat; she could feel the heat in her breasts. Dread lowered like a pall; she should have stayed with Mrs. Quince; she wasn't so certain that she could handle this dangerously dark man whose choice of costume hinted at his reckless nature.

A sense of panic gripped Royall, blinding her to the bright, colorful costumes, muting the blaring trumpets and strumming music until it became one note, high and shrill, reverberating in her ears, rushing through her veins. The ground seemed to be coming up to meet her when strong arms gathered her close, holding her, steadying her. Swallowing hard, she gently extricated herself from his embrace. She was trembling, knew the buccaneer was aware of it. Her body felt scorched where his hands had touched her.

Ripe. That was the word that came to Sebastian's mind. *Ready* was another. And he was just the man to turn opportunity his way. Yet, there was something about this woman that told him she was not a garden variety streetwalker. There was an air of fine breeding about her. Nor would a whore become so shaken and quake or tremble just because he had had his arms around her. Where did she come from? Who was she? A woman too long starved for love, he told himself, hungry for the pleasures of bed. She moved like a sleek, jungle cat, waiting, watching . . . Moisture beaded on his brow. He had known more than one jungle cat who would kill a man for intruding into her domain. Cats were graceful and wild, ferocious in their stalk of prey. The jet black eyes took on a speculative look as he watched her. He would never become a woman's prey, never be devoured. He was his own man and always

29

would be. Yet, it would be amusing to see how close he could get to those claws without getting scratched. After all, he had lived in the jungles and he knew a trick or two himself. Males were dominant; they always won. Still, he found himself thinking that he should never turn his back on this hungry creature beside him.

Chapter Two

Evenings in Brazil descended with suddenness, the sun dipping low over distant hills, not to rise again until the following day. This evening was no different, but Royall was having such a wonderful, exciting time that she failed to notice the darkness until lanterns in windows were lit and blazing torches lined the streets.

She had supposed that once the parade was over the buccaneer would gallantly take his leave of her, but that was not the case. Instead, he had led her through the narrow, winding streets of the seaport city, following one gay party after another. There was always another delicacy to be tasted, another wine to be sipped.

Streets and byways were filled with people, most of them natives, dressed in wild colors and garish headdresses. Some of them had even painted their bodies and faces in pagan ritual. Musicians seemed to be on every street corner, beating drums and playing flutes, creating strange melodies that stirred the blood and dulled the senses. Any fears she had entertained concerning the buccaneer were abated, replaced with an easy camaraderie they both enjoyed. He graciously pointed out unusual sights, told her of the myths and legends behind some of the songs and dances, and patiently explained the traditions of Mardi Gras.

It was with some alarm that Royall noticed that their path had led them to a distant part of the city where there were no shops and only occasional pubs. It was difficult to find a white face among the hordes of people, save for her own and the buccaneer's, but the wine she had consumed was too heady, quelling her fears.

"Soon it will be midnight," her buccaneer told her, his mouth close to her ear to be heard over the din. "All celebration will cease; everything will be quiet, marking the onset of Lent. Come with me, I know a place where we can have a late dinner. You must be hungry."

Royall nodded, agreeing, averting her gaze from him. She should go back to the ship, back to the protection of her cabin, away from this handsome rogue whose eyes told her he too was hungry, but for something else besides food. As the night had worn on, she had become increasingly aware of his hand on her arm, of his arms around her waist as he had led her through a dance . . . aware of the man himself, of his height, his warm, deep voice. But mostly, aware of his eyes always on her, searching her face behind the mask, dipping lower to where fair skin was revealed by her gown's wide-cut bodice. She should go back to the ship, but some inner urge, some drive and need of her own, compelled her to agree, to go with him, to follow her adventure through to the end.

Like two children, they ran through the streets, dodging people, scurrying through alleyways and shortcuts that would take them to where he was leading. The buccaneer was obviously familiar with the city, just as he was familiar with the language and even the native dialects. Either he was a seaman who visited Rio often, or he himself was a native of the city. When he spoke English, there was an accent in his voice, making it slightly exotic and pleasant to her ears.

Royall was breathless by the time he stopped, pulling her into a doorway and into his arms. She could feel his breath upon her cheek as he looked down at her.

"Do you know how beautiful you are? It's almost midnight, time for unmasking."

Before she could protest, he held her captive with one hand and with the other removed her mask. "I knew you were beautiful, and you are." Slowly, deliberately, his mouth closed over hers, his hands cupping her face, fingers tracing gentle patterns where their lips met.

Setting her away from him, he removed his own mask with a brush of his hand. He laughed, showing perfect, gleaming white teeth. His face was square, his features chiseled, his laughing mouth sensual. There was a slightly exotic tilt to the corners of his dark, heavily lashed eyes which were margined by thick, unruly brows. "And what had you expected, lovely, a devil behind the mask?"

Royall laughed, throwing her head back, revealing the slim, long column of her neck. "A devil is a devil, mask or no. And you, sir, kiss like the devil himself."

"And where did you come by this knowledge?" he challenged. "Or would that be revealing professional secrets?"

She felt her face flame, feeling as though it could light the darkness like a candle. He had practically accused her of being a streetwalker—a prostitute! Lowering her head in shame, she thought, what else *should* he think? Proper ladies did not attend celebrations like Mardi Gras alone and unescorted. Nor did they accept the company of a stranger and spend the entire day with him, drinking and eating and allowing his eyes to devour her. And proper ladies didn't thrill to that excitement they found in those stranger's eyes.

As soon as he had spoken the words, Sebastian could have cursed himself. He wasn't ordinarily the kind of man who reminded a woman, even if she was of dubious character, that her morals were less than acceptable. He wanted to apologize, say he was sorry, take back the words. She was insulted, as well she should be, and it showed by the way she lowered her head, hiding her face. This golden lioness was a sensitive woman, and he was a dolt.

Royall was at a loss for words. She *should* hate him, protest that she was indeed a respectable woman who was only seeking a small adventure, a lark, an afternoon of gaiety. But she found she couldn't hate him unreasonably, not after seeing his almost instant remorse. Besides, what did it matter who he thought she *really* was? This was someone who didn't even know her name, would never know it. Someone she would never see again in her lifetime. And it was exactly what she wanted. To deny it would be to lie to herself. To be truthful, she had even contemplated drugging Mrs. Quince to obtain these few hours of anonymity and freedom. Even before leaving the ship she had secretly hoped she would meet someone exactly like the buccaneer, someone who would find her attractive and whose eyes would tell her that he wanted to make love to her.

His arms reached out for her, bringing her close to him. No words were spoken; none were necessary. Gently, she felt his lips in her hair, on her cheek, in silent apology. Whoever this buccaneer was, he was no clod, no rakehell, riding roughshod over a woman's feelings. In fact, his behavior all day had been exemplary and above reproach. A gentleman. Something she had never expected from a rough seaman.

Tenderly, his fingers lifted her chin, raising her lips to his own. His arms tightened about her, pressing her closer to his chest, crushing her breasts against him. His body was hard and muscular. Royall's arms encircled his back. Without reason or logic, she felt safe and secure in his embrace, and she faced her tumultuous emotions

34

with directness and truth. She wanted this man. Wanted him to make her the woman she knew she could be—the woman her husband had never known existed.

Looking into his eyes without a trace of coquettishness, she was aware that she could drown in that incredibly dark gaze and emerge again as the woman she wanted and needed to become.

Seeing her moist lips part and offer themselves to him, he lowered his mouth to hers, touching her lips, tasting their sweetness, drawing from them a kiss gentle, yet passionate. He robbed her of her senses, and searing flames licked her body, the pulsating beat of her heart thundered in her ears.

When he released her, his jet eyes searched hers for an instant, and time became eternal for Royall. From somewhere deep within her a desire to stay forever in his arms, to feel the touch of his mouth upon hers, began to build to crescendo, threatening to erupt like fireworks. Thick, dark lashes closed over her sparkling golden eyes, and she heard her own breath come in ragged little gasps as she boldly brought her mouth once more to his, offering herself, kissing him deeply, searchingly, searing this moment upon her memory.

She kissed him as she had never kissed another man—a kiss that made her knees weak and her head dizzy. She knew, in that endless moment, that this man, this buccaneer, belonged to her in a way no other man could ever belong to her, for however brief this time together would be. She had found him: a man who could make her senses reel, her passions explode, who could promise the fulfillment she had only dreamed could be hers.

The buccaneer's gentle fingers caressed her cheek softly and seemed to know what she was feeling. "There are needs of the soul that go beyond the hungers of the body, little cat." His voice was deep, husky, little more than a whisper. "Will you come with me and be mine, if only for the night? Only you, my cat, can make it a night for all eternity."

His answer was in her kiss, in the sweet pressure of her body. His hand cupped her throat, feeling the abandoned rhythm of her pulse, sending a scorching streak of fire through her, and she knew that this night was decreed by the fates that had sent him to her. He took her hand in his and led her from the doorway out into the streets that were quieter now. Only scattered little bands of people were still singing and dancing; the sounds they made seemed to come from so far away. Her senses were filled with him, and while they walked they were silent, each feeling the presence of the other and the effect this nearness had on their rioting emotions.

She had no idea where he was taking her, didn't care. She knew that tonight she would go to the ends of the earth with this man whose lips worshipped her own and whose hands were gentle, so gentle.

As he measured his steps with hers, he found himself studying her profile and appreciating the finely molded nose that was only slightly up-turned, and in perfect balance with her high, intelligent brow. Her golden wealth of hair was piled atop her head, giving her added height, but he saw that she was a petite woman, just barely grazing his shoulder, and he knew that beneath her voluminous skirts he would find that she was perfectly proportioned, full and womanly, neither too plump nor too thin. Her proud breasts strained against the bodice of her gown and promised to be round and high, fitting nicely into the palm of a man's hand. He found he was eager to take the pins from her hair, to see it flowing down her back, to run his hands through the strands of luminous gold. But it was to her mouth that his eyes always returned, full, ripe, mobile. A mouth that clung in a kiss, a mouth made for kissing; the touch of it upon his was soft and cool, and he knew he could lose himself in that tempting confection.

Royall walked beside him, knowing he was looking at her, appraising her, liking what he saw. And she bloomed beneath his gaze, held herself proudly and erect. With this man there would be no pretending, no false modesty; she knew he would not allow it.

Unlike MacDavis with his still Puritan morals, this man would expect her to yield to her passions, demand that she delight in the pleasure he gave her. She knew that this night would not end with her wanting and needing something that had no name, something that could leave her crying with frustration and loneliness.

The buccaneer's pace slowed, and he led her into a dimly lit hostelry that she guessed was patronized by travelers. Beyond the anteroom she could hear the muffled sounds of drinking and eating and the melodious strumming of a guitar. Before the innkeeper could greet them and survey them with a curious eye, the buccaneer turned and replaced the mask that he had removed from her face an eternity ago in the darkened doorway. She fumbled with the side wires, attaching it firmly to her hair, grateful for the return to anonymity.

The next few moments passed like a blur. She was vaguely aware of the innkeeper's curious glances and of the buccaneer's quiet authority that tolerated no questions. In every way he was protective of her, his very demeanor forbidding any casual, offhanded remarks the innkeeper might have been prompted to make.

Securing the key to a room above, the buccaneer led her up the stairs, keeping a steady hand on her elbow, shielding her from the prying glances of anyone passing through the anteroom.

Behind the closed door of their rented room, he took her in his arms, hungry for the touch of her, the feel of her. Hidden from curious eyes, his lips claimed hers and worlds collided.

His mouth became a part of her own, and she heard her heart beat in wild and rapid rhythms. They strained toward each other, imprisoned by

38

the designs of yearning, caught in an embrace that ascended the obstacles of the flesh and strove to join breath and blood, body and spirit.

Forcing a restraint, he led her over to the bed, sitting her down and removing her shoes. Quick and capable fingers reached beneath her gown, pulling at her garters, slipping the silky stocking down her smooth legs and off her feet. She allowed him to unbutton the back of her gown, helped him remove it from her shoulders, and stepped out of it, glad to be free of its confines and thrilled to expose more of her flesh to his touch. Petticoats and chemise followed, along with restricting stays and undergarments. And each item of clothing he took from her he replaced with a kiss, a long, teasing kiss, on parts of her body that had never known a man's hands, much less his lips.

Gently, in the darkened room, he lay her back against the pillows, leaning over her, nuzzling her neck, inhaling the heady fragrance that was hers alone. Blazing a hot trail from her throat, his lips covered her unguarded breast, and she shivered with exquisite anticipation. She became unaware of her surroundings, oblivious to time or place; she only knew that her body was reacting to this man, pleasure radiating outward from some hidden depths within herself. She allowed herself to be transported by it, incapable of stopping the forward thrust of her desires, spinning out of time and space into the soft consuming vapors of her sensuality.

Her emotions careened and clashed, grew confused and wild, her perceptions thrumming and beating wherever he touched her. And when he moved away from her, leaving her, she felt alone, bereft and grieving. When he returned, she was whole again, wanting and needing, wanting to be needed. He had stripped his clothes; the feverish heat of his skin seemed to singe her fingers as she traced inquisitive patterns over his arms and back and down over his sleek muscular haunches.

She had never touched a man this way, not even during her marriage to MacDavis, who had always worn a nightshirt. But somehow she knew she could have touched a thousand men this way and none would feel the same to her as this man. None would have the unexpectedly smooth skin that tantalized her fingers and tempted her to seek the hard, rolling muscles that lay beneath. No other man could possess this soft furring on his broad chest that tickled her nose and brushed her lips, nor the long, hard length of thigh that her wandering hands had found and explored.

Suddenly, the room was too dark, jealously keeping the sight of him from her eyes. She wanted to see him, to know him, behold the places her fingers yearned to find and her lips hungered to kiss. "The lamp," she whispered, hardly daring to make a sound, afraid to break the spell. "Light the lamp." She hardly recognized her voice; she sounded husky, throaty, sensuous, even to her own ears. "I want to see you," she whispered brazenly. "I want to know you, like this . . . naked.

All of you." It was a plea, a demand, exciting him with its fervor, arousing his desires for her to a fever pitch.

Soft, golden light flooded the room, and he stood there before her, just out of her reach. Her gaze covered him, sizzling and searing, lingering at the swell of his manhood and grazing over his flat, hard stomach. Dark patterns of hair molded his form into planes and valleys, covering his chest and narrowing to a thin, elongated arrow that seemed to point below. Thighs thick with muscle supported him. His haunches tapered and broadened again for the width of his chest. But it was to his nether regions that her gaze traveled again and again before stretching out her arms, beckoning him to her.

He was filled with an exhilarating power that came from the knowledge that she wanted him, unabashedly and unashamed—the power that only a woman can give to a man when she reveals her desires for him, welcoming him into her embrace, giving as well as taking, trusting him to take her to the realms of the highest star, where passion is food for the gods and satisfaction is its own reward.

When he had lit the lamp, he looked down at her, seeing her, and was held in the spell of her gaze, watching her eyes travel the length of his body. Her lips parted, full and ripe, revealing the pink tip of her tongue as she moistened them. She was leaning back against the pillows, one knee bent, hiding her most secret place from his sight.

Breasts proud, their coral tips erect, invited his hands and his lips and tapered to a slim, graceful torso where a fine feathering of downy hair caught the light, gilding her body with a soft, shimmering glow. She was beautiful, this lioness with the hungry eyes, beautiful and desirable, setting his pulses pounding, unleashing a driving need in him to satiate himself in her charms, to quell this hunger she created in him and to salve an appetite for her that was ravenous and voracious.

He stepped into her embrace, felt her arms surround his hips, was aware that she rested her cheek sweetly against the flat of his stomach, rubbing it against his soft, curling hairs. His hands found the pins in her hair, impatiently pulling them, removing them, eager to see its golden wealth tumble around her shoulders and curl around her breasts. Silky spun gold, scented and clean, rippled through his fingers, tumbling and cascading, following his hands, down the smooth length of her back and onto the pillows. She lifted her head, looking up at him, her golden eyes heavy with passion. He had been right in calling her a lion, a wild cat of the jungle. Dark lashes created shadows on her high cheekbones; upward winging brows delineated her features. The slim, lithe body, tinged with gilt, tempted his hands, invited his lips.

Her teasing touches fleetingly grazed his buttocks and the backs of his thighs, slipping between them and rising higher and higher. She watched him as she touched him, aware of the masculine hardness of him, feeling it pulsate with anticipation of her touch. And when her hand closed over him, a deep rumbling sounded in his chest, coming from his lips in a barely audible groan.

He lay down beside her, reaching for her, covering her breasts with his hands, seeking them with his lips. But her appetite for him had not been satisfied, and she lifted herself onto her elbow, leaning over him, her hair falling askew over her shoulder, creating a curtain between them.

Hesitantly, she touched him again, running the tips of her fingers down his chest, hearing his small gasp of pleasure. The flat of her palm grazed his belly, and her lips blazed a trail following her hand's downward sweep.

The swell of her hips and the rounded fullness of her bottom filled him with a throbbing urgency. Nothing short of having her, of losing himself in her, would satisfy. He was afraid the touch of her lips would drive him over the edge, past the point of no return. Impatiently, he drew her upwards, pushing her back against the pillows, trapping her with his weight. He wanted to plunder her, to drive himself into her, to slake his thirst, knowing that his needs could be met only in her.

Her mouth was swollen, passion-bruised and tasting of himself. Her arms wound around him, holding him close as she pressed her nakedness against him. His hands made an intimate search of her shoulders, skimming the long, silky length of her back, following the curve of her spine and over her bottom.

A warm, golden warmth spread through her veins, heating her erratic pulses. Her hair became entangled around her neck, and he lightly brushed it aside before resuming the moist exploration with his lips. His mouth lingered in the place where her arm joined her body before tracing a pattern-less path over her full, heaving breasts. She clung to the hard, sinewy muscles of his arms, holding onto him for support, afraid she would fall into a yawning abyss where flames were fed by passion.

His hands spanned her waist, tightened their grip and lifted her above him. His mouth tortured her with teasing flicks of his tongue, making her shudder with unreleased passions. She curled her fingers into his night-dark hair, pushing him backward, away, pleading that he end the torment, only to follow his greedy mouth with her body, pushing her flesh against it, relieved when it encircled the whole peak.

A throbbing ache spread through her, demanding to be satisfied, uncontrollably settling in her haunches, making her seek relief by the involuntary roll of her hips against the length of his thigh. He held her there, forcing her bottom forward, driving her pelvis against him.

Suddenly, he shifted, throwing her backwards, coming on top of her, looming over her. For a thousand times, it seemed, his lips and hands traveled her body, starting at the pulse point near her throat and seeming to end at her toes. He found certain places that pleased him, hunted for those places that pleased her.

He whispered Spanish love words, praising her beauty, celebrating her sensuality. Her body seemed to have a life of its own and she succumbed to it, turning, opening, like the petals of a flower. His searching fingers adored her, his hungry mouth worshipped her. Lower and lower his kisses trailed, covering the tautness of her belly and slipping down to the softness between her thighs.

She felt him move upon her, demanding her response, tantalizing her with his mouth, bringing her ever closer to that which had always eluded her and kept itself nameless from her. Her body flamed beneath his kiss, offering itself to him, arching and writhing, reveling in that sensation that was within her grasp, reveling in her own femininity.

She felt as though she were separated from herself, that the world was comprised only of her aching need and his lips. Exotically sweet, thunderously compelling, her need urged him on, the same need that lifted her upwards, upwards, soaring and victorious, defeating her barriers, conquering her reserves, bringing her beyond the threshhold of a delicious rapture that she had never dreamed or suspected even in her fantasies.

And when his mouth closed over hers once again, he tasted of herself. He had proved her a woman and had not cursed her for it. He had allowed her to rise victorious in her passions, leaving her breathless and with the knowledge that there was more, much more. She was satisfied, yet discontent; fed and yet famished. She wanted to share the ecstasy he had given her, participate in that sharing, and only with him.

Grasping her hips, he lifted her as though she were weightless. He brought her parted thighs around him, and when he drove downward, she felt as if she were being consumed by a totally different fire. A fire that burned cooler, leaving sensibilities intact. Yet, there was that same driving need deep within her, deeper and more elusive than she had experienced the first time. She struggled to bring herself closer, needing to be a part of him this time, needing him to be a part of herself. These fires burned deeper, brighter, fed by the fuel of his need for her, of his hunger to be satisfied.

A single, golden tear glistened on her cheek. She was triumphant, powerful, a woman. In this man's arms she knew she had been born for this moment, that all her life had been leading up to what she was experiencing with this magnificent stranger. He had taken her out of herself, revealed a world of wonder to her, where arms and lips and bodies were meant for the loving. He had shown her the secrets of the universe and she had learned them, proudly, head high. He had taught her that she was a woman and exalted with her, carrying her with him to the heights beyond the stars.

Afterwards, they slept in each other's arms, and even in sleep their lips sought and their hands soothed. Twice again, before the light of day, he took her, each time finding a new and exciting variation to their lovemaking.

Royall was sated, filled with the wonder of her new-found sensuality. Her body ached in places she had never known she possessed, and with that ache came a joy. She had found herself, felt she at last knew herself, and all the dark secrets were banished, exiled by the hands and lips and body of a mysterious buccaneer.

Shortly before dawn he nuzzled her neck, holding her close. "I don't want to leave you, *mi poca leona.*" These last words he whispered softly, calling her his little lioness. "I must leave Rio on the outgoing tide and still have affairs that must be attended to."

She could sense that he didn't want to leave her, and it made her feel closer to him. But he said he must, and she felt it would be irrelevant to tell him that her own ship sailed very shortly. For a moment she held him close, knowing she would never find another man like him in her lifetime. But last night had been made for memories, and she would cherish every one.

Chapter Three

Everywhere she looked the bright Brazilian sun illuminated the pageant of humanity on the rough-hewn wharf in the seaport city of Belém.

Hawkers were everywhere, crying their goods

at full voice. Sailors mulled about from one stall to another, quarreling about the prices and paying them all the same.

Beggar children followed the sailors, pulling on their sleeves or tugging at their trouser legs, begging for a sweet or imploring the men, through gestures, to visit and buy something at their families' stands.

While merchants haggled over the prices, Indian women, long skirts wrapped about their slim bodies, vied for the best of the merchandise. All about was color and teeming life. It was the most exciting sight Royall had seen since Mardi Gras in Rio, and a far cry from her native New England.

She took particular notice of the Indian women. They were lovely to her eyes—smooth, dark skin, not black like the Negro, but a nut brown, great dark eyes, and straight black hair tied at the back. They wore bright colors and patterns that enhanced their complexions, and Royall felt pale beside them.

She noticed a few of the women appraising her, and she felt herself blush under their impertinent stares. A few of them spoke to one another, nodding in her direction.

Mrs. Quince, noting her embarrassment, translated their light, musical language for her. "They say you're beautiful; they call you the golden girl. These Indians are always impressed with fair skin and light hair. They envy you."

"And I was just thinking how lovely they are. They make me feel pale in comparison."

"Well, dear, you know the saying, 'the grass is always greener.' Come, we must inquire about our accommodations on the paddlewheeler. One mustn't trust to reservations. Drat this outlandish chair," the woman complained testily. "If these wheels get caught between the cobblestones, poor Alonzo will be without a wife. A wheelchair, they call this contraption," she continued to mutter as Royall pushed her from behind. "I call it a curse! Push, Royall! And keep a firm grip. The Lord protect us, I won't feel safe until we set foot in Manaus!"

At the name of the exotic city, Royall felt a tingle and a quickening of her senses. "Manaus," her geography text had read, "a treasure trove of wealth and culture, glistening beneath the Brazilian sun. Erected on the banks of the Amazon on the wealth from the rubber boom, deep in the mysterious jungles of Brazil."

Settling her bandbox on Mrs. Quince's lap, Royall squared her shoulders and started to push the rattan wheelchair in the direction of the low-slung buildings at the wharf's edge.

A small boy dashed past her. As she swung sideways to avoid colliding with him, she noticed a tall, dark, hatless man staring at her. The boldness of his gaze was disturbing, and she rushed forward to escape his rudeness.

". . . You'll be delighted with the paddle boat. It's just what a young girl needs. Gaiety and music. Our paddle boats here on the Amazon rival those on your Mississippi for luxury and food and entertainment. This will be a chance to wear your loveliest gowns."

Royall smiled as she watched Mrs. Quince's pale, slate-colored eyes light with anticipation.

After booking passage on the *Brazilia d'Oro*, Royall guided Mrs. Quince toward the wharf. "We can have our trunks transferred to the *Brazilia* when we board."

The gangplank stretched ahead of them, waiting for the purser to validate their boarding passes. Rosalie Quince was engaged in a lively conversation with the agent when, for a second time, Royall became aware of eyes staring at her. Boldly, she looked around. Her heavily lashed, gold-flecked eyes lifted to the promenade deck. Staring down at her with a cool, mocking gaze was the buccaneer from the Mardi Gras.

God in heaven, what was he doing here on board their ship? He couldn't be sailing with them. He just couldn't. Memories of Mardi Gras flooded through her as she struggled to gain control of her composure. This couldn't be happening to her. She raised her eyes slightly. He was leaning nonchalantly against the rail, never taking his gaze from her. Royall's back stiffened. She stared back, her eyes bold and just as mocking. A pity, she thought, that the sun was so blinding that it was making her squint. Or was it the starkness of his white tropical suit? She found herself craning for a better look and was immediately annoyed with herself. What did he think? As if she cared what the arrogant bastard thought. How dare he look at her that way? Make her feel conspicuous and embarrassed. A small, sick curl of heat wormed in her stomach. This couldn't be happening! The buccaneer was supposed to be aboard a ship in Rio, sailing out of her life forever. If she had ever suspected that their paths would cross again, she would never have allowed herself to be compromised this way. Impertinently, refusing to allow him to get the better of her, she tilted her chin upwards, continuing her bold stare. A tumble of dark hair, ruffled by the soft wind, grazed his brow. He brushed it aside impatiently, never taking his eyes from her.

Again, Royall was struck by his handsomeness, his masculinity. And if appearances were not deceiving, he was still very interested in her. More for deviltry than for any other reason, she lowered her left eyelid in a seductive wink, a smile tugging at the corners of her mouth. He straightened and nodded his head imperceptibly, acknowledging her small flirtation.

Rosalie Quince turned to face Royall. "Did you ever see a more beautiful thing in your life?"

Mistaking Mrs. Quince's words, Royall laughed. "No, Mrs. Quince, I can truthfully say I have never seen anything quite so. . . so . . . dashing."

Rosalie Quince grimaced. "I don't believe I've ever heard of a ship called dashing before. Whatever, it's of no mind. I do so love these paddle-wheelers."

Royall's eyes were following the tall man on the

51

promenade deck. "I've only seen pictures of them," she replied distractedly.

"Is anything wrong, Royall?"

"Wrong? Of course not, Mrs. Quince." She couldn't allow the garrulous Mrs. Quince to suspect that there was a man aboard the paddlewheeler arousing her interest. Worse yet, what if he approached them and revealed his acquaintance with her? No, she assured herself uncertainly; surely he would not be that much of a boor. Or would he?

Royall watched the people boarding the steamboat. Her eyes took in the bright white vessel with its red and gold painted rails. The smokestacks were painted a bright orange, and the gangplank itself was a bright green. Anywhere else these colors would have been overstated, but on the graceful paddlewheeler they were exactly right.

A steward came and relieved Royall of her bandbox, and she followed him as he expertly guided Mrs. Quince's chair up the bright green gangplank to the promenade deck of the *Brazilia*. Royall held tightly to the hemp rope handrail as she ascended the slanting plank. She was still not sure of her "land legs," and she felt she would be more secure on board ship on her "sea legs," which she had learned to command over the several weeks' journey from New England to Brazil. She wondered vaguely if it were possible to become "land sick." She had certainly felt queer since her return to solid ground. Or was it the buccaneer's influence on her? She said as much to Mrs. Quince.

"Oh, lord a mercy, yes, child. I, too, am feeling the effect of our long sea voyage. The layover here in port hasn't really helped. We'll be much more comfortable aboard the *Brazilia*. Truthfully, I can hardly wait to arrive at my plantation where I can be at my leisure and take life slow."

Royall found it hard to believe Mrs. Quince ever took life at a leisurely pace.

They followed the steward to their respective cabins. The small, dark man opened the doors and led them into a cool, dim stateroom, furnished in quiet elegance. The theme of the room was that of a casual summerhouse, all cool greens and pale petal pinks. A deep rose carpet accentuated the light color of the draperies. Hanging from the low ceiling was a glittering crystal chandelier properly scaled to the diminutive proportions of the cabin.

Mrs. Quince's stateroom was similarly furnished, except that the carpet was a deep crimson.

"They will do nicely, won't they? Royall, do you hear me?"

Royall wasn't listening to Mrs. Quince. Instead, her attention was directed toward the open doorway where she had glimpsed a tall figure dressed in a white suit. It had moved from the doorway just as she lifted her eyes.

"Excuse me, Mrs. Quince, did you say something?"

"I was just saying these staterooms will do nicely, don't you think?"

"Yes, very nicely indeed."

"Child, you seem tired. Perhaps you should lie

down and rest. You'll feel more like yourself and you'll be able to enjoy the evening's festivities."

"Perhaps you're right. I do feel a little tired."

"I thought so. Why don't you go into your room and rest. I'll make certain our luggage is brought aboard."

Royall sank down on her bed. Her innards were churning ominously, making her feel decidedly green at the gills. It was impossible! Impossible! He couldn't be here, aboard this ship, traveling with them, his obvious destination Manaus. It was close, too close for comfort.

Her thoughts raced, discarding one possibility after another. What would he do? What would he say? Was he a gentleman or not? Would he dare to refer to their meeting in Rio de Janeiro? Would he flaunt their intimacy?

Questions boiled in her brain, and no solutions made themselves clear. At last, she decided there was only one possible course of action. Royall threw herself back against the pillows. There was only one choice. If he should dare to approach her, she would ignore him. Pretend that he was mistaken about knowing her. It would take daring and the skill of an accomplished liar, but her reputation was at stake.

Why? Why, when for once in her life she had followed her own instincts, her own desires, should fate decree she would be haunted by her impetuosity? Fool! Fool! she cursed herself, beating her fists against the coverlet. Why couldn't I

54

have listened to Mrs. Quince, stayed aboard the clipper ship, and drowned myself in lemonade?

Royall squeezed her eyes shut and turned over on her side. He was brash, insolent, a rogue without conscience! She should have known he was no gentleman—staring at her that way, smiling at her! A gentleman never reminded a lady of her indiscretions. His eyes had seemed to devour her, and in public no less! Shame filled her, bringing heat to her cheeks. But then her traitorous memory reminded her of the way his dark gaze had covered her the night of Mardi Gras. The way his hands had touched her, pleasuring her, bringing her beyond the threshold of desires and passions that she had only dreamed of but had had no experience with. His lips had burned her skin, scorching a trail from her breasts to navel and . . . beyond. Tender lips, demanding lips, glowing dark eyes, gentle exploring fingers . . . Stop it! Stop it! her mind screamed, even while her body betrayed her, needing, wanting to feel those lips, know those hands again. And somehow knowing she would.

Her agitated thoughts demanded action. Jumping up from the bed, she prowled the room like a caged lioness. Mrs. Quince was right; sleep, she needed sleep. With shaking fingers, she unpinned the scandalously tiny hat that matched her gold and navy pinstripe dress from atop her shining, golden head. Next came the dress, the shoes and petticoats. Stripped down to pantaloons and chemise, she closed the louvers on the tiny draped portholes, darkening the room and muting the bright colors. It seemed that since arriving in Brazil she had been assaulted by color, all colors, intoxicating in their intensity. The colors of the Mardi Gras . . . no, she would not think of that now. If possible, she would never think of it again. Pulling the last of the pins from her hair, allowing it to tumble down to her waist, she flung herself on the bed, determinedly closing her eyes, banishing all thought, seeking sleep.

After awakening from her brief nap, Royall felt refreshed and found herself excitedly anticipating the coming evening aboard the river steamer. From all indications it would indeed be exciting. Already she could hear strains of music from the distant orchestra, the tune reminiscent of Mardi Gras.

Quickly, she made her ablutions and sat before the kidney-shaped, organdy-skirted dressing table to arrange her hair. Beneath the bevy of hairpins, ribbons, and dusting powder, she spied her silver-backed hairbrush.

Lovingly, she picked it up and held it to her cheek. Somehow, it brought her father closer to her. It had been his last gift to her before he died. She once again felt the deep, aching gap in her life, a loss more devastating than even losing MacDavis. Perhaps after a time it would narrow, its sharp edges becoming less jagged and easier to bear. She studied the back of the brush. It was heavily engraved. Her slim, oval finger traced the words "Reino Brazilia," the name of the rubber plantation to which she was traveling. It was from this same plantation that her father had come by his wealth. Now it was to be her new home.

Twin lines formed between her finely arched brows, and for an instant she felt as if she were moving through time. Her thoughts slid backward, placing her once again on the clipper ship that had brought her to this exotic land.

The wind had been blowing gently, rustling the sheaf of papers she had carried with her to the mid-deck. Settled in her chair, she attempted to make some sense of her father's portfolio. It had all been carefully explained to her by the family lawyers, but she had been so filled with grief that their words were only a jumble, and the papers she had signed had passed beneath her pen in a blur.

It was there on the mid-deck that she had come across a ledger that her father had used for his personal journal. Leafing through the pages, she found the ledger opened to the last few entries: those written just before Richard Harding's death.

Melancholia brought stinging tears to her eyes, and she fought them back in an effort to read the neat, small script. Something caught her eye, some oddly worded phrase that she couldn't comprehend. She then turned back to the preceding pages and scanned the lines. Nothing really, some mention of dates and appointments, a few others about a purchase of French wines for the cellars. Here:

Heard from old Farleigh's lawyer today. Suppose the old codger finally retired and began to remember his old friends. Still, if what he tells me he suspects is true, I shall have to alter my plans concerning Royall's future. This will take prompt investigation.

Then another entry, two weeks later:

Morrison, Farleigh's lawyer, seems to know what he is talking about. The evidence certainly would seem to point to that. . . . Still, I cannot believe Carlyle would be guilty of such action. It is not indicative of the young boy I once knew . . . Am waiting to hear from Morrison again!

Another entry, a month later:

Yes, it is true. Carlyle has not abided by my wishes to comply with Princess Isabel's Ventre Livre law, and I will not condone his actions. From recent correspondence with him and from other sources which have come to my attention, I tend to believe Morrison's accusations. This is not all. From searching my memory, I seem to remember my dear friend complaining to me of his son. Something about the boy cruelly beating a slave to death. There was some talk of disinheriting the boy.

And among the last entries:

More and more I search the past; now I am quite convinced Carlyle was responsible. I must arrange for a major upheaval in my plans for Royall. I am going to dissolve my holdings in Reino Brazilia and let Carlyle Newsome be damned!

Royall couldn't understand what she had uncovered in the ledger, and it was too late to do anything about it anyway. She was already on her way to Reino Brazilia, Brazilian Kingdom. Richard Harding had died before he had had a chance to sell his share of the plantation. She pushed the chilling phrase that she had read in the ledger away from her thoughts. Father had always been overprotective; still, something was amiss.

Rifling through her bandbox now to find a fresh length of ribbon, she came across the letter that Carlyle Newsome had sent her upon the news of her father's death. She knew its flowery phrases by rote.

My dear Royall,

I am much saddened by the news of your husband's death. I know his passing is a great burden to you. I can only offer you my sincerest condolences in your time of grief.

Your father was a much valued business partner and greatly respected and honored by my father. I remember having met your father only once, when I was but a boy.

This letter is to extend to you a warm invitation to the Reino Brazilia. It will be your home.

Enclosed are sailing dates for ships leaving New England, also instructions for your travel.

If you can arrange to book passage on the *Victoria*, you will have the pleasurable company of Mrs. Rosalie Quince, who is returning to Brazil. She will bring you as far as Reino Brazilia. Her own plantation is but ten miles from here.

My sons, Carl and Jamie, extend their condolences and wish you a safe, speedy journey.

My sincerest wishes,
Carlyle Newsome

Coming back to the present, Royall found herself annoyed once again at Carlyle Newsome's letter. It said all the right things, but what it didn't say was that Royall now owned one half of Reino Brazilia. That what appeared generously offered hospitality was nothing more than her right to look into her investments. Pulling the brush through her hair, she scowled into the mirror. Enough of these dark thoughts. She would deal with "the Baron," as he liked to call himself, when the time came. For now, she had more urgent problems: the sudden, unexpected appearance of the buccaneer. This was a new life with new opportunities, and she meant to make the most of it! Still, the buccaneer occupied her thoughts as she dressed.

Enough of all those dark thoughts. This was a new life with new ideas. With this new life, the first thing she had to see to was her person and her hair.

She finished her hair in the popular style of the day. Her coif of golden curls, pulled back from her smooth brow, Grecian style, was swirled into huge coils at the crown of her head. The style accentuated her graceful, long neck and softly rounded shoulders.

Choosing a gown of fine silk in a dark amber color, she held it close to her body and admired her reflection in the long looking glass behind the armoire door. Its rich, gleaming folds were perfect for an evening of entertainment. Excitement eliminated the need for rouge, and she applied only a touch of pomade to her full mouth. Would he notice her? How could he help but be aware of her?

Gathering up her reticule and cashmere shawl, she stole a final glance in the glass. Unashamedly, she appraised herself, liking what she saw. She smiled, remembering Mrs. Quince interpreting the native women's chatter and saying they called her golden girl. She thought perhaps she should feel conspicuous for her fairness in a land where most everyone was dark complected, but she recalled the eyes of the buccaneer on her and she tingled deliciously under the remembered feel of her body against his.

Pulling herself from her thoughts, she turned away from the glass.

"Yoohoo, Royall, are you dressed?"

"Yes, Mrs. Quince, I'm ready to go." The door opened, revealing Mrs. Quince sitting primly in her wheelchair. "I think I'm finally able to maneuver this dratted contraption," Rosalie Quince sighed as she worked the oversized wheels with the palms of her hands. A handsome woman, she had chosen a deep burgundy silk gown that complemented her rounded figure.

"Royall, you look absolutely breathtaking. You'll turn every head when we enter the dining room. I hope you're prepared to parry the notorious flirtatious natures of our Brazilian gentlemen."

Royall pushed Mrs. Quince's chair out of her room and onto the promenade deck, laughing over Mrs. Quince's amusing observations about the amorous nature of the Latin.

The dining hall was full to brimming when they arrived. "Oh, dear, I underestimated the number of passengers who will be having dinner here the evening of the sail. I hope we won't have to wait too long for a table. I'm famished."

Royall was quite content to wait, however hungry she felt. The dining hall was sumptuous, approaching the point of garishness. Deep red carpeting, gilt-edge picture frames of questionable taste, floods of gloriously gowned women and scrupulously tailored men graced the hall. Crystal chandeliers cast a warm glow over the tops of the tables, causing iridescent shimmers to reflect from the jewels worn at the ears and throats of the ladies. After the sterile efficiency of the *Victoria*, which had brought them to Brazil, it was a welcome sight to Royall's eyes to feast on the opulence and splendor of the *Brazilia d'Oro*.

A heavy-set, stern-looking maitre d' approached them.

"If you will permit, mesdames, it will be an hour before you can be seated at a table. Perhaps you would like dinner served to you in your rooms?"

Mrs. Quince turned to look at Royall to view her reaction. Seeing the disappointment on her face, she answered, "No, we'll wait. However hungry I am, I would not care to disappoint my young friend on her first night on an Amazonian river steamer."

The maitre d's stern look vanished, and he braved a small smile in Royall's direction. He offered Mrs. Quince a slight bow as he took his leave.

The music had started to play again, and Royall turned to see the orchestra. The musicians were seated on a dais above the main floor of the dining hall. They were attired in bright red waistcoats and black trousers. She was surprised to see that all the musicians were Indian. They played the popular tunes so well, one would have thought they were English or American.

A movement caught her eye, and she lowered her gaze to the main floor. There, seated in an alcove, was the buccaneer. Suddenly, their eyes met and held. She tore her gaze away, then quickly found herself stealing another look. He was on his feet and coming toward her. Inexplicably, her heart beat faster, making her feel as though the pulsing in her throat was choking her. Her eyes followed his hindered progress through the crowded room. He was no longer looking at her; he was looking beyond her, and inexplicably her heart fell. As he approached, she noticed again how tall he was. Well over six feet, if her guess was correct.

Mrs. Quince made a slight gasping sound behind her. "Why, it's Sebastian. We're in luck. I was right! It was you on the wharf in Rio!"

He gracefully climbed the four or five steps to the level on which they were standing. He smiled, white teeth gleaming in his darkly tanned face; his eyes were black . . . Indian black. "Mrs. Quince! I had not expected to see you until sometime next month. Had I known you were traveling on the same vessel as I, I would have invited you to join me at dinner much before this." He was suddenly aware of Mrs. Quince's wheelchair, and his brows lifted in question.

"Oh, posh, Sebastian, don't ask questions and make an old woman feel more foolish than she is. I've broken my ankle. I'll be fine in a few weeks, I promise you."

In a gallant gesture, he leaned over her hand and pressed it to his lips. "I am so sorry, Senora Quince. May you return to yourself soon."

"I'll feel more like myself as soon as I've had dinner, Sebastian. Whatever are you doing in Belém at this time of year? One would think you were too busy getting your rubber to market to treat yourself to a sojourn in the east. However, I am sure, never has one been so happy to see you as I am. The maitre d' informs us it will be at least an hour before he can seat us to dinner." At her last words, Mrs. Quince turned to Royall.

Sebastian's eyes followed Mrs. Quince's gaze, and he turned to Royall and gave a slight courtly bow. "Royall Banner, allow me to present Sebastian Rivera to you. Royall has been widowed recently and is journeying with me to the plantation, Sebastian."

"How do you do, Senora Banner." Sebastian's eyes formed questions and then seemed to find the answers. He wasn't surprised to find that Royall was a widow; it explained so many things. The night of Mardi Gras he hadn't been surprised, thinking she was a prostitute, to find that she wasn't a virgin. What had surprised him was her obvious lack of experience, her innocence. A smile formed on his lips. Royall had all the untouched innocence of a virgin, blended with a natural inclination for passion. No doubt her husband had never delved the wells of sensuality this woman possessed. Poor man, he found himself thinking, going to the grave never knowing what an exciting woman warmed his bed. The grin broadened; Senor Banner's loss was Sebastian's gain.

His eyes flashed at her; twin circles of jet bore into her being. She felt breathless and struggled for control. Never had she met so handsome and dynamic a man.

Regaining control, she answered, "How do you do, Senor Rivera. And that's Royall with two L's."

Sebastian's eyes became hooded. He remained silent for a moment. Was she daring him to expose her? Or was she simply mocking him? How sweet and innocent she looked standing next to Senora Quince. His heart thumped in his chest as she boldly returned his gaze. There was no point in denying the fact that he found her exciting. She was indeed a sleek jungle cat.

"Ladies, please do me the honor of joining me at my table," he said urbanely.

Mrs. Quince, in the abrupt manner to which Royall had become familiar, answered for them. "I thought you would never ask. But I warn you, if you hadn't, I would have invited us anyway. So it's just as well you did, Sebastian!"

The twin orbs of jet glowed at Rosalie Quince. "Based on our long acquaintance, I've no doubt you would, Senora. However, let me assure you, the pleasure is all mine." His words were directed to Rosalie Quince; his gaze was for Royall alone. A gesture, a word, and two stewards lifted Mrs. Quince, complete with wheelchair, down the few steps to the main Salon. Offering his arm to Royall, they followed behind the steward pushing the chair to Sebastian's table.

The conversation was lively, owing much to Mrs. Quince's jocularity and loquaciousness, not

66

to mention her constant references to her wheeled chair. The dinner of stuffed lamb and rice was delectable, and the wine Sebastian chose to accompany the meal was the perfect complement to the savory courses. In spite of her previous misgivings, Royall found herself relaxing in his company, in fact enjoying it.

When the waiter came to take the order for dessert, Mrs. Quince uttered a small squeal of delight. "At last," she sighed. "Sebastian, I can't tell you how many months I've hungered for *clea'ho.*"

"I can well imagine, Senora Quince. I understand guava is not a popular fruit in America."

At this exchange Royall frowned. She did so hate to be left out of any conversation.

"Dear, Sebastian is referring to my passion for the favorite dessert of Brazilians—guava paste and white cheese. Do you think you would care to try some? Or perhaps you would like to have a Blessed Mother?"

Royall frowned again. "What is a Blessed Mother?"

Sebastian and Mrs. Quince laughed, but at the embarrassed look on Royall's face, Sebastian's features sobered.

"Senora Banner, forgive my rudeness. Senora Quince and I are enjoying ourselves at your expense, I'm afraid. A Blessed Mother is what the natives call certain little pastries. They're very similar to French petits fours. The Indians usually

67

serve them on religious holidays, hence the name, 'Blessed Mothers.' "

"Oh, I see. Perhaps I shall try a Blessed Mother, if you don't mind." Seeing the apologetic look on Mrs. Quince's face, she broke into a mirthful smile. If Sebastian Rivera could act as though nothing had happened between the two of them, then so could she.

"It would seem Senora Banner also has a teasing sense of humor. Senora Quince, I can't tell you how I'm looking forward to this journey up the Amazon. Thanks to Mrs. Banner and yourself, I believe I'm the only gentleman aboard who is so fortunate as to be honored with the company of two such lovely ladies."

"Sebastian, save your speeches for the dance floor. My ankle is aching me. Please don't hesitate to ask Royall to dance for fear of leaving me alone at the table." Mrs. Quince pressed her hand to her lips to stifle a demure yawn. "As soon as I have finished my dessert, I fear it will be all I can do to keep my eyes open. Therefore, I shall have one of the stewards take me back to my cabin and entrust you to see that Royall is properly entertained. I have no wish to act as a duenna, I can assure you. I've known you long enough, Sebastian, to feel it quite proper to leave Royall in your care."

Oh, Mrs. Quince, if you only knew how wrong you are, Royall thought.

Sebastian nodded. "I shall be delighted to act as escort for Senora Banner."

Sebastian turned his eyes toward Royall and smiled. Somewhere within her something stirred, making it hard for her to breathe.

He had kept his eyes on her throughout the dinner, ruining her appetite. What was he looking for when he peered so deeply into her eyes? Why was it so hard for her to keep her eyes from meeting his? She didn't like the strange emotions his presence evoked.

The music began to play again, a soft, haunting tune with which she was not familiar. Waiters busied themselves quenching the candles burning brightly in the chandeliers above the tables.

A huge black man, dressed in bright gaudy trousers and an orange silk shirt open to the waist, proceeded onto the dance floor and squatted, placing a pair of drums between his knees.

The flutist played a haunting melody, rising an octave above the other instruments. Suddenly, on the dance floor were two other natives, a man and woman, both dressed in flamboyant costume. They assumed a stiff, yet graceful pose and waited for the music to reach its end.

The dining hall became quiet; the diners waited expectantly.

"You are in store for a treat, Royall," Mrs. Quince whispered. "This is, if I'm not mistaken, the trio that has been taking Rio de Janeiro by storm. They're from Africa and I understand they're quite a success. I suppose they're on their way to Manaus to play at the opera house."

"Shhh," came a command from behind Mrs.

69

Quince. A woman gestured with her hand and turned Royall's attention toward the dance floor.

The dancer began to move, swaying her hips in rhythm to the music; the man followed her lead. The drummer beat a slow rhythm, which became imperceptibly faster as the dance continued. The music took flight, the flutist now reaching low, mellow notes and then soaring to unbelievably clear, high-pitched tones.

The dancers followed the rhythm, swaying, rocking, becoming faster till they were swirling together, holding each other close.

Royall had never seen anything like this. She had been to New York once with her father, to the opera and the ballet, but somehow she could not imagine even the sophisticated New York society of the year 1877 accepting these dancers at their ballet or opera house.

Her attention was attracted to the woman dancer. Tall and lithe, she was now arching herself backward, her expression one of ecstasy. The light of the few candles remaining was caught by the beads of perspiration on her arms and throat, creating miniature diamonds.

The melody and rhythm became heavy, surging to a rapid crescendo. The music stopped; the dancers remained absolutely still, a dramatic tableau. The diners were hushed. Royall glanced around and saw men pulling at their collars and women fanning themselves rapidly. Within herself, Royall felt a remembered excitement. She returned her attention to her own table. Mrs.

Quince appeared mesmerized by the dancers; she was staring fixedly at them. Sebastian Rivera was staring at Royall. His gaze was penetrating, probing. Royall returned his look boldly. She felt beautiful under his gaze, warm and sensuous. He was remembering the same as she was. This man made her aware of herself, of her beauty, of her womanliness.

Their eyes locked. Deep, deeper. He gazed, she felt, into her soul and she welcomed him. How well she remembered.

Minutes later, Mrs. Quince retired to her cabin with the aid of a steward. Royall and Sebastian spoke of inconsequential things and shared the enjoyment of each other's company. Along toward midnight, Sebastian acquiesced to the lateness of the hour and suggested a stroll around the deck before escorting Royall back to her cabin.

Royall felt drained. Why was he playing this charade? Not one mention of the Mardi Gras. He was behaving the perfect gentleman. Acting as though he had just met her. It was damn insulting. She should get angry and do something, say something to shake his manly composure. He had made wild, passionate love to her, and now he was treating her like a casual acquaintance. Exasperated with her own contradictory thoughts, she eagerly accepted his invitation for a stroll. She couldn't keep things straight in her head. One minute she was praying that he would never refer to the night of Mardi Gras, and the next she was cursing him for pretending she had never spent the night in his arms.

The night was shimmering with stars. The Southern Cross was clearly visible, and Sebastian pointed it out to her. Silence fell between them. Royall sighed. If she had to play the game, she would. What an awful waste of time.

"What are you thinking of, Senora Banner?" His voice was a low-pitched purr.

"I was just thinking that home in New England, it is late February, and the full force of winter is holding fast. Here, it is eternal summer. It's hard to imagine a world so big it can have two seasons at the same time. New England always seemed the world to me. Now, here I am in Brazil on a riverboat, sailing up the Amazon to a city I'd not heard of till a few months ago. Traveling with Rosalie is an experience." That should slow down your game a bit, Sebastian Rivera, she thought nastily.

"Yes, Rosalie Quince sees the world through the sharp eyes of a child. Every day is an adventure for her, and she shares that adventure with those around her."

"I know exactly what you mean. When I first met her, she put me completely at ease. She is truly a great lady." She wanted to scream, to beat at him with her fists. The last thing she wanted to talk about was Rosalie Quince.

"In more ways than you know. When Senora Quince came to Brazil years ago with her husband, Alonzo, she braved fever and famine to work at his side in the wild rubber forest. If it weren't for her strength and perseverance, Alonzo is the first to admit, he would have turned away from Brazil to find his fortune elsewhere. From wilderness and a thatched-roof hut Rosalie Quince carved a civilization out of the jungle. It was she who induced the Catholic missionaries to come to the wilds of the rubber forests to educate the Indians. It was she who founded the first hospital for Negroes and Indians. Manaus looks upon her as the grande dame of its society, and a dinner party during the social season is not a true success unless she makes an appearance.

"Rosalie Quince has worked hard all her life, and sometimes I think it rankles her to have so much leisure time on her hands. Still, I think if she had the opportunity, she would gladly wrap her head in a cloth and work in the fields alongside her Indians as she once did. She's a remarkable woman, and I, for one, consider myself fortunate to know her and be recognized by her."

"I'm glad you have told me this about Mrs. Quince, Senor Rivera. Rosalie never would have revealed it herself; although I must admit I guessed at what you've told me. Only a woman who has known hardship can have the capacity for unselfish understanding. And this I found in Mrs. Quince. I've been the beneficiary of her maternal instincts. I've felt she privileged me by substituting me for her daughter Suzanne."

"You're correct in considering yourself privileged. Tell me, how did she find Suzanne when she went to America?"

"Very well, I think, though I know she misses her sorely."

A brisk breeze swept across the deck, and the dampness of the night air gave Royall an involuntary shiver.

Sun-bronzed hands gently tucked Royall's shawl more closely about her. How strong and capable his hands looked. The faint aroma of his cheroot and some tangy, unnamed scent wafted about her. She shivered, not with cold, but with memories.

Dark eyes stared down at her. Royall correctly interpreted the look and flushed, grateful for the near darkness. His voice, when he spoke, was mocking. "Come, Rosalie will never forgive me if I allow you to catch a chill."

Royall lowered her eyes, feeling a glorious warmth steal over her, warmth from Sebastian's mocking eyes and tall, muscular body. Without warning, she found herself suddenly in his embrace. He said nothing as he brought his face close to hers, making her light-headed with excitement. Lightly, his lips grazed hers.

A current of emotions swept over Royall. Her body tingled; her pulses throbbed.

His lips were hard and demanding. Hungry. She responded, her lips as feverish as Sebastian's. Suddenly, he released her. Royall felt shaken. Surely he wanted more, just as she did. The brazen thought did nothing for her composure. She stared into dark eyes that held a promise. Was her own gaze also full of promise? Promise of . . . of . . . she refused to name the emotion that was sweeping all reason, all thoughts aside. She wanted this man. She knew without a doubt that her new life would never be complete unless Sebastian Rivera was entwined in the strands of her very being. He was her destiny. She could almost feel it, taste it filling her.

Their soft footfalls outside Rosalie Quince's stateroom made her smile. Then she heard Royall's stateroom door close and the sound of Sebastian's boots going back down the companionway to the rhythm of his satisfied whistling. Was a match in the making? If so, she was delighted. If not, as yet, she would give romance a helping hand. A gentle prod, so to speak. Sometimes Sebastian could be so mule-headed, especially when it came to women. Women like Royall Banner didn't enter a man's life every day of the week. In fact, rarely did they enter a man's life. There was something special about Royall, something that set her apart from the other women in Rosalie Quince's circle of friends. It wasn't her golden beauty either. What was it? Rosalie hated it when things or thoughts eluded her. Well, whatever it was that made the young woman different would come to her one of these days when she was least expecting it. She would forget the gentle prod and concentrate on a well-deserved kick in the right direction. That was something Sebastian would understand. Rosalie Quince sighed deeply, and much to her own amusement, she found that she missed the lumpy and narrow bunk in which she had slept during her long journey on the *Victoria*. "Ridiculous," she chided herself. "How a body could miss that foul excuse for a bed is beyond me."

Even as she muttered the words, she wriggled slightly, seeking the familiar hole which she had worked into the cotton mattress that served for bedding on the clipper ship.

Silently, reverently, Rosalie Quince whispered her evening prayers before closing her eyes. She had lain in bed resting until she heard the footsteps; then, knowing the girl was safe, she felt able to sleep.

According to habit, she saved her prayers for her last thoughts. While still a young girl, she had developed the knack of sorting her thoughts and mulling them over as one will do before sleep; then, when she felt all that could be done for the day was done, she would whisper her words to God and close her eyes for the night.

As she began her "God-blesses," as she had done since she was a child, Suzanne's name came to her lips. Darling Suzanne, the only child of Rosalie's marriage. The journey to America, in spite of her cheerful demeanor, had been taxing and tedious. No longer young, Rosalie Quince nevertheless could not bear her daughter to endure childbirth among strangers. Even though the "strangers" were the girl's in-laws, Rosalie felt the need to protect Suzanne from whatever her new life cast her way and once again, perhaps for the last time, draw her daughter close and help her through the pain.

It was not easy for Mrs. Quince to admit to herself that perhaps she had seen her beloved daughter for the last time. After all, she was not young, and she could feel the hot, humid jungle drain away her strength more and more, year after year.

Her arms ached for Suzanne, and she could again see the slim, young girl standing on the wharf, waving good-bye. It remained unspoken between mother and child, the fear of never again holding close one who is loved so dearly.

A sound from the companionway shook Rosalie from her reverie. Aboard ship, Rosalie Quince had taken an immediate liking to her traveling companion, perhaps to defray the pain of being separated from Suzanne; nevertheless, Royall proved to be a young woman of warmth and charm.

Rosalie's maternal instincts, torn so savagely by her separation from Suzanne, were able to find refuge and comfort in the tutelage and protection of Royall Banner.

Finishing her "God-blesses," Rosalie impatiently brushed a tear away from the corner of her eye, plumped her feather pillow, and fell back to render her keeping to the angels for the night.

Royall awakened leisurely. This had been the first night in several weeks that she had not felt herself cramped into a short, narrow bunk. She stretched her long, slim limbs, luxuriating in the feel of the fresh muslin sheets.

A feeling crept over her, one of happiness and anticipation. She had fallen asleep with the thoughts of the exciting evening she had spent with Sebastian Rivera and Mrs. Quince, and now she looked forward to another.

She lithely jumped from under the covers and hastened to make her ablutions as though she could not wait to face the day. Humming softly to herself, she rummaged through her trunks and cases looking for exactly the correct costume for her first day upon the luxurious Amazon steamer.

Finally, choosing an aquamarine moiré silk morning dress, she sat before the mirror to dress her hair. She freed the thick blond masses from their ribbons and began to brush the snarls and tangles from it.

It fell almost to her waist, cascading around her white shoulders. Every time she dressed her hair, she reveled in its wealth and sheen. She couldn't help but remember when she was a young girl of thirteen. She'd suffered from a fever and the doctors had insisted on cutting her hair. "It saps her strength." She could still hear the dour physician's voice and her father's murmured cry of dismay at this radical treatment. For months after that Royall had refused to venture from the house. It was not until her hair grew back to a decent length that she allowed her father to buy her a frivolous bonnet, and she shyly accompanied him for a ride in a hansom through the city park.

Now, as she dipped her fingers in the pomade and stroked them through her hair, she could bless the doctor who had issued the order. Her hair had grown back in a very short time, and where once it had been fine and silky, now it was heavy and glossy, obedient to the will of her brush. Royall considered it her most valuable feature.

As she was placing the last of the pins in her coiffure, Mrs. Quince knocked at the door. "Yoo-hoo, Royall, are you awake?"

"Yes, Mrs. Quince. I've just finished dressing my hair."

Rosalie Quince maneuvered the chair into the room, still in her dressing gown. "Dear, would you prefer breakfast here in your stateroom, or would you prefer to eat on deck with the other diners? Perhaps you would enjoy a view of Brazil as you sip your coffee?"

"I'd like that very much, Mrs. Quince. I didn't get to see much of it yesterday."

"I thought as much. It will only take minutes for me to dress. Perhaps you would come into my stateroom and lace my stays for me?"

Twenty minutes later Mrs. Quince and Royall were seated at a small table on the upper deck of the riverboat. Royall, in her aquamarine gown, had turned every head as she made her way through to their table. She adored the attention she was receiving and only hoped Sebastian Rivera was close enough to notice.

The richness of the moiré silk and the vibrant hue of aquamarine set off Royall's golden skin and turned her blond hair to gold. Conscious of the admiring stares, she followed Mrs. Quince's wheelchair and seated herself. Every nerve in her body was tightened to alertness. Then she felt, rather than saw, Sebastian Rivera approach them.

"Good morning, ladies. I trust you rested well?" His tone was light and casual, his eyes sharp and piercing. Royall exalted in their uncompromising approval as he surveyed her. He had noticed.

"It seems Senora Quince, I am in that unfortunate position in which you found yourself last evening. There is no available table."

Rosalie Quince, a smile playing about her thin mouth, lowered her head in a mock curtsy.

"Please, Sebastian, I entreat you to join us for breakfast."

"I warn you, Senora Quince, had you not done so, I would have invited myself," he chided as he winked at her.

Remembering Mrs. Quince's words from the evening before, Royall laughed openly. "It would seem, Mrs. Quince, that Senor Rivera has quite a memory for conversation."

Feigning annoyance, Mrs. Quince replied sullenly, "Yes, so it would seem."

"Tell me, Senor, how is your memory concerning other matters?" As soon as the words were out of her mouth, she could have died. She must be insane to remind him, to practically give him permission to acknowledge what had occurred between them.

He met her head on, brows lifting, dark eyes daring, a crooked grin twisting his mouth. "I assure you, Senora, my memory serves me very well." His gaze flicked over her arrogantly, saying more than his words that he remembered her quite well indeed.

Sebastian signaled to the waiter to bring a chair to the table. His poise and authority did not escape Royall. Once seated, he directed his full attention to his companions. "Tell me, Senora Banner, has Rosalie fully prepared you for the rigors of plantation life?"

Before she could answer, Mrs. Quince interrupted. "The rigors of life in Manaus would be more the case, Sebastian, and you know it." Turning to Royall, she began to explain. "I'm sure, dear, you've heard of the decadent society of Paris. Well, let me assure you, Manaus will soon rival that European city for its gluttony and distasteful displays of garish accoutrements. I, for one, much prefer the quiet, serene life on the plantation. I could well do without splendiferous-gowned ladies and men who tipple the most expensive wines. Were it not for the fact that I am sure it is only to flaunt their newfound wealth, I might accept it more gracefully. But this society is so ostentatious that it is actually perverse." Turning to Sebastian, "And the less said of it the better. Were it not expedient to maintain a townhouse for the sake of Alonzo's business dealings, I assure you I would not set foot in that devil's shrine."

Sebastian, who had heard this same point of

81

view at other times from Mrs. Quince, smiled and commiserated with her. "I, too, prefer plantation life. And you're right; the less said, the better. I wouldn't want to discourage Senora Banner before she has had a chance to decide for herself."

"I assure you, Senor Rivera, it would take much more than the evils of Manaus to discourage me in my opinion of Brazil." She half-turned in her seat to admire the view along the shore. "From what I've seen of your country, the only word with which I could describe it would be *lush*."

The waiter arrived and Sebastian ordered quickly. Royall found it hard to concentrate on her plate under Sebastian's scrutiny. He watched her in open admiration. A table close to theirs was occupied by three gentlemen. Their admiring glances directed toward Royall brought a scowl to Sebastian's face, and he glowered at them, causing her to experience a delicious tingle. Jealousy? It serves you right, Sebastian Rivera.

With a last sip of coffee Sebastian grudgingly excused himself, saying, "I have a meeting to attend in the lower lounge, but I would like it if both you ladies joined me for dinner."

Mrs. Quince accepted quickly for both of them.

Royall watched Sebastian's graceful movements as he took his leave. "Shall we indulge ourselves with another cup of this marvelous coffee, Royall?" she heard Mrs. Quince break into her thoughts.

"Yes, please, Mrs. Quince, and perhaps another wheat cake." Anything to occupy her thoughts, anything to drive Sebastian's image from her mind.

Chapter Four

"Another wheat cake? Why, you hardly touched . . ." Mrs. Quince broke off in mid-speech. She grinned at the blushing Royall like a cat that has just discovered a mouse in the pantry. "Yes, of course, dear, another wheat cake."

Most of the tables were empty by now, and the waiters were clearing away the debris left behind.

Royall attacked her breakfast and was putting the last crumbs into her mouth when Mrs. Quince said shortly, "He's a bastard, you know."

Mrs. Quince's proffered statement brought about the desired results; Royall choked on the crumbs.

"What . . . who?"

"Sebastian, of course." Mrs. Quince's penetrating look sought out Royall's opinions. "Why do you tell me this? What concern is it of mine?" She tried to act blasé and was determined Mrs. Quince would not get any satisfaction from her scandalous remark.

All the while Rosalie Quince was peering into Royall's gold-flecked eyes to measure her mettle. It was a cruel thing to do, but Sebastian was dear to her, and it would be best to see what stuff Royall was made of before he lost his heart completely to the golden girl. She liked Royall very much, "exceedingly fond," some of the sophisticates from Manaus would call it, but she liked Sebastian also. If the matter of his bastardy would put the girl off him, it would be best to know it now, not after when real damage could be done to both.

"I only tell you this because I have eyes, and I wouldn't want you to hear it from anyone else. To be fair, before you make any judgments, I want you to hear me out.

"Society in the jungles of Brazil is much different from that to which you are accustomed. Here we are swayed by what a man makes of himself; his beginnings are of little consequence. The natives and the Negro slaves so outnumber us English-and Portuguese-speaking people, it is only a matter of better judgment that we not hastily cast aside a member of our society for something as trifling as dubious parentage."

To her knowledge, Royall had never listened to a conversation in which the subject was illegitimacy. She couldn't bring herself to question. Mrs. Quince answered her unasked inquiry.

"Oh, yes, dear, Sebastian's mother was a native, an especially beautiful girl with a sweet disposition. She was devoted to her son until her death. As to his father, that is unknown. I doubt if even Sebastian knows who his father is. Although some say it was Farleigh Mallard, who left Sebastian a failing plantation and a barely adequate income— just enough to send Sebastian across the ocean to England to complete his education. When he returned from England, he took up the reins, so to speak, and worked day and night to make the plantation the thriving holding it is today."

"But why do you tell me this, Mrs. Quince? Don't you like Senor Rivera? You seemed so glad to see him, and your manner is quite friendly."

"Good Lord, child. Of course I like him. I'm quite fond of him, actually. Even when he was a small boy, there was something intense about him, as if he were fated to be a powerful man. The men also think a great deal of him. They consider him most honest and reliable. I'm glad to see he is finally accepted into the society in which he belongs."

"What do you mean, 'finally'?"

"Be it because of his Indian mother or just plain humanity, Sebastian's sympathy is with the Indian. When the plantation began to thrive, he freed his slaves and began to pay them a small wage in return for their labors. And labor they do. They honor Sebastian; they love him. He is their redeemer; their god here on earth. It is unheard of for a master to free slaves in these parts."

"Unheard of?" Royall was incredulous. "But my father was jubilant because Princess Isabel passed the law of Ventre Livre. I remember reading about it in my school books. When the law was passed saying all slaves were to be free when they reached the age of sixty, my father told me it would be a matter of generations before all men in Brazil were free!"

"You are right, dear. In 1871 the Ventre Livre law was passed. This provided that all children born of slaves after 1871 would be free as well as all slaves that belonged to the State or the Crown. But unscrupulous plantation owners are only concerned with their rate of profit. They cannot find it in themselves to pay even a small wage for the work they have been getting for the price of spoiled food and a miserable thatched hut. Don't be shocked to come across deplorable conditions here in Brazil. Many of us are petitioning for the emancipation of all slaves. As of yet, the government feels the economy is too shaky. But if enough of us raise our voices, we will have to be heard. Sebastian is a great example for abolition; he owns no slaves and yet his plantation yields the most rubber."

"How can these unscrupulous plantation owners keep the Indian at work? Surely they want to see their children free men?"

"Most certainly. The Indian's love for his children is unequaled. Yet, there are those owners who say, 'If the child will not work in the field beside his parents, there is no room for him here. Put him out!'

"Parents don't want to be separated from their children, so they stay on and work for the owner, even those over sixty who might want to consider themselves free. Where can they go? Old and worn, who would give them work? No, they stay on at their plantations and labor till they drop dead in their tracks."

"What of you and Mr. Quince? Have you freed your slaves?"

"We have, those born after '71. But they are still too young to work in the fields, so it has not strained our budget. And those old folk who are sixty and over, they have nowhere to go, so we give them light chores around the garden or in the dairy with the livestock, and they are grateful to have the food we feed them, and just to stay with their families. Besides, we treat our help most humanely. The conditions under which they live are far superior to those on many plantations.

"Sebastian is forever trying to induce the owners to improve the conditions of their slaves and raise their standard of living. He is indeed worthy of the adulation of his help. Kindness is his bylaw. He is the guardian of the downtrodden people. Make no mistake, though; when he is dealing with the rubber traders, he matches their ruthlessness. He is, on the whole, honest, but he is not to be put upon and cheated. He is wise and compassionate, truly a remarkable man." Mrs. Quince picked at a piece of lint on the front of her gown and said distractedly, "I had wished at one time he would be my son-in-law. But it was not to be. I can take comfort in the fact that none of the other doting mothers of debutantes seem to be making much headway. I suppose it might seem strange to you that a mother might welcome a man born on the wrong side of the covers for her daughter's husband. But remember, I told you: Society here is very different from that which you have known."

Royall smiled and gazed reflectively toward the

water. She felt the light touch of Mrs. Quince on her arm. "Forgive me, Royall. I wanted to tell you this in as kind a way as I knew how. I startled you in the beginning, but it was for a reason. I'm proud of you for coming from so sheltered a life and accepting things as they are here. I can see it now. You will give the plantation life some sparkle. All the young men will be after you like flies to a honey pot."

Royall laughed aloud. As long as Sebastian is the fly, she thought secretly.

That evening Royall dressed with extra care. Annoyed that her hair kept turning into unexpected curls, she tugged and pulled and combed and smoothed until she achieved the effect she wanted. A high coif, not too high, but higher than she was accustomed to wearing. That afternoon she had buffed her nails till they had a soft gleam that enhanced her oval-tapered fingertips. The bath, which the stewards on the paddlewheeler brought to her after many trips back and forth to the galley, carrying the heated water in great jugs, had been scented and taken leisurely.

Picking through her wardrobe, she chose a smoky rose silk gown with a puckering of ribbons at the bodice. "Simplicity itself," the New England dressmaker had sighed. It was of classic design, soft folds falling unhampered from the slightly elevated waist. A drop neckline left her arms bare and showed smooth, flawless skin against the muted color. Against her tawny hair, its contrast was striking. She picked up the ostrich plumes that were popular, and then abruptly threw them back again on the dressing table. She would feel foolish and flighty wearing them. She knew they had been a mistake when the dressmaker insisted they would be a perfect foil against the simplicity of the rose gown. A simple pendant of quartz was all the accessory she felt she needed. All Sebastian would like to see her in. She did not take him for a man who liked to see women dressed in "gadgets," as her father had called them. As she sorted through her dainties to select a fresh handkerchief, she thought again of what Mrs. Quince had revealed to her that morning. What a strain he must have lived under, although he seemed to fare with it very well. A doubtful parentage was not exactly a boost to a man's career, and she was delighted for him that he had overcome its burden.

She stood before the mirror and studied herself. The gown was perfect, but she had doubts about the hairdo. Was it too high? Too affected? "No, silly," she told herself, "you'll do just fine. No sense trying to be what you're not! Still . . . no, it's fine," she assured herself. Before she could change her mind she hurried down the hall. "Mrs. Quince, are you ready?"

Sebastian was waiting for them outside the dining room. He was handsome in a dinner jacket of white gabardine with snowy frills on his shirt front. His deep tan and dark hair were in startling relief against the whiteness of his dress. He turned in their direction and saw them. His eyes fell on

Royall and seemed to drink her in. Her patience in her dressing was well rewarded. He kept his eyes on her face as he bid them hello, and it was with effort that he drew his attention to Mrs. Quince.

With little conversation, he led Royall into the dining room, a steward pushing Mrs. Quince's chair. The table was the same one as the previous night, and he explained that he had reserved it for the entire journey.

"I wish we had thought to do the same, Sebastian. Were it not for you, we would have been in that din waiting for a table," Mrs. Quince said, looking toward the doorway where a myriad of people stood waiting to be seated.

"I repeat, Senora Quince, the pleasure is all mine." This he said as he looked in Royall's direction. She felt her skin grow warm under his gaze. Why could this man make her blood race through her? Why did she find herself at a loss for words in his presence? Why was she acting like a schoolgirl instead of a poised widow who had had the benefit of an education and profited from a finishing school, not to mention the lovemaking they had shared? Why, when she wanted to be at her best, did she find her confidence in herself falter? But then, when he looked at her as he was doing now, her fears disappeared and she could feel herself preen under his attention. Her pulse would quicken and the very air she breathed would exhilarate her being. She felt herself fill out—a woman, nothing more, a woman. His kind of woman?

Sebastian picked at his dinner, feeling nourished by Royall's presence. He watched her. Slim and lithe, poised, quiet. Not babbling on, the way some girls did. She was gracious, almost queenly in her bearing. He, Sebastian Rivera, sometimes described as the most eligible bachelor in Manaus, felt as though he had feathers instead of a backbone. Yet, there were times when she looked at him, waiting for him to answer her question, or looking to him in conversation, when he felt he could be all she would ever want him to be. A man whose opinion was valued, whose words meant something. He believed she measured his words, listened to him. Not like most other women he had known, who patiently waited for him to finish his sentence just so they could lead the talk back to themselves. Or perhaps, while he was speaking, were wondering if their hats were on straight or their hair falling out from some of those outlandish coifs they wore, or were fidgeting with their gloves, or, worse, giggling in punctuation at the end of his every statement. This was a woman who was interested in him and what he had to say, what he was thinking. Nothing would ever convince him she was feigning interest. A man could tell those things. And in her deference to him, he found he weighed his words more carefully, pondered his judgments, considered his banter. He enjoyed himself, liked himself. He felt good to be with her, more a man, and always the memories of the night they had shared. Was she too remembering? He had been wrong. This young lady was different. If he wanted more to come of their relationship, and he admitted to himself that he did, he would have to tread softly.

After dinner Sebastian escorted Royall to the top deck. The night was sultry, and from where they stood, the sound of the great paddle wheel was a low whoosh as it propelled the luxurious boat through the dark waters of the Amazon.

The stars hung in the black sky, shining their dim, celestial light upon their faces. The moon at its first quarter was like an orange slice, precariously teetering in the heavens.

Royall breathed in the heavy scent of the tropical air. She became lost in the moment, entranced in the magic of the Brazilian sky, warm in the nearness of Sebastian.

He watched her as though from afar. Inwardly he groaned with longing for her and silently cursed himself for being at a loss for words. As he watched her, a breeze lifted itself across the water and blew against her. The soft folds of her gown were drawn against her, revealing the sensuous lines of her body. The breeze caressed her and wafted in his direction, bringing with it the scent she used. It reminded him of the earth, the sky, and the river he loved.

She turned to face him, somewhat embarrassed by her long silence, shy that her emotions were all too evident, afraid he would sense her desire.

His expression, as he looked at her, made her

feel giddy; she was aware of his feelings and reveled in them. The embarrassing silence became a silent understanding—no words were needed. He approached her as she turned to look out over the water. His arms slipped around her and held her close. She could feel his warm breath against her cheek and she pressed herself closer to his chest.

Suddenly, his lips came down hard on hers, straining, loving, wanting her more than he'd ever wanted a woman. And she was responding to him as urgently as he hoped she would. In their ardent embrace, he caressed her full breasts through the soft silk, feeling their rosy crests grow taunt with desire, feeling her body meet his with unrestrained passion. He kissed her hair, her neck, her eyes, as she clung to him, her heart pounding, throwing caution to the winds, wishing it would never end. He wanted to take her right there on the deck, but knew he wouldn't. With an inward groan, he let his passion subside and held her gently to him as her breathing relaxed and she leaned against him quietly, wanting more than his passionate kisses—wanting his love.

A lifetime passed, and she gave an involuntary shiver.

"You're becoming chilled. It's late. Come, I'll see you to your cabin."

Silently, she acquiesced and allowed him to lead her down the ramp to her stateroom door.

The door was hardly shut behind him when he

took her in his arms again. "So, my little lioness, the hunter has you in his arms at last."

She thrilled to his words, trembled to the low, husky sound of his voice. He had dropped the cool, courteous tone of the casual acquaintance, and he was once again that stranger, the wild, hot-blooded buccaneer she had known in Rio de Janeiro.

He wanted her naked, wanted to feel her skin warm against his hands. Quickly, he undid the buttons on the back of her gown, helping her to remove it. His hands touched newly exposed flesh, always leaving it warm with the heat from his lips. He placed her hands on his belt, invoking her silently to return the favor. Their garments fell away like dry leaves from a tree, until they were both naked and wild as a winter storm in their hunger.

They tore at each other, each seeking that which the other could give. There on the silken coverlet, they devoured each other with fevered lips and grasping fingers.

When their passion was abated, they touched mouths with lips swollen with passion and tasting of the salt of blood and tears. They lay together feeling the warmth where their bodies touched, and when they sought each other again, it was with tenderness. Gentle mouths, delicate fingers, exploring, caressing. Passion quickened within her, and Sebastian calmed her with his touch and soothed her with words known only to lovers.

He was gentle with her, so gentle, evoking in

her a golden warmth that spread through her loins and tingled her toes. His movements were familiar, reassuring; his touch on her naked breasts, light and lingering.

He gentled her passions the way he would gentle a wild cat, with a sure touch and a soft voice. He tamed her wildness, yet loved her wild; he quieted her cries with his mouth, and yet evoked moans of passion with his caress. When passion flamed again, it burned pure.

Sebastian cradled Royall in his arms, a strange expression in his ebony eyes. Only with this woman could he experience such fulfillment, such deep contentment. This girl, no, this woman, with the strange name could match his ardor and without reservation would give herself totally to him. He felt an insane desire to leap from the narrow bunk and shout to all the passengers that he had found a part of life that was missing. How beautiful she was. How gentle she could be, and then she would become a raging riptide, swirling and crushing his volcanic outpourings until the molten lava and thundering waters were a marriage of one. This was a woman. His woman.

Imperceptibly, his embrace tightened. Royall smiled into dark eyes that mirrored her soul. Sebastian's thumb traced the delicate skin over her sooty lashes. She was a sleepy angel. His angel. He would never let her go. Never. She belonged to him, always had, ever since that night in Rio. Now, he must make her his forever.

His tone, when he spoke, was a husky caress.

"You're the most beautiful woman I've ever seen. Lovemaking gives you the aura of an angel and the soul of a lioness."

"Mrs. Quince would probably call me a wanton."

Sebastian threw back his head and laughed, a deep, boisterous sound that was music to Royall's ears. His smile was almost boyish. "Our lovemaking was just that. Making love. Just as it should be. No restrictions, no reserves. A meeting of a man and a woman who need to become one."

Royall sighed deeply. She never wanted to leave this bed, leave Sebastian's embrace. His hard, manly body that molded itself to hers was so comforting, so right. How wonderful that she hadn't felt compelled to make any apologies, any explanations for her behavior in Rio at the Mardi Gras. Sebastian seemed to instinctively know that her marriage had been stultifying, smothering her in supposed respectability. To say that she was a widow was enough for him. To know that she had experienced her first fulfillment as a woman with him, ended all questions.

Was it possible that she could love him, love Sebastian Rivera, the man? Even as she thought it, she knew it was true. She loved him fiercely, with every fiber of her being. Now, for the first time in her life, she knew what it was to be loved by a man. She savored the feeling, almost tasting it. She never wanted to feel differently. And pray God he felt the same way.

Again, Sebastian's hand traced the delicate lines

of her face. "Sleep, *mi amor*," he whispered huskily. "We'll awaken in each other's arms."

Royall snuggled deeper into the crook of his arm, her cheek against his chest. Her thick lashes fluttered and then were still. A smile tugged at the corners of Sebastian's mouth. Dark eyes closed in dreamless sleep.

It was Royall who stirred first. She woke, completely alert. She wanted to stretch her long, slim body but negated the idea. For now she would content herself with savoring the nearness of the man laying beside her. How handsome he was, how virile. How tender and yet savage. What did it matter if she had wanton desires or if he had dubious parentage? Nothing mattered save the two of them. She stirred slightly, affording herself a better look at his face. He appeared relaxed, contented in sleep and yet vulnerable. A sudden surge of desire and longing stirred within her. She wanted him, needed him again, again. She shifted her position slightly and leaned toward him. Strong arms pulled her lithe body on top of his. Hungry mouths searched, found and conquered in the dimness of the cabin.

Spent, Sebastian and Royall fell back against the bedding, their bodies glistening with perspiration. It wasn't possible that perfection could be equalled and surpassed, but it had been. Sebastian let his mind soar to dizzying heights as he ran his hands through his unruly hair. There were no words. He gathered her close, devouring her with his glistening body. He would never let her go, he thought savagely. He would fight to the death anyone who tried to take her from him. She belonged to him; he decreed it. "I must leave you now; it will be dawn soon. Rosalie is an early riser and would question my exit from this cabin at this particular hour."

"I wish you didn't have to leave, but I understand," Royall said softly, already mourning his departure.

"I will always be near you, *mi amora*. Senora Quince's plantation is very near to mine." Gently, he nuzzled her neck, all the while twining his sun-darkened hand through her hair.

"Sebastian, I won't be staying with Mrs. Quince. She's been my traveling companion and only that. I can see how my friendship with her has misled you. Actually, my destination is the Reino Brazilia. It's been in my family for years, and I've inherited half of it from my father. Baron Newsome invited me and is awaiting my arrival."

Royall could feel Sebastian's arms stiffen. Something was wrong; she could sense it. He was holding her as though she were a dead, lifeless thing. Gone was the warm, open closeness, and in its place was an icy stare. Sebastian's firm, square jaw was set as though cast from bronze, and his eyes had narrowed to slits. The hostility emanating from him frightened her.

His thoughts wheeled and skidded; his emotions rocketing with them. It couldn't be! Reino Brazilia! Why was this the first time he had heard of it? Why hadn't Rosalie Quince told him, knowing him as she did and how he felt? Carlyle Newsome, calling himself the Baron, waiting for Royall. Royall owning half of Reino Brazilia. Owning it. Living from it. Letting it feed her, clothe her, educate her!

Royall wanted to say something, to question him, demand an explanation for the reason she saw hatred in his eyes. But his face forbade it; his actions prohibited her from uttering a word.

Silently he rose from the bed, extricating himself from her embrace with harsh, quick motions. She watched as he dressed, hoping to hear him offer an explanation, hoping he would allow her to ask him what she had said, what she had done.

He said nothing, dressing with as little wasted motion as possible. He flung his jacket over his shoulder, leaving his tie loose, his shoes unlaced. His words were clipped and bitter, offered as he opened the door and closed it behind him. "I plan to erase you from my mind. You would be wise to do the same."

Bewildered and humiliated, Royall watched him leave, heard the sound of the door closing, and felt as though it were the lid on her coffin. Without Sebastian there was no life, no air, no anything.

Royall tossed and turned, tormenting herself with questions as to what she had done, said, to make Sebastian turn from her as he had. It was when she told him she was half owner in Reino Brazilia that he had changed. An overwhelming loss shrouded her, seeming to steal all the light from the world. An inner spark of self-preservation ignited. "Damn you, Sebastian Rivera. I did nothing to warrant this misery. I want an explanation and I want it now!"

Without another thought she leaped from the bed and riffled through her clothing. Quickly, she bathed her eyes and face in the cool water from the ewer. She cared nothing for how she looked. What she wanted was answers. All that was important was to find Sebastian and set him straight about a few things. Things like how she loved him. All womanly instinct told her that this wasn't the time for pride. She knew she loved the tall, dark-haired man, and she would give everything she owned to prove to him that he felt the same way. Hadn't she heard his whispered love words? Didn't she know the hurt that lay in his heart concerning his birthright?

Less than half an hour later, Royall was dressed in a light green, striped dimity dress, and her hair was brushed simply back from her face into a casual knot. Forgetting her hat and ignoring her gloves, she stormed her way down the companionway to Sebastian's stateroom. She raised one daintily shod foot and kicked at the door while she banged on the upper half with her fists. "Open this door, Sebastian. I have to talk to you! Do you hear me? Damn you, Sebastian, stop making a fool of me and open this door. I want to show you your little lioness has claws."

Silence. Total and complete. Royall pushed the door and was surprised to find it unlocked.

Empty! No sign of Sebastian anywhere. No boots near the door; no waistcoat hanging on the hooks; no traveling bag; no razor. The soft face cloth and toweling were folded neatly. The coverlet on the bed was free of wrinkles. Where could he be? One of the ship's valets was coming down the companionway carrying a gentleman's suit. He seemed startled to find her standing in Senor Rivera's empty room.

Quietly, Royall asked him if he had seen Senor Rivera.

"Yes, Senora, Senor Rivera left the ship with the mail boat. There is a small town not far from here. No doubt he will join the next riverboat that comes up the river in a few days."

Back in her own stateroom, Royall sat for a long time, remembering, wishing the tears would come to cleanse her, make her feel better, but they wouldn't. A sharp rap sounded on her door and for an instant her hopes lifted. Sebastian! He hadn't left after all!

Rushing to the door, she flung it open, expecting Sebastian to take her in his strong embrace and tell her he was a fool. The steward who stood outside her door had a strange expression on his face when he saw her features fall and the misery creep into her eyes.

"Senora Quince has sent me to tell you she is on deck for breakfast and wishes you to join her."

Royall nodded, incapable of speech, knowing that she wanted to see Mrs. Quince and ask her why Sebastian should behave the way he had.

Royall threaded her way through the tables and sat down across from her traveling companion, who was liberally spreading jam on a breakfast roll.

"Mrs. Quince, something terrible has happened." Quickly, she told how Sebastian had left her so abruptly after she told him she was going on to Reino Brazilia. Protecting her privacy, she deliberately omitted how intimate she and Sebastian had become.

The older woman placed her breakfast bun on her plate and raised her eyes to meet Royall's tormented gaze. She laid a comforting hand on Royall's slender fingers, ceasing their agitated fumbling. "I'm afraid this is all my fault. I wanted the two of you to enjoy one another's company and become friends. I purposely misled Sebastian, never telling him you own part of Reino Brazilia, and now you must suffer the brunt of my deception. I'm so sorry, child. Forgive a meddlesome old woman who doesn't know her place. Sebastian is the one person in the world I should never have . . . Well, it's over and done with now. I meant no harm, Royall, believe me, I didn't. I was so certain things would work out."

"Mrs. Quince. Please, just tell me what did you do? I don't understand. I forgive you; just tell me so I can right the wrong that's been done!" Royall cried wretchedly.

Royall watched the older woman gather her thoughts together and waited expectantly for the woman's next words. If Mrs. Quince could explain why Sebastian had left her as he had, perhaps it was something which could be amended.

"Royall," Mrs. Quince began hesitantly, "there is tremendous animosity between Sebastian and Carlyle Newsome. They greatly differ in their beliefs of how the workers should be treated. I know it seems a feeble reason, but there's something else. Something I can't explain." Mrs. Quince lowered her eyes and seemed to measure her next statement. She lifted her head slowly and watched for Royall's reaction. "I might also tell you, for you will only see it for yourself, there is a *very strong resemblance* between Sebastian and the Baron. Some even whisper that Sebastian is Carlyle Newsome's son."

Royall gasped and said nothing, her mind in a whirl. Regaining her composure, she said hotly, "But what has that to do with me? Surely Sebastian can't blame me for his differences with the Baron! And as for how the slaves are treated, that is none of my doing!"

"I know, dear. It's most unfair. But you must understand; Sebastian has been at odds with Reino Brazilia for as long as he can remember." Then Mrs. Quince sniffed and cheerfully stated, "Men are as difficult to understand as women, if not more so!"

Sometime shortly after midday a note was delivered to Mrs. Quince, stating that Sebastian had left the riverboat when the paddlewheeler stopped at a riverport for water. The note was short and clipped. Mrs. Quince and her traveling companion were to have the use of his table in the dining room since he would have no further need for it. His signature was a large scrawled *S*.

The hastily scrawled note set Royall's teeth on edge. The rejection and hurt she felt prior to the delivery of the note was now replaced with searing hot anger. If this was the way he wanted it, then so be it. There would be another time and another place, and at that time and at that place *she* would be the one who had the final word.

Royall looked out over the calm water. The bright sunshine that had warmed her, brought life to her, now seemed clouded, and a chill clutched her heart. She would not admit to herself that the sun had dimmed for her, that the emerald green of the Amazon had turned dark and murky. She would wait for her time and her place. And then, as gamblers said, the odds would be in her favor.

Chapter Five

Royall thought she could not endure another moment of the drive to Reino Brazilia. The rough, corded roads caused the wagon to lurch first to one side and then to the other, leaving her body bruised and battered.

She sat in the back of the wagon, surrounded by luggage and carryalls. Too exhausted even for sleep, she peered through the darkness, trying to acquaint herself with their position. At last, giving up all hope of recognizing the dark shadows and resigning herself to the total blackness, she settled against one of the trunks and concentrated on the pool of yellow light that haloed through the thick humidity, throwing a feeble circlet of illumination upon the dry, caked roads.

Mentally she counted the trunks and valises and carryalls that surrounded her. Her eyes came to rest on the largest of the trunks, and she envisioned its contents. She saw herself, in her mind's eye, packing the simple gown she had worn on the riverboat, the gown that she had worn that last evening with Sebastian. Self-disgust washed over her. Why should I think about him? Why should I care? Mrs. Quince, knowing the hardship of the journey for Royall, silently cursed the fact that the comfortable coach that was to meet them had broken a wheel, forcing them to ride the baggage wagon Alonzo sent to meet them at the dock.

Royall had been so quiet the last hour that at times Mrs. Quince was certain the child had fallen asleep. Lifting the lamp high, allowing the yellowish light to fall on the girl, Mrs. Quince saw Royall seated among the luggage, wide awake, eyes staring into nothingness, a tight expression on her full mouth.

Damn you, Sebastian, for being the pig-headed fool you are, she thought. And damn you, Rosalie Quince, for trying to put your nose in where it doesn't belong! It would have taken a fool not to recognize the attraction the two young people held for each other. Whatever made you think you could play matchmaker. You old, foolish woman!

Determined not to allow Royall to sit and brood, Mrs. Quince started a spate of patter and succeeded in prying a few half-hearted replies from Royall.

"We're almost here now, child," Mrs. Quince announced as the wagon suddenly veered to the right. "A few yards more and you'll be home."

Mrs. Quince tapped Royall on the arm. "We're here, my dear. Come now, and the wagon master will help you down. One of the servants will fetch your baggage."

Royall nodded wearily as the kindly lady embraced her and kissed her good-bye. Mrs. Quince was going on to her own plantation several miles away.

"I'll send you a note in a few days' time. Best get a good night's rest now." She gave Royall an affectionate embrace.

"But aren't you staying here for the night?" Royall heard herself ask. The weariness in her own voice surprised her.

"No, dear. Since I'm this close to home, I want to go on. I long for the sight of my husband, Alonzo, and I confess a great desire to rest these old bones in my own bed."

Strong arms helped Royall alight from the wagon. She swayed momentarily as she tried to stand erect. She could feel the blood coursing through her still cramped legs. Unobtrusively, she stamped her feet to hasten the return of circulation. While doing so, she peered through the darkness to observe her surroundings.

A full moon shone upon the clearing around the house. It was one story high, a sprawling affair, quite different from the neat brownstone buildings found in New England.

The veranda seemed to encircle the house; white arched columns supported the porch roof and appeared luminescent in the moonlight. Dark shadowy shapes graced the foundation, and a fresh scent emanated from them. Tall trees leaned toward the house and rustled in the warm, soft, tropical breeze.

Gentle arms helped her up the stone steps to the veranda of the dark, silent house. The figures pulled a chain and a bell pealed somewhere within. Moments later, the door was opened by a tall, light-skinned figure holding an oil lamp. Royall felt, rather than saw, the dark figure of the servant leave her side. The tall form with the lamp beckoned her into the house.

Royall struggled to look alert, but the effort was too great; she didn't care at that moment what kind of an appearance she made. She was bone tired; all she longed for was a bed and oblivion. In the morning she would look at her new home. For the moment she had all she could do to remain awake long enough to follow the tall silhouette to her room.

"I am Elena, the housekeeper," the silhouette announced. She made a motion for Royall to follow her as she held the lamp high to light the way down the dark passageway. Royall needed no second urging. She followed quickly behind the regal back of the housekeeper. The woman opened a door and held up her hand for Royall. She supposed Elena meant for her to wait until the room was lighted. Suddenly, the room was ablaze with a bright yellow glow. Royall squinted against the glare. She hadn't known what she expected in the way of furnishings, but this light Regency furniture was not it.

It was clearly a woman's room, done in pale beiges and warm rose tones. The creamy lace bed hangings wafted gently in the warm breeze from the open French doors, which were screened with nettings.

Feeling eyes upon her, Royall turned to face the closed expression of Elena. "I'm Royall Banner," she announced in a friendly, weary tone.

"I have prepared for your arrival for many weeks, Senora Banner. I know who you are!"

Royall was surprised at the cultured, musical voice. She did not miss the coldness of the words, however. She looked into the dark eyes and felt instinctively that the housekeeper did not like her, but she was too tired to care. She thanked Elena for the obvious care taken with her room and proceeded to the edge of the tester bed.

Elena watched the beautiful girl through inscrutable eyes, then turned on her heel and left.

Royall reached down to undo her shoes and removed them. The small task wearied her, and she lay back on the bed.

The next thing she knew, there was soft sunlight streaming into the room. Glancing toward the windows, she noticed that during the early hours of the morning someone must have entered her room and closed the doors to ward off the morning heat. The sheer bed hangings were drawn against the bright light, giving the room a soft, muted atmosphere.

A quiet knock sounded at the door, and Royall bade the unknown visitor to enter. Elena strode through the door carrying a tray. Delicious aromas tantalized her appetite. Coffee! Royall sighed as she thought how good it would taste. She uncovered the plates and looked with interest at the thin, pink slices of ham, an egg, a small pot of marmalade, and fresh rolls crowned with a mound of yellow butter.

Elena looked at the tousled girl on the bed and let a smirk of rejection touch her lips. She spoke, however, in a quiet, civilized manner. "The *ninas* will be here shortly with your bath water and to unpack your baggage." Finishing her brief statement, she let her cold eyes linger a moment longer and left the room as quickly and as quietly as she had left it the night before.

Royall was bewildered by the coldness in the housekeeper's tone. As she ate her breakfast, she reviewed in her mind a conversation she had had with Mrs. Quince on the riverboat concerning the mysterious Elena. They had been sitting on deck enjoying the breeze blowing over the water. She had known that Mrs. Quince was trying to divert Royall's mind from thoughts of Sebastian. The talk had come around to the servants on Reino Brazilia and, of course, Elena.

"This is only gossip, of course, but no one seems to know exactly where she came from. Oh, there have been many stories, but who knows the truth?" Mrs. Quince shrugged. "One story goes that she was born in Haiti, that her mother was a Negress, a slave on some estate. Her father was a white man. This would explain her coloring, although to be as light-skinned as she is, it would seem likely that her mother was at least a quadroon, and I suspect there is native Indian blood in her somewhere. Elena is not at all black. In fact, she has a beautiful tawny complexion, large green eyes, and long silky hair, which she wears in two coils over her ears. She is truly a beautiful woman, and she appears to have breeding. She carries herself like a duchess. She was a servant before the Baron's wife died, and since that lady passed on with the fever, Elena has managed the household for the Newsome family. At one time it was whispered that she was the Baron's paramour."

Royall fell back against the pillows, chewing on the tender ham and thinking about that conversation. Mrs. Quince had certainly been correct in saying Elena was a beautiful woman. And now, in retrospect, Royall was surprised that the housekeeper was so young. She appeared to be in her thirties. She must have been little more than a girl when she came here to the Reino.

From thoughts of Elena her mind wandered to

110

Sebastian. Where was he and what was he doing? What was he thinking, feeling? Did he really put her from his mind. How could he forget her? Tears stung Royall's eyes as she stared around the room. If she couldn't forget him, how could he possibly forget her? He had no right to be so angry. She had done nothing except to say she was part owner of Reino Brazilia. All she had been guilty of was loving him and giving herself to him. It was so difficult to believe that Sebastian Rivera would hold her responsible for circumstances at the Reino. Still, Mrs. Quince had told her about the bad blood between Sebastian and the Newsomes. And it was apparently well known that he abhorred slavery. It made no sense at all that he held her responsible, no sense at all! Damn Sebastian Rivera!

Her train of thought was broken by the entry of four little Indian girls, *ninas*, carrying pails of steaming hot water. One of the girls removed a screen from the far corner of the room and pulled out a large tin tub. The little girls poured the steaming water carefully into the tub and left the room. In a few moments they were back again with more water.

"Very good, *ninas*," Royall said approvingly as she rummaged in her carryall for the decanter of bath salts and poured in a generous amount. As she started to undo the bodice of her dress, four solemn pairs of eyes watched her. Royall looked at the little girls and felt momentarily unsure of

111

what she was to do next. Surely, they didn't mean to help her!

"All right, *ninas*, you may leave. I'll call if I need you." No one moved. Evidently they didn't understand English. Now what do I do? she wondered. No one was going to watch her bathe, little girls or not!

She took the girl closest to her by the arm and ushered her to the door. The other three stood rooted to the floor. The child by the door had tears in her great black eyes. "What did I do?" Royall wailed.

Solemn eyes looked at her. One plump little girl raised a fat finger and pointed to the girl by the door. "You no like?"

Royall was shocked. "Of course I like her. I just want to take my bath in private!"

"We help," the plump little girl giggled.

"But I don't need any help."

"We help," the girl repeated stubbornly. The children advanced toward the frustrated Royall. The child by the door stood mute, tears streaming down her face.

"All right, come here," Royall smiled. "You can help too." The child rewarded her with a bright, toothy smile.

Before she knew it, Royall's clothes were stripped off and she was submerged in the water. She was soaped and scrubbed till her skin tingled. The plump little girl attacked the golden tresses. "Pretty," she stated, the others nodding happily as they continued their vigorous scrubbing.

Royall wondered how long the bath ritual was to continue. "Lord a mercy!" she muttered, parroting Mrs. Quince's favorite expression.

Her exclamation made the girls giggle; evidently they were familiar with the lady.

The first little girl held up her hand and said, "You wait; we bring more water." Royall sighed; where could she go in this condition? She smiled wanly at the girls as they trotted from the room. Fervently, she hoped the water was for rinsing and not more soaping. She looked at her rosy skin and winced. "I must manage to get a softer bath brush!"

The door opened, and giggling *ninas* carried the pails into the room. They looked at Royall sitting in the tub, covered with soap lather, their bright, dark eyes glittering in merriment. Apparently this is the part they enjoy best! Royall thought.

One of the children made a motion for Royall to get onto her knees so that they could pour the water over her. "When in Rome, et cetera," Royall muttered. She did as instructed, and as she felt the first torrent of water, she heard one of the girls giggle at her repeated exclamation, "Lord a mercy!"

Royall choked on her laughter at her own expense. Soon she was toweled dry, her long hair wrapped in a turban. Her skin felt tingly and renewed. Suddenly, the plump little girl had a jar in her hands, and she watched in fascination as each girl helped herself to a portion of the thick, fragrant lotion.

"Oh, no!" Royall cried. What was the use, they would have their way. She let the girls rub her legs and arms. When they made a motion to remove the towel, she clutched it like a lifeline.

The plump little girl looked at Royall, her dark eyes dancing. "Lord a mercy," she chanted. Evidently this was her battle cry. Royall gave in gracefully.

Soon the girls had her dressed in a light, yellow-sprigged dimity that somehow was miraculously free of wrinkles. She was then ushered out to the wide veranda and gently placed in a rattan chair. The turban was removed from her head, and the girls stood like bright, precocious squirrels. They cocked their heads first to one side and then to the other. They appeared to reach some sort of agreement, for the plump child took the brush and started to brush out Royall's damp hair.

As soon as it was free from tangles, they sat down at Royall's feet and looked at her expectantly. Royall felt perplexed as she looked at the children helplessly. The plump one seemed adroit at reading her mind. She looked up at the sun and then pointed to Royall's hair.

"Oh, I see. You want my hair to dry and then you will fix it. Very good," she laughed. She wondered how she would look when these small children finished with her. Possibly better, she thought as she remembered their experienced fingers when they bathed her.

"What are your names?" she asked. At their

blank expressions she pointed to herself and said, "Senora Banner." Then she pointed to the girls.

"Nessie," said one, the smallest.

"Rosy," announced another, the one with the great black eyes.

"Blodgett . . . no! No! . . . Bridget," corrected the tallest child.

The last, the plump one, announced, "Moriah."

"What strange names for Indian children. Where did you get those names?" Royall asked, smiling. Moriah giggled, and Royall gave it up. However was she to communicate with these children?

When her hair was dry, Moriah jumped up to brush the long golden strands. She stood behind the chair while the others sat crosslegged in front of Royall. The little vixens, Royall thought. They're the approval committee, and they take their job seriously. From time to time they squinted and nodded, mostly in the affirmative. Moriah kept up a running report and the girls again nodded. Nessie, the smallest, ran to get the hand mirror. "You see?" asked Moriah proudly.

Royall looked at her reflection. She was amazed at the artfulness the child had exhibited. The light golden tresses were piled high on her head with a single curl falling over one shoulder. At her ears, tiny tendrils of curls were permitted to escape the pins.

They awaited expectantly for her reaction. She smiled and repeated their names. "Lord a mercy," she laughed and embraced the children. Unnoticed, Elena had entered the room and now watched the scenario on the veranda through icy, green eyes.

With a loud clap of her hands the housekeeper dismissed the now subdued children. They scurried from the room, but not before the jolly, pig-tailed Moriah turned her head and gave Royall a precocious wink. Royall could not believe her eyes and had to stifle a laugh at the little Indian's defiance.

"How old are the children?" she asked the housekeeper.

"They are ten years old, Senora Banner. Were they satisfactory?"

"Most definitely. They're very experienced for girls so young."

"I have trained them myself," the housekeeper said coldly. "Master Jamie is waiting for you on the east veranda. The Baron and Carl are out on the plantation. They asked me to extend their warm welcome." If possible, the cultured, musical voice was more aloof than before. "We dine at half past eight, Senora Banner. Dress is formal." She glided from the room with a grace Royall envied.

Royall followed the housekeeper down the hall and out to the veranda.

"You must be Mrs. Banner! I'm Jamie Newsome," he said, bowing low.

"I'm happy to know you," Royall said, returning his smile. "I've come a long way to meet you."

He rose to full height. Handsomely tall and of muscular build, he was an impressive figure for a young man barely in his twenties. His blue eyes smiled into hers and he impatiently brushed back a lock of springy, fair hair from his wide brow.

"It's my pleasure to have you here. May I call you Royall?"

"But of course. And I'll call you Jamie. Let us sit. I'd like you to tell me about the plantation," Royall said, seating herself on a rattan chair. "Why is it that you're not out on the plantation with the other men?"

Jamie looked momentarily angry. He became engrossed in rubbing the thumb of his left hand between the index and middle finger, and then he pulled himself to attention. "Father wanted someone from the family to be here to welcome you and to show you around on your first day," he said off-handedly. "Besides, they're dealing with the rubber merchants today and father didn't want me aro—" Suddenly, Jamie flushed and changed the subject. Royall pretended not to notice the slip of tongue. Jamie then spoke of the plantation and the changes that had come to pass since he was a child. "Every year we have more rubber and better markets," he said. It sounded as though he were repeating a much learned school lesson.

Royall spoke of the Indian girls and asked Jamie how they came to have such Christian names.

"That is Father Juan's doing. He's a missionary and he has converted most of the Indians around here. Christian people, Christian names," he shrugged. His eyes sparkled as he spoke. "They're wonderful," he smiled, "quick, bright, and eager to please. Especially Moriah. She's a quick little bird, isn't she?"

Royall thought back to the precocious wink and agreed with Jamie.

"How many Indians are there on the plantation?" She asked.

"Over three hundred, and about half as many Negroes."

"Do all the plantations have that many workers?" Royall asked, avoiding the word *slave.*

"Some have more. Sebastian Rivera has, in all, only one hundred. Somehow he gets more work out of the one hundred than we do with the three hundred we have," he said frowning. "Of course, you must have heard he gave his slaves their freedom. I am sure Mrs. Quince must have told you," he smiled.

Royall nodded. "Has the Baron considered doing the same?" she asked.

Jamie looked shocked. "He says he gets no work from them now. What would they do if they were given their freedom?"

"How long does he think he can hold off?" Royall questioned. "Mrs. Quince tells me it's only a matter of time until slavery is totally abolished, if Princess Isabel has her way."

"She never will!" Jamie roared, startling Royall to silence. Noting the shocked expression on her face, he continued in a quieter voice that he visibly struggled to control. "At the moment we're having a little trouble with our slaves. We hear they're planning an uprising. But we hear that very often. Sometimes I think they spread the rumor themselves just to irritate the Baron. Especially when we have a large shipment to get out to the rubber traders."

Royall glanced at the table next to Jamie. "How beautiful," she said, admiring an array of wooden soldiers.

"They're collector's items," Jamie said proudly, handing her one of the brightly painted figures.

Royall admired the artistry and commented on the fine detail. "How many do you have?" she asked.

"Seventy-six in all," Jamie told her. "I hope to reach one hundred one day soon."

"I've never seen such fine soldiers, even in the States. You must be very fond of them," Royall said.

"I am, Royall. They're my most treasured possessions. I've been collecting them since I was a small boy." Quickly, he changed the subject. "Would you like to take a walk through the garden before the heat gets unbearable? Later, after lunch, I'll give you a tour of our Casa Grande." He extended a long arm and helped Royall from the chair. They walked down the steps, the perfume of crepe jasmine heavy in the air.

Royall expressed delight over the abundance of sweet-smelling, lush flowers. Jamie explained how difficult it was to keep the jungle from creeping up to the door. "The lawn gets shorter and shorter every year," he laughed.

Within an hour the heat and humidity reached a soaring point, and Royall felt light-headed.

"We had better go back," Jamie said, noticing her pallor. "I shouldn't have kept you out so long. You have to get used to the heat gradually." Royall secretly felt she would never grow accustomed to this strange land, as she walked behind Jamie on the narrow footpath.

Settling themselves in a dim, cool room of the Casa Grande, Jamie rang for Elena and requested cool drinks. Royall sat and rested her head on the headrest behind her chair. It appeared to be a conservatory of some sort, and she promptly asked Jamie what the room was used for.

"It used to be what my mother called her morning room. We moved her spinet in here after she died. Mostly, it's never played. I come here sometimes just to see if I can remember her. She died when I was two years old," he explained. Royall felt puzzled at the quick, choppy way he spoke.

Royall asked no more questions as the housekeeper offered her a tall, cool-looking drink. She tasted it, and her mouth puckered. "What is it?"

"Lime and papaya juice. We find it an excellent thirst quencher."

Royall agreed. A trifle tart for her taste, but she supposed she would get used to it. "It's so pleasant here in the house," Royall remarked. "What a contrast to the heat outside."

"That's because the walls are more than a foot

thick and the roof is tile. Would you care to see the rest of the Casa Grande?"

When Royall nodded, Jamie jumped to attention, ready to guide her.

The Casa was laid out in the shape of a U; the building surrounded a small courtyard paved with cobblestones and artfully landscaped with tropical shrubs and trees. Throughout, the furnishings were baroque in style, embellished by touches of gilt. Royall found she was appreciative of her room with its simpler Regency furniture. The Baron's taste was much too ostentatious for her liking. Jamie pointed out different objects, and she carefully complimented them, seeing how he was enjoying his role of tour director. As they circled back to the morning room, he remarked, "It's almost a perfect copy of the original, down to the details."

"What original?"

"The original Casa Grande. Grandfather lived there. When he died it burned to the ground. Father had this one built soon after. The first Casa was about a mile from here. Father didn't build on the old foundations because he felt it advantageous that we be closer to the river." His speech about the old Casa was spoken as though he were reading it from a Cook's Tour pamphlet.

Lunch was served in a cool, dim room in the back of the house. Royall was surprised at the quality of the fine English china, and commented on it.

"It was my mother's," Jamie explained. "We

have many fine pieces, as you will soon see." The lunch was light and pleasant. A sweet salad of guavas and oranges with pineapple, then some thin slices of cheese with wafer-thin slices of bread and another glass of the lime-papaya juice completed the meal. Jamie escorted Royall to her room for the siesta and told her he would join her for tea at four and promised a horseback ride later.

Royall lay down with the thought of resting only. Soon her eyes closed and she was sound asleep. The oppressive heat had had its effect and enervated her. She woke drenched to the skin. Quickly, she shed the damp clothing and made a mental note to remove her outer clothing when she next took a siesta. Changing into a light riding habit, she entered the conservatory where she had promised to join Jamie for tea. As she neared the door, she heard a low-voiced conversation from within and was about to retrace her steps when she heard her name mentioned.

"Your father won't like it if you take the Senora riding. You know he doesn't approve of your horsemanship, Jamie."

It was Elena. She sounded quite bossy and even petulant. "Why not wait till Carl returns and you can go together?"

Royall stood quietly, listening shamelessly.

"I'm sure, Elena, that Royall is an accomplished horsewoman. You don't have to worry that she'll fall from her horse. I'll watch over her," he said coldly. Royall thought that with such a blunt statement the housekeeper would have considered herself dismissed, but she continued to argue the point, her voice lowered, musical cadence gone.

"If you disobey your father again, Jamie, I fear he will not order the new soldiers for you," she said firmly.

"Then I'll order them myself. I'm no longer a child, Elena, as you well know. I intend to keep my promise to take Royall riding after tea. See that you fetch it immediately," he ordered imperiously.

Royall felt it was time to make her presence known. She retreated a few steps and stepped heavily on the tile floor, her heels making a clicking sound.

"I hope I'm not late, Jamie," she said, entering the room. The austere housekeeper glanced at Royall with hostility as she left the room. She returned almost immediately with two fine cups, a pot of tea, and a tray of pastries.

"I think it's a little cooler, don't you, Jamie?" Royall asked.

"Yes, it usually starts to cool off around tea time. It's the best part of the day."

Royall had two cups of tea and several of the flaky pastries. Jamie seemed to have an insatiable appetite. He continued to eat pastries until the plate was empty. He smiled sheepishly at Royall's look.

"They're my favorite," he remarked, then burst out laughing. His laughter was contagious, and Royall joined him.

"But not too good for the waistline," she said playfully.

"That doesn't worry me," he smiled again as he finished his fourth cup of tea.

"Is that your favorite, too?" Royall asked with humor. He nodded happily as he set his cup down and stood up to shake the crumbs from his trousers.

Royall followed him through the kitchen area and walked out into the pebbled courtyard where two saddled horses stood waiting. Jamie helped Royall mount and they set off, Jamie in the lead.

Royall rode a dappled gray, and Jamie a high-spirited chestnut gelding. He seemed to ride with ease. She wondered vaguely at Elena's warning him against disobeying his father. It had sounded like a warning. Suddenly, Jamie veered to the left and reined in the startled gelding. He dug his heels into the flank and the animal reared and pawed the air. Jamie continued to pull on the reins, and the horse fought all the harder. Royal felt frightened. There didn't seem to be anything on the ground to startle the horse. Jamie freed the reins, and the horse quieted as he pawed the ground and nickered softly.

"What happened, Jamie?" Royall asked anxiously.

Jamie's face looked contrite. "I don't know. One minute he was fine and the next he was in the air."

"You should never pull the reins as you did; you only frighten him more," Royall said quietly.

"I know. He was just out of control for the minute. Don't badger me. Come, let's ride a little farther. See, over there?" he said, pointing a finger in an easterly direction. "That's the beginning of Sebastian Rivera's property."

Royall looked in the direction Jamie pointed and wondered where Sebastian was at this moment. She had not long to find out. Jamie dug his heels into the flank of the gelding, and the horse snorted and took off at a gallop. At first glance it was evident that Jamie did not have a good seat. He'd been turned sideways to speak to Royall when the horse broke into a run.

Royall followed but the speed of the animal was frightening, and she felt helpless as she watched horse and rider plunge ahead.

Suddenly, another rider came into view, took in the scene, and spurred his horse after the runaway gelding. Minutes later both riders returned. Sebastian Rivera led the now docile horse carrying Jamie.

He nodded indifferently to Royall, but the way her white riding habit molded itself to her slim, supple curves did not escape him.

"Does the Baron know you're riding his gelding?" Sebastian asked Jamie quietly.

Jamie turned sullen and ignored the question. Sebastian shrugged and looked as though he hadn't expected an answer anyway.

Royall remained as mute as Jamie. Why should she say anything and have him turn it around to suit his satisfaction? Who cared what he thought anyway, she muttered viciously under her breath. She had been insulted and humiliated enough by him to last her a lifetime.

"You are trespassing on my property," Sebastian said coldly. "Come, I'll ride back with you to the boundary line to be sure that you get home safely."

"There's no need for you to play duenna for Royall or myself. I'm perfectly capable of seeing that we both get home safely," Jamie said petulantly.

"It's not your friend that I'm concerned about, Jamie. I want to be sure you get back where you belong. Senora Banner has proven that she can do just about anything." His tone was so cold Royall thought her blood would freeze in her veins.

Jamie's head drooped as his gelding fell in behind Sebastian's blue black stallion. Royall marveled at the horse and the man who rode him so effortlessly, knowing no other man would have been able to ride the huge black beast with the agility Sebastian displayed.

From time to time Jamie turned in his saddle to glare at Sebastian, who completely ignored him.

Royall's back stiffened. What business was it of Sebastian's if Jamie rode the gelding or not? He had a perfect right to chastise them for trespassing, but that was all. And why did he ask if the Baron knew that Jamie was riding the gelding?

Suddenly, Sebastian turned and stared at Royall. Actually, she thought, it looked as though he was staring through her, a glint in his ebony eyes.

When he finally spoke, it so unnerved her she almost fell from her mount. How could he sound so brutal, so cold and hard when they had shared . . . What was he saying? She had to pay attention.

"Senora, there's no telling what might have happened to you if I hadn't come along when I did. It's not wise for you to ride here in the jungle until you are more familiar with the terrain, and it would be best if you rode with an experienced horseman, which Jamie, as you can see, is not. In short, this property is off limits to all who reside at the Reino Brazilia. Is that understood, Senora Banner?"

"Perfectly," Royall hissed through clenched teeth.

Sebastian reined in his horse. "This is as far as I go with you. I doubt very much if the Baron would appreciate me escorting his son and guest to his plantation." The black eyes were slate colored now in the afternoon sun, almost murky, as he once again gazed past Royall's head. Swinging the huge stallion effortlessly, he headed back in the direction from which they had just come.

Royall turned in the saddle and hissed, "You're an insufferable bastard, Sebastian Rivera!"

Without moving a muscle Sebastian shot back, "And you, Senora Royall Banner, with two Ls, have both names correct."

Royall seethed all the way back to the plantation, barely hearing what Jamie was saying. "You know I would never let anything happen to you, Royall. Why, we just met and already I like you very much. I want us to be friends. Sebastian hates my father, so he hates me too."

Royall nodded absentmindedly. She knew that intentionally he wouldn't have let anything happen; unintentionally was another matter.

Leaving the horses with one of the stable boys, they entered the cool, dim house through a side entrance. It appeared to Royall that Elena crept up on them as they entered the long hallway. The look of relief on her face was unmistakable. Relief for Jamie, no doubt, Royall thought sourly, still smarting from Sebastian's arrogance.

"Did you have any trouble, Jamie?" He merely shrugged, and Elena didn't bother to question Royall. The tall, stately housekeeper looked at her but spoke to Jamie. Perhaps I am invisible, Royall thought as she remembered how Sebastian stared through her.

"There will be heavy rains before the dinner hour is here. Perhaps you had best remove your soldiers from the veranda." Jamie's eyes lit up at the mention of his hobby, and he went immediately to do her bidding.

The housekeeper again pierced Royall with a black, malevolent stare.

"I don't want you to ride with Jamie ever again, Senora Banner. Is that understood?" she asked frigidly.

Royall looked puzzled. "But why, Elena? He did nothing wrong!"

"There's no reason for me to explain to you the

128

way of anything. I have said you are not to ride with Jamie. Do you understand?" she asked, her eyes bright and piercing.

Royall murmured yes to the demand. She didn't understand, but she did mean to find out. She loved to ride, but if that pastime was to be curtailed, she would find some other form of entertainment. She felt the housekeeper's eyes on her back as she made her way down the hall. From the way things were going, this was not going to be one of her better days.

Once inside her room she removed her riding habit and lay down on the chaise. She remained so, puzzling over the strange behavior of not only Jamie but also Sebastian and Elena as well. None of it made sense. She wished that Mrs. Quince and her treasure trove of information were here. A knock sounded on the door, and the little Indian Moriah came into the room carrying a tall drink. She held it out shyly, and Royall accepted it.

Royall patted the foot of the chaise for Moriah to sit down. "It's all right, Moriah. I've given you permission. Come, I want to know how much English you speak. Tell me, who teaches you?"

"Father Juan," the child answered shyly.

"I see. Do you also get to know your numbers and your letters?"

"Yes, and Nessie too."

"What of Bridget and Rosy?"

"Elena says no," the child said, her face still and quiet.

"Doesn't the Baron have anything to say of it?"

"No, the . . . the . . . Elena says no," the child repeated stubbornly.

"Are you and the others to be my maids?"

The child nodded. "We take care of you," she said happily.

And who takes care of you, little one? Royall wondered. "Where are your mother and father, child?"

A frown crossed the little face. "My mother and father work on Regalo Verdad, for Senor Rivera."

"Then why is it that you aren't with them?" Royall questioned in disbelief.

"The Baron sold my parents to Senor Rivera but would not let me go. Elena wanted to train me for this plantation. Senor Rivera is trying to buy me."

"How could they sell the parents and not the child?" Royall felt nauseated. "Can't something be done?" she asked. "And the others, Rosy, Bridget and Nessie, where are their parents?"

"Also on Regalo Verdad. Senor Rivera bought them all at the same time. They were all sick with the fever and the Baron says they are no good. He sell"—she floundered for the word—"cheap," she said triumphantly.

Royall's blood boiled. "How could this be? When was the last time you saw your parents?" she asked angrily.

Moriah held up three fingers.

"Years?" Royall demanded incredulously.

The child nodded.

"Well, we will just see about that," Royall

shouted, angry in outrage, causing the child to cower. Instantly contrite, Royall cradled the small head in her lap. "I didn't mean to frighten you, little one. I'm angry that this could happen to a child," she tried to explain.

"I cost many dollars," the child added proudly.

"Who told you that?" Royall demanded.

"I heard Father Juan say to Senor Rivera." The round face puckered as she tried to remember. "Not enough to buy me," she said. Royall understood. No matter how much Sebastian Rivera offered, the children were not for sale.

The child rose to leave. Royall, sunk deep in her own thoughts, barely noticed. If I own half of this plantation, then I own half of all the slaves and that includes the children. Granted, the Casa belongs to the Baron, but the profits and the plantation we share equally. Then I should have some say in the matter. Indignation welled within her, making her temples throb. They were only children, hardly more than babies! She couldn't, wouldn't, accept the fact their parents had been sold, separated from them when they were barely seven years old. Mrs. Quince had told her the natives were fiercely protective of children and family. Then how did this happen? And how could Sebastian Rivera, for all his supposed mortality and ethics, have allowed it to happen? At least, Royall told herself, the little ones seemed well cared for, that at least was something to the good.

Royall opened the carryall that rested beside the bed and withdrew the folded papers she had studied on the ship, hearing the stiff crackling as she opened them. She didn't pretend she understood them, and thought that perhaps Father Juan would be willing to translate them for her. She knew they were legal testaments of her share in Reino Brazilia, and now she needed more specific information, delineating her exact legal position.

Walking out to the wide, shadowy veranda, she picked up the novel she had tried to read during the voyage, but couldn't concentrate any better now than then. Her mind was in a turmoil, her emotions rioting, whirling in a hundred different directions. Weary, she rested her head back against the rattan chair, watching the sun go down over the vibrant green treetops. The scent of crepe jasmine was like a heady wine, hanging in the air, cloying in its sweetness.

Eventually, Moriah and Bridget returned to the darkened room, lighting kerosene lamps, flooding the room with light. "Time to dress, Senora," Moriah smiled.

Royall rose heavily from her chair, feeling as though the weight of the world were on her shoulders. The little girls helped her dress quietly, each sensing the golden lady's depression. They liked the way the Senora's hands reached out and touched their cheeks, and they were puzzled by the deep sorrow they saw in her golden-flecked eyes.

Royall glanced in the mirror, satisfied with the amber gown she had worn that first evening to dinner on the riverboat. Pushing back thoughts of Sebastian, she adjusted a fold in the rich fabric and thanked the girls, calling them *ninas*, and making them giggle with her attempts to learn the language.

Royall entered the expansive library where two men stood talking earnestly. Jamie apparently felt excluded from their conversation and moped in a far corner of the room, leafing through the pages of a book with obvious disinterest.

A distinguished-looking man in his middle years sensed her presence and turned toward the door. He studied her briefly, his penetrating gray eyes observing her from head to toe, lingering ever so fleetingly at the swell of her hips and the rise of her bosom. Royall felt a faint blush beneath his admiring scrutiny and was transfixed beneath his gaze, which was just short of insolent.

He was tall, slenderly built, yet a strength of physique was apparent in his well-set shoulders and slim tapering torso. A shock of dark hair framed by gray feathering at his temples caressed a shapely, regal head. His face was darkened by the sun, making his light gray eyes appear almost luminescent by contrast. A full, sensuous mouth, now smiling at her, revealed strong, even white teeth, accentuated by a small, carefully clipped moustache.

A woman finding herself so pointedly admired by such an attractive man, could consider herself flattered, but watching him, Royall became uneasily aware that there, in the Baron's handsome face, was the strong and undeniable resemblance to Sebastian Rivera.

"Welcome, welcome. Welcome to Reino Brazilia!" He stepped forward, graceful as a dancer, and took both her hands in his. Gallantly, he bent and pressed his lips to the back of her hand. "Come, I would like to present my son Carl," he introduced the tall young man he had been speaking with, "and of course, you've already met Jamie."

Royall smiled in return, uneasy beneath those flashing gray eyes.

"Jamie tells me you went for a ride this afternoon," Baron Newsome said smoothly. "My dear, I would much prefer you didn't ride until you're more familiar with the plantation." His tone was soft, concerned, but nevertheless, Royall recognized it for the order it was. To her own disdain, she found herself nodding in compliance and looked at Carl, who was observing her over the rim of his wine glass, a speculative expression in his dark eyes, eyes that were startlingly similar to Sebastian's. There was truth to the gossip Mrs. Quince had related to her, Royall thought as she accepted a glass of sherry from the Baron. There was a definite family resemblance between the Newsomes and Sebastian Rivera, and one would have to be blind not to see it.

Carl engaged Royall in conversation, asking her about her trip from New England. "I've never been farther than Belém," he told her slightly regretfully. "Someday, soon I hope, business will

134

take me to Rio de Janeiro. How did you like that city?"

Memories of Sebastian shivered through her as she answered, and pushing them aside, Royall recounted as much about the city as she remembered. Carl seemed so interested, so eager for word about places and things outside his life here on Reino Brazilia. He was a pleasant young man, Royall decided, and definitely attractive. A younger version of the Baron, with his dark hair brushed back from an aristocratic brow that gave emphasis to his finely structured features and high-bridged nose. He, like his father, was slim and lithe, almost languidly elegant, quite the opposite from Jamie's muscular bulk.

Bringing her attention back to himself, seemingly annoyed with Carl's thirsty interest for places and things beyond the Reino, the Baron spoke of the coming festivities in Manaus and how exciting they would be. "It's the beginning of the opera season and we, the committee for the opera house, have sent for some of Europe's finest performers. I own a townhouse, useful for business. But more about that later; first you must concern yourself with having a costume made for the ball."

Elena broke into the conversation by announcing dinner, and without further words, the Baron took Royall's glass from her and placed it on a marble-topped table.

Jamie rushed toward her, his arm extended, offering to escort her into the dining room. With quiet grace, the Baron stepped between them, casually placing her hand on the crook of his arm. A sulky expression played about Jamie's mouth, and for a moment, Royall thought he was going to verbalize his objection. "Gentlemen," the Baron stated in an authoritative tone that broached no objections, "I believe dinner is served."

It was a quiet meal. Carl added very little to the conversation. To the annoyance of his father, he seemed lost somewhere far beyond the limits of the plantation. Jamie sat with lowered eyes, picking at his food, sulkily clattering the flatware against his plate and setting his glass down roughly, nearly spilling its contents.

In the uneasy atmosphere, Royall herself was without an appetite, despite the deliciously spiced freshwater shrimp and light fluffy rice. She was grateful for the strong Brazilian coffee that ended the meal and was served in the conservatory where they gathered near the delicately feminine spinet.

"Do you play?" the Baron asked hopefully.

When she replied that she did, Jamie bounded across the room to her, begging her to play. She demurred at first, but after gentle coaxing, she accepted the invitation, running her fingers down the keyboard.

As she played love ballads, Jamie sat as though hypnotized by the soft music, and the Baron lounged in a rose brocade armchair, his head resting back, his eyes watching her through lowered lids.

Carl stood by the open doorway leading to the veranda and the gardens beyond, a slight frown on his face. A faint breeze carried the scent of jasmine and was pleasing to his senses; the delicate music and feminine fragrance made him melancholy for his sweet, dark-haired Alicia.

Carl had no stomach for what he had been ordered to do once Royall stopped playing the piano, and he wished she would go on playing forever. But there, that was further proof of what the Baron claimed was his foolish romanticism. Also, he knew he had to follow his father's orders if the Reino were to be saved.

Carl's thoughts wandered to Alicia and her desperate situation. If only he could bring her here to the Reino, marry her, take care of her. But the Baron wouldn't hear of it. Since the death of Alicia's father, her financial position had gone from bad to worse. An accident, the charitable chose to call it, but anyone knowing the true circumstances knew if for what it was: suicide. A further blot on Alicia's eligibility, as far as the Baron was concerned.

"The girl is an unsuitable match!" the Baron had objected. "Find yourself a rich wife, one who'll bring her bounty to the Reino!"

The plantation, always the plantation! How could he measure the value of a damned lot of humid air, sodden ground, and a forest of trees, compared to sweet arms clinging tenderly, moist, fragrant breath against his cheek, and warm, promising lips?

"What better solution?" the Baron's argument

continued. "Royall Banner is just the rich wife you need!"

"Why do I need a rich wife?" he'd railed. "The Reino has everything, gives us everything!"

The Baron's face became muddied, almost black with rage. "If you weren't such a dolt, you would have seen it for yourself! Richard Harding, Royall's father, has been partner in this plantation since I was only grown halfway to my own father's knee. Now his daughter has inherited, and if she demands an accounting of her holdings, she will discover that it is *her* money that's been used for administration and for these luxuries that you find so enjoyable! Over the years I've been sending false reports to Mr. Harding while our profits have been mounting in the bank. If the girl were to ask for an accounting, to which she has every right, the game would be up. Paying her rightful share would pauperize us, Carl," he told his son, a slight curling of his lip to show his scorn, "and then where would the Newsomes be? We, the ones who have built this land into the little kingdom it now is?"

Carl was speechless. He'd always known his father was less than honest in business dealings, but he'd never suspected that the Baron was no better than a thief.

"Now you see why you will obey me. You will court this Royall Banner and make her your wife. Call it a business merger, if you like. Either way, the Reino will belong totally to the Newsomes. As

I see it, your duty is to me and the plantation, leaving you no choice."

Carl inwardly cringed at his own cowardice, pleading with the Baron to allow his marriage to Alicia. "Never!" the Baron had roared. "Never will I permit a son of mine to neglect his duty to the family, to himself, and to Reino Brazilia. If you must have this little chit, then have her. Take her, love her, keep her. Surely, in her desperate circumstances Alicia would invite a bit of assistance from you for something so trifling as her virginity. Do what you will, but if I were to disinherit you—for any reason—do you still feel Alicia would welcome your attentions? I think not, my boy. She'd soon hurry on to greener pastures." The Baron allowed himself a smile, seeing that he'd already won the argument. Carl would do as he was told, just as he'd always done. In his victory the Baron couldn't help turning the knife a bit further. "Son, a beauty as fragile as Alicia's can't be counted upon to last past her mid-twenties. No, son, however I see it, you're the loser."

An icy stare descended on Carl, and he was frozen by its calculating coldness. He knew the Baron wasn't making the idle threats. Disinherit him he would; then how could he help his Alicia?

While Royall continued playing at the spinet, Carl's thoughts were rioting through his head. His hand wandered again to his pocket, which held a note from Alicia, and his hand felt as though it held fire as his fingers touched the crisp, scented paper.

It was an answer to a note he had sent her explaining that they had a guest at Reino, so he wouldn't be able to see her until the next week. In the note he had expressed his love for her and promised the days would drag until he saw her again and held her in his arms.

Carl watched his father rise and applaud Royall's excellent touch at the piano. A quick glance in Carl's direction, and he found himself moving toward her, offering his congratulations and inviting her for a stroll on the veranda.

Jamie made a move to accompany them, but the Baron called him back, explaining that tomorrow his younger son was to accompany him to the rubber tradings held at the river wharf.

Jamie wasn't impressed with the invitation; he was still hearing the lovely music Royall had created, and he wondered if his own mother had played the same songs and somehow believed so. He'd finally been rewarded for coming to the conservatory, where he'd always felt close to her.

Carl and Royall walked in companionable silence around the great veranda, and he graciously asked if she'd care to ride to Mrs. Quince's plantation later in the week. "In the trap, of course. But we'll have to leave early to get ahead of the day's heat. We can return at night, if that meets your approval."

"Why, thank you, Carl. I'd love to see Mrs. Quince again and see how her ankle is mending." She liked Carl but suspected that something was deeply disturbing him. There was something in his eyes, a certain loneliness, that kept his face in shadows.

"Then it's settled," Carl said briskly. "What do you think you'd like to wear to the masked ball in Manaus? Or are you going to be like the other women I know and keep it a secret until the last?"

"I have no idea, really," she answered truthfully, trying to keep her mind from Mardi Gras in Rio and Sebastian Rivera's hot, flaming embrace.

Royall looked at the star-filled night and suddenly thought of the heavy rains Elena had predicted. "Elena said there was going to be rain tonight."

"Tonight?" Carl asked, puzzled.

"Yes, she told Jamie to take his soldier collection from the veranda because it was going to rain before dinner."

"I see," Carl murmured. "In two or three days the rains will hit, making it steamier and hotter than before. But it won't rain tonight. It's time to go in," Carl remarked as they found themselves before the French-paned doors. "Good night, Royall." Quickly, before she realized what was happening, she felt a gentle kiss on her cheek. Then Carl turned on his heel and motioned for Jamie to follow him. Royall watched the brothers leave the room, and a strange dread descended over her. Something was off center here, but she couldn't put her finger on it.

Picking up a lighted lamp, Royall started down the hall to her room. She was surprised to find

141

her bed turned down and her nightgown laid out. The little girls had been at work again. There was a fresh bowl of cut flowers on the small table by the bed, and she wondered which of the children had picked them. She knew it was Moriah—plump, little Moriah with the dark eyes and the fat pigtails.

Chapter Six

In his townhouse in Manaus, Carlyle Newsome looked into the mirror over his massive dressing table and worked his features into something resembling a smile. Deftly, he smoothed the iron gray wings at his temples and frowned slightly. He would find time during his trip to Manaus to visit his barber for a trim. He drew his upper lip down to see how much of the short hairs of his moustache had grown, anticipating a quick clip with the tiny scissors. Amazing how the wealth of hair atop his head was turning gray while his moustache remained coal black. He did look the distinguished plantation owner, he told himself smugly. Gentry, quality, and wealth always showed on a man. He was all that and more, he thought with a grim satisfaction. Perhaps he wasn't as wealthy as some of the other plantation owners, but he soon would be, once Carl married Royall Banner. Then it would all be his own, to do with as he pleased. A vague stirring in his loins at the thought of Royall made his neck warm.

She was a beautiful woman, too beautiful for Carl. He himself could appreciate her to the fullest. Carl could never even dream to attempt to unleash the passions beneath her golden facade. After all, he thought complacently, hadn't he trained Elena in the bedroom arts? And scores of others besides, white as well as dark-skinned, women who were only too eager to please him? Only his wife, of all the women he had known, had been less than enthusiastic in her bedroom duties.

The Baron's fingers, when they withdrew his pocket watch from his trousers, were trembling. He always knew this excitement when about to make a new conquest. He liked to think of it as a game with himself the winner. Carlyle Newsome always won, and it would be no different with Alicia.

Straightening his cravat over his fine lawn shirt, he expertly centered his diamond stick pin. Alicia. Always a lovely girl, even if he'd always considered her frail, with hardly a mind of her own. Yet, he'd noticed the alluring curves beneath the stylish gowns she wore, and there was no doubt concerning her fine breeding. With a churlish grin into the mirror as he slipped into his tropical weight white suit, he considered that he was being disloyal to Carl. Immediately, he negated the idea. Loyalty was for sons to demonstrate toward their fathers, not the other way around. Besides, Carl should have no complaint. Hadn't he seen to it that his son was made the better of the bargain by allowing him to console himself with Royall's golden promise?

Alicia Stanhope was not the girl to enhance the Newsome fortunes, but the Baron had contemplated other uses for her. The first opportunity had been seized upon months ago when he had first learned that Richard Harding's widowed daughter would come to Reino Brazilia. That was the day the Baron had deliberately set out to ruin Leslie Stanhope. One of the traits he most respected about himself was that he could think quickly in a crisis and act accordingly. And have an alternate plan, should something unforeseen spoil his original thought. Nothing in life could be left to chance. He smiled urbanely at his reflection, satisfied.

Before leaving the townhouse the Baron paused for a moment in the handsomely appointed foyer, then stepped out into the cobblestoned street that was lined with tall palm trees and gave a welcome show of green against the pink brick buildings that were familiar in Manaus. He was right in deciding the time had come to take a mistress. After all, he was still a young man by most standards. Fifty-three was hardly the tip of the crest.

A mistress would solve many problems, especially intimate ones, ones that had been plaguing him for this past year. Any fool could see that what he needed was a steady woman, not these hasty alliances with the whores on Viajar Arbol or quick trips across the compound to his bedroom by some slave girl whom Elena sent according to orders. Giving his shoulders a mental shake, he left the townhouse in search of the apothecary shop where Alicia had an upstairs apartment.

When the carriage stopped in front of the meager little apothecary shop, the Baron stepped down and ran a delicate finger over his moustache. So, this was what the lovely Alicia had been reduced to—living in a furnished apartment above a shop. The building itself appeared neat and even quaint, but in a year or two there would be rubble piled in the alley with half-dressed, screaming children with running noses, milling around outside, begging for coins. The shop was just two blocks outside the lowest quarter of the city, and it wouldn't be long before the neighborhood caught up with it. Alicia Stanhope deserved her circumstances, if for no other reason than being born into a spineless family. The girl was stretching beyond her station in life to suppose she was good enough for the heir to Reino Brazilia. She could never be woman enough to carry on the responsibilities as mistress of the Casa. The time had come to settle the matter irrevocably. Carl was so besotted with her fragile beauty, he couldn't see beyond the end of his nose. It was up to him, the Baron, to take matters into his own hands and see to it that Carl would never again want to set eyes on Alicia Stanhope.

Nonchalantly, Carlyle looked over his shoulder, striving to give any passersby the impression that he was waiting for someone. Quickly, he opened the street level door and climbed a steep, narrow flight of stairs to the second floor. With the head of his walking stick he rapped several times on the door at the head of the stairs, listening for sounds within. It would be just his misfortune that Alicia wasn't at home. He rapped again, impatiently, and then kicked the door. It swung open, taking him by surprise, leaving him feeling foolish with his foot still in midair.

Alicia Stanhope stood there, her hand clutched to her throat, her mouth opened in a frightened silent scream.

"Don't just stand there, Miss Stanhope, aren't you going to invite me in?" His voice was as smooth as oiled silk, disarming her, bringing color back into her cheeks.

Alicia stepped backwards, her breathing quickened. What was Carl's father doing here? "Of . . . of course, please come in. It's just that . . ."

"You weren't expecting anyone, especially me, is that what you were about to say?" the Baron said coolly, enjoying her discomfort.

Alicia's shoulders squared imperceptibly. Her pansy blue eyes took on a glassy appearance, as though brimming with tears. "More or less," she answered, turning her back on him, allowing him to follow her into the scrupulously neat but poorly furnished apartment.

The Baron was aware of the defiant turn of her head and her stiffly held back. Who did she think she was, to present this attitude to him? She should be licking his boots to get him over to her side of things.

She led him into the front room that faced out onto the street. Worn red velvet draperies shunned the sun, dimming the room and making it cool. Several pieces of furniture that he recognized from the Stanhope household were attractively placed around the small room, along with bric-a-brac and books, also, no doubt, saved from the auctioneers.

"Please sit down, Baron. May I offer you a cool drink? I have papaya and lime. I usually don't have visitors, so I don't keep spirits in the house."

"House?" the Baron sneered incredulously. "I hardly call this a house, Alicia. And you say you don't keep spirits? Why, dear child, my information tells me you entertain quite frequently. Or do your clients bring their own refreshment? Let's not fence, Miss Stanhope, I know that since you've found yourself reduced to this . . . this hovel, you've had to survive by whatever means presented themselves to you. I think they call it the oldest profession. No, no," he raised a hand to stay her objections. "Prostitution has its merits in every society, even our own."

Alicia's face drained of all color. Had she heard him correctly? Where had he gotten such an idea? Her tongue felt thick in her mouth when she tried to object. "You're a cruel old man, Baron Newsome. I refuse to listen to this slander, even if you are Carl's father!"

"Come, come, Alicia. Why not admit that you're no longer that simpering, overprotected daughter of that whimpering fool, Stanhope.

147

You've become a woman of the world, and we should be able to discuss matters coolly and logically." His gray eyes fell on her, covering her from head to toe. It was plain to see why Carl thought he was in love with her. Smooth, burnished dark hair was pleasingly arranged about her pale and delicate features, and those remarkable pansy blue eyes flashed from behind incredibly long black lashes. She was taller than most women he knew, aside from some of the Indians, and she carried her height well, with a fluidity of motion that was emphasized by her long, slender limbs, gracefully rounded arms, and a high, girlish bosom. He had always thought her to be in delicate health, but she was showing her strength by glaring at him, daring him to continue with this conversation. Looks could be so misleading.

"There's nothing to discuss, Baron. I'd appreciate it if you'd leave my home before I repeat this conversation to Carl." Her voice broke and a tear slipped down her cheek. She'd always known the Baron objected to her match with Carl, but this went beyond the common grounds of decency.

Carlyle settled back in the overstuffed horsehair chair, crossing his legs, demonstrating his intention to stay. "Dear Alicia, I have no intention of leaving, so save your hysterics for some of your gentlemen callers who might find them fetching. Now, listen to me very carefully. I've forbidden Carl to see you ever again, so you will not have the opportunity to tell him of this dilemma you find yourself in. And, dear girl, I want you to know that I mean what I say. To show you what lengths I will go to to prevent your marriage, allow me to tell you that I am the one who is responsible for your living in this rat trap. I alone am responsible for your financial problems. I am responsible for your father's lost fortune; however, I refuse to take the blame for his death. That he did by his own hand. He was a weak and ineffectual excuse for a man. Weak, ineffectual men breed weak, ineffectual children."

Rage swelled in Alicia. She couldn't believe what she was hearing. Let him say and think what he would about her, but not her father. Her father had been a caring, generous, loving man. Perhaps he hadn't had the cold, ruthless business sense of the Baron and some of the other plantation owners, but she wouldn't have wanted him any other way. She held his memory dear and close to her heart. "You are a vile excuse for a man," Alicia screamed. She leaped from her position on the love seat to pummel his chest with clenched hands. "I don't care what you say about me, but I won't allow you to slander my father. Do you hear me?" she continued to scream as she pounded away at the Baron's chest.

Carlyle grasped both of Alicia's flailing fists and held tight. Slowly, he forced her heaving body closer to him, bringing her face to within inches of his own. Cold, slate gray eyes stared unblinkingly into soft, moist velvety ones. His voice was low, almost a caress, when he spoke. "I've come here to right the wrong I've done you. I plan, along with a little help from you, to take you from these wretched surroundings and permit you to live in my townhouse. I plan to settle an allowance upon you so that you can once again have the necessities of a decent life. There's no point in even thinking about Carl. My son and I have come to a complete understanding. He has given me his word that he will not set eyes on you again. You see, Alicia, he knows where his place is, and it's at Reino Brazilia. Shortly, the banns will be announced and he will wed my ward, Royall Banner. Carl is used to the good life, fine food and wine, elegant homes, and a woman that hasn't been tarnished as you have. In other words," his voice dropped to a husky whisper, "if you don't agree to my suggestion, Alicia, you will find yourself not only without clients but also without a place in which to entertain them. You'll be walking the streets like the other ladies of the evening. I trust we understand each other." Gently, he released Alicia's hands. He smiled to himself as she went limp and fell to her knees at his feet.

This was a bad dream; this surely couldn't be happening to her. How could one man be so evil? Carl. Carl couldn't be marrying Royall Banner. He didn't love Royall, he loved her, Alicia. Fear settled in her stomach as she raised beseeching eyes to the Baron. "Please, you must not do this to me and to Carl. We truly love each other. Carl's your son, and he loves me."

"Carl loves money and the fine life. Come, child, sit here beside me." Alicia recognized the words for the iron command they were. Awkwardly, she rose to her feet and then settled herself primly on the sofa. He had to leave so she could think. She had to get her wits together and sort out all of the things he had just said to her. Think, she had to think. God in heaven, this man had just turned her world upside down. He had made insane accusations, said foul, filthy things to her, and then said he wanted to right a wrong and at the same time forbid her to see his son ever again. Think! her mind screamed.

Tears of humiliation coursed down her cheeks as she felt rather than saw his well-manicured hand cup her breast. A shudder ripped through her. Not Carl's father. He couldn't . . . he wouldn't . . . take advantage of her.

Alicia felt flesh touch flesh. Now she knew what the saying meant when someone said their flesh crawled. "I see that you understand," the Baron said suavely. "As long as you cooperate, Carl will never hear about your, er, shall we call them, escapades? Now," he said, cupping her breast with hurting fingers, "I'm certain you can see my logic. You have nowhere else to turn besides myself. Without me, you'll find yourself out on the streets begging for a living. I'd like it if you were ready by noon tomorrow. I'll have my carriage waiting outside the shop to take you to my townhouse."

Alicia wanted to cry out that he was hurting her. She knew her flesh would hold the bruises. She was beaten, and she knew it. Without Carl there was no one, no one. No friends, nothing. Thanks to the Baron her father had died in disgrace, leaving countless debts, many of them owed to former family friends. No one could help her, and without Carl nothing had meaning. He had turned from her, bending to his father's will, leaving her alone.

"Now that wasn't so hard, was it?" the Baron smiled, assuming Alicia's silence was her acquiescence. "Fix your gown, Alicia, before I change my mind and stay for the remainder of the day. There will be time enough soon for us to get off on the right footing."

Alicia shivered. She knew exactly what he meant when he said they would soon be on the right footing. Hastily, she righted the bodice of her mauve dimity gown. Her tears had long since dried on her face. What did anything matter anymore? At least she knew she would have clothes on her back and food in her stomach. She would have to allow her mind to go to the pretend world her mother had traveled before her death. The world where there was no feeling, no caring, no loving. One just existed from one day to the next. Nothing mattered now. Her world, as she lived in it, no longer existed. Without Carl, there was nothing.

Chapter Seven

The early morning ride through the jungle was an exhilarating experience that Royall knew she would not soon forget. The smell of the tropical flowers was intoxicating, and the dew lay heavy on the lush green foliage, causing it to sparkle in the bright sun. Soon it would dry off as the light became more intense. Scarlet and emerald birds shrilled and cackled as they flew through the dense forest.

Carl pointed out a large python that lay coiled, dozing in the sun. Briefly, he gave Royall a lecture on the snakes of the jungle, especially the poisonous ones, how they attacked and what to do if it happened. Royall shuddered and knew that if a snake ever bit her she would lay down and die.

"That's one of the reasons why we don't want you to venture into the jungle until you know the terrain and can handle yourself. Never fear, it will not take long to learn the ways of Brazil." Carl smiled at her uncertain look.

They chatted happily, and Carl gradually lost the worried look with which he had started out. Royall was eager to see Mrs. Quince and have a picnic breakfast at her plantation.

When they arrived at the Quince plantation, Rosalie was overjoyed at the arrival of her neighbors, and Royall felt that Carl was embarrassed by such a blatant display of emotion. Royall was pleased to see that Mrs. Quince's ankle was mending nicely. The woman carried a walking stick and the wheeled chair had been discarded.

"Come, my dears," Mrs. Quince cried happily. "I also have another guest for breakfast. I can't quite believe my good fortune this day." Royall and Carl followed the aristocratic lady into the dim house and onto the veranda. Seated at the table, his plate piled high with food, sat Sebastian Rivera. He stood and gave a slight bow in Royall's direction. Royall recovered quickly and smiled coolly, surprised at his appearance.

"Isn't this good luck?" Mrs. Quince asked happily. "Not one visitor but three! This year promises to be very exciting with the opening of the opera," she continued enthusiastically. "It'll be a welcome change to live in town and visit with friends. I look forward to it every year."

Carl frowned at the sight of Sebastian Rivera. He wished he'd known the man would be here and had arranged for another day to bring Royall to visit Rosalie Quince. Now he had to go through the social amenities for their sakes. It would be too rude to allow his feelings toward Mrs. Quince's guest to show. Carl found himself studying Sebastian's face as he always did when he was in Rivera's company. The squareness of the jaw, jet black hair, not just dark like his own, but most of all, the sense of power he emanated; power of the same intensity but of a different nature than the Baron. Was it possible, could it be that Sebastian was as much the Baron's son as he was?

Was that the real reason behind the Baron's hatred for Rivera, and not Rivera's stand on the slavery issue or the man's obvious Indian heritage?

Briefly, Carl remembered those days when he and Sebastian had been boys, stealing out into the jungle to play with one another, each knowing the risk they took if the Baron should discover them. Those had been good days, days when hatred and prejudice had been left to the adults. Even today, Carl knew a secret admiration for Sebastian Rivera and personally agreed with the general consensus that he was an honorable man with acute business sense.

"Carl," Rosalie Quince addressed him, breaking him away from his thoughts, "Sebastian came here last night to tell Alonzo and myself that there's fever on Reino Brazilia. Is this true?"

Royall's ears pricked up and she watched Carl, waiting for his answer. The man appeared shocked, whether at the news or the fact that Sebastian was the bearer of the news was not clear.

"There are a few sick Indians, but the Baron doesn't think it's the fever," Carl answered calmly, aware he was under Rivera's scrutiny.

"What do *you* think, Carl?" Mrs. Quince persisted.

"I haven't been down to the compound myself. Other business has prevented me."

Rosalie Quince frowned, making it evident that she could not accept Carl's excuse. "How sick are they? How many?" she demanded sternly.

"Four, I believe, and they've been off work only three days."

"Is there any improvement in their conditions?" she persisted. An outbreak of fever would affect every plantation owner on this side of the Amazon and was not to be dealt with lightly.

"I don't know, Mrs. Quince. The Baron seems to think it's all part of a rebellion, and he doesn't believe they're sick at all." Plainly, Carl didn't hold with the Baron's beliefs. He was decidedly uncomfortable under Mrs. Quince's questioning, and Royall actually felt sorry for him. Poor Carl, if he would only stand up for his own beliefs, he'd like himself better.

"It wouldn't surprise me, Carl, if fever was present on the Reino. Alonzo has told your father many times, and so has Sebastian, to clear out those lowlands and drain the marsh. The very air down there is lethal. The Baron promises but never follows through. There'd better not be another outbreak of yellow jack. We'd all suffer the losses."

Royall listened attentively. Rosalie Quince was accusing the Baron of neglecting his sick. If he could separate children from their parents, she could very well believe he was just as cruel in other ways. Royall decided this was another matter she would look into. If the Indians' welfare depended upon the owners of the plantations, she meant to have a hand in it. Mrs. Quince was looking at her as though she could read her mind, and a challenging glint shone in her sharp eyes.

"Royall, Sebastian must leave now, and this carnfounded ankle of mine still acts up. Would you be so kind as to see him out?"

"That won't be necessary," Sebastian hastily interjected. "I've known my way around your home since I was a boy."

"Hush now, Sebastian. I won't be said to be lacking in social graces. Royall, dear, please see Senor Rivera to the door."

Royall was being manipulated and she knew it, but having no other recourse, she stood and smoothed the skirt of her riding habit. She moved through the veranda doors into the cool interior of the house, aware that Sebastian was following closely behind.

"The front door is this way," he told her when she turned the wrong way into the corridor. "You seem to know as much about Mrs. Quince's house as you do about the condition of the *slaves* on *your* plantation!"

Royall turned on him, heat flaming in her face. "That's not fair, Senor Rivera. I've only just come to the Reino, and I'm only beginning to guess at the condition of the workers."

"Save me your explanations, Senora Banner," he said coldly, his black eyes flashing, his lips curling in a churlish sneer. "You and your father lived off the profits from the Reino for many years. It was your business to learn how those profits were made. And knowing, I doubt it would have made much difference. What matter if a man's life is hell on earth when compared to a new hat for that beautiful golden head of yours."

She wanted to lash out, slap the contempt off his face and replace it with the bloody slash of her nails. "You didn't know my father, Senor Rivera! He would have thought the slavery here abominable. In America he was an outspoken emancipationist!"

"And did your father have holdings in the South that depended upon slave labor?" His face was so close to hers, she could feel his breath on her cheek, feel herself locked in those night dark eyes.

"N-no, he didn't, but . . ."

"Exactly. It's easy to be an emancipationist when one's fortune doesn't depend on it. And if I'm not mistaken, living in the North, he merely adopted a popular opinion. Having interest in a plantation south of the Equator where his friends and acquaintances couldn't see the deplorable conditions for themselves, your father was quite safe, wasn't he?" His hand gripped her arm, pulling her toward him, forcing her to look up at him and see the hatred there in his face.

"And you were safe, also, weren't you? Your lovely patrician nose never had to smell the stink of the Reino's compounds, and you never had to see the suffering. You only knew that nothing was denied you. Education, travel, clothes—all bought for you by the miserable lives of the slaves on Reino Brazilia!"

His voice was a deep growl, menacing and threatening. Royall tried to pull away, wanted to run away, hide from that murderous glint in his eyes. But she was helpless, caught in a vise, unable to run, even to speak.

"Ever since I was a boy, I've hated the Reino for what it did to my people, what the Baron and your father did. And God help me, but I want to hate you too!" His breath escaped in an audible groan as he seized her with both hands, pulling her hard against him. He frowned, tipping his head to one side, watching her with the alertness of a panther.

She wanted to escape, needed to hide herself from the rage in this man's eyes, from the bitter set of his mouth. He was posing a threat, but of what she wasn't certain. With supreme effort she pulled herself free, turning and running down the corridor, not knowing where it would take her, only praying there was safety on the other side of the door.

She ran faster, holding her skirts, her booted feet striving for purchase on the slickly polished floor. Reaching the door, she pulled it open. Like something in a bad dream, he was behind her, slamming the door shut with one hand and seizing her with the other.

"Let go of me!" she panted with desperation, struggling wildly against his grip. "Stay away from me!"

"If only I could!" he said harshly, his voice barely above a moan, tightening his hold on her, holding her fast, preventing her wild twistings to gain freedom. He seized her shoulders, shaking her violently, making her think her head would snap off.

His eyes blazed with fire and his mouth tightened into a grim, forbidding line, a muscle leaped wildly in his jaw. Before she could take another breath, he subdued her struggles by pulling her arms behind her back, crushing her against him. His height and massive shoulders made her feel helpless and insignificant, and sudden fear seemed to heighten her senses in spite of a dull roaring in her ears. She was aware of the clean, masculine scent of his cologne, of the feel of his chest, rock hard and impervious against her. He stalked her deliberately, finding the moment to lower his head and seek her mouth with his own. Despite the strength of his hands holding her captive, his lips were tender, teasing, stilling her fears before they crashed down upon hers again, searching and demanding, evoking her response in a bruising possession.

Royall's knees buckled under her, making her hold him for support. His lean, masculine body emanated a heat that penetrated her clothes and seemed to burn her flesh.

Roughly, he pushed her away from himself, an expression of self-disgust banking the fires in his eyes. She felt herself sinking, crumpling to the floor. For a long moment he stood looking down at her, feet spread wide apart, his stance telling her that she was helpless against him, that he could take her if he chose to, that he hated her and hated himself for wanting her.

Without a word, he turned, walking down the corridor to the front door. He opened it, a bright shaft of golden light outlining his stiffly held frame and proud dark panther's head. And when he was gone and she was left there in the dim shadows, she felt as though he had taken something of herself with him. Some vital part of herself that she had only discovered in his arms in the quiet after Mardi Gras.

She shivered in the dim coolness, knowing she should hate him for the way he used her, for what he thought of her. Her eyes burned, but no tears slipped down her cheeks. Her heart seemed to choke off all air and her pulses pounded with despair. She would never really hate Sebastian Rivera, she admitted. He hated enough for the both of them.

What seemed to Royall like hours later, she finally composed herself enough to go back out onto the veranda where Mrs. Quince and Carl were waiting for her. Rosalie's sharp eyes must have seen that something was amiss with her guest, because she turned to Carl after a moment and said, "Carl, why don't you go to the stable and see the new foal? Royall and I need some time for women's talk."

Royall was thankful for the woman's lack of tact when Carl stood to leave, an expression of chagrin on his face. He stood for a moment looking down at Royall, concern shadowing his eyes. "Is everything all right? You took so long seeing Rivera to the door."

Smiling, she tried to reassure him, even though her pulses were beating in crazy rhythms. "Of course, why shouldn't everything be all right?" she challenged.

"I just thought it took you so long to come back out here, and I know how Rivera feels about the Reino. If he said anything or did anything . . ."

"Carl, Royall said everything was fine. She probably needed to refresh herself after the long ride. Didn't you, dear," Rosalie made her excuse.

Taking the hint, Royall agreed, daring to meet Carl's curious glances head on. Forcing herself to smile brightly, she added, "You go on and see the foal. I'll come down after a while. I think Mrs. Quince wants to try to pry out the secret of what I'll be wearing to the Masquerade Ball."

When they were alone on the veranda with the bamboo blinds closed to ward off the sun, cool papaya drinks in their hands, Royall immediately questioned Mrs. Quince about the little girls on the Reino.

"It's sad, isn't it? Unfortunately, it's also true. Carlyle doesn't treat his Indians and blacks with a shred of humanity. The living conditions are deplorable! Sebastian has been trying for the last three years to get the children." Suddenly, something bright green swooped onto the porch and settled on Mrs. Quince's shoulder. "Lord a mercy! Lord a mercy!" it squawked in a raucous voice.

"This is my parrot. Bartholomo, meet Royall Banner."

"Where's my sweetheart?" he chanted again, making Royall laugh.

"At least he's someone to talk to during the day before Alonzo comes home," Mrs. Quince said, laughing at herself, fine lines radiating from the corners of her sharp blue eyes.

"Tell me, child, how do you like it at the plantation? What did you think of the Baron?"

"He's been most courteous. I've only seen him at dinner. And of course, Carl has been very gallant."

"And Jamie?" Mrs. Quince asked, her tone suddenly sharp and her eyes bright.

"He's very nice and friendly. He took me horseback riding, to everyone's disapproval. Evidently he's not an accomplished horseman. The Baron has forbidden me to ride with him. Jamie was quite angry. He acts like a spoiled child from time to time. But I like him."

"And the housekeeper?"

"She, too, has forbidden me to ride with Jamie, and I think she takes too much upon herself. And yes, she doesn't like me. You were right, Mrs. Quince. I've tried to be friendly, but she's so cold and unbending. But tell me, Mrs. Quince, what's this about a fever on the plantation?"

"Sebastian rode here last night to ask Alonzo if he knew of any cases of yellow jack at Reino Brazilia. So far, it's only a rumor. A rumor I hope isn't true. The last epidemic we had was also on the Reino and it spread to our plantation. We lost seventy-two Indians and forty-five blacks. I can't recall the number the Reino lost, but it greatly exceeded ours. It's the Baron's fault. He's never adequately cared for the Indians. He expects them to work day and night under the worst conditions."

Royall sensed Mrs. Quince's dismay over the loss of life, and recalled Sebastian telling her of Mrs. Quince's long struggle to improve the natives' living conditions. She also recognized the woman's hostility toward the Baron and his indifference to the slaves.

The parrot suddenly set up a furious squawking. "The Baron is a nitwit. The Baron is a nitwit." Mrs. Quince laughed uproariously. Royall joined her as the great, beaked bird flew from its soft perch.

"As you can see, he's heard it so many times, he picked it up. When the Baron is here, I have to hide him in the shed," she said, wiping her eyes on the hem of her skirt.

Sebastian Rivera rode from the Quince plantation as though the hounds of hell were on his heels. He cursed himself for his lack of control, for giving into his passions. And that's what his feelings were toward this Royall Banner, this golden-skinned woman from the north. Of all the bad luck, to run into her and Carl Newsome at Rosalie's house. The thought of Royall and Carl together brought his mouth down in a frown. Everything had seemed innocent enough . . . yet, he didn't want to see Alicia hurt. Sebastian was well aware of the relationship between Carl and Alicia, and although he didn't entirely approve of the girl's choice, he wished her well. She'd need all the luck in the world if she married Carl and went to live on the Reino Brazilia with the Baron.

Sebastian had known Alicia since she was a little girl, and he'd always enjoyed doing business with Leslie Stanhope, her father. He'd been shocked to hear that Stanhope had shot himself when his business was lost, and something in his gut told him the Baron was at the bottom of it. The Baron and Reino.

Aware of Alicia's circumstances, Sebastian had tried several times to help her through her financial difficulties. The estate left to her was penniless, and there were staggering debts besides. But Alicia, being proud as well as pretty, was confident that she would soon be married to Carl and her problems would be over. For her sake, he hoped she was right.

Unbidden, his thoughts returned again to Royall. Just another pretty face, he told himself. All golden and soft. She wouldn't last long in this torturous climate before picking up her skirts and hightailing it back for New England. He shook his head angrily as he spurred the horse forward. Memories of long, delicate fingers and creamy golden skin flashed before him. Damn her, damn her! She didn't know what work was! Senora Royall Banner was from a wealthy family who had

165

servants like his own mother, to wait on her hand and foot.

The thought of his mother made him grit his teeth. She'd labored all her life just to keep him with her, and that was the deepest love Sebastian could ever know. He tried, unsuccessfully, to set aside all memory of his dubious parentage. A man was a man and what he made of himself. That was something that that finely bred American woman with the golden hair would never appreciate. Proper lineage, proper parentage, would be all-important to her. If she knew he was a bastard, she'd no doubt ingnore him and cast him from her society. Yet, there was a small, niggling doubt. She'd certainly been earthy and worldly in Rio de Janeiro when she'd cried out for his lovemaking and seared his body with her own burning kisses. And then on the riverboat when he'd believed she was Rosalie's guest. She was so sweet, so gentle . . . Damn him, he'd even thought he was in love with her. Royall Banner was part owner in the Reino, he reminded himself harshly, remembering the old adage of birds of a feather. He punctuated his disgust by biting the lip off a fresh cheroot and forcefully spitting it out.

A thought came to him. Last evening at dinner, Rosalie had told Alonzo of Royall's share in Reino Brazilia. Well, he, Sebastian, would just sit back and wait to see if she took a hand in management. He knew he could depend on Rosalie to explain the conditions at the Reino. Then and only then would he see the stuff Royall Banner was made of.

Muscular thighs gripped the sides of his horse, and he spurred the animal forward. He wanted to ride, fast, too fast to think.

It was time, he told himself, for a trip into Manaus and the sloe-eyed beauty he kept in residence at his townhouse. He smiled to himself when he thought of the coming evening and the pleasure it would hold for him.

Back at the Quince plantation, Carl joined Royall and Mrs. Quince on the veranda and contributed to the conversation about the coming opera season and the festivities.

"Royall, I must have a party for you when we're in Manaus. I insist you stay with Alonzo and myself. Leave the men to their own devices in Manaus and say you'll stay with me. We can have the party for you right there in Manaus while everyone is in town. What do you think, Carl?"

"I think that's a very good idea. I'm certain Royall would much rather spend the days with you than wait at home for the Baron and myself to finish business." Carl's mind was racing. Bless Rosalie Quince for suggesting Royall stay with her while in Manaus. At least he'd be able to find the opportunity to see Alicia and spend some time alone with her. His father's plan of having him marry Royall was just that, as far as Carl was concerned. All he needed was to go through the motions and wait for the right opportunity to make his father change his mind. He was sure of it. He had to be, because facing a life without Alicia was like facing a long, dark eternity where there was no light.

The rest of the day passed quietly. With the matter of the party settled in favor of the townhouse, talk ranged from parties to plantation life and the servants, Indians, and blacks. Mrs. Quince cautioned Carl again to warn the Baron on the living conditions of the Indians. And she asked whether the Baron had decided about the children. Would he return them to their parents at the Rivera plantation?

Carl shook his head and said the Baron wouldn't part with the girls.

Royall looked from one to the other. "The children will be returned to their parents," she stated quietly and firmly. "I won't have that on my conscience." Mrs. Quince and Carl stared at her in surprise. Approval replaced the look of surprise on Mrs. Quince's face. Royall waited expectantly for some comment from Carl. None was made. Instead, Mrs. Quince announced an early tea. She knew the young people wanted to leave in order to arrive home before dark.

Royall's thanks for the lovely visit were effusive. Carl was more formal and more quiet than usual.

On the ride back to the Reino, Royall had the feeling that he wanted to say something but didn't know how. Bluntly, she asked him what was troubling him.

"Royall, I don't think you should have made

such a rash statement about sending the little girls back to their families. The Baron runs the plantation, and he'd never tolerate your interference. A woman has no say in the running of the plantation."

"Even if the woman owns half of said plantation?" Royall asked coldly.

Carl stammered as he again tried to persuade her to let the matter drop.

"Carl, I mean to see that the conditions of the Indians and the blacks are made livable and tolerable. I couldn't live with myself and take my living from their suffering. I don't see how you, as a man, can condone it. Evidently, the other plantation owners don't do this, and they still show a profit and survive."

"It's the Baron's way, and so far he's been successful. I wouldn't interfere if I were you," he said quietly.

"Well, I'm not you, and I do mean to take a hand," Royall said sharply.

Carl let the matter rest, and the remainder of the trip passed in silence. Royall's thoughts were of Sebastian, and Carl's were of Alicia and his love for her.

Chapter Eight

Royall dressed hurriedly and fidgeted while Moriah brushed her hair. She wanted to speak to the Baron before dinner, before her determination flagged. She wanted the matter of the girls settled and to arrange for an accounting of her holdings. Feeling nervous and a bit light-headed, she knew the meeting would not go well, as Carl, in his own way, had tried to warn her. Still, she had to try. Her father would have expected it of her. She demanded it of herself.

She waved the little girls away and lightly dusted her cheeks with rice powder. Playfully, she put a dab on each of the little girls' faces. They giggled as they looked at each other.

Quickly, Royall left the room. The sooner she faced the Baron, the sooner it would be over.

She entered the library just as Carl was announcing they had had a pleasant outing.

Royall tightened the muscles in her body. She walked over to the Baron and said, "May I speak to you, sir? I feel it is a matter of some importance." The Baron looked at the beautiful, golden girl in front of him and smiled.

"My dear, you sound so serious. What could make you this serious on such a beautiful evening?"

She felt her determination weaken before the hard, glittering gray eyes. His presence commanded her full attention. She lowered her attention from his compelling gaze and focused on his square, clean jaw and neatly trimmed moustache. She could feel him tensing, waiting. At her hesitation he studied her, admiring the stylish green watered silk gown that displayed her femininely sloping shoulders.

She was about to speak when he licked his lower lip, his eyes straying to her bosom. He reminded Royall of the old tomcat the cook had kept in her spotless kitchen. The old tom would lick his lips just that way when the cook was about to pour him a saucer of cream. Only the tom's glittering green eyes would betray his excitement as he slowly and deliberately licked his whiskered chin.

Royall plunged ahead. "I've heard rumors today about the sick Indians. Is this true? Are we threatened with yellow jack?"

"My dear," the Baron said, concern on his face, "Rosalie must have been inventing tales. There are several Indians who 'say' they're ill," he said, wagging a finger in the air. "I'm sure they're contemplating a rebellion of some sort. There have been vague threats that have reached my ears the past several days."

"But what of the living conditions? I've heard they're deplorable."

The Baron puffed out his cheeks in outrage. "Who tells you these lies? Answer me," he demanded.

Royall stood her ground firmly. "I heard it at Mrs. Quince's plantation. The lady herself spoke of it."

"I'll wager she got her information from her neighbor to the north," the Baron replied, his mouth tight.

So, he already knew of meeting Sebastian at Mrs. Quince's. Evidently Carl had reported the details of their visit.

"Sebastian Rivera was there, yes. He no more than said hello and then good-bye. Mrs. Quince told me that once before yellow jack broke out on Reino and it spread to the other plantations and many lives were lost."

The Baron snapped his fingers; the sound hung heavy in the still air. "One cannot concern oneself with the insignificance of slaves."

Royall felt a rage rise in her chest, but she fought to control it. She couldn't afford to lose her temper now. "Are you telling me, sir, that there is no fever here at Reino Brazilia?"

"But of course, my dear. That is exactly what I'm telling you. There's no need for you to concern yourself with the management of the plantation. You and your father have for many years lived luxuriously and comfortably from the Reino Brazilia, and your father never once questioned my methods. The details are much too complex for you to even begin to understand."

"Sir, are you insinuating that I'm not capable of handling my own affairs, and that I wouldn't understand them if I tried?"

The Baron smiled coolly. "No, my dear. However, I feel that it's not something for you to concern yourself with I'll run the Reino the same as I always have. Let this be the end of the discussion," he said abruptly.

Royall was still her father's daughter. "One moment, sir. There are several other things I wish to discuss." She trembled at the audacity she had shown. Squaring her shoulders, she faced him head on. "There is the matter of the children. I want to know why they aren't with their parents on Regalo Verdad."

"The children remain here. They're part of a debt owed to me by their parents." His speech was smooth, but a muscle in his cheek had begun to jump. Royall knew he was angry. So be it; so was she!

"It's my understanding that Sebastian Rivera has offered to buy the girls for any price you named."

"There's no need to discuss the matter, and, my dear, I want you never to mention the name of Sebastian Rivera in Casa Grande again."

Royall felt herself flush. She looked at Jamie, who was watching her. He appeared upset. He was rubbing his thumb and fingers together nervously and was trying to catch his father's eye. The Baron ignored him and continued to stare at Royall.

"I repeat. The children are not for sale and never will be. Is that clear?" he asked in a dangerous voice.

Chagrin, humiliation, and defeat ran up Royall's spine. Again, she looked at Jamie. He was now relaxed, his fingers still. Surely he didn't enjoy her humiliation, or was he suddenly relieved that the little girls would remain at the Reino?

Refusing to give up, Royall ignored the flush that traversed her body and said brazenly, "I trust, sir, that I can depend on an accounting of my share of the plantation before the opera opens."

There was a determined edge in her quiet voice. She gathered up the bottom of the gown and advanced to the dining room at Elena's entrance to announce dinner. She didn't wait for one of the men to escort her. She was mistress of this plantation and she would do as she pleased. She looked into the dark eyes of the housekeeper and could not fathom the expression—admiration or hate? She carried herself regally and stood by the chair, waiting for Jamie to seat her.

Dinner was a dismal affair. The Baron had struck a note of fear within her, and the ominous phrases in her father's ledger swam before her eyes. Carl tried his best to make lively table conversation, but his heart obviously was not in it. Jamie told them about a new order he had placed for five soldiers from England. They were to be made expressly for him and would arrive with the next sailing.

Royall picked at the food and answered when spoken to. She felt like a schoolgirl who had been reprimanded.

The Baron chewed his food slowly and methodically and concentrated on the slim girl opposite him. What did this chit of a girl know? How dare she order him about! Actually, *order* was too strong a word. It was all Sebastian Rivera's doing. He knew the man was behind all the questions and the innuendos.

The girl was probably smitten with Rivera, just as many women appeared to be. Royall Banner was going to be trouble; he could feel it in his bones. If Carl didn't take interest, soon the plantation would suffer. As he chewed, he contemplated the accounting Royall had requested. There was no way he could refuse. To do so would be illegal and make him look less a man. He looked at the girl coldly and was revolted by all she stood for. He hated her in that moment as much as he hated Sebastian Rivera; both were a threat to Reino Brazilia, his kingdom in Brazil. And that was exactly what he had made it: his kingdom, where he was king and ruled supreme. Royall looked up into the Baron's cold, hate-filled expression. She felt her innards tremble and didn't hear the question Jamie asked her.

The Baron repeated the question for her benefit. For the life of her, she didn't know what he said. She nodded and asked to be excused, pleading a headache. The three men watched her exit, concern on their faces, concern for three different reasons.

As Royall passed the Baron's chair she suppressed an urge to scream like Bartholomo had, "The Baron is a nitwit; the Baron is a nitwit!" Once she reached the hall, she raced on light feet to her room. Passing Elena in the hall, she didn't stop to give her a second look. Once in her room Royall flung herself on the chaise and let the humiliation wash over her. Just because she was a woman, the Baron considered her incompetent. More than that, she was sick with herself. She should have stood her ground, forced the issue, badgered the imperious Baron and the devil take the hindmost.

A knock sounded on the door, and Royall bade the caller to enter. It was Jamie, a frown on his face. "Does this mean you won't play the spinet this evening?" he asked wistfully.

"Not tonight, Jamie. My head aches too much." In truth, her head had begun to throb like a drum.

"Couldn't you take something? I've waited all day for this evening, just waited for you to play," he almost shouted, then immediately gained control of himself. "I'm sorry," he said, "that was foolish of me. I love music."

At the moment Royall couldn't have cared less. She waited for him to leave. Evidently he had something else to say. She waited.

"Aren't you happy that the girls are to remain here to take care of you?" He looked so concerned that she nodded. Anything so that he would leave. Royall closed her eyes in pain as he quietly left the room.

When the headache disappeared she would again get out the packet of her father's papers and read, and she would understand them if it took her till morning. Once the decision was made, she dropped into an uneasy sleep. The girls awoke her later in the evening and helped her dress for bed. She climbed between the crisp, cool sheets, her resolution postponed till the morrow.

Downstairs the Baron was having a heated discussion with Carl. "I want no more foolishness with the girl Alicia. Didn't I tell you to put her out of your mind? She's penniless. We don't need a pauper added to this family."

"But, father, how do you cut love out of your heart?" Carl pleaded. The Baron looked at his son and his lip curled in distaste. He knew the boy would botch the job.

"You *must* do it. I am your father and I *command* you to obey me." Carl nodded, his eyes wretched with the task before him. "The chit wants an accounting. Did you hear her? And what am I to do? I warn you, Carl. If you haven't succeeded, I'll take other measures. Which brings me to another matter. You won't be going to Manaus for the opening of the opera. There are affairs that need attention in Belém. I'm making the arrangements in the morning. So, you'd better get busy and convince that little interloper she wants to marry you. Going to Belém can be your wedding trip." The Baron threw back his head and laughed, a dry, nasty sound. How easy it was to arrange other's lives. With Carl in Belém the poor fool would never know that his precious Alicia was ensconced in the Newsome townhouse, bed partner to his own father. And once he did discover who had become Alicia Stanhope's protector, it would be too late; he'd already be married to Royall Banner.

Carl's shoulders slumped. He wouldn't be going to Manaus to see Alicia after all. He wanted to rebel, hit someone or something! Marry Alicia and go off somewhere with her and the Baron be damned. But tradition was too strong and his up-bringing too rigid.

Carl cringed before the verbal attack as though it had been physical. He knew what his father meant by "other measures."

Jamie sat on the sofa listening to his father's sharp words. He wondered what had made the Baron so angry; hadn't Royall agreed to everything he had said? He let his mind wander to the new order of the additional soldiers. It would bring his total to eighty. He didn't hear Carl's weak reply promising to do his best.

Royall spent her days with Jamie and her evenings with Carl. At first she had spent many hours inspecting the Casa Grande. She picked the colorful tropical flowers and arranged them artfully in every room of the Casa. When she tired of the flowers, she would make her way to the kitchen regions and hesitantly make suggestions to the cook. Surprisingly, Elena made no attempt to interfere. When boredom set in, as Royall knew it would, she decided to teach Jamie the piano. He wasn't an apt pupil and would have been content to have her play for him by the hour while he sat and dreamily listened. It puzzled Royall that his help wasn't needed on the plantation. The Baron actually seemed glad that he spent whole days in her company.

It had become increasingly clear to her that Jamie was irresponsible and childish, incapable of decision. Elena actually mothered the tall, husky, young man and controlled him with an iron hand, tempered with tenderness. Lately Elena seemed to be losing that control as Jamie became increasingly rebellious. Often he would do something or say something that would anger Royall, but all it took was one of his bright, sincere smiles and she found herself forgiving him. Jamie was an incredibly handsome young man, beautiful, actually, and when he apologized, his manner was especially engaging.

Carl was an attentive suitor. And he had fast become a suitor. On long, quiet evenings under the alluring tropical moon, Carl and Royall sat in the small pergola in the back gardens. He was pleasant company after the long day with Jamie and, unlike his brother, was extremely well read and quite knowledgeable about the functions of rubber. He even described some ideas of his own for the practical use of the gooey substance drawn from trees.

Royall enjoyed her evenings with Carl because his excitement was contagious, and she found herself a sounding board for his more innovative ideas. She became quite fond of him; he was dear to her if only for the fact that he respected her intellect, acknowledged that she even possessed an intellect! A rare thing in an age where a woman was thought blessed if she possessed tiny feet, slim ankles, a narrow waist, and a pretty face. Having these, a woman had no need for a brain. Indeed, society decried a woman who professed to have one.

Royall knew that several times Carl had been on the verge of asking for her hand. Skillfully, she had so far avoided a direct confrontation. She was fond of Carl, but she didn't love him and his attentions were fast becoming worrisome.

She paid rapt attention to the lessons that Jamie and Carl taught her regarding the jungle, and the Baron finally decreed she could ride alone.

Royall arose early with the knowledge that this was her first day of freedom. For it was freedom! She could go and do as she pleased. In truth, all she planned to do was go for a ride alone, without Jamie or Carl. She was so excited she could barely close the hooks on her riding habit. Quietly, she slipped from the room, her carryall in hand. She was going to the Regalo Verdad, Sebastian Rivera's plantation. A note had been delivered from Mrs. Quince telling her of the expert needlewoman that Sebastian employed as his housekeeper. It appeared from the letter that Anna, for that was her name, had agreed not only to make Royall's costume, but also Mrs. Quince's, who was to be at the plantation awaiting Royall's arrival. She had journeyed there the day before and had spent the night, the note ended.

Royall slipped from the house quietly and ran on light feet to the stable. Dawn was just breaking. She looked at the gray pink light and shivered. By the time she had her horse saddled it would be completely light. Saddling the dappled gray with clumsy fingers, she fought the urge to look over her shoulder to see if anyone was going to stop her. Her preparations completed, she mounted the gray and led him in a slow trot through the courtyard. Once on the jungle trail, she spurred the horse gently, and it responded to her hold on the reins. She felt as free as the colorful birds with their shrill, raucous cries. Picking her way carefully over the vine-strewn ground, she felt her seat was firm, and she felt quite comfortable on her high perch. She nibbled on a ripe papaya, tossing the pit away. She rode at a fast canter and within the hour was on property that belonged to Sebastian Rivera.

Royall stopped her horse at the end of the long drive leading to the Casa Grande of Regalo Verdad—in Spanish it meant the True Gift. Taking her mount for a slow canter up the drive, she stopped once again as she came within sight of the house. Like the Reino's Casa, it was low and white with Spanish arches creating the veranda. Its roof was red tiled, and there was a luxurious growth of greenery surrounding it. Unlike Reino Brazilia, everything seemed lovingly cared for, tended with the gentlest of hands. The drive that approached the house was carefully laid brick, and at the far side Royall could see several old Indian men patiently laying the dusty pink oblongs into the striking herringbone pattern. A black woman wearing a colorful tignon wrapped around her head stepped out into the drive to shake an Indian-made rug. She sang in full-throated glory, her voice carrying across the distance in lyrical melody. When the woman lifted her eyes and saw Royall, she waved a happy greeting.

Compared to Regalo Verdad, the Reino was a dismal, lonely place. Here, children played on the back lawns and fresh laundry flapped in the breeze. Women and children seemed to all be happily engaged in their work, and although they moved slowly, as the Indians had learned through the ages to survive the climate, they were all clean and smiling.

Small children gathered around her as she slipped from her horse onto the mounting block and handed a tall, age-bent black the reins. He offered a wide, toothy grin. "Welcome, Senora, welcome to Regalo Verdad."

The atmosphere here was an uplifting one, and Royall hadn't realized how much she missed seeing a friendly smile on someone's face. A little girl came running up to her, *"Hola, Senorita,"* she said with a giggle. *"Como se llama usted?"*

Royall laughed at the small child who expected her to speak more Spanish than she could. *"Hola, nina. Me llamo Royall Banner."*

"My name is Mary," the child answered in clear, precise English. "Have you come to see Senora Quince?" Leading Royall up to the house and waiting by the heavy, carved door, "You are very pretty. Someday may I touch your hair?" Her dark eyes lit with eagerness that made Royall laugh.

"You may touch it now, if you like." She bent her head and felt the child's little fingers touch her curls. "I love your pigtails," Royall told her, twitching one of her fat braids.

"Pigtail?"

Royall laughed with delight. She held the heavy braid and explained that it was called a pigtail in the United States. The child giggled over the new word. Royall watched as she rolled the word over and over on her tongue. The door was opened by the housekeeper, who ushered Royall into a wide, cool-looking room. Immediately Royall spied Mrs. Quince drinking a cup of coffee, her host beside her.

Once again Royall was struck by Sebastian's resemblance to the Baron. The same square jaw, the set of the eyes. Consciously, she drew her eyes away from his face. Her breathing quickened as her legs turned to jelly.

As she entered, he arose and extended a welcome to his Casa Grande, but his eyes remained cold and aloof. Immediately he excused himself and left the ladies to their dressmaking. He informed his housekeeper that he would be back in time for lunch and, if she had time, to prepare it. The dark-skinned housekeeper smiled and said, "Be gone with you, Sebastian. When you return, it will be ready. As you well know, I am quite capable of doing two things at one time." Sebastian smiled, and his handsome face transformed completely. Royall envied the easy camaraderie he had with his housekeeper. Why couldn't he smile at her like that? He had once—so long ago she could barely remember.

The ladies then entered into an animated discussion about the ball and the costumes they would wear.

"What will you be wearing, Mrs. Quince? Or are you keeping it a secret?"

"No secret, Royall. I don't wear a costume. I'm far too old for that. I'll just go as plain old me."

"Don't consider yourself old, Mrs. Quince," Royall pretended to scold. "And as for being plain, nothing could be further from the truth."

"Our new neighbor is right, Mrs. Quince," Anna, the housekeeper, broke in. "You have character and respect. Aren't you the most respected lady in Manaus?" Then, turning to Royall, "Mrs. Quince does not want a costume, but you, Senora, are young and should dance all the night. Have you thought of what you would like to wear? You are so light, so fair, you remind me of . . . of what I have seen in Senor Rivera's books. The goddess Diana. The huntress."

Royall was speechless.

"It is settled then," Mrs. Quince burst out. "Diana you will be."

Anna watched the golden woman and said, "I will outdo myself in making your costume. It will be small payment for the kindness you have shown my daughter."

When Royall looked puzzled, Mrs. Quince explained. "One of your little handmaidens, Nessie, is Anna's daughter."

The rest of the morning was spent searching through Sebastian's books for a picture of Diana wearing something that was proper to wear in public. Then they discussed material and fittings, and it was noontime before Anna departed for the kitchen to prepare lunch.

When they were alone, Mrs. Quince turned to Royall and asked, "Tell me what you think of Regalo Verdad. No small difference from the Reino, eh, Royall?"

"It's magnificent. And happy, such a happy place."

"Sebastian's heart and soul are in this plantation. I think he's worked harder than any man in Brazil to make it what it is, including my own Alonzo."

Anna announced lunch, and the two women followed her to the dining room, where they were immediately joined by Sebastian. He seated the two women and then took his place at the head of the table. He bowed his head and said grace. The light luncheon of fresh fish was a tasty delight. For dessert there was a fresh fruit sponge cake. The inevitable strong Brazilian coffee followed.

Mrs. Quince, always a matchmaker at heart, suddenly spoke. "Sebastian, my dear, why don't you take Royall for a ride around the plantation? Anna has finished with her for the moment."

Royall flushed a rosy crimson at the blatant approach of her matchmaking. Sebastian Rivera frowned, but being the gentleman he was, could do nothing but agree. He told Royall to wait on the veranda, and he would have her mount saddled. He returned within minutes.

Royall looked up at the tall man. "I apologize for Mrs. Quince. She means well but I'm sure you must have other things to occupy your time than taking me riding. I can sit on the veranda if Mrs. Quince feels that I am in the way."

Sebastian looked at the golden girl and felt some of his hatred fade. She looked so lost, so alone. "It's my pleasure, Senora Banner," he said coolly. He helped Royall mount, and her dappled gray followed the black horse.

"It's a magnificent animal you ride," she said in a friendly tone, hoping to draw him into conversation. Sebastian merely nodded.

They rode in silence and soon came upon what looked like a village. The stone huts were white-washed and clean. Small children scampered around happy and healthy. The women wore bright clothing; they too looked happy and healthy. The jungle had been cleared from the center of the little village. Everything seemed to have its place. The people greeted Sebastian, smiles stretched from ear to ear. It seemed that Sebastian had a personal word for each. And he appeared to know everyone's name. He reached a long arm down and scooped up a small Indian boy and swung him onto the horse. He spurred the great black beast around the small clearing, and the child giggled and laughed with glee. His mother smiled at this display of affection from the owner of the plantation, and Royall felt in awe of this great man at her side; yet, he mystified her. He set the child down and called out in the Indian tongue. Three women came to stand by his mount and looked at him expectantly. Sebastian introduced Royall and told them she lived on Reino Brazilia and that she knew the children.

Hope, despair, and love were mirrored in the women's faces, but they said nothing. They stood still and waited for her to speak. She tried, but the words were thick in her throat. She tried again. "Dear God in heaven, what do I say?" She looked at Sebastian. He returned her look mockingly. She would receive no help from him. She looked into the expectant faces of the women in front of her and suddenly the little village was quiet. They all waited for her answer. "The *ninas* are happy. Father Juan is teaching them their letters and numbers. Moriah is happy and laughs a lot." One of the women, evidently Moriah's mother, beamed a smile, tears in her eyes. The others asked of Rosy and Bridget. Royall tried to speak quickly, but her choking emotions caused her to stutter. Sebastian did not fail to notice, but he said nothing. If Royall was part owner in Reino, then she was just as responsible as the Baron himself.

Royall stared at the three mothers and cleared her throat.

Finally, she managed, "They will be returned to you. I give you my word." Suddenly, the women were grasping at her legs and crying happily. Royall looked at Sebastian but could not read anything in his expression. "I *will* see to it that the children are returned," she said coldly to the tall man. "I don't give my word lightly."

"It's not your word that I doubt, Senora Banner. It's that of Carlyle Newsome. And," he said darkly, "he has given *his* word that the children will *not be returned. . . ever!*"

"Well, Senor Rivera," Royall said hotly, "I have given you my word. And," she said imperiously, "that is the end of that." She reined in the gray and started off at a brisk canter.

Sebastian caught up to her effortlessly. There was a new expression on his face as he studied the proud head and the stately carriage of the golden girl. She had spirit and determination, he'd give her that.

"Tell me, Senora Banner, when do you plan to marry Carl Newsome?" It was a question he casually tossed out, but he'd been thinking about it. Knowing the Baron, it wasn't unlikely that the man would want to incorporate Royall's share into his own. And what of Royall? Was she contemplating marriage into the Newsome family, wanting the whole pie instead of half?

"I'm afraid you have been misinformed. I am not now, or in the future, contemplating marriage with Carl. Somehow I would have thought you weren't the kind of man to listen to gossip," she said, her voice frigid, her eyes level.

Sebastian looked at the girl and didn't doubt her for one moment.

"And to clarify one more matter, Senor Rivera—" She made his name sound like a disease. "—when I marry it will be because I am in love. I'll have no marriage arranged for convenience's sake. Is that understood? The man I marry must be a man, and above all else, he must love me as I love him, a man to father my children. Not a man who lies and takes advantage of a woman's most tender emotions. In short, Senor Rivera, the man I marry will be the direct opposite of you! You used me! I was nothing more to you than a convenient whore. It was a mistake I'll never make again."

Royall flushed from head to toe. Dear God! Had she said those things aloud? So be it. She was her father's daughter; she would speak her mind. She had certainly done that!

Royall spurred her horse forward, leaving a stunned Sebastian staring after her.

He watched her ride ahead, a grin on his face. She was a spitfire! A survivor.

Suddenly, Sebastian saw a long vine hanging in the path of her cantering horse. She was heading for it at a fast pace, unaware of the danger. He dug his heels into his stallion's flanks, spurring the beast forward. Lunging to Royall's side, he reached for her and grabbed her from the saddle just as her mount cleared the vine.

Royall found herself in a most unladylike position. In order to extricate herself, she would either have to wiggle out of his grasp and fall to the ground, placing her in an embarrassing position, or she would have to let Sebastian pull her up next to him, placing her face inches from his own.

Sebastian looked at her curiously, watching her indecision, then decided for her, pulling her up, hard against him.

Sebastian's eyes laughed into Royall's. The jet circles glinted in amusement at her obvious predicament. She faced him boldly, brazenly.

Amusement died in him as he became aware of her nearness, of her womanly scent mingling with the perfume of her hair. The sun made a nimbus of gold around her head, and he held her more tightly, finding himself marveling at the lightness of her, the slimness of her waist. The contact of her body against his thigh was warm, a tingle of slow-burning fire. Golden flecks were dancing in her eyes, heightening the pink flush of her smooth cheek. Bending his head lower, lower, until he could see the slight pulse at the base of her throat, he kissed her, this golden goddess, and she was responding in the way he remembered, had dreamed: deeply, searchingly, passionately.

His lips were soft and warm, hard and demanding. Royall responded to him and felt herself lifted in a surge of emotion. It was as before, his kiss; nothing had changed except that it left her hungrier than before for his arms, his touch. She wanted to forget everything, everyone. She wanted to return to that night of discovery in Rio when he had been her teacher and she had been his most ardent student.

Sebastian broke away first, looking down into

her face, seeming to want to memorize her features, his own eyes unreadable. Long, thick lashes threw smudgy shadows on his high, tanned cheekbones and his mouth, that mouth that could caress so softly, so tenderly, was drawn into a hard, thin line. For an instant, Royall thought he might apologize, and when he didn't, it further added to her confusion. She couldn't understand the man who obviously wanted her, reaching out for her time and again, only to put her aside, seeming to hate himself for the hungers she stirred in him. He must enjoy what they shared between them, the kiss, the nearness, the same searing of the flesh and the senses; and yet, he always put her away, withdrawing from her, leaving her confused and feeling abandoned, always giving himself the upper hand.

Royall flushed with shame. Why did she always reveal so much to him? Why did she always give him the satisfaction of knowing how his touch, his nearness, affected her? He was used to having his own way with women; it meant nothing to him. If he did keep a woman in residence in Manaus as Jamie had told her, he certainly had no use for her! Rejection made her tongue sharp.

"Put me down," she told him, her voice a raspy whisper. "Don't put your hands on me again! I don't need you, Sebastian Rivera, and I don't need your approval either. Not about my being part owner in Reino or my personal life. I'm used to taking care of myself. You've used me, and I'll even admit that I fell eagerly into bed with you, but that was another time and another place. I thought I'd never see you again. And when I did, I was fool enough to think we had something between us that was right and good. I was wrong. You only care about your so-called principles and your goddamned plantation. I'm learning to hate you, you . . . bastard!" Hot tears scalded her cheeks.

"That's true, at least. I am a bastard," Sebastian said coolly, apparently unruffled by her attack.

"At least we agree on something," Royall shot back, hating him for his composure, hating herself for her outburst. "And for your information, I've known all about you from the moment I saw you on the paddlewheeler, and it never made that much difference," she snapped her fingers in his face, enjoying the glowering menace she saw in his black eyes. "You made it a difference. Let me make myself clear. I called you a bastard for the way you've treated me, not because you were born on the wrong side of the covers. Now that I've had my say, leave me alone. I'll find my own way back to the house. I don't need you. I never needed you!"

Royall mounted her gray, feeling his eyes on her as she headed back to the Casa. Coming into the courtyard, she slid from her mount and raced into the house, needing to be with someone, anyone, who could protect her from Sebastian Rivera.

Mrs. Quince and Anna looked up, startled at

her entrance, concern in their motherly cluckings and demands, "What's happened?"

Royall had plopped herself down into a sea-green armchair and stared straight ahead, her face a mask of stony indignation. Sebastian strode into the room, his steps long and determined. "Where the hell are you, Royall?" he demanded at the top of his voice. When he found himself under the attacking glares of Mrs. Quince and his housekeeper, Royall swore she saw a crimson stain creep up his face.

"What did you do, Sebastian Rivera? What did you do to our Royall? Can't you see she's a lady? What gives you the right to speak to her that way?" Mrs. Quince voiced her objections. "What have you done to upset her? Tell me, you big oaf!"

Sebastian suffered the verbal abuse of his neighbor much as though she were his own mother. Even his housekeeper took up the cry.

Sebastian stood first on one foot and then the other, damning himself for following Royall into the house and walking right into the spiders' parlor. He twirled his flat-crowned hat with his hands, eyes riveted on the floor.

"Sebastian, I demand an answer! Look at her! She says nothing; she just stares!"

"I kissed her," he said defensively.

"Ahh!" the housekeeper breathed with satisfaction.

"Lord a mercy!" exclaimed Mrs. Quince.

Royall bolted out of the chair, facing him, hands on hips, face flaming. He was grinning. Grinning!

193

He *could* smile now that her two companions seemed to be on his side.

She was the picture of defiance. Golden hair wind-torn and disheveled framing her face, eyes flaring, mouth set. "If you ever lay a hand on me like that again, Senor Rivera, I promise you you'll pull back a bloody stump!" A tear, crystal and pure, coursed down from the corner of her eye and glistened on her cheek.

Daring a glance at the housekeeper and Mrs. Quince, he saw them staring at him with cold, hostile expressions. He had made the golden girl cry!

He stomped from the room muttering something about vaporous women. He decided then and there he would go to Manaus and Aloni. She, at least, wouldn't behave as though she hated him just because he kissed her!

Chapter Nine

The Baron's townhouse in Manaus was built of pink bricks, made from the light colored clay indigenous to the northern bank of the ever-flowing Amazon River. Imported black wrought iron decorated the facade, bellying out from the front windows and marching like little sentries around the tiny front garden.

The inside, like outside, was cleverly decorated and immaculately kept. Consisting of three floors, as were so many of the homes in Manaus, it mimicked the houses surrounding St. James Park in London, England. Fireplaces in every room were used only during the rainy season and then more to burn off the excess moisture than for heat. Carefully laid parquet floors were covered by vibrantly colored carpets that, like every luxury in Brazil, were imported from Europe at great expense.

The front parlor looked out onto the street and was decorated in deep jungle greens and hibiscus against a backdrop of the palest yellow silk walls. Dark teakwood tables gleamed with care and polish and reflected the objects d'art skillfully displayed.

Alicia was dressed in a femininely ruffled pink wrapper, her slim legs propped on the sofa, high-heeled slippers dangling off her tiny feet. She eyed the brandy bottle on the table in front of her, liking the way the shaft of sunlight penetrated the glass, lighting the liquor within. The tip of her tongue moistened her lips. She looked at the bottle with longing, with actual desire.

Vaguely from somewhere in the back of her numbed brain, she likened the feeling to the times she had eagerly anticipated Carl's arrival at her home. There had been a need in her then too, a need for Carl. But that was all gone now, she had to make it be all gone. Now she was involved in an affair of a different nature. A love affair for the sticky sweet brandy and a deep, abiding hatred for Carlyle Newsome. It was the former that made the latter bearable. Without a moment's hesitation, she sipped the fiery liquid, relishing the taste, welcoming its effects. Putting the glass to her lips once again, she gulped it down and quickly poured herself another. Soon the Baron would arrive and she needed to be numbed, drunk, oblivious. And when it was over, perhaps a merciful God would let her sleep. Sleep.

The past several days, between drinks she had engaged in a self-debate upon whether or not there was a God. If so, how could. He have allowed this to happen to her? How could He have made her so weak, so lacking in character? It was because she knew that Carl was lost to her whatever she did, Alicia told herself. The Baron would see to that. Also, she had this damnable addiction; it was called eating, needing a place to live, clothes to wear . . . his father's sanction. And once the Baron convinced his son that Alicia's reputation was severely lacking, Carl would have turned his back on her anyway. "There's no God," she said slowly and distinctly, satisfied with her decision.

Where was Carl now? What was he thinking? What was he doing this very moment? If she could only have a glimpse of him, touch him. . . She stared at the brandy bottle again. All I have to do is walk out the front door and run in front of the first passing carriage. Or walk down to the river . . . The thought was so appalling, she reached for the bottle and gulped its contents. Her eyes watered as she gasped for breath, and a trickle of brandy dribbled down her chin into the cleft between her breasts.

Alicia became slowly aware of someone watching her, imagined she could hear the sound of breathing. Whirling around, she found herself face to face with Carlyle Newsome. Standing suddenly, feeling the blood rush from her head, she struggled for a haughty expression and knew she failed miserably when the Baron smirked.

"Drinking again, Alicia. It's most unbecoming, and I find it takes the edge off our passion. You reek!" he told her with disgust. "Go to your room and make yourself presentable. I'll be up shortly, and I want you in control of yourself. I didn't come here to witness your drunken orgy. I suggest you hurry and do as I say."

Deep hatred for herself and for the Baron swelled in Alicia's breast. How could she be sobered just by the sight of the man? She must have drunk half that bottle, and here she was mentally alert and cripplingly sober. The brandy had failed her. She looked at the bottle with a senseless accusation.

The Baron smiled. Seeing her looking at the bottle, he picked it up and held it aloft, tantalizing her with the shimmer and sparkle within the glass. "This, my little pigeon, will be your reward if you do well this evening. If you don't, all spirits will be removed from the house or locked away from your reach. I learned that trick from my father when he was training a hunting dog. When the pup obeyed, he would give him a piece of meat. When he disobeyed, he gave him nothing. The dog soon learned how to behave. The way I expect you to behave. You understand, don't you, Alicia?"

"Perfectly," she answered quietly, twisting her hands behind her back, wringing them in a silent agony. At this moment the brandy became all-important, an anesthetic to blunt the sharp edge of reality. She would cheerfully kill to know for certain she could have it. It would be hers; she would earn each and every drop.

"I'll see you shortly," the Baron told her, satisfied to see her vanquished. "And, dear, add a little scent. It does delicious things to me."

Carlyle walked around the decorative parlor after Alicia fled up the stairs. He felt magnificent. He *was* magnificent, in perfect control of his life and, even better, in total command of the lives around him. The last pleased him the most.

It puzzled him that he hadn't considered placing Alicia in his townhouse sooner than he had. It was something he should have moved upon as soon as he confirmed that the interfering Royall Banner was coming to Brazil. He should have taken a mistress, at any rate, much sooner. He was well on his way to solving his temporary impotency, he knew it; he could feel it in his bones.

Allowing his eyes to sweep the room, he knew a gratification for having done well for himself. Certainly, to all appearances, he was as successful as the most prominent plantation owner, Alonzo Quince, and as much as Sebastian Rivera, bastard that he was. No one would ever have to know that his yield from his trees hadn't lived up to his expectations for the last four or five years. No one, including Royall Banner.

Considering outside appearances, anyone could see that his furnishings both here in Manaus and at Reino were of the finest quality and in the best of taste, imported at great expense from America and Europe. The monstrous chandelier hanging in the center of the room and its twin in the dining room had taken ten men to install. His eyes traveled farther around the room to fall beneath his proprietorial glance. Gold and silver bowls held fresh tropical flowers, and in the rich amber shine of the parquet floors was further accoutrement of the care his servants took with their master's belongings.

Pouring himself two fingers of fine, imported Scotch, the Baron liked the look and feel of the fragile crystal goblet he held in his hands. Elegant hands, like Elena's. A pity his housekeeper at the Reino had been born among the lower classes. She would have been the perfect hostess, the perfect accessory to his already perfect life. The piercing gray eyes dropped to the glass. Only the stem of the wafer thin goblet remained; whisky ran down his trouser leg, dropping into a little puddle at the tip of his gleaming black shoe. Small pinpoints of blood dotted his palm. A snowy handkerchief materialized and he deftly wiped at the blood, a snarl pulling his mouth downward. Elena: just thinking about her made his pulses pound and made him lose his tightly held self-discipline. At times he thought he hated her, hated the sight of her, hated the constant reminder of her presence in his household. But he realized he needed her, that she was a valuable asset both in controlling Jamie and seeing to the running of his household. And, he admitted, he couldn't bring himself to part with her, to allow her her freedom. Thinking about Elena stirred his loins, and his eyes went to the central staircase.

Carlyle strode into the dressing room adjacent to the master bedroom. Swiftly, he removed his clothes, replacing them with a burgundy dressing gown that waited for him on the back of the clothespress door. He adjusted the silk belt and knotted it. A piece of paper followed his hand from the inside pocket of his waistcoat, and he slipped it into the pocket of his robe.

The Baron thrust the bedroom door open, knowing he would see Alicia cowering as usual in the huge four-poster bed. "Alicia, darling," he purred, "I thought you might like to see something I have in my pocket." He played with her emotions cat and mouse, aware that she knew full well what he was talking about. "It's a letter from Carl. I stopped the messenger that was to bring it to you. Later I'll allow you to read it." Carefully, he watched her expression, delighting in the intensity of her anticipation. The letter, coupled with the brandy, should work to his favor, and Alicia would go beyond what she considered her duty to him.

Desperately trying to control herself, Alicia asked calmly, "What does Carl have to say, Baron?

I don't understand why you don't let me see it before. I want to see it now! It's mine, give it to me!"

"Later, darling," he soothed unctuously, "trust me." The robe slithered to the floor, and Alicia knew she was lost; there would be no chance of seeing the letter if, in truth, there was a letter. She averted her eyes from his nakedness, her heart pounding with fright as she visualized the intimate acts she would be made to perform. Imperceptibly, she moved over as far away in the bed as she could.

The Baron stretched out luxuriously, and Alicia was hugging the far edge of the bed as she read the lust in his eyes. She would have to pretend again, pretend that it was Carl lying beside her, that it was Carl's flesh she would touch, caress. She would pretend she was a captive and she was being brought before the king, who was Carl. Whatever Carl wanted, she would give. Gladly. She had to remember that it was Carl's hands that would touch her, open her body to ravaging kisses and intimate caresses. Not ever the Baron.

"Dance for me, Alicia."

"But . . . no music . . ."

"Dance!" Alicia recognized the iron command.

Alicia left the bed and began to move, her movements at first slow and awkwardly embarrassed and gradually becoming more sensual and provocative as she swayed to an unheard tune. Her slim body lent itself to wantonness as she brought into play her proud high breasts and rounded hips.

Graceful arms lifted over her head as she had seen the Indians do so often in their rituals, softly clapping her hands to an increasingly rapid rhythm. As she twirled around the room, her tiny feet barely touched the floor, her hands, reaching and eloquent, caressed her body, driving the Baron to the edge of the bed. Perspiration beaded on his forehead as he stared at Alicia's undulating body. When he reached for her with a quick, groping hand, she seemed to throw her body into a frenzy of gestures that bordered on the immoral, knowing what he demanded, giving it to him.

Aided by the alcohol, feeling as though she was somewhere a world away, her fingers tore at the buttons on her dressing gown. It slid to the floor, and she demurely covered her breasts that were still hidden from his sight by the dainty camisole. Slowly, inch by inch, she opened the satin ribbon that held her swelling flesh prisoner.

The Baron rolled over on the bed, his eyes glazed as he stared at the expanse of skin that was suddenly free of confinement. Alicia danced closer, following a silent drum beat in her head, a knowing smile playing across her lips. This was her love, Carl, wanting her, desiring her as he always had in her dreams.

Suddenly whirling again, she stood even closer to him, tantalizing him, just out of his reach, freeing her breasts, baring them completely for his eyes. He gasped as he reached for her, her small, delicately formed body, losing her again, seeing her back away a step, her breasts with their rosy crests pointed and erect. She swayed ever closer until she was directly in front of him, her movements seducing him, flaunting her body without restraint. Slowly, she exposed a long, shapely leg from between the open front of her lace petticoat and languidly thrust it out, withdrawing the silk stocking from thigh to toe. Tossed away, it fell near him, brushing against his agonized face. She followed her action with the other stocking, hearing him groan, hearing him beg, "Now, come to me, Alicia, come to me."

Instead of obeying him, she dropped her petticoat at her feet, and from the deep groans coming from the bed she knew he was beyond control. Gliding gracefully to his bedside once again, she allowed him to touch her.

He swallowed hard; his half-closed eyes devoured her, his hands clutched for her breasts, her thighs, her legs; low, animal sounds escaped him.

Perspiration dripped from his face, and he felt the blood soar through his veins as the pressure in his loins became unbearable to him. He reached for her, clutching at her soft, dark hair, covering her mouth with his own.

He mounted her, knowing that this time the same blood that pounded through his veins would erect his failing manhood. Wild frustration flooded through him as he rolled over onto his stomach to hide his body's defeat. He had been so sure!

Exhausted, Alicia lay quietly, waiting for his

next move. He rolled over onto his side, playfully nibbling at her breasts. Determined to overcome his impotence, he let his hands trace her silken body, searching out the coveted moistness between her thighs. In desperation, he strained every fiber of his being to produce the tightening of muscles, the throbbing of his genitalia that was necessary to satisfy his wants. At Alicia's scream of despair he fell back in resignation, ignoring her, totally absorbed in his own black thoughts.

Alicia lay back with her eyes squeezed shut. She needed the brandy, craved it, almost more than she craved the letter from Carl. Was this then going to be her life from now on? God, help me, she cried silently.

Covering herself with the edge of the sheet, Alicia lay beside him for a long time, listening, waiting, anticipating a return attack. He didn't move, not a muscle, and his face was turned away from her. But she could hear his labored breathing, sense his desperation, could almost feel his stiffly controlled rage for having failed. Again.

The sun dipped low, only long burnished shadows, slanting through the draperies. Hours had passed, and it was with relief that she heard the Baron's deep, even breathing, signifying sleep.

Alicia crept out of the bed and quickly threw on her dressing gown and raced down the stairs to the parlor. Her hand clutched the brandy bottle to her breast for a moment before she brought it to her lips. There was no way she could have poured the desired liquor into a glass, not when she was shuddering from the scene she had just been through. Coughing and sputtering, she downed a second hearty swallow.

I should kill him. Kill him for what he's done to Carl, to me!

When Alicia peered intently into the clear bottle, she wondered how it could be empty so soon. In her drunken state she reasoned that the idea of killing Carlyle Newsome was the only logical method of freeing herself, freeing Carl. Muttering softly to herself, she tottered down the dark corridor to the kitchen. Rummaging through the cabinets, she found her weapon. Holding the butcher's knife in her slender, shaking hand, she was shocked at the length and weight of the wicked-looking blade. No matter where this knife went in, the Baron would breathe his last breath. He had to die, she thought vehemently, imagining the soft sink of flesh beneath the shining blade.

With stealthy determination, she climbed the stairs, quietly covering the distance between the door and the bed. She was surprised at how steady her hand was as she brought the weapon above her head. One quick plunge and it would all be over. Forever.

"I wouldn't if I were you, darling Alicia. Did you think I would allow you to murder me in my own bed?" The thought struck him as funny and he laughed loudly, a mean and ugly sound. "I smelled the brandy as soon as you reached the door. Put it away and get into this bed. I have other ways to make you behave. What a precious little pigeon you are, darling Alicia. And what a fool!"

Forcing her down onto the bed, he held her with his weight. His lips trailed between her breasts, moistly covering her throat and then down again. "I'm doing this for Carl," he whispered. "You aren't half good enough for him, you know. You're not a woman. A woman could excite me, propel me to a climax. I knew I made the right decision when I forbid Carl to marry you. You're going to have to try harder, Alicia darling. Try and try until you succeed. Now, lay very still and listen to me while I tell you that I've sent Carl on business to Belém. He won't be coming back for quite a while. And when he does, lucky boy, he's going to marry my little ward, Royall Banner." On and on his voice droned, talking to her as though in ordinary conversation. And all the while his hands were on her, demanding, coaxing, exploring. And with each touch Alicia died a little, her flesh growing cold, her body stiff. There was no more pretending, no afterglow from the brandy. She should have turned the knife on herself. As much as she hated the Baron, she hated herself more!

Chapter Ten

Royall sat in her room at Reino Brazilia, contemplating her next move with the Baron. Exasperated because her efforts to have the children rejoin their mothers at Regalo Verdad had been thwarted, she was determined to find something with which to bargain, something that would sway the Baron's thinking.

Opening the valise that contained her father's papers, she examined them, searching for the title rights to the Reino. There were phrases she hadn't understood when she had looked at them last, and she had decided to bring them to Father Juan in the hopes that he could shed some light on them. It wouldn't be to her benefit to ask the Baron or to inquire of his lawyer. They would just put her off and tell her not to busy her pretty little head about it. No, Father Juan would be the best one to answer her questions.

Placing the papers back in the valise, her hand brushed against a hard-bound book—her father's ledger.

Pushing aside the flood of renewed depression, she opened the ledger. Instantly, she thought of Mr. Morrison, the lawyer who had written to her father and informed him of . . . what? What exactly did Mr. Morrison tell her father that induced him to repudiate the Baron? Surely it was not only because Princess Isabel's Ventre Livre law was being ignored. No, there were hints of something that Richard Harding could not forgive. Her eyes glanced over the words "cruelly beating the slave till his death."

Royall felt cold waves race up her spine. Behind those glinting, steel gray eyes was a killer.

Carefully, she replaced the ledger and laid the

valise on the floor of the clothespress. She intended to go to the kitchen and speak to Elena. Perhaps the housekeeper would be able to tell her where she could find Mr. Morrison.

The kitchen was dim and cool, shuttered from the heat of the day. Elena appeared to be busy, instructing the Indian cook and sorting through the pantries, making a shopping list. Noticing Royall, she lifted her dark head and faced the intruder with aloof hostility.

"Elena, I'd like to speak with you a moment if you have the time. I need some answers to a few questions. Now, Elena!"

Elena set aside her pen and approached Royall, her manner coolly respectful. Royall modulated her voice, slightly apologetic for the harsh tone she had used.

"Yes, Senora Banner, how may I help you?"

"Just last evening I remembered my father speaking of an old acquaintance, a Mr. Morrison. I was wondering if perhaps you might know where I can find him. I understand he was a lawyer and has since retired."

"I may be able to help you, Senora," said Elena, her black eyes glinting with unspoken curiosity. It gave Royall some satisfaction to know that Elena's facade of seeming indifference could be pierced.

"Senor Morrison was once barrister to the Newsome family, when the Baron's father was alive. He was a frequent visitor to the Reino when the Baron held residence in the old Casa Grande. Since the old man's death and the burning of the original Casa, I've not seen him. It has been years since I've heard his name mentioned in this house. The Baron does not welcome Senor Morrison here; he had a falling out with the gentleman soon after the death of his father. I assure you, Senora, the Baron would not take kindly to the idea of your seeking Senor Morrison." At this last, Elena's voice grew stern with warning.

"I don't much care if the Baron takes kindly to the idea or not, Elena. He has no jurisdiction over whom I may or may not see. Now, answer my question, Elena: do you know where I can find Mr. Morrison?"

Elena's eyes were guarded and she lowered her voice to a degree above a whisper. "You will find Senor Morrison at his townhouse in Manaus, Vengar de Soltero, the Avenue of Bachelors. It's the large house with stone lions at the foot of the stairs."

"Thank you, Elena. Please have the groom saddle my horse; I'll be going for my ride today as usual."

Royall spurred the horse forward. It was time to inspect the living quarters of her Indians and blacks. Sebastian hadn't said the words aloud; still, she knew what he meant. "Go look and compare. See where your living comes from." Well, she would see and she would see now! She allowed herself to remember the day he had pulled her off her horse and into his arms. She could feel herself flush, knowing the hot sun had nothing to do with the warmth that spread over her body.

She was so engrossed in her thoughts that she didn't notice Jamie until he rode in front of her and startled her. Quickly, he reined in his mount and laughed. "I'll give you a penny if you tell me what you're thinking," he teased.

Royall smiled. "Just about my costume for the ball."

Jamie's face lit up at the mention of the ball and costume. "What are you wearing, Royall?" he coaxed.

Royall wagged a finger. "You'll have to wait and see, Jamie Newsome," she teased back. "Jamie, does Elena know you're out riding? You know your father has forbidden—"

"I'm a grown man and I'll do as I please. I don't have to listen to anyone!" he told her, sulkiness distorting his handsomely carved face. Then Jamie smiled secretively. "Tell me where you're riding to this morning."

"I plan to look over the workers' compound. Would you like to come with me?" She decided not to press him about his disobedience. He would have to answer for his own actions.

Jamie looked shocked. "Does my father know where you're going?" he asked nervously.

"No, Jamie. I didn't think I needed permission to inspect land that is half mine," she said, her tone bitter.

Jamie looked at her and seemed to be at a loss

for words. Nervously, he rubbed his thumb and forefinger together.

"It's not far now, just around the . . ." As they approached the small village, Royall could hear voices. She strained higher on her mount to see into the clearing.

As they rode nearer, she couldn't believe the sight that met her eyes. She had never seen such squalor. At the sound of the horses' hooves, the noise abated. Children, as well as men and women, stood quietly; they wore rags; their faces were blemished with sores. They huddled together, staring with hate-filled eyes at the two mounted figures. The open hostility was so obvious that Royall wondered how Jamie could sit so still and quietly. The hostility was for him. Of this she was sure. The men had blank, hopeless looks on their faces. The women stood mute; their children whined in hunger. Royall felt physically sick as her eyes wandered around the village. The sanitary conditions were so inadequate, the stench made her eyes water. God in heaven! The blacks, separated across the compound from the Indians, were in the same circumstances. The only difference was that they looked ill, physically very ill. A mound of dirt behind the squalid thatched huts caught her eye. She knew immediately what it was. A grave! As her eyes continued to wander, she noticed two more fresh mounds. A tall black walked into the middle of the clearing, and Royall closed her eyes in shock as the lash marks and welts on the man's back glistened in the bright sun. She took fast hold of her composure and demanded to know how many people were sick. No one answered her. "Jamie," she called. "Come here. Ask them how many are sick. Immediately!"

Jamie looked angry for the moment but obeyed her command. "A dozen or so," he replied shortly.

"What is being done?" she demanded furiously.

Again Jamie spoke. "The overseer was here," he said shortly. "He says they are just lazy, they're not sick," he said happily.

"Not sick! They all look sick to me," she said, her voice rising shrilly.

Again, she spurred her horse forward to observe. In the far corner of the clearing she noticed a penlike enclosure. She spurred her horse toward it and looked at the dozen or so small children sitting on the ground playing in the dirt.

"Why are these children in this pen?" she demanded of Jamie, her eyes shooting sparks.

"We're breeding them. They're the best. They get the best food and the best clothing. They're the pick of the litter," Jamie giggled.

"They're nothing but babies," Royall gasped. The women were standing quietly about, hate and fear rode rampant across their faces. Never in her wildest imagination had she ever seen such misery and human suffering. These were human beings without a glimmer of hope, and there was nothing but hard labor and squalor for them on their horizon. She thought of Sebastian and his village, and understood why he hated the Reino and its owners; the difference was night and day.

"Why are you so angry, Royall?" Jamie pleaded.

"Don't you think I have a right to be angry, Jamie?"

"Why, Royall?" Jamie said, snapping his fingers. "They're just slaves."

"Don't you ever snap your fingers at me again, Jamie. Do you hear me? Not ever," Royall shrilled as she spurred her horse from the clearing. "Not ever again!" she shouted.

Royall ached with a physical as well as a mental pain as she pondered the problem. She felt nausea wash over her when she thought of all the fine things she had in life and that all the advantages were bought with the sweat and the deaths of these downtrodden people. She took solace in the thought that her father had had no knowledge of where his fortune had come from. She was sure that if he had known he would have made complete revisions. Her heart heavy, she thought how like her father she was. If he would have done something, then so would she. But at the moment she was helpless! Being Richard Harding's daughter and MacDavis Banner's wife had taught her that the only way to meet opposition was from a position of strength. First, she had to learn exactly what her position was and find the only man who could help her learn exactly what that was—the lawyer, Mr. Morrison.

While Jamie led the panting, sweating horses

to the stable, Royall climbed wearily up the veranda and fell into the rattan chair. She didn't know how long she had been sitting there when her attention was caught by the sound of voices. Momentarily confused, she listened to the voices coming from indoors. It appeared that Jamie and Elena were arguing over something. She knew she should get up and leave; she didn't like eavesdropping, but the heat stifled her and she sat mute. It was impossible; Jamie's high-pitched whine could not be ignored.

"They say they're too busy to play, Elena," he complained. "Father and Carl are too busy and you don't have the time. Royall is angry about the Indians in the compound and she doesn't want to talk to me. What's there to do? You gave Moriah and Nessie too much work to do, and I'm lonely," he pouted.

"Jamie," came the tender reply, "why don't you get your soldiers and set them up on the veranda? Soon it will be cooler and I'll bring you a drink."

"I don't want to get out the soldiers! And I don't want a cool drink! I want someone to play with me!"

"The servants are all busy. You know they have many chores, Jamie. You must understand that this is a very busy plantation, and the work load is heavy. Everyone has to do his share. Besides, boys should play with boys."

"There are no boys to play with," Jamie sighed

logically. "Moriah is so pretty and she feels so soft."

Elena paused. "Have you touched her? Jamie, answer me. Have you touched Moriah?"

"I just pinch her arm," Jamie pouted.

"Jamie, how many times have I told you? How many times have I warned you that Indian fathers get angry when you want to 'play' with their little girls."

"Stupid Indians! No one cares, and no one sees me!" A loud crash followed the petulant outburst.

Royall sat quietly, her mind racing at the strange conversation taking place between Elena and Jamie. Her heart chilled as she began to recall the times she had seen Jamie playfully tug at Moriah's fat braids or the hair of one of the other girls. She also remembered the frightened expressions on the girls' faces at his seeming playfulness. She had thought it was because he was the Baron's son and that they were afraid to offend him. Now. . . she shuddered; she knew differently. Jamie was a little boy who couldn't or wouldn't grow up, imprisoned in a man's powerful body.

She could hear running feet; Jamie ran down the steps ignoring the heart-rending cry from Elena. "Jamie, come back. Come back, Jamie." Royall sat quietly and didn't move. There was no need for her to intrude into a family matter. Now she was beginning to understand many things as she listened to Elena sob heartbrokenly from inside the Casa.

215

Elena slumped into the hard wooden kitchen chair and wept as she hadn't done in years. But these tears weren't healing; they were tears that raked up the past from the still graveyard where she had buried it. Jamie *had* to learn, *had* to understand, must see that his lack of self-control and self-discipline were leading him into danger. They might even take him away.

She sobbed anew as she thought of what her life would be without Jamie. He was all she lived for, and life without him would be unendurable. Wiping her tears on the hem of her apron, she thought how strange it was that she had come to love him as though he were her own son, but there had been a day when she hated the fat, pink-skinned baby. And it was all Carlyle Newsome's fault! She loathed the man who pompously named himself the Baron, taking for himself the title that the people had bestowed on his father with great love and respect.

Thinking of the Baron brought a natural progression of thought to his dead wife, Senora Catarine. When Elena had first come to Reino Brazilia, Carlyle had brought her, bringing her from Rio de Janeiro to his home on the Amazon. He had taken her as his mistress, and she believed she loved him. She also believed him when he told her he no longer slept with his wife. Then the English, white-skinned wife had become heavy with her second child, and Elena was ordered to become handmaiden to the Senora. She was ashamed when she remembered the coldness and lack of sympathy she had shown Senora Newsome, and she remembered the vague little cruelties she had shown on the day of Jamie's birth, when the Senora had been in such agony to bring the lusty second son into the world. But in spite of Elena's indifference, the Senora had recovered and had transferred the newborn's care over to Elena.

A rush of memory made her wince as she recalled the day the Baron and his wife had gone off in the carriage to a neighboring plantation, leaving Jamie with her. Angry and insulted with the circumstances that had demoted her from paramour to servant, Elena had left the toddler unattended, and when she finally returned to him, he had fallen from his chair and lay still as death and unconscious for four days. But Jamie wouldn't have been the first baby to die on the Reino.

Elena also remembered with bitterness and hatred her own stupidity the day the Baron had ordered her to get rid of the life she carried within her. He didn't want any bastards in this house, he told her. She had killed her own child—and then had been expected to nurse the Newsomes' white-skinned child.

It had become evident to the most casual observer that Jamie didn't function as well as his older brother had at the same age. He appeared slow, clumsy, growing at a normal rate, yet not developing mentally. When he was six years old and the retardation could no longer be denied, Senora Catarine had taken to her bed and pined. Within a year she was dead, and Elena's hatred for Jamie's father continued to increase with each passing day. Guilty because of her own negligence, she appointed herself Jamie's guardian, and she had come to love him as much, she was certain, as she could ever love a child of her own.

How proud and arrogant and in love she had been with Carlyle when he had taken her for his mistress. Nothing else had mattered, only her love for him, a love that was great and all-encompassing, forgiving and loyal. But he had killed that love, leaving her an empty shell of a woman whose whole existence was centered upon protecting the child he had placed in her care.

Now this, Jamie's preoccupation with the four little girls the Baron insisted on keeping at the plantation. She'd seen the way he liked to touch them, witnessed the expression in his eyes. Jamie was only a boy in a man's body, but even boys had sexual drives and hungers. How much better it would be if Senora Banner had her way and the *ninas* were sent back to their parents. Especially for Jamie. Then there wouldn't be anything or anyone to tempt him.

Elena had told the Baron of Jamie's increasingly disturbing appetites, and his answer had been a coarse laugh. "Why, Elena, you surprise me! What a delicate choice of words. And tell me," he whispered as he clutched her arm, squeezing it painfully, "why do you feel you must be delicate with me? Haven't we known moments when delicacy was abandoned for something more basic and infinitely more exciting?"

His hard gray eyes peered into hers meaningfully, stirring all the old, hot memories. "And as for Jamie," he had continued, apparently enjoying Elena's embarrassment, "why else should one amass a fortune if not to bring to one's son those things he desires?"

Elena had pulled away from his grasp and quickly took her leave. Behind her, his cruel laughter echoed raucously, sending shivers up her spine and a fuller determination to protect Jamie not only from himself but also from his father.

Chapter Eleven

Sebastian took the steps to his Manaus townhouse two at a time. He was eager to see Aloni, and the hassle at the docks hadn't done his humor any benefit. Aloni knew how to soothe his ruffled temper.

As he thrust open the door, she came running to greet him; her small, lithe figure was in his arms, and she was kissing him, murmuring soft endearments. Waist-length black hair hung over one shoulder, and he could smell its sweet fragrance and feel the smooth as silk skin as her arms twined around his neck.

Pulling away from him, Aloni looked up at him from her diminutive height, staring at him with her mahogany dark eyes, her full moist lips parted over her dazzling white teeth. "Come," she said softly, her voice childlike, "I will prepare you a cold drink."

"It's not a drink I want, Aloni," he whispered hoarsely, pulling her back to him. She giggled seductively, this woman that was more a child, and sighed seductively. "Handsome master, tell Aloni what it is you want. Tell me, Sebastian," she coaxed enticingly.

"You little tease," he answered huskily, a familiar surging need coursing through his body and seeming to center in his nether regions.

Playfully, she struggled away from him, skipping up the first few steps to the bedroom. Sebastian bounded after her in hot pursuit, laughing at her little game. This ritual never failed to amuse him.

He followed her to the top of the stairs and saw article after article of clothing being thrown through the open doorway in accompaniment to her squeals of expectation.

First her tiny slippers, and then her petticoats —faster and faster the garments flew through the air. He dodged a high-flying chemise and marveled at her agility in undressing herself so quickly.

When the assault of clothing ended, he strode into the dimly lit bedroom on cue; it was cool from the shutters being drawn against the afternoon sun. His eyes adjusted to the half-light and found her laying atop the bed, waiting.

Sebastian stood before her appraisingly, removing his shirt, deliberately fumbling with the buttons, watching her eagerness build. Through slitted eyes, their gazes locked. His hands went to his straining trousers, his movements slow, watching, filling his senses with the sight and scent and anticipation of her.

The pink tip of her tongue moistened her lips and, as always, he was struck by her beauty. Her lean, supple body never failed to excite him; her sensuous lips promised fulfillment; her oblique, almost oriental, eyes measured him knowingly, without coyness. Aloni realized the impact her beauty had on him, and she capitalized on it.

He stood before her, fully aroused, wanting her, enjoying the sight of her small, uplifted breasts with their chocolate-colored nipples. Aloni lowered her eyes and held her arms out for him.

Sebastian stood in front of his shaving stand, trying to avert his eyes from the reflection that bore a startling resemblance to his enemy, the Baron. Out of the corner of his eye he noticed Aloni's image in his shaving mirror. Her eyes were narrowed as she studied him. He steeled himself against her onslaught of questions; he had heard them so often. "Is not Aloni pretty? Why can't I go with you? Are you ashamed of your Aloni?" And on and on she would whine, until he was dressed and ready to leave. At that point she would change her tactics for fear he would order her from his house, and she would once again become his sweet, undemanding Aloni.

"I think maybe Aloni will be leaving." A practiced sob caught in her throat.

Sebastian turned to face her, angry at her words.

Aloni's eyes were now mere slits. "It is true. I think maybe Aloni will have to leave. My Sebastian has thoughts for another."

"What are you saying, Aloni? I have no thoughts for another." Even as he said the words, he knew he lied. It was true; their lovemaking had been clouded by his thoughts of Royall. At one point he had almost moaned her name in his desire.

"It is true. Sebastian has found another, I feel it here," she said, dramatically touching her heart. "Is it one of those milk-skinned, overfed ladies you see at the opera house? No, Sebastian would not care for a fat lady. Perhaps," she said shrewdly, "it is the golden girl I have heard spoken of in the marketplace."

Sebastian ignored her bid for reassurance. "Enough, Aloni," he said angrily.

"It is," she said whiningly. "It is the golden girl! I knew it, I feel it. Now you will discard me like one of your dirty sheets."

Angry at the insight of his mistress, Sebastian snatched up his jacket and strode from the room.

Aloni followed him, small sobs catching in her throat. Anger welled up in him, and he felt the urge to slap her, to still the words that tumbled from her petulant mouth. Immediately, he was contrite and ashamed of the impulse. What's gotten into me? Have I gone mad? Within him beat the answer: Royall Banner.

"I have business, Aloni. I'll be back this evening. Have something light for dinner. Perhaps we can go to the Chaucer Gardens tonight and dance. Would you like that?"

He knew Aloni would like it. She was always begging him to take her out. "Aloni has no need for these pretty gowns. Aloni never goes anywhere where she can be seen," she would pout.

He watched her face light up. Another time he might have been pleased with himself. Now he couldn't care one way or another if Aloni was happy or not. All his spare thoughts were of Royall and the brief time they had spent together. If the truth were known or if he cared to admit it to himself, he was tiring of Aloni and her childish, clinging ways. For a woman of twenty-four she was often infantlike in her behavior.

She came to him and threw her arms around his neck and kissed him gratefully. "You make Aloni so happy!"

"Be ready when I get back," he said curtly.

He strode out to his waiting coach and instructed the driver, "Vengar de Soltero, Lawyer Morrison's offices."

Sebastian settled back in the comfortable coach as it made its way through traffic to the Avenue of Bachelors.

Damn. When would Aloni grow up? Never, he answered his own question. It grated on his nerves to hear her use her name instead of the personal pronoun. Damnation, he swore silently, couldn't he think about anyone but the golden-haired cat? Settling back further in his seat, he pushed his thoughts away from Royall and toward the meeting with his lawyer friend, Victor Morrison.

Sebastian leaped from his coach and strode toward the pink brick building Victor Morrison called home.

Lawyer Morrison's manservant smiled at Sebastian as though he were glad to see him. He was. Azus had been with the Morrisons for many years, a family retainer, and Azus knew how bored Senor Morrison had become with the retired life. Not enough of the old gentleman's friends came to call, and Sebastian had always been one of his favorites.

"Senor Morrison has a caller at the moment, Senor Rivera, but I'm certain there meeting will end shortly. If you care to wait in the drawing room, I'll fetch you a glass of the master's favorite brandy."

"Yes, Azus. I'd like that. A caller? Anyone I know?"

"I don't know, sir. I've never seen the lady before, although Senor Morrison was quite pleased when I announced her."

Resisting the impulse to impose on Azus' friendship and cajole him into revealing the name of the caller, Sebastian accepted the snifter of brandy and sat back to light a cheroot.

Minutes later, the door to the drawing room

swung open. Victor Morrison entered the drawing room, in the company of Royall Banner.

Sebastian's face turned dark, and Royall's expression matched his.

"Sebastian. How nice to see you! When did you arrive in Manaus?" Victor Morrison demanded.

"Several days ago," Sebastian said curtly, his eyes on Royall.

"Forgive my manners. Mrs. Banner, may I present Sebastian Rivera."

"Senor Rivera and I have already met, thank you, Mr. Morrison. How are you, Senor Rivera?" Royall inquired perfunctorily.

"Well, Senora Banner, and yourself?" His tone equally cold.

"Well." As if he cared how she was.

Victor Morrison frowned, bewildered by the ensuing silence. One would have thought these two handsome people would find much to talk about.

"Mr. Morrison, thank you so much for seeing me today. I'll be in touch within the week," Royall said quietly.

Was Sebastian mistaken, or did Royall's golden-flecked eyes hold a warning message for Mr. Morrison?

When his servant closed the door behind Royall, Victor Morrison joined Sebastian in a snifter of brandy. "I wasn't aware that you knew Senora Banner, Victor. You certainly are an old rake. I should have guessed you would know every lovely young woman who arrives in Manaus." Victor

225

Morrison's eyes grew serious as he measured Sebastian. "I'd like it if you watched over her for me, Sebastian."

Sebastian almost choked on a swallow of brandy. "You can't be serious, Victor! Watch over *her!* Damned if I will!"

Shocked by this sudden outburst, Morrison could only stare at Sebastian, mouth agape. "But surely you can do this for an old friend," he pleaded. "I've never known you to refrain from the company of a beautiful woman?"

"I've been in Senora Banner's company, Victor, and I've found her to be a lovely lady, although a devious one."

Sebastian felt duty bound to explain his attitude in regard to Royall. His lip curled in distaste as he described how he had felt himself deceived that Royall was a guest of Mrs. Quince. "I tell you, Victor, had I known she was traveling to the Reino, I would have cut a path a mile wide to stay away from her. And now I'm given to understand she is part owner in that den of unpardonable injustice to humanity."

"Sebastian, the girl has only been here a matter of weeks. Surely you can't blame her for the injustice that has run rampant on the Reino all these years. That girl is within a hair's breadth of trouble! Judgement tells me she'll be in need of a friend. And these sources that informed you that Royall Banner is part owner in the Reino, have they also informed you that she's trying the will of the Baron in order that four children be permitted to return to their mothers? And have they told you of her misery because of the condition of the slaves on the Reino, and of her guilt because her own life has been one of ease and luxury at their expense?" Seeing Sebastian's look of embarrassment, Victor Morrison softened his tone. "I knew her father, Sebastian. Richard Harding was a man to your liking. He never would have allowed the deplorable conditions on the Reino if he had known of them. Take pity on her, Sebastian, and me. Please watch over her."

"I'm afraid the damage is done, Victor. Senora Banner has reacted accordingly to my hostile behavior. She can fend for herself, take my word for it."

"Perhaps," Victor said soberly, a knowing gleam in his eye. "Nevertheless, you could be very unobtrusive, couldn't you?"

Sebastian smiled and heaved a sigh. "I suppose I could." He felt ridiculous because of the way the idea pleased him.

Royall leaned her head against the back of the seat and rubbed a hand over her weary brow. So much, and yet nothing. Mr. Morrison had revealed very little to her about the mysterious words in her father's ledger. "Now is not the time," he had insisted. But she had extracted a promise from him to tell her something soon. She thought of his round, kind face narrowing into deep lines of concern. Why did men feel they had to coddle women? Why couldn't they be honest and frank?

Still, Mr. Morrison had been helpful in explaining the finer points of her partnership with the Baron. Even Morrison couldn't be sure where the line was drawn. Tired, beaten . . . and then to meet Sebastian! A small groan escaped her, and she forced back her frustration. A commotion in the street caught her attention. Several blacks were erecting a papier-mâché tower that was painted in garish colors. Festival was two days away, and no one in Manaus felt less like celebrating than Royall.

Chapter Twelve

Manaus, for the week of the opera opening at least, had become a tropical Vienna. Music seemed to be everywhere, played on street corners and by marching bands; native minstrels wandered the streets begging coins for their songs; violinists and pianists displayed their talents at the numerous parties and soirees held in the performers' honor; and dark-eyed Latin singers, *cantante*, serenaded much like Christmas carolers did in Royall's New England.

From Europe artists and performers had traveled up the Amazon, tenors and sopranos, orchestras, all bound for the flagrantly opulent theater for the performing arts in Brazil. The trip was arduous, the cost to the opera guild, which seemed to include everyone in Manaus, was astronomical. But worth every penny. Sophistication and culture had come to Brazil.

In preparation for the festivities, Royall had moved to Manaus with Rosalie Quince, making herself at home in her friend's townhouse. Now, as she sat before the mirror putting the finishing touches to her hair, a heavy tap sounded on the door and Mrs. Quince strode briskly into the room. "Royall, aren't you dressed yet? The DuQuesnes are expecting us in thirty minutes! You'll have to hurry or we'll be quite unfashionably late."

"I'm not going. You can tell the DuQuesnes for me that I have a very fashionable headache, and I can't join them for still another night of revelry." Royall's tone was hostile and tinged with weariness.

"What are you saying?" Mrs. Quince squawked. "You can't disappoint the DuQuesnes; the table will be uneven, and I'm afraid it would take another century of festivals for Tilly DuQuesne to recover."

Royall laughed, delighting in Rosalie's scorn. It was comforting to know that she, too, was bored and disgusted by the endless suppers and parties of Manaus's elite society.

"Mrs. Quince, it delights me to know that your feelings are the same as mine. You alone make this social parade bearable for me. It's the only thing that keeps me from running screaming back to the Reino."

"I know, dear. Suzanne hated it too. But as I

used to tell her, it's what's expected of us. Duty calls and all that posh!" she sighed.

"How do you do it every year? I'm warning you, friend, if I have to look at another gilt-edged anything, I'll reward myself with a case of the good old-fashioned vapors. The gowns, the perfumes, the jewelry!" she exclaimed. "The Queen's own jewels are trinkets compared to the rings and fobs and stickpins the men wear. And those geegaws the women wear!"

"I understand, but try to understand these people yourself. They're wealthy beyond imagination, thanks to rubber. And they've no outlet for their money and the frustrations that the remoteness of this part of the world imposes on them, aside from their homes and their dress. Take pity on them. If they were in America or Europe or somewhere civilized, they wouldn't need this show of success. But here, in the wilds of Brazil, it seems to bring them a feeling of security."

"Homes! You call those decorated mausoleums homes? I'd sooner live in a thatched hut than in one of those painted, pretentious galleries of bad taste and worse art. The ceilings in the drawing rooms alone could rival the Sistine Chapel. Last night at the Beaumonts' I found myself eating through an orgy of an overseasoned, overcooked, nauseating seven-course meal while waiting for Mrs. Griswald's bosom to pop out of her gown and land in the tapioca pudding. And it all took place under the sweetly smiling gazes of the painted cherubs perched on the stone pedestal above her head."

The women laughed together, trading gossip and catty remarks about the other women. To Mrs. Quince's relief, Royall continued primping, obviously forgetting her oath not to attend the dinner.

Royall was regal with her golden curls piled above her smooth brow. Her skin shone with health, and the sapphire of her gown complimented the golden flecks in her eyes.

Clasping a necklace about her slim, graceful neck, she thought better of it and instead fastened a small topaz brooch to her bodice. Satisfied with her reflection, she slid her narrow feet into a pair of sapphire blue slippers.

"It's time to go, Mrs. Quince. We certainly don't want to be unfashionably late to the Du-Quesnes."

Rosalie Quince wore her most victorious smile as she followed Royall from the bedroom. The art of persuasion had always been one of her strongest virtues, she thought smugly.

"Mrs. Quince, can you help me with these little hooks. I can't seem to reach them," Royall called.

"In a moment, dear. I'm just about ready."

Royall sat before her mirror winding the gold ribbon through her intricately braided hair. She and Mrs. Quince had left the DuQuesne dinner, as had all the other guests, to come back to the Quince's townhouse to dress for the masquerade.

"I'll never understand," she muttered to herself, "why they begin a ball at the ungodly hour of ten-thirty." A deep sigh escaped her; she wasn't looking forward to the festivities, knowing Sebastian would be there. It galls me the way every woman in town makes cow eyes at him. One would think he was some sort of god. It didn't occur to Royall to think that her anger stemmed from simple jealousy. Senor Rivera this, and Senor Rivera that, she snarled to her reflection. And what did he do? The bastard accepted it as his due. Arrogant, disgusting . . . man.

Royall's eyes darkened till they were dancing flames. How well she recalled the scene at the Roswells' dinner party the evening before last. Sebastian had been paying compliments to the Roswells' pudgy, dull, giggling daughter, and Mrs. Roswell beamed a satisfied smile toward the disappointed mothers whose own daughters shot covetous looks at Nancy. And Sebastian loved every minute of it! Loathsome man! As if he could be interested in a dullard like Nancy Roswell.

And then to leave the poor lovesick girl to move on to another, and no doubt regale her with the same practiced compliments he had paid to Nancy! Several times Royall had seen Sebastian glancing her way, and once he deliberately moved over to a circle of women with whom she was talking and asked Cynthia Taylor to dance, greeting all in the circle and pointedly ignoring her. It was a public slap in the face, and one she wouldn't soon forget.

Rosalie Quince stepped into the room, her gaze meeting that of the grimacing girl.

"Royall, is something wrong? Are you ill? I know the duckling sauce was rich, but I swear I didn't see you take more than a bite! Ah, I can see Anna has outdone herself with her needle. You're lovely, young lady, simply lovely!" she said brightly.

Royall flushed with Mrs. Quince's complimentary words. She turned to face her reflection and stared at herself with unbending scrutiny. The soft white gown was empire in its lines, so popular during the reign of Napoleon's Josephine. Gold ribbon outlined the sever V of the neckline and crossed over her bosom to wrap around her midriff several times over. The stark white of the shimmering silk was offset by heavy gold bracelets worn on her upper arm, and complemented the gold kid slippers on her slim feet. In her hand she would carry a miniature bow and arrow. To pierce Sebastian Rivera where it would do the most good, she thought sourly.

Mrs. Quince's eyes swept Royall's golden head, down to the kid slippers on her feet. "I'm sure when the ancients spoke of 'Diana the Huntress' they could never have imagined her to be as beautiful as you are."

"Mrs. Quince, I wish you would stop referring to me as beautiful. I appreciate your kindness, but I'm sure you're much too extravagant in your praise."

"Nonsense, child, when one gets to be my age,

one has the privilege of speaking one's mind and posh and tother with all the amenities. You'd better be careful this evening, you'll find yourself in the midst of lovesick young men and irate old mothers, not that it would be such a surprise to you. I've seen the effect you have on the young gentlemen here in Manaus, and I can assure you, you'll not be lacking for partners this night! Sebastian will find himself hard pressed to get near you."

Rosalie Quince fumbled with the tiny hooks at the back of Royall's costume, giving the girl more time to study herself in the glass.

Mrs. Quince was truthful in her judgment, Royall thought smugly. She knew she looked her best in Anna's handiwork. The dress accentuated her petite figure, and the severe neckline revealed a bosom more ample than her spare form should allow. If there was one thing that would draw a man's eyes, it was a woman's bosom.

"Royall, we'll have to hurry. Alonzo is downstairs waiting for us now." Royall only half listened to the gray-haired lady whom she had come to love.

"That man," Rosalie complained. "Sometimes I think he has a clock for a brain. You know how he hates to be kept waiting."

Royall faintly listened to Mrs. Quince grumble until they reached the main staircase. Mrs. Quince suddenly became still. She stood there beaming down at her husband, Alonzo. He stood at the foot of the stairs and gazed upward at his wife. It

234

was not the first time Royall had been a witness to the love the Quinces had for each other. Alonzo was a tall, pink-cheeked man with silvery white hair. Watery, faded blue eyes held a tenderness for Rosalie that was still evident after so many years. He clearly adored her, and the feeling was noticeably reciprocated. When they descended the staircase he lavished compliments on Rosalie's choice of dress, a pale blue satin, and only as an afterthought did he think to compliment Royall on her costume.

There was no way Royall could feel affronted by his lack of enthusiasm regarding her costume. Instead, she felt lighthearted, as always, at the steady, deep love that was shared between them.

The carriage turned into the Parradays' circular drive, where the ball was to be held. The traffic of carriages suddenly came to a standstill.

"Alonzo, I'm supposed to be on the receiving line. As a judge, it's one of my duties."

Alonzo Quince glanced at his wife and smiled, and Royall felt the unspoken recriminations of Rosalie's habitual tardiness.

"I can see where we're going to be tied up here for a while. Why don't you and Royall step down now and walk to the front. It's just a short distance."

"Alonzo, I never cease to marvel at your astuteness. Of course, we'll walk!" Royall could see this was just what practical Mrs. Quince intended all along, but she allowed her husband to claim the idea for his own. Alonzo proceeded to assist his wife and Royall. While he gave orders to the coachman, Royall turned to see Mrs. Quince favor her with a decidedly conspiratorial wink.

Rosalie tugged at her arm as they approached the bright lanterns lighting the entrance to the Parradays' palatial home.

Royall's eyes flicked over the crowd. Her gaze settled on the Baron peering into the distance, searching the melee of carriages, no doubt searching for Mrs. Quince's party. As they approached the main entrance, he turned suddenly and saw her. Shouldering his way through the throng, he was beside them in a matter of seconds.

"Royall, you're beautiful!" He nodded his greetings to Mrs. Quince, remarking on Rosalie's choice of gown. "I'm sure you have duties to perform, Mrs. Quince, as you're one of the receiving line. I'll see to Royall."

Mrs. Quince sniffed her acquiescence and went up the marble steps to the ball. Her bearing was regal, that of a dowager queen. It was silently understood between Alonzo and Royall that she, by her very actions, had dismissed the Baron.

"I think we might be wise if we waited for the crowd to thin. I don't want to see you trampled in this melee of party goers," the Baron said in an intimate tone. Deftly, he guided her to the side, out of the way of the arriving guests.

Royall felt a chill run down her arms. She didn't like his tone, nor did she appreciate the way he was touching her arm. His touch somehow in-

236

ferred an intimacy she had no intention of sharing. Imperceptibly, she moved her arm, only to find the Baron's grip become tighter. "You are quite beautiful, Royall. I know that every man's eyes will be on you this evening. How fitting that you should come as Diana. Many times since you arrived at the Casa I've found myself equating your beauty with that of a goddess."

"Yes, I know," Royall said haughtily. "What I mean, Baron, is that I know that I look beautiful, and others beside yourself have said the same. I fear all this attention is going to my head. As a matter of fact, if you'll excuse me, I feel a trifle light-headed. I'll just find the powder room. Perhaps there's some other young lady you can . . . help." Without another word Royall extricated herself from his grasp. She jostled her way through the crowd, intent on finding Rosalie Quince. Anything or anyone just so she wouldn't have to be in the Baron's company. If necessary, she would hide out in the powder room all night just so she could avoid him. Her skin prickled as she remembered the feel of his hand on her arm, pressing ever so slightly into the side of her breast.

Inside, her intention of finding the powder room was forgotten. The gaily decorated ballroom was ablaze with gaslights. A monstrous chandelier suffused its lights into shimmering rainbows on the merrymakers dressed in jewel colors. Brilliant crimson chairs lined one wall for the ladies. Opposite the gilt chairs were two thronelike chairs decorated with tropical flowers of all descriptions.

Within minutes Royall's dance card was full, save for two dances that she hoped Sebastian might claim for himself.

The voice was neutral when she turned to see who was addressing her. "I'm glad to see that your headache is better, my dear. Or was it that you were light-headed with all the guests milling about. Young people are so resilient." Royall cringed. His voice when he spoke again reminded Royall of oiled silk. She realized that she detested Baron Carlyle Newsome and dreaded even the thought of having to dance with him.

"My dear, allow me," he said reaching for her dance card.

"Oh, Baron, I'm so sorry, but the card has been filled." Quickly, she raised it to the deep cleft in her bosom. Two bright spots of color dotted her cheeks as she kept her hand over the tiny dance card with its sky blue tassel falling into the cleft.

"Why, I do believe you're flirting with me," the Baron said unctuously. "You realize, of course, that you must dance with me, otherwise it will look peculiar. If you care to look around, you'll notice that people are staring at us. Smile, my dear. Smile like you mean it."

Royall recognized the iron order. Her first thought was to defy him and run from the room. Instead, she let a slow, wicked smile play around her mouth. "Why, Baron, is it your intention then to have me cross off another name on my card?" Playfully, she flicked the card near his face. One heavily lashed eye drooped in a wicked wink.

Quickly, she whirled around . . . straight into Sebastian's arms.

"I was beginning to think you had forgotten that this was your dance, Sebastian!" Quickly, she lowered her voice. "Smile, damn you, and show lots of teeth. I told the Baron . . . never mind what I told the Baron. Dance with me and use both feet. Don't say anything," she managed through clenched teeth as Sebastian whirled her onto the dance floor.

"Why didn't you just attack me? You would have gotten the same notice," Sebastian said mockingly.

"Oh, my, that is funny," Royall trilled as she tried to stare over Sebastian's broad shoulder to see where the Baron was.

"I guess you know you're going to be the scandal of this soiree. Most women don't go around snatching men from other partners."

"Then I just started a new trend," Royall exuded a confidence she wasn't feeling. "You aren't smiling. Do it, damn you, or I'll kick you where it will do the most good. Do you want me to end up like . . ."

"Is this what you mean," Sebastian grinned as he stretched back his lips to show glistening white teeth in a ghoulish grin. "What seems to be your problem anyway? I thought the Baron looked most attentive. After all, he is your—"

"Shut up, Sebastian, and dance. You aren't exactly light-footed. You've stepped on my toes twice. Just keep your nose out of mine and the

Baron's business. You're just doing me a tiny little favor."

Sebastian threw back his head and laughed. Royall was mortified. "So, I stepped on your toes. I can only do one thing at a time. First, it was smile, show my teeth, then dance, and all the while I'm to be careful so you don't kick me where it will do the most good. Darling lady, I am just a mere man. As for that tiny favor, how many times are you going to call upon my services in payment for that little romp we shared aboard ship?"

"Shhh," Royall hissed. "That's all it was to you, wasn't it? A romp. Damn you, Sebastian, you really are a no-good, lascivious—"

"Smile, Royall with two L's. People are staring at you. Be sure to show lots of teeth. Another thing, you really aren't too old for a few dance lessons. You've taken the shine from my evening shoes. Clumsy women bore me," he said, yawning in her face.

Royall's eyes narrowed. She felt herself relax. Before Sebastian knew what was happening, Royall complained at the top of her voice, "How dare you make such an obscene suggestion in my presence? It gives me great pleasure to answer you in kind." Before she could think twice, she brought up her knee with all the force she could muster.

"Excuse me, pardon me, please let me through," she begged as she weaved her way through the crowd on the dance floor. When she finally found the powder room, she thought she would faint.

"Lord a mercy, child, what have you done. I have to admit this little soiree was dying on its feet, but was it necessary to set a bonfire to re-kindle it? Royall, was it necessary . . . What I mean, did you have to . . . It's quite possible that you've maimed Sebastian for life. You can't . . . it isn't . . . *Royall*, young ladies just do not do what you did, especially in front of hundreds of people."

"Mrs. Quince, I have become very fond of you. In some respects you're like a mother to me. How-ever, in this one instant, you'll have to allow me my . . . What I did was well deserved. In years to come every mother in this room will thank me. Their daughters are now safe from his lechery. Find Jamie for me and have him meet me outside on the veranda. He can take me home now that I've disgraced myself. Make my apologies to the Parradays."

Head high, cheeks flushed, Royall sailed through the doorway. She looked neither to the right nor to the left. Voices buzzed about her as she made her way through the central foyer out to the wide veranda. What if he was really hurt? Romp! Damn his soul to hell. Clumsy! Angry sparks spewed from her amber eyes. Just let one person say just one thing to her in Sebastian's defense and he would get the same thing.

Taking deep breaths, Royall managed to calm herself while she waited for Jamie.

Jamie's face wore a look of concern as he waited patiently for Royall to acknowledge him. She turned; this was the first time she had seen his costume. "Jamie, you look marvelous. I should have known you would come dressed as a toy soldier. No doubt every young lady in the room has her eyes on you."

"I'm afraid not, Royall. The young ladies have eyes only for Sebastian Rivera. They swoon at his feet. Sometimes it makes me sick. They don't even want to dance with me unless my father tells them they have to. Why do you want to go home? Do you have a headache, or did someone step on your toes?"

"Both, I'm afraid. Are you sure you won't mind missing the ball, Jamie?"

"No, I won't mind. Sebastian managed to get sick or something and every woman in the ballroom is squealing in agony. The men are mooning over him and cursing at the same time. Did you see what happened to him? I tried to find out what happened to him, but no one would tell me."

Royall shrugged. The less Jamie knew, the better.

A sudden, viselike grip on her arm caused Royall to gasp in fright. "Now that you've made a spectacle of yourself, I suggest you come back to the ballroom and try to act like the lady you're supposed to be. Don't confuse my words as a suggestion. They're an order. I will not have my family humiliated in such a manner, although I think Rivera deserved exactly what you gave him. Now," the Baron said, holding up his hand to forestall her objections. "I know that it is going to be very embarrassing for you, but you must do it."

Royall flinched. How right he was. It wasn't any order, nor was it a suggestion. Pure and simple, she recognized it for what it was: a threat.

Assuming her most haughty expression, Royall walked ahead of the Baron as Jamie trailed in their wake.

The music began; the Baron held her around the waist and smiled down at her, and she found herself whirling across the floor. The Baron was a well-practiced dancer, and she fell gracefully into the rhythm of the waltz. "Where is Jamie? Is he still here?"

"He's here. Look, there he is, looking for you, no doubt, to add his name to your dance card."

Royall followed the Baron's gaze. Jamie stood on the perimeter of the ballroom, his bright red soldier's uniform with brass buttons and insignia gleaming in the light.

"I'm not surprised at his costume," Royall said quietly, feeling more at ease with the Baron now that he had loosened his arm around her waist.

"Yes," the Baron replied just as quickly. "As you can see, I don't care for the costumes, that is why I am wearing my dinner jacket. But Jamie wouldn't miss an opportunity to dress."

Royall felt the Baron was leading her on, and she rose to the bait. "But surely you don't consider yourself old?"

Immediately, he tightened his hold of her; he

smiled down at her. "I'm glad you don't think so, Royall . . . so glad," he whispered meaningfully.

At once she became uncomfortable, remembering his intimacy with her when she first arrived. Disgust washed over her, and she concentrated on the dance.

Carlyle Newsome led Royall across the floor, feeling her lithe form in his arms and reveling in the sensation. She was the most stunning creature he had seen in years. She made all the other women appear dowdy and frumpish compared to her natural grace. He had watched her, studied her, compared her through the midst of the countless parties they had attended since the season began. And always she carried herself with an ethereal poise and an air of sublimity. Her brash tongue and undignified actions could be overlooked and forgiven. Damn fool, that Carl! Here he was with the most beautiful girl in Brazil his for the asking, and he would prefer that mouse, Alicia!

As the Baron held Royall, he felt a stirring within him, a familiar chord being struck. He wondered why it had never occurred to him to have Royall for his own. He was only slightly past fifty, not too old for someone as mature as Royall.

Daringly, he held her close to him, and maneuvered her into the reverse position. As he dipped her backward, he could feel the soft protuberance of her breasts, feel her slim torso bend beneath him. He heard the sharp intake of her breath and misunderstood it for excitement.

When they straightened, he laughed softly and was startled to see her annoyance flush on her face. "Sir," she said sharply, "I do not reverse! It's unbefitting a lady!" Her golden-flecked eyes glittered angrily. There was no mistaking the dislike for him in her voice or the trace of disgust in her look.

Had they been anywhere but here, he would have struck out at that disgust and changed her superior attitude to one of subservience. She would lose her smug look when he slapped her dignity from her and left her cringing at the mere sound of his voice. In that moment Carlyle Newsome knew enmity for Royall, a hate tinged with fear. She caught him unawares and rendered a forceful blow to his image of himself as a man.

Suddenly, he threw back his head and laughed, drawing attention to himself from the other dancers. Let Carl have her; she deserves him, the thin-blooded New England miss who dared to demand an accounting of her inheritance. They deserve each other! The thought brought on a new burst of laughter from deep in the Baron's throat.

He's mad! Royall thought. She had seen the cruel glittering in his gray eyes and it frightened her. Before she could give it more thought, the music stopped and she was being led by the Baron to Mrs. Quince.

Later in the evening, Jamie approached her to claim his dance. He was resplendent in his costume, and his courtly manner was impressive. Still, Royall couldn't help but remember the conversation she had overheard between Jamie and Elena. She really didn't want to dance with him but realized she had no other choice.

Jamie danced surprisingly well, and soon Royall was lost in the music. "When will you be returning to the Casa, Royall? I miss your playing the piano."

"I'll be back in a day or two, Jamie." She smiled up at him. Once again Royall was struck by Jamie's handsome good looks. Sandy-colored hair, thick and glossy, a strong, firm jaw. Whereas Carl was handsome, he was more the dandy, but Jamie had a rugged handsomeness, like Sebastian. She furtively glanced at Jamie again; yes, she thought she might have been mistaken, but no, there it was—a marked resemblance to Sebastian. Royall looked away quickly, not wanting Jamie to see her staring at him. Sudden anger rushed through Royall. She was angry with Sebastian for his foolish attitude about his parentage, angry with the Baron for his lewdness. She could well imagine how he had used Sebastian's mother and then tossed her aside. It was slowly becoming apparent to Royall as it had to other people that it was most likely the Baron was Sebastian's father. Suddenly, it dawned on her: could this be the reason the old Baron had disinherited Carlyle Newsome, as she had learned from her father's ledger and then from Victor Morrison? It would appear the dates would coincide. From what she knew of her father's old friend, he would demand that Carlyle do his duty by the girl, and perhaps because he had refused to do that duty, the old Baron had disclaimed him as his son. She meant to find out more about this mystery. "Tell me, Jamie, did you ever know your grandfather?"

"Oh, no. He died before I was born. It was just after father came back from England; that was where he met and married my mother, you know."

"I heard rumors, Jamie"—here she tread carefully—"that your grandfather had disinherited your father. How is it then that he came back into your grandfather's good graces?"

"Oh, I don't think he ever did gain the old man's good graces. Once Carl told me that father owns the Reino because no other will could be found, and therefore all properties reverted back to the natural son." To Royall's knowing ears, it sounded like another of Jamie's well-learned school lessons.

"But surely if your grandfather truly disinherited your father, the properties would not have reverted back to him?" Royall said, testing his knowledge.

"I don't know, Royall. That kind of thing doesn't interest me. It doesn't seem real, somehow. But take my toy soldiers, they're real. I had this costume copied after one of my favorites. It's the kind the British officers wore during the Crimean War." Noting Royall's preoccupation with his grandfather, Jamie offered, "I could take you for a ride to see the old plantation if you like. It's not far from the new one. As a matter of fact, father copied it line for line, room for room. I think I told you this once before, didn't I?"

"Yes. But I would very much like to see the old ruins. There was a fire, wasn't there?"

"Yes. It makes me sad to think of it. Grandfather died in the fire, you know."

Royall's eyebrows shot upward, "No. I didn't. I just assumed he died from old age."

"Oh, no," Jamie's face turned pale. "We Newsomes always die a violent death."

"Jamie! Who told you that?"

"No one. But I like to think it's true, then I could show everyone how brave I really am."

"Don't talk foolishness, Jamie."

"Well, it's true, Royall. Moriah and her friends think I'm a sissy, but I'll show them!"

At the mention of the little girls Royall's blood ran cold. The feel of Jamie's fingers on her back chilled her, and she was fearful of the determination in his voice.

Royall was delighted when the music came to an end. She was glad to be with Mrs. Quince, who could always be relied on to say what she meant. There were never any veiled meanings from that candid lady.

Jamie escorted Royall back to Mrs. Quince, and she was pleasantly surprised to find the grand lady in conversation with Mr. Morrison, the attorney. At Royall's approach, Mr. Morrison stood and received her warmly.

"I don't want to interrupt, Mrs. Quince. You and Mr. Morrison seemed very deep in conversation. If you have something you wish to discuss privately, I'll excuse myself."

"Quite the contrary, dear," broke in Mr. Morrison. "Mrs. Quince and I were discussing you, as a matter of fact."

Royall glanced from one face to the other. "If that's the case," she demurred, "I'm sorry to be the cause of a disagreement."

Chapter Thirteen

"Nonsense, child. It was merely that we don't agree on the time and place to tell you something that we both feel you have a right to know." The look on Mrs. Quince's face caused Royall some alarm.

"Whatever it is, I can see you consider it serious." Slowly, she lifted her eyes to the old lawyer. "Is it what we discussed at your home earlier this week?" Surely, it couldn't be about her earlier antics on the dance floor with Sebastian.

"It is," came the brief reply.

"As it happens, I was just discussing the matter with Jamie. I, too, think it abhorrent that the Baron has never claimed Senor Rivera for his son, but since he has not and Sebastian has inherited Farleigh Mallard's properties these many years now, I feel it's a matter of beating a dead horse."

Abruptly, she turned on her heel to search for her next dance partner, leaving Mrs. Quince and Mr. Morrison with stunned expressions. As Royall searched the dance floor, she could feel the heat burning her face. "I must look a sight," she thought. After all, she attempted to excuse herself, it is like beating a dead horse. Why can't they just let it rest? All these reminders about his heritage can't be comforting to Sebastian. Perhaps if the ugly stories had been allowed to die years ago, he wouldn't feel this rage toward the Reino and everyone on it. Including me, she thought sorrowfully. Another glance at the dance card told her that this was the waltz she had saved for Sebastian. Poor Sebastian, it would be a long time before he did any dancing. Fresh anger boiled up within her, and she fled to the nearest balcony to escape the din of people around her.

On the balcony, overlooking the Parradays' extensive rose garden, Royall breathed deeply. The night air was exhilarating, so cool compared to the heat of the day. Almost at once she could feel herself relax, feel the strain of the past few days seep from her body. She leaned over the marble railing to reach out for a rose that had climbed up to the balustrade.

"Careful, better let me get that for you."

Royall spun around, almost losing her footing, to look into the dark eyes of Sebastian Rivera. Nervously, Royall looked around to see if any of the other guests were in evidence. He would kill her, she could feel it in her bones. By all rights he should be there lying in pain, gasping for breath and hating her for what she did to him.

"I've decided to be magnanimous and allow you

to apologize to me for your behavior on the dance floor."

"Then you'll have a long wait because I never intend to apologize to you. You deserved what you got and more."

Sebastian ignored her. "I should have dragged you by the hair across the room, taken you outside, and given your bottom a paddling. In fact, I think I'll do it right here and now. *You* deserve it!" he said emphatically.

"You wouldn't dare!" Royall hissed as she imagined the scene with all the men laughing and cheering him on. He wouldn't dare! She knew he would. Her mind raced. She had to flirt with him, make him forget his threat. Plead with him, even resort to going down on her knees. "I must say," she said coyly, "you look quite elegant in your costume. Anyone dressed as grandly as you shouldn't waste his time on someone like me, whom you consider nothing more than a . . . romp. Go inside where the ladies are all waiting for you." She gulped at the cold look on his face. She had meant to flatter him, cajole him, and here she was, adding fuel to the fire.

"It's true what you say, that I'm in demand," Sebastian said airily. "However, since I've tasted your delights, the others are less tempting."

"You're insufferable," Royall spat. "Why aren't you maimed?" she asked as an afterthought, totally candid.

"I was wondering when you would get around to asking about my well-being." His raven's wing eyes dipped to the golden bow and arrow she carried. "For Diana the huntress, your aim fell short of the mark."

He casually reached out and captured the rose, plucked it, and proceeded to break the thorns from the stem. Royall watched him out of the corner of her eye. He was dressed in a black suit with a short, snug-fitting jacket over a snowy white cambric shirt. A bright red satin band encircled his slim waist, topping off narrow trousers. A black sombrero, tilted at a rakish angle on his head, gave his square jaw emphasis.

"Here, I give you beauty without the barb."

"Is that supposed to mean something, Senor Rivera?"

"Nothing personal, I assure you." Royall hated his condescending tone.

"Are you prepared for the evening's final entertainment before us, Senora Banner?"

"Us, Senor?"

"Yes, us. I understand you've been judged the most fair and therefore the queen of this ball. It is rather fitting; after all, you are Royall with two L's."

Royall gasped. "How can that be? How do you know?"

"One has a way of finding out these things. Especially since Mrs. Quince warned me and gave me directives on how I was not to embarrass you with my surliness, even after what you almost did to me. It's amazing how forgiving other people can be about my body. I'm to be a gracious partner and put aside all feelings, save those that are complimentary."

"You, why you?" Royall couldn't believe that Mrs. Quince had told Sebastian that she, Royall, was voted queen of the ball. On second thought, she could if Sebastian was voted king. Lord a mercy! She hoped not. She couldn't endure his sarcasm for the rest of the evening. "Are you the king?"

"That is correct, Senora. I am to be your king. Just remember to act surprised when the announcement is made. I know I can rely on your abilities as an actress."

"How dare you!"

"Oh, yes, before I forget, do steer clear of Senora Roswell. It seems as though the dear lady exerted her pressure to have me named king. Dear soul felt assured that her daughter, Nancy, would be named queen. A bit of matchmaking has been going on in the Roswell household, it seems. When she hears you've been named queen, I'm sure the fur will fly. Your fur, and never fear, Senora, I assure you, you'll find me the most attentive of kings."

"Oh, you . . . you . . ."

"What? What am I, Senora? I warn you, your opinion of me is becoming tiresome." He reached for her arm as it rose to strike him.

"Answer me, Royall, what am I? Am I a person to live off the misery of another human being? Am I? A little sarcasm would not be alien to you, I am sure. And as to being an actress, aren't you, and a convincing one? Who would have supposed the day you went riding with me on Regalo Verdad that it was to distract me from the sabotage taking place elsewhere? Yes, that's what I said—sabotage!" She was a better actress than he'd guessed. "Don't you think I can add two and two together?" He jerked her arm viciously. "That nasty little fire was started at the opposite end of the plantation from where we were riding. Luckily I've got good men working for me, and all that was lost was a week's work. It could have been a year's work, and well you know it."

He held her arm in a fierce grip, squeezing till she cried out in pain. Immediately, he seemed contrite and released her. She stood there, looking at him in disbelief, puzzled over his statement. Actress or no, he felt desire for her well up within him. Before either of them was aware, he had pulled her to him, crushing her lips beneath his in a tempestuous, burning kiss.

She fought him, pushing him away from her, feeling his burning lips above hers, lingering. She felt the brutality ebbing and something else taking its place, something demanding and sweet and yearning. With a will of its own, her body clung to his, her lips answering his demand. Without removing his mouth from hers, he sighed deeply; she could taste the wine punch he had been drinking, heady, tangy. She felt herself spinning as though she were in a whirlpool and Sebastian was her lifeline.

Roughly, he pushed her away, his jet eyes peering deeply into hers. In a half audible groan she heard him murmur, "She-devil," and he pulled her to him for another kiss, this time more searching. When she felt herself stir in his arms, he put her away from him, almost knocking her off her feet. She saw on his face a white, tight-lipped anger. Angrily, he strode off, leaving her alone on the balcony. Royall stared at the crushed rose at her feet, trampled beneath his foot, just as she was.

Royall didn't know how long she stood alone on the lonely balcony overlooking the rose garden. She was faintly aware that another dance was beginning, and somewhere a young man would be searching for her to dance with him. She couldn't go in there, not the way she was feeling. At a sound behind her she turned to see Victor Morrison.

"Here you are, my dear. I've been looking for you. This may be the last chance we have to talk before you go back to the plantation. There's something I feel I must tell you."

Royall brought herself to her senses. She could see the old lawyer was struggling with indecision. "It's most unpleasant, but Mrs. Quince assures me you have the mettle to take it."

"I think I do, Mr. Morrison."

"I'm sure of it, Royall." He seemed to stiffen; he came closer to her and put a hand on her arm. "Your father was a friend, both of mine and the old Baron Newsome. Old Farleigh Mallard knew him also, and always had the kindest of words to say about him. I think a daughter of Richard Harding can listen to the truth and bear it."

He gazed at her with a stern expression on his face. Whatever the subject was the lawyer had to discuss with her, Royall knew it was serious.

"Tell me, Mr. Morrison. I'm not a woman prone to vapors."

"Ahem. Yes. Remember you came to me and asked that I help you discover your rights to Reino Brazilia? Yes, of course, forgive an old man. However, you also asked me about some cryptic phrases your father wrote in his journal concerning correspondence I had had with him before his death. Now, mind you, child, I have no proof. However, I wrote to your father that I had reason to believe that the Baron, Carlyle Newsome, murdered his father in cold blood and destroyed his will."

Royall gasped, her hand flying to her mouth.

"I said I've no proof. However, it's my belief that this is true. I'm only telling you this, Royall, because I fear that if Carlyle would kill his own father to gain Reino Brazilia, what might he do to you if you started to assert your rights as to your inheritance? Think on it, child. It's a matter of record that the Baron has frequently outspent his credit. Yet somehow he always manages to pay off his debts. Never mind the technicalities; it's simply this: I have reason to believe the Baron has been using your share of the estate for personal debts for some years now. Your poor father was given to believe that his share of the money was being vested in the plantation. According to the figures to which I have access at the bank as a trustee, this is untrue.

"I want you to hold off demanding an accounting of your share until you hear from me. The situation, as it stands, could place you in danger."

Suddenly the music coming from the ballroom sounded discordant to Royall's ears.

Chapter Fourteen

Alicia dragged herself around the gilt and baroque sitting room. Absently she picked up one object after another, pretending to look at it. Her hands trembled as she carefully handled the priceless objects. She was pretending again, just like yesterday and the day before that. She had been pretending ever since she had come to live in the Baron's townhouse. She had just replaced a rare porcelain dove back on one of the small tables when the delicate chime of the clock startled her. If she had been holding the dove, it would be in shards now. She swallowed hard, forcing her throat to work against its will. She knew what she needed, and she needed it now. Her eyes scuttled around the room, finally coming to rest on the liquor cabinet at the far end of the room. All she had to do was walk across the room and remove the stopper on the decanter and take a drink. It was wrong. Her mother hadn't had to resort to liquor in her pretend world. All she had done was sit in a chair and close her eyes, and everything and everyone ceased to exist. She had tried that, but it didn't work for her. Carl's face always swam before her weary eyes. Memories haunted her, of how close they had been, and then, as always, the humiliating scenes she had to remember of the hours she spent in the Baron's bed. The liquor was the only thing that could blot the hateful face of the Baron from her mind. If she was lucky, and she knew she wasn't or she wouldn't be in the predicament she was in now, she could drink herself to death and never have to worry again.

Her hands were trembling so badly she had to clasp them together. She glanced down at her clenched hands, seeing the knuckles stark white against the sky blue gown she wore. She wanted a drink. She needed a drink. She was going to take a drink and then another and one after that, until she finished the bottle. To hell with Carl. To hell with the Baron. To hell with everything. What kind of man was Carl to lie to her as he had? He couldn't have truly loved her if he permitted his father to lead him around on a leash. Sebastian, next to her father, was the only man fit to live and breathe. The rest were all vile, perverted bastards. Her teeth clenched together, she crossed the room and reached for the sparkling cut glass decanter. Quickly, she removed the stopper, brought the bottle to her mouth, and drank deeply. She swallowed, waiting for the fiery liquid to hit her stomach. She needed that, she told herself, pouring another jolt into her snifter. Once she finished that off, she would cry a while, curse the Baron and sleep, hoping to see Carl in her dreams. When she woke, she would come downstairs and repeat the process all over again.

Her pansy eyes narrowed to slits. Today was supposed to be different . . . or was that yesterday, or tomorrow? Sooner or later she'd remember. That she'd remember anything at all struck her as funny, and she flopped down on the sofa, laughing in hysteria. If the Baron could only see her now. Fresh waves of laughter rolled over her. He'd throw an unholy tantrum because she was unable to perform. He should only know that the only way she could perform for him was to half drown herself in brandy.

Tears slipped from her eyes. Why couldn't she be a little girl again? Have a mother and father to make things all better again? Have friends, friends like Sebastian, whom she had trailed after since she could walk. Beautiful, beautiful Sebastian. If he could see her now, he'd be appalled, but he'd understand. Sebastian always knew what to do when things went wrong; he could fix anything.

That was what she was going to do today. She was supposed to visit Sebastian. Just yesterday she'd been looking out the bedroom window and had seen his carriage drive past the house, so he must be in Manaus.

A fresh roll of laughter erupted. What would Sebastian think if she showed up on his doorstep drunk? Hiccoughs overcame her as she struggled to her feet. No one could ever fool Sebastian. When he got a whiff of her, he'd probably catch fire. The thought delighted her as she tripped around the room, swirling her skirts. "I know—hic—that you must think I'm under the weather —hic—but actually I'm feeling rather well as of late—hic—"

Making her way to the door by willpower alone, she was determined that she'd see Sebastian. Hadn't she always had a talent to rise to any occasion? And this was an occasion—hic!

Holding onto the door for support, Alicia squinted. Damn, when had it begun raining? She'd need her cloak and, of course, her ruffled parasol. Wouldn't Sebastian be surprised to see her.

She carefully placed one foot in front of the other as she made her way to the small utility area outside of the sitting room. She struggled with a lemon yellow cape until she had it wrapped around her. She fished around inside the urn for her parasol, coming up with the one with scarlet bows on the handle. A rich gurgle of laughter made her double over when she caught sight of her reflection in the looking glass. If Rosalie Quince's parrot should light on her shoulder, passersby would be hard pressed to discover where the bird left off and she began.

Alicia blinked. At least the damnable hiccoughs were gone. She repeated her careful progress back into the room. Her bleary gaze fell on the liquor cabinet and the two half-empty bottles. She pondered the problem for a moment. She could pour one into the other, or she could drink it. On the other hand, it was a long walk to Sebastian's house and it was raining. She might want to stop along the way, and if she did stop, she would be thirsty. The problem was, and she admitted to herself that it was a problem, could she carry the parasol, watch out for puddles, read the street signs, and still carry the two bottles? It wasn't an insurmountable problem. She finally solved it to her satisfaction by downing the contents of one of the bottles and carrying the other under her cape.

The minute she stepped outside, the torrential rain sluiced through her flimsy parasol, drenching her to the skin. She tossed the parasol onto the road and started off to the right, hoping she was going in the right direction. Merchants stared at her through their shop windows. They shook their heads and looked at one another. A woman in her cups wasn't something you saw every day of the week or even once a year, for that matter. And a woman in her cups, staggering down the road in a heavy downpour, was even worse.

What seemed like hours later, Alicia climbed the steps to Sebastian's house. "Sebastian Rivera, let me in your house immediately!" she shouted above the whipping rain. Getting no response to her order, she uncorked the decanter and took a healthy swallow. "Open this damn door, Sebastian," she shouted again. Another swallow from the bottle, and the hiccoughs were back. "Damn you, Sebastian, you see what you've done. You made me get the hiccoughs again. Open this door before someone thinks I'm drunk. Sebastian!"

The door swung open and Sebastian Rivera blinked. "Christ almighty! Alicia? Jesus! Alicia, what the hell has happened?"

"I thought you were never going to open this damn door. Do you have something illicit going on in here? Look, Sebastian, I brought some refreshments with me. It took you long enough to open the door. I thought for sure that some of your neighbors would see me out there and wonder at my—hiccough—my condition. I have . . . I have . . . these . . . hiccoughs . . . from walking in the rain, and then—hiccough—you let me stand out there—hiccough—in the rain and now they won't . . . won't . . . go away. Oh, Sebastian, I had nowhere else to go, no one to turn to— hiccough—I had to come . . . come here . . . I knew you . . . knew you would . . . you have to help . . . please . . . Sebastian . . . you have to help me . . ."

"Alicia, what happened?" His voice was tender, brotherly, as he bent down on one knee. Taking her hand in his, he brought it to his cheek. "I'll help you, Alicia. Just sit there for a moment and I'll fetch my housekeeper." When he returned with a rotund, jolly honey-skinned woman, Alicia was fast asleep, her hands folded under her cheek like a small child. Sebastian scooped her up and was startled to find that she weighed less than a child. How much weight she had lost; she felt all bony and thin. Gently, he laid her on the bed and spoke softly to the housekeeper. "Take care of her, and be gentle."

Sebastian sat in his study, Alicia's bottle of brandy in his hands. What in the name of all that was holy had made Alicia show up at his door drunk! Something told him that this wasn't the first time she'd looked for answers to whatever was bothering her at the bottom of a bottle.

When he'd arrived in Manaus, he'd gone around to her apartment over the apothecary shop and learned that she was gone. Knowing that Carl Newsome was in Belém, Sebastian had thought Alicia was with him.

Hour after hour, Sebastian sat, waiting. He'd determined he wasn't moving until Alicia woke and told him what her problem was. He was beginning to doze off around midnight when his housekeeper tapped him on the shoulder and pointed to the upper level. Hurrying out into the hall, he ran into Aloni.

"Sebastian, why do you banish your Aloni to her room? Why is that woman here in this house?"

"Not now, Aloni. I've got too much on my mind. Go to bed. I'll talk to you in the morning."

As he took the carpeted stairs two at a time, he heard Aloni complaining behind him. "You don't love your Aloni anymore. Why didn't you take Aloni to the masquerade . . ."

Ignoring his mistress, he came to a halt outside Alicia's door. Cautiously, he opened it a crack to see Alicia weeping into her pillow. It made him feel inadequate to see a woman cry.

Drawing up a gold brocade chair beside the bed, he gently reached for her hand and covered it with both of his. "Alicia. What happened? What's made you so unhappy? Tell me, let me help you. You're safe here, if that's what you're worried about. No harm will come to you. We've been friends since you were a little girl. Come, wipe your tears and we'll talk."

What he said was true. That was why she had come to Sebastian. It was no longer important to hide her shame. In the beginning, yes. Now she didn't care anymore. Sebastian would understand. She groped for the snowy square of linen Sebastian handed her. She dabbed at her eyes and then blew her nose lustily. "I suppose I'm pretty much of a mess," she said swallowing hard. "Do you think I could have a drink, Sebastian? Not water," she added hastily.

Sebastian frowned. How could he refuse her anything? But he had to. "No, Alicia, spirits aren't what you need right now, and I've a feeling that that's how you've been trying to solve whatever problem it is that's plaguing you. You can't think and act clearly when you're under the influence. Tell me what's troubling you and how I can help. I don't think I need to remind you that any confidence you share with me will stay with me."

"I know that, Sebastian, and you're right. Spirits aren't what I need right now. Now I need a friend." Staring him straight in the eye, she recounted what happened to her from the day the Baron first visited her. She left nothing out, spared herself no shame. She neither cried nor excused herself in any was. That was what frightened Sebastian.

A rage as black as hell ripped through Sebastian as he heard her out. When she finished with her tale, her eyes pleaded with him for forgiveness. At first she thought he was angry with her, then he stood and curled his fist into a tight ball. Before she knew what was happening, he lashed out at the armoire, splintering the wood. His face showed no pain, just vile disgust. The emotion, she knew, was directed at the Baron, not herself.

"My God, why didn't you come to me in the beginning? Why did you suffer so? I would have killed the bastard cheerfully and then danced on his grave. Why, Alicia, why did you wait so long?"

"Because I couldn't bear to see the look on your face. I thought you would believe the rumors that have been circulating that I was a prostitute. Sebastian, surely you understand. And then I started to drink, just to drive what was happening to me from my mind. Yesterday, I saw your carriage drive by the house. I wanted to run after you right then and there and tell you to take me away, but I was too drunk to make it to the door. In the beginning you were back on the plantation, and there was no way for me to get there, and above all, I was afraid of the Baron. Please, Sebastian, say you understand and forgive me."

"Of course, I forgive you, and I do understand. My housekeeper is going to bring you some food shortly. I'm going downstairs to think. This can't go on. Something has to be done. We'll talk again in the morning. Good food and sleep are what you need most. In the morning we'll both have clear heads and know how to deal with this matter, and you have my word, Alicia, we will deal with it, head on if we have to." Gently, he kissed her on the cheek, and then, tenderly, he brushed back a stray tendril of hair from her forehead. "We'll speak later."

"Sebastian," she said in a frightened voice. "Have you seen Carl? Is he all right? Please, you must tell me, is he going to marry Royall Banner?"

Sebastian stared at her for a moment. "I don't know, Alicia, but I promise you I'll find out. The last time I saw him, he appeared . . . distraught. You know, I have never concerned myself with Newsome affairs unless they affected me in some way. You're not to worry. He isn't married yet. We both know that you're the girl he's always loved. Even when we were children, we all knew."

"Not any longer, Sebastian," Alicia whispered. "It's too late now, for everything." Her voice was flat, dead, sending a shiver of dread through him.

"Don't talk like that, Alicia. It's never too late."

"Yes, yes, it is! Don't you see! I'm not good enough for Carl if I ever was. Not any longer . . . not after what I've done. . . no . . ." Emotionlessly, seeming to have drained herself of tears, Alicia gave him a level look that cried hopelessness.

"Alicia, you did what you thought you had to do. I'll kill Carlyle for it, I swear."

266

"No, don't, Sebastian. Don't ever, promise me! Promise me!" Her fingers clutched him, tearing at cloth and flesh, demanding, needing to hear him promise.

"I don't want you wasting your life for me, Sebastian. I'm not worth it. I'm not worth anything anymore." The expression in her eyes, more than her words, made him frightened for her. If he didn't do something and do it soon, Alicia would die, by her own hand.

"Alicia, little darling, don't torture yourself."

"Go away, Sebastian! Go away! I can't bear to have you look at me! Please, please go away." She buried her face in the pillow, staring blankly at the far wall, a part of her already dead.

Without another word Sebastian closed the door and headed for his study. He had lied to Alicia. Sometimes there was nothing to do but take a drink and hope it would make the world right side up. The Baron himself had been circulating the news that when Carl returned from Belém an engagement was to be announced. And as he said it, he had allowed his gaze to find Royall.

One drink led to two and two to three. Three raced into four, five, and six, when dawn broke. He felt sober. Sober enough to want to kill the bastard named Carlyle Newsome. He knew that the only reason he had consumed so much liquor was because he needed the courage to do what he was going to do as soon as it was full daylight. There were some things a man could do and some he couldn't do without the crutch of alcohol to get

267

him through the tight moments. He told himself that Alicia was the only person in the whole world who could make him go to Royall Banner for help. But he would make it perfectly clear from the beginning that he was only seeking her help for his friend. There was no way he would ever approach her on his own behalf for any matter. But for Alicia he would subject himself to anything, as long as it would help her. He wondered fleetingly if he looked drunk.

He blinked when he stood up. There didn't seem to be any feeling in his legs, at least none that he could feel. He stomped his feet several times until he felt the tingle start in his toes and work its way up his legs. He was alive. Now, if he could just ride a horse, his problems were solved. The Quince's townhouse had been one of the first built on the outskirts of town. If he rode in from the back, he would go unnoticed. He would simply go around to the kitchen area and have one of the servants fetch Royall. It sounded too simple. He must be drunk, he thought as he mounted the russet gelding he kept at the stable behind his townhouse. He couldn't allow himself to dwell on the Baron or he would forget his intentions to bide his time. This was no time to kill anyone. That would come later, at the proper time. If only his head would stop its infernal pounding, maybe he could think clearly.

By the time the gelding picked his way around to the back of the townhouse, Sebastian's face wore a look of pain. All he could say for Royall

Banner with two L's was that she better not give him a problem, for if she did, he would be forced to abduct her in broad daylight. Alicia needed a woman to talk to, and he had decided that Royall was the one to do the listening. Royall was the only woman he knew who had come to terms with her own sexuality, and she was worldly, mundane, able to pick up the pieces and go on with her life!

The cook walked out to the courtyard to watch the lone rider. Her round, chocolate eyes widened when she noticed his identity. She waited for him to speak and then just nodded.

Royall was just tying the sash of her dressing gown when the cook entered her room. Motioning with her hand for Royall to follow her, she led her to the wrought iron balcony that overlooked the courtyard. Perplexed, Royall stared about and then let her eyes drop to the courtyard. Sebastian! What was he doing here? Something was wrong! The cook pulled her by the arm to show that she was to follow her down the stairs and out to the courtyard. When the old woman placed a cautious finger to her lips, Royall understood. No one was to know Sebastian was here. What could he want with her at this time of the morning?

Royall stepped outside, a shaft of sunlight capturing her in its golden rays and lighting her hair to spun gold. It was long, hanging down around her shoulders, and Sebastian remembered that first night in Rio when he had thought of little else besides pulling the pins from her hair and running his fingers through it.

She wore a scarlet dressing gown that was form-fitted, tiny jeweled buttons running down the front to the hem. It was partially opened at the wide, open neck, and from the hem to mid-thigh. When she walked, it revealed a silky expanse of a well-turned leg that set his pulses racing.

She stood before him, tapered fingers lightly touching her throat, golden-flecked eyes penetrating into his. She was beautiful, this golden girl, and he needed her. More for himself than even for Alicia.

"What's wrong? Why are you here?"

"Just shut up and get on this damn horse," Sebastian ordered briskly as he suddenly remembered why he was waiting for her.

"Why?" Royall demanded. "I'm not even dressed."

"I've seen you in a lot less," Sebastian leered and almost fell off the horse. "Come over here. I hate to admit this, but I need your help and what you're wearing won't make any difference."

Royall advanced a little closer. "How do I know you're telling me the truth. And why should I do you any favors after the way you've treated me? You're drunk!" she all but shouted, and then immediately clapped her hands over her mouth.

Sebastian tried for a sweeping bow from his saddle. His head reeled as he straightened, his back stiff, his face haughty and cold. Carefully, he brought his index finger to his lips. "Shhh. I don't want anyone but you to know. Now, get on this damn horse before I fall off and make problems for both of us."

She felt deliciously wicked as she reached up for him to help her. She seated herself as comfortably as she could, feeling the hardness of his chest against her body. Clenching her teeth, she refused to think of the other times the same feeling swept over her. Sebastian's arms circled her, holding her firmly against him. He liked the feel of her softness next to him.

"It's not necessary to hold me so close, Senor Rivera. I realize that the only reason you're doing so is so that you won't fall off this horse, so please spare us both the indignity of me helping you once you fall. I'll leave you in the middle of the road."

"Testy this morning, aren't we?" Sebastian grinned drunkenly. "Don't worry, Royall, with two L's, I'll not mark you in any way. I've seen chickens with more meat on their bones. You're skinny," he said slowly and distinctly.

Royall seethed and fumed. "And Senor Sebastian, as in bastard, I've seen roosters who have been done in by chickens, so watch that tongue of yours."

Sebastian threw back his head and laughed uproariously. "I never thought of myself as a rooster somehow."

"What a pity. You should recognize the smell, though. You smell quite gamey to me," Royall said viciously.

"I've been drinking, that's why. I was in such

a hurry to fetch you that I didn't bother to . . . It's none of your damn business, Royall with two L's, why I smell like I do."

Royall suppressed a smile. She must be insane to go riding with him at the crack of dawn, dressed in her dressing gown. What could possibly be wrong at his townhouse to make him come for her as he had? She tried again. "Why did you come for me? Tell me what's wrong. I demand to know, or I'm getting off this horse right now and pulling you with me. You're so drunk you'll never be able to get back on. Now tell me!"

"All in good time. I thought I told you to shut up. I hate to hear women whine. It's so . . . so . . . annoying."

"I wasn't whining," Royall sputtered. "You know, you really are an insufferable—"

"Bastard," he finished for her. "I never denied it. I even told you I was a bastard myself. Honesty has always been my motto," he said piously.

"You're disgusting. Aren't we there yet? Why is this animal going so slow?"

"Because my head is pounding, for one reason. The second reason is that this animal is carrying two people. And the animal had just recently been castrated. Is there anything else you want to know?"

Royall clamped her mouth shut, swearing to herself that she wouldn't say a word, never ask another question. He always told her much more than she wanted to know!

She felt his hands around her waist through the

272

scarlet silk of her dressing gown and became increasingly aware of the fact that she hadn't a stitch on underneath. Her long bare legs were stretched out, the wind lifting the skirt and exposing her skin to his greedy eyes. His hand clutched her tighter, so tight she thought she'd never draw another breath. His face was in her hair, his lips nuzzling the back of her neck. And she loved it.

"We're here," he said at last. "Now, was that so bad? Get off and go in the house. My housekeeper will find something for you to wear. I wouldn't want her to get any wrong ideas about this little ride."

Royall slipped to the ground, her face suffused with rage. "I don't believe what I'm hearing. You care about what your housekeeper thinks, but you rode me through town in my dressing gown. You are . . ." Words failed her completely.

"You're giving me a headache," Sebastian said coolly. "Go in the house. I'll be in shortly, after I see to the animal."

The kitchen area was dim and cool in the early hours of the morning. Royall looked around, conscious of her bedroom attire and hating the position in which Sebastian had placed her. She must be out of her mind to follow him so blindly. All she had to do was turn her back on him the way he had turned his back on her aboard ship. Refusing to follow him would have been simple. Where was the housekeeper? Advancing farther into the kitchen, Royall cleared her throat. Everything was neat and clean. A long, sharp knife rested alongside a bowl of ripe papayas, and mangos sat on a rough table ready to be prepared for the first meal of the day. She felt ridiculous as she called out, "Yoohoo," using Rosalie Quince's favorite yodel. There was no reply. Well, what had she expected? Sebastian was drunk as a lord, and probably didn't know if he even had a housekeeper. For all she knew he could have abducted her with some devious plot in mind. What a fool she was. There was nothing to do but wait and see if someone answered her call or go in search of Sebastian.

"May I help you?" a light, musical voice inquired. Royall swung about to see its origin. Beautiful almond eyes stared into Royall's startled gaze. At first glance she thought she was looking at the perfection of a China doll. Waist-long hair, resembling a length of ebony satin, graced a small head that was in direct proportion to the rest of the tiny body. The only words that came to Royall's flustered mind were *exquisite miniature*. She felt dowdy and overgrown.

Uncomfortably aware of her appearance, Royall found her tongue sharp. "Fetch me some suitable clothing," she ordered imperiously. In all her young years she had never known a housekeeper who looked like this porcelain decoration.

The rosebud mouth on the miniature doll tightened imperceptibly. Her voice, when she spoke, was disdainful as was her gaze. "I hardly think my clothing will fit you. I suggest you fetch it yourself. Perhaps the housekeeper has something . . . suitable."

Royall stared at the China doll, not fully comprehending her words. If she wasn't the housekeeper, who was she? Oh, no. Sebastian wouldn't humiliate her like this. Surely, he wouldn't dare bring her to his house while his . . . his . . . whatever she was was in residence. *He dared! He would! He did!*

Just then, with both women's eyes shooting sparks, a plump, jolly-looking Indian woman entered the kitchen. Royall's blood boiled as she recalled the tiny girl's words, "Perhaps the housekeeper has something . . . suitable." Goddamn Sebastian to hell. He truly was a bastard to subject her to this confrontation. "You come with me, missy, Senor Rivera tell me you coming early this morning. I take you to other lady now and bring breakfast for both of you. Other lady wait upstairs."

Royall's blood continued to boil. "Now just a damn minute here!" she exploded. What did that bastard think he was doing? "I'm not going anywhere, not until I know what is going on around here. You," she said pointing a long finger at the carved doll, "don't open your mouth again until Sebastian gets here. I'm surprised at you that you would . . . that you could. . . Why, you're nothing but a child, a baby actually. Make me some coffee," she ordered the housekeeper. "Now!"

Two pairs of eyes stared at Royall. Hastily, the housekeeper set about making coffee, while the

275

girl in her flawless white silk wrapper gazed at her with eyes that clearly did not belong to a child. She seemed amused and annoyed at the same time. Royall was infuriated.

Royall was tapping her foot angrily on the brick floor of the kitchen. The housekeeper was busily clanking pots and pans while the tiny girl drummed on the door frame with two-inch-long fingernails. Sebastian picked that moment to enter the kitchen. His black eyes took in the scene at one glance. A grin stretched across his lips and was banished instantly when Royall leaped from the chair. "What are you doing sitting here?" he demanded arrogantly.

"I'm sitting here because I feel like it. And I feel like having a cup of coffee. When I finish the coffee, I want a carriage that will take me back to my own house. I hope I make myself clear." While her comments were addressed to Sebastian, her eyes were on the girl in the silk wrapper. "If you think for one minute that I'm going to be a party to your . . . your lascivious pastimes, you have another thought coming. How dare you bring me here with . . . with . . . her!" Royall shouted.

Sebastian grinned widely. The plump house-keeper wore a decided smirk. The tiny girl gri-maced, marring her perfect features.

"You talk more than any female I ever came across," Sebastian muttered disgustedly. His gaze shifted to Aloni. "Go to your room," he said coolly.

At first Royall thought the girl would defy Sebastian. Instead she favored him with a level look, turned, and left, but not before Royall saw the hatred leap from her eyes. As if she cared.

"That's it, order everyone around. Arrogant bastard," Royall hissed.

"I can almost imagine what you're thinking, but you're wrong. Believe me. I brought you here for a reason. Upstairs in one of the bedrooms Carl's bride-to-be is waiting. She needs someone to talk to, another woman. I thought you might be able to help her; after all, you are a worldly woman and that's what she needs right now."

Royall backed off a step and then advanced until she was standing inches from Sebastian. "That has got to be the most insulting thing you have ever said to me. I wouldn't do anything for you if you were the last person on this earth. Who," she hissed through clenched teeth, "is more worldly than that . . . that . . . decadent child who was just here? How dare you call me worldly." Unmindful of the housekeeper's sharp ears, Royall rushed on. "You're nothing but a . . . a perverted, decadent, miserable . . ."

"Charming, dashing, handsome bounder," Sebastian finished for her. All signs of drunkenness were gone. His movements were sure and steady, his gaze cold and mocking as he stared down at her, enjoying her anger. She was quite the most beautiful woman he had ever seen, even when she was in the throes of rage.

"Ha. That just shows how stupid you really are. I, for one, never heard anyone say such things about you. It's solely your opinion," Royall shot back.

"But that's the only one that counts. Enough of this nonsense. Personally, I don't give a good goddamn how you feel or what you think. I brought you here for a very real reason. Believe me, if there had been anyone, I repeat, *anyone* else I would have gone to them. Since there wasn't you were the only choice. Listen to me carefully because I won't repeat myself." Quickly, he recounted Alicia's story, deliberately leaving out the Baron's name. That he would deal with in his own way, in his own good time.

Royall was thunderstruck at Sebastian's words. She could only stare at him with wide eyes, begging him to tell her it was all a poor joke. When he returned her cold-eyed stare, she knew that Sebastian would never jest about something so important as the dear childhood playmate who was like a sister to him. Rage, hate, pity, every emotion known to her flooded through her being. "You see," she squawked hoarsely, "men can't be trusted. I never heard of anything so vile . . . so degradingly inhuman. I demand that you tell me who the man is who made Alicia do this! I demand to know. I'll kill him myself before he gets a chance to practice his wicked ways on some other poor female. Sebastian Rivera," she stomped her foot, "I demand that you tell me now."

"Shut up, Royall. I will handle the matter. You would only botch the job, and I want to be the one to make the bastard suffer as Alicia has suffered. All you have to do is talk to Alicia and help her in any way you can. Woman to woman. I'll say one thing for you, you do have a glib tongue . . . among other things."

Royall ignored what she thought were his compliments. "Then I want your promise to at least allow me to be in attendance when you do the fiend in. Give me your promise or I'm going home."

"I thought I told you to shut up." Wearily, he brought his hand to his forehead. "Why is it you women feel you have to screech and squawk at every comment a man makes? You should talk softly, caressingly to a man. You should be gentle and compassionate."

"You can just stop telling me to shut up, Sebastian. God gave me a mouth and I intend to use it. If there was a man around, perhaps I would take your advice. You," she said piercing him with a speculative eye, "don't count. And don't tell me what to do again. Do you understand? I'm not deaf, dumb, and blind. I know where my duty lies and I'll do it. And," she said triumphantly, "the only reason you have a headache is because you were drunk. A drunken headache, they're the worst kind. For shame, Sebastian Rivera," she said disgustedly.

"If you don't shut up, I swear I'll . . ."

"You'll what?" Royall shouted. "You're in no condition to do anything. You're fortunate you can stand erect. I find your behavior insulting and degrading. I don't even want to be in your company. What do you think of that?"

"I think you need to be taught a lesson, and I'm just the one to teach you. Like that night aboard ship. I did teach you a thing or two, if memory serves me correctly. You certainly were an apt pupil." Sebastian leered at her, his intentions clear. She watched him with narrowed eyes as he advanced a step and then another.

"Now look, Sebastian. Perhaps I was a little hasty in my tirade. You're suffering from your headache, and I wouldn't want to add to the pounding in your temples." Royall backed off, her eyes trapped, her heart pounding. "You wouldn't take advantage of me in my position. You said Alicia needed me and I'm ready to . . . to help her. I know exactly what you're thinking and you aren't going . . . ever again . . . I told you I hate you . . . you hate me . . . you even walked out on me and made a fool of me . . . Get away from me, you . . . you . . ." She babbled on as she backed deeper into the kitchen.

Chapter Fifteen

Royall retreated into the kitchen, watching him advance after her. There was intent in his eyes; she could see the muscles bunching beneath his white cambric shirt, saw his arms reaching out to her, to capture her, to bring her hard against him in an angry, malevolent embrace.

"Don't, Sebastian. No. I don't . . ." Roughly, he seized her, demonstrating his strength, holding her fast, making her his prisoner. At his touch Royall felt herself stiffen. What was the look in his eyes? "Take your hands off me, Sebastian!" she cried, her voice tinged with fear. "Let me be!" she insisted, wrestling loose.

No sooner had she gained her freedom than she was running for the door. She knew defeat when Sebastian's fierce hold imprisoned her again.

"And what is this?" he mocked. "The golden girl afraid of me? A mere man?" he smiled churlishly.

"Let me go, Sebastian! I hate you this way!" she cried defiantly.

"*This way*, is it? And how is it you like me, Royall with two L's?" His voice was controlled fury, his eyes glittered like fragments of glass.

"God help me, but I wonder what I ever liked about you!" Her tone matched his for venom.

"Would you like me to remind you?" he smiled crookedly, wickedly. His hands on her shoulders burned through the scarlet silk of her dressing gown, searing her flesh as he pulled her against him again.

"Sebastian! Leave me alone! Don't touch me!"

"Make me," he taunted, his lips so near hers, his breath fanning her cheek.

"Don't do this, Sebastian. Let go of me!"

"Do what, little cat, *mi poca leona?* Take you in my arms, hold you this way? You love the things I do to you, to your body."

281

"You're a pig!"

"No, love, a man. A man whose mouth and hands can stir you, can leave you panting, purring like the cat you are." His grip became stronger, pressing her against him, making her aware of the lean hardness of his thighs, the flatness of his belly, holding her until she thought it would be impossible to draw another breath. His voice was smooth, yet his tone harbored a vengeance.

"Tell me, Royall, should I press my lips to that most secret place where your passions flare and your body turns to liquid fire?" He needed no answer, refused one. He wrapped his arms around her, grabbing hold of the long tumble of gold that fell below her shoulders and yanked her head backwards, lifting her face, baring her mouth to his hungry kiss.

Royall struggled, feeling him tug at her hair, clamping her lips shut, refusing his kiss, feeling his teeth biting against her mouth, his tongue demanding entrance.

"Tell me how you love the things I do to you, Royall," he taunted, pressing her downward, knocking her legs out from under her, holding her against the rough brick floor, his face only inches away.

She brought her arms up in defense, wedging them between herself and Sebastian. Her struggles were useless, she was defenseless as a child. He seized her wrist, pulling her arms upward over her head, keeping them there.

"Tell me, little cat, my little lioness, tell me.

Do you like it when I caress your flesh?" He transferred possession of both her wrists to one of his, leaving him a free hand that delved into the neckline of her dressing gown, covering her bare flesh, cupping her heaving breasts. "Do you love it when your breasts swell, filling my hand, their tips standing erect beckoning my lips? Admit it, you love it, don't you?"

Against her own will, her body betrayed her. Even before he said the words, she could feel her flesh swell, seeming to reach for him, proudly rising, tempting him. Royall refused to speak, to give him more ammunition.

His knees forced their way between her thighs, the rough fabric of his trousers scraping the tender skin that her half-open, rucked-up dressing gown exposed. His lips were where his hands had been, torturing her, teasing, evoking in her a response she desperately wanted to deny.

Again, claiming her lips with his own, he slowly traced the outline of her mouth with his tongue, moistening it, penetrating it. A tremor passed through her to him, exciting him, spurring him to continue his assault. He could feel the perfect symmetry of her figure beneath his fingers. He was familiar with the purity of her breasts narrowing to her tiny waist. Her skin glowed amber in the morning light filtering through the kitchen window, tantalizing him, whetting his appetite for more, always more.

He felt the change in her when his lips traced moist patterns on her throat, felt the heat in her loins pressed so tightly against his own, and he knew he had won. The power was his; Royall was his! He could never have enough of her. The freshness of her skin, the spun gold of her hair, the sweet curve of her breasts and thighs. Every inch of her was created by the gods to entice him, to fever his passions, to make him dissatisfied for any other woman.

Her legs wound round his hips, clinging in a honeyed embrace, and he knew a sense of coming home. Of a familiar welcome that he had tasted before. Her hips followed his, moving against him, making demands beyond her will.

He was lost in her, adrift in a golden sea. He released her wrists, half expecting her to curl her fingers into claws, to rake his face, to vent her rage. Instead, she forced her hands between their bodies, creeping lower, fumbling with the fastenings on his trousers. She wanted him with a hunger that was expressed in searching lips and seeking tongue. Soft moans of desire emanated from her, singing passion's sweet song.

His night dark eyes glowed with exaltation as he entered her and she trembled beneath him, opening herself to him, imprisoning him in love's tender sheath.

Royall whimpered softly, relishing the weight of him, loving the sound of his husky whispers when he told her of her beauty, and how he loved the feel of her body, the scent that was hers alone.

He crushed her mouth beneath his, savoring her, tasting the ambrosia of passion's promise.

Slowly, tantalizingly, he withdrew from her, entering again forcefully, making her cry out, anticipating the rake of her nails on his back as she realized what his next move would be. Sebastian rolled over onto his back, bringing her with him.

She felt his muscular torso between her knees, knew the sweet fulfillment at the center of their embrace. His fingers worked the few remaining buttons of her dressing gown, drawing the scarlet silk apart, seeing her body outlined in stark golden relief against the vibrant color. His hands possessed her breasts, cupping their firmness, teasing their rosy crests. She arched beneath his touch, throwing her shoulders back, offering herself to him.

Fire sparked where their flesh was joined, and her movements were instinctive and unstudied, arousing him beyond the limits of his control.

A waterfall of gold cascaded forward over her bared shoulders, hiding her breasts from his view. Impatiently, he took hold of it, reluctant to remove his hands from that precious flesh they had held captive. Pulling, persuading, he drew her downward, seeking her mouth with his own, eliciting from her a fevered response that quickened the movements of her hips, carrying him with her into a rapture that transcended the limits of the flesh and became a fusing of the spirit.

Head high, chin lifted to a level denoting confidence and pride, Royall turned toward Sebastian, holding his eyes with her own, feeling his returning gaze penetrate and warm her. They climbed the long, curving staircase and walked down the wide corridor leading to Alicia's room, side by side. Sebastian didn't touch her; he didn't have to. She could feel his warmth, his own wonder, experiencing it as though it were her own. Something had changed between them. She no longer felt the deep, abiding hurt and rage that had consumed her all these past weeks. Whatever this new feeling was, it was fragile, gossamer thin, easily penetrated, more easily destroyed.

Sebastian's voice was deep and husky when he spoke. "This is where Alicia is staying. I'm certain she's sleeping, but she wouldn't mind if you woke her." He looked down at Royall, whose hand was gripping the door knob. She met his gaze and smiled, reassuring him, silently pledging to do her best to help his friend.

"I want you to know something, Sebastian," she whispered. "I don't expect you to understand this, but I'm not really doing this for you. I'm doing it for Alicia and myself, and pray God I can say the right things, get through to her. And," she continued, looking directly into his tortured black eyes, "I want to say that Alicia is indeed fortunate to have you for a champion. Whatever is or isn't between us, I want you to know how I feel." Not allowing him time for an answer, she pushed open the door and closed it behind her and tiptoed across the room to Alicia's bed.

How frail she looked, almost ethereal. Soft, dark hair was scattered on the pillow, and her piquant face was troubled, even in sleep. Blue smudges of weariness were beneath her eyes and blemished her peaches and cream complexion.

Royall hated to wake her, but Sebastian seemed to think it would be better for Alicia to talk to someone than to sleep. Touching the girl lightly on the shoulder, Alicia stirred, her breathing harsh and tormented. Alicia woke, her eyes wide and frightened. "Alicia, it's all right," Royall soothed. "You're in Sebastian's home. He brought me here to talk to you. I'm Royall Banner," she said quietly.

Alicia closed her eyes and leaned back against the snowy whiteness of the pillows. Oh, Sebastian, her mind rebelled. How could you do this to me? How could you want me to talk to the woman Carl is going to marry? Tears gathered in her eyes.

"Sit up, Alicia, and we'll talk. Sebastian has told me why you're here and why you came to him. I know it's going to be hard for you and that you feel ashamed, but I want you to put that aside. I want to help you, and I want to be your friend. Sebastian has told me how dear you are to him, and we both know he wouldn't subject either of us to this meeting if he didn't think it was necessary."

Alicia was silent, staring at this beautiful woman with the wealth of golden hair. Imagining her in Carl's embrace. Seeing Royall's full, ripe mouth and seeing Carl's lips caress it—it was too much. Too humiliating! Sebastian, what are you doing to me?

"Alicia, I must tell you right from the beginning that I have no intention of marrying Carl. How could I? He's never asked me! Alicia, Carl has never treated me as anything but a friend. He's never made any advances toward me, and deep in my heart I've always felt he loved someone else. You, Alicia."

At the girl's incredulous expression, Royall hurried on. "I know the Baron would like a marriage between Carl and myself, but I'd never marry anyone unless I truly loved him. I've made that mistake already and I won't make it again. Carl is a wonderful man, tender and sweet, and obviously in love with you!"

Gratification came in seeing Alicia's pansy blue eyes brighten, and then fall back into the shadows of misery. "I should be happy to hear what you've told me. I was so confused . . . when I was told that Carl was going to marry you . . . Oh, please, go away," she cried, deep sounds of sorrow, like an inexorable tide, coming from her as she rocked back and forth, hugging herself. "Don't you see, now it's worse! So much worse! I'll never be able to face Carl again. How can I tell him what I've done? He could never love me again, never! No man could ever love me."

Royall moved to the bed, taking Alicia in her arms. Waiting for this new wave of misery to subside. "Alicia, there's no need for you to tell Carl. He'd never have to know. Why would you tell him?"

Alicia shook her head, "I could never lie to him. I love him."

"And for that reason you should never tell him, and he'll never hear it from anyone else either. Sebastian will say that you've been here under his protection the whole time. And if a word of scandal should ever reach his ears, he'll make it known that he'd kill the man who's spread such lies. Besides, this man, whoever he was, wouldn't want to be ostracized from society, and that's exactly what would happen. Do you understand?"

Alicia nodded in agreement. "But I'd have to be honest with Carl."

Royall was angry. Her fingers dug into the soft flesh of Alicia's arms and she threw her back against the pillows, following her, putting her face only inches from the girl's. "I thought you said you loved him!" she hissed, venom spitting from her lips.

"I do. I do."

"Then why would you want to hurt him? Are you so weak that you can't carry your secret by yourself? That you'd need to lay it on Carl's shoulders and make him miserable?"

Eyes widening, Alicia's mouth formed an O; she shook her head in denial. "But . . . but . . ."

"No buts, Alicia. Sebastian told me you were made of strong stuff, and this only happened because you were miserable and frightened that you'd lost Carl forever. You were stupid, Alicia; you should have gone to Sebastian to tell him what that man was trying to make you do. But no, you wanted to wallow in your own misery and compound it, triple it, kill yourself with it! You were stupid, but I know that we all make the wrong choices sometimes. But do you really want to burden Carl with it? Do you want to cheat him of his happiness just because you cheated yourself out of yours? Needing to confide in Carl isn't love, Alicia, it's selfishness. If you need to punish yourself, Alicia, find some other way. Some way that won't punish Carl in the bargain!"

Alicia seemed to crumble in Royall's arms. Holding her, Royall softened her tone. "It will have to be your secret, now and forever. Soon the time will come when memories will fade because Carl is at your side and you'll hold his child in your arms."

Drawing away, pushing Alicia from her, Royall stared deeply into the girl's eyes. "You're young, you're resilient. You've survived the worst and you can't go back now! You're safe now, Alicia. And Carl will keep you safe and you'll be able to go on with your life as it was meant to be!"

"Royall, do you really think so? Do you really believe it?"

"You know I do! With my whole heart."

Alicia's thoughts whirled, coming again and again to the Baron. How could she marry Carl and live in the same house as the Baron? Would Carl ever leave Reino Brazilia?

"I couldn't stay here, Royall. I want to leave Manaus . . . and the memories. What . . . what if Carl doesn't want to come with me? What if he obeys his father and cuts me out of his life? How can I live without him? And those vicious rumors about me. . . saying I'm a prostitute . . ." her words rambled.

"A prostitute!" Royall gasped. "Silly girl! Don't you think that Sebastian would be one of the first to hear any rumor like that? This man, whoever he was, lied to you. He tricked you so he could force you into doing as he wanted. You must believe in yourself, Alicia, before anyone else can believe in you. You must stand on your own two feet. And as for Carl, I've my own ideas about him. I've told you he never mentioned marriage to me, regardless of the pressure the Baron exerted. What does that tell you, Alicia? That his father hasn't won, that Carl is a man who is learning to stand up for himself and what he wants, regardless of the Baron. Otherwise, I'm certain he would have proposed long before this."

Alicia's eyes were bright with tears, tears of realization and a growing hope. "Oh, Royall," she hugged her, "how can I thank you. Dear Sebastian, for bringing you here to me. And to think how many hours I've spent hating you, jealously thinking Carl loved you. And now that I know you, I wonder that Carl didn't fall in love with you; how could he not?"

Royall smiled. "Because his heart belongs to you. He loves you."

"Royall, are you certain I shouldn't tell Carl?"

"I'm certain. It would be cruel, to both of you. Women are strong. You, Alicia, are strong!"

"How will I ever be able to thank you, Royall? Sebastian was right, you've done me the world of good. Thank you. Perhaps some day I may be able to help you."

"You may at that. I'm going to leave you now. You need more rest. Your eyes are heavy. I think you'll sleep a restful sleep now. We'll talk again when you're feeling better. And at that time," she wagged a finger at Alicia, "I expect to see a bloom in your cheeks. I want your promise."

"I promise," Alicia said wanly.

"Alicia, is that your cape on the chaise?" At the girl's nod, Royall asked if she might borrow it.

"But of course. I'm afraid it's a bit wrinkled. I arrived here in a downpour."

"It's of no matter. I can't go back in my dressing gown. Your cape will do nicely. I'll be sure it's pressed and returned to you."

"Burn it, please. I want no further reminders of where the cape came from," Alicia said harshly.

"Sleep now, Alicia. We'll talk again."

Royall was almost at the top of the stairs when she heard her name being called. "Yes?" she questioned turning around. The child from the kitchen! Sebastian's paramour. What did she want!

"My name is Aloni." Royall said nothing as she narrowed her eyes. She didn't like the stiffness of the tiny girl, nor did she like the dangerous look in her eyes. "Sebastian belongs to me." Still Royall said nothing. The girl seemed confused by her lack of response. The musical voice rose an octave.

"You will never take him from me, and if you try, I'll kill you."

"What makes you think I want Sebastian? Don't ever make the mistake of threatening me again, for if you do, I may be forced to take you over my knee and paddle your backside till you can't sit down for a week. If you want to be treated like an adult, I suggest you start acting like one." Good lord, where was she getting all of this advice she was ladling out in such large doses. "Step aside!"

Aloni's breath came out in a sharp hiss. "I saw you in the kitchen with Sebastian. I saw you both!"

Royall was stunned and momentarily taken off guard. She had seen . . . had heard . . . God in heaven! She had to get out of this house! Now! Damn you, Sebastian Rivera, she muttered under her breath.

"He could never love you," the woman-child said hatefully. "We belong together. You will never take him from me."

"I don't want him. You can have him! You can have all of him," Royall shot back as she made a move to go around Aloni.

"He has tasted your passions now, and he will compare them with mine. Aloni does not like it when he will do that."

The thought of this woman-child comparing passions amused Royall, and the cat in her emerged. "Be careful, Aloni. If a comparison is made, you would lose."

"You lie! You white-skinned old woman!" Aloni spat, her fingers curling to claws.

Gone was the amusement and in its place rose anger, white hot and searing. It was the word "old" that Royall objected to. "You deserve one another, you and your master. You're both cut from the same bolt of cloth. Now, let me by, you whining infant!"

Aloni raised her hand and pushed Royall back against the wall. Royall's eyes widened at the strength behind the slender arm. Her eyes narrowed. If Aloni wanted a battle, she would give her one. Royall brought up her hand and slapped Aloni square across the side of the face. Aloni retaliated by grasping Royall's long blond hair and yanking till tears came to her eyes. She tugged and pulled with vicious pleasure. "You damn little bitch, I'll teach you a lesson you'll never forget!"

A second later Royall had her hair free and had knocked Aloni to the floor. The woman-child shrieked and screamed for help from Sebastian. "If you don't shut that petulant mouth of yours, your teeth will be rattling around," Royall gasped as she straddled the tiny form on the floor. Both of Aloni's hands were held at the wrist with Royall bending over, her face inches from Aloni's terrified face. "Call me *old* now. Let me hear you say it again. Say it!" Royall shouted angrily.

"Say what?" Sebastian's voice thundered. "What the hell is going on here? Christ, don't you women ever shut up? I'm going back to the plantation for peace and quiet. One of you better tell me within thirty seconds just what the hell this is all about, or I'll take both of you over my knee. Speak!" he roared.

Royall struggled to her feet. With a flourish she whipped the lemon-colored cape about her, all the while staring disdainfully at Sebastian. "The infant on the floor needs a wet nurse and a sugar tit." This she said with her mouth pursed as though she were sucking on a sour lime. "Don't even try to explain, for I have no desire to hear any explanation. This is the last insult I will suffer at your hands, Sebastian Rivera. Now, get the hell out of my way before I knock you down those steps and then walk over you. Now!"

Royall gathered the shreds of dignity around her and left, feeling both pairs of eyes piercing her back—one pair hate-filled and the other confused.

Chapter Sixteen

The Quince townhouse was ablaze with lights shimmering through the long French glass windows and laying golden pools on the cobbled street outside. People were arriving for the party given by the Quinces in honor of their guest, Royall Banner. Jewels glittered, taffeta gowns rustled, men were attired in their most dashing best. Carriages were tended by the footmen, and music, full and glorious, filled the night, sweeping over the slate rooftops from Rosalie's back garden, where the party was already in progress.

Royall stood to Mrs. Quince's right on the receiving line, patiently allowing herself to be formally introduced to people she had met a hundred times over during the past ten days since the opening of the opera. The party itself was an informal buffet. Long tables, covered with snowy white cloths, were tended by servants and laden with foods of every description. The hour was late by most standards, nearly eleven o'clock, near the witching hour, because everyone had attended the performance of Verdi's *Rigoletto* before coming to the Quince residence.

Royall shifted her weight from one foot to the other. Damn if her feet didn't hurt. She wanted nothing more than to just creep up to her room and pull off her clothes and sleep. But Rosalie had gone to considerable trouble to make things as nice as possible for her young guest.

In spite of herself, Royall found she continually watched the entrance to the lantern-lit garden, watching for Sebastian. She had seen him earlier from the Quince box at the opera. He had brought Alicia with him, and the girl had looked lovely in a pink gown striped with silver. Royall had once or twice glanced their way. Alicia had caught her eye and waved a greeting. Sebastian had not turned his head, not even to offer a smile to Rosalie.

Royall hadn't seen him since the day he'd practically kidnapped her to bring her to Alicia, and she admitted to herself that her eyes were hungry for the sight of him.

"Royall, darling, how nice to see you again," a masculine voice greeted her. Turning, she saw the Baron standing there, his gray eyes smiling into hers, something behind the smile making her blood run cold.

"Baron," she murmured, feeling very ill at ease with him since he had danced with her at the masquerade ball. The man had become too familiar and that, combined with what Mr. Morrison had told her, was enough to make her flesh crawl.

"The festivities are almost over," he told her, smoothing his iron gray hair over his temples. "It will be nice to have your company again at Reino Brazilia. It's very lonely at my townhouse," he went on. "Carl is in Belém, and Jamie has insisted on staying in the apartment behind my offices near the wharf. I'm quite alone," he told her meaningfully. "Why don't you come and stay with me for the remainder of our time here in Manaus?"

A shudder captured Royall. He had mentioned the very thing she'd been dreading. Somehow she managed a smile, adroitly swinging her eyes to the woman behind the Baron, offering a greeting, dismissing him completely. But the man stood his ground and refused to move on to Alonzo Quince, who stood beside her in the receiving line.

"Aquamarine does wonderful things for your hair, Royall," he told her, his eyes moving over her familiarly. "You're more stunning than ever this evening."

"Thank you, you're very kind." Her voice was flat; she felt herself shrinking inside. She didn't want his attentions or his flattery, she just wanted him to move on, to go away. Lord in heaven, how was she going to tolerate this man once they were all together again on the Reino?

She heard him laugh, a wide grin splitting his face, showing his dazzling teeth. "Kind, Royall? No, I don't think so. At least I've never considered myself as such."

He'd been drinking, and he frightened her. Some chord was struck, something was off center—in addition to being inebriated, he seemed half mad!

Alonzo Quince came to the rescue. "How do you do, Baron Newsome. It's been so long since I've actually had a moment with you," Alonzo grasped the Baron by the arm and led him away. "Have you managed to ready the rubber shipment to the East? We've had some diff . . ." As their voices faded, Royall felt herself relax. Was this how Alicia had felt when that nameless man had exercised his control over her? Suddenly, the night was too warm and she needed something to blot the sudden perspiration of her upper lip. She admitted that it wasn't the heat or the party; the Baron was the reason she had broken out into a cold sweat.

Shortly afterwards, Sebastian arrived with Alicia. They spoke for a moment with Rosalie before

298

moving on to Royall. Alicia's eyes were alive and dancing. For an instant she slid her tiny gloved hand into Royall's, and then, dropping all pretense, wrapped her arms around Royall's shoulders and hugged her. Sebastian watched the display of feminine affection and found himself smiling. He took the opportunity to look at Royall, finding her lovely in her watered silk aquamarine that heightened the gold of her hair and the honey amber of her skin. His hand itched to reach out and touch her, to hold her in his arms. . .

"Sebastian has been wonderful," Alicia was telling Royall. "I'm going to stay in his townhouse even after he leaves for Regalo Verdad in a few days. He's so generous! When Carl comes back from Belém, Sebastian will tell him where to find me."

"That's wonderful," Royall murmured, truly happy for Alicia. She felt Sebastian standing there looking down at her, but she refused to lift her eyes to him. Their last meeting, which had ended in a hair-pulling match with his paramour, had been a final humiliation.

Rosalie Quince broke in. "Royall, most everyone is here now. Why don't you go and mingle with the guests? You must be as hungry as I am by this time. I've got my mouth watering for a thick slice of that lamb."

"Then I'll come with you, Mrs. Quince," Royall said hurriedly, hoping her relief wasn't too obvious to Alicia. She really liked the girl and didn't want to offend her, but Sebastian's nearness was making her claustrophobic.

Sometime later, Royall was sitting on one of the iron benches resting her feet and watching the party from a distance, when she caught sight of the Baron. He held a drink in his hand and was staring across the crowd, his stance one of frozen motion, his silver gray eyes spewing menace. Royall followed his gaze, stretching her neck to see the recipient of his stare, expecting it to be Sebastian. When the dancers changed positions, she had a better view and was shocked to see a slim, dark-haired girl in a pink-silver-striped gown locked in the terror of his gaze. Alicia!

Thought rioted and rambled through Royall's brain. Before she could formulate an opinion of what she'd witnessed, a cry went up among the crowd. Shrieks were coming from an open doorway leading to the garden. Royall looked to the source of the commotion and heard the words: "Yellow jack!" Instantly, a man she did not recognize was surrounded by every man at the party.

"It started on the Reino and is spreading to every other plantation! I saw it with my own eyes! They're falling down dead!"

"When did you see this?" The harsh cold demand was from Sebastian Rivera.

"Yesterday. You can be sure the situation has worsened by now."

Royall suddenly found herself standing beside Rosalie Quince. "We'd best start at once for the plantation," Rosalie called to her husband,

Alonzo. The portly gentleman needed no prodding as he strode from the room. The other men followed suit. Not so Sebastian Rivera and the Baron.

"It's ridiculous!" the Baron shouted, his face mixed shades of crimson. "Who is this ridiculous person who dares to come here uninvited and start such a malicious rumor? I demand an explanation!" he said, grasping the man by the open collar of his shirt.

"This is my foreman, Jesus Alvarada," Sebastian said coldly. "If he says there's yellow jack on the Reino, then it's true. He knows what the fever is. He lost a mother, father, and two children, not to mention a wife," Sebastian said, his face a mask of fury. He looked to the foreman. "And ours? What of ours?"

"One child is poorly. I don't know at this time if it's the fever or not."

"Has the child been isolated from the others?"

"I saw to it, sir. It was the first thing I did," the foreman replied.

"Good. Come, Jesus, we have a long ride ahead of us. I remember only too well the last time the fever struck."

Sebastian's tone was contemptuous when he turned and spoke to the Baron. "Is it your intention to stay in town while your plantation is wiped out? If so, be prepared for the other owners to take matters into their own hands. I warned you time and again. You ignored me as well as the others. Now you see the results of your ignorance," he said ominously as he strode from the room.

"Sebastian, wait," Royall implored.

"For what? For more people to die needlessly? Use your wiles and charms on the Baron; it will do you more good. You're just as responsible as he is. Everyone has a day of reckoning, and this is yours, Senora Banner."

Tears stung the amber eyes. Would he never believe her, trust her? Whatever the Baron did or didn't do, she knew *her* duty! Her gaze left Sebastian's retreating back to settle on the mask of rage the Baron was presenting to the room at large.

"How dare that bastard speak to me as if I were one of his common workers!"

Shock coursed through Royall. What had she expected? Everyone had tried to warn her, and while she had listened, she had done nothing. Sebastian was right; this was her day of reckoning. The Baron had no intention of returning to the plantation. From the expressions on the women's faces, they weren't surprised. After all, how many times must they have heard their husbands and sons talk about Reino Brazilia and the Baron?

"Do what you want, Carlyle, but I'm leaving for the Reino." Her voice was cold and bitter. "Sebastian said I'm just as responsible as you, and while you don't take your responsibility seriously, I do. Now get out of my way, and don't try to stop me."

"Bravo, child!" Mrs. Quince chortled. "If you

need me, call upon me at any hour. You promise, Royall."

Royall embraced the older woman before she fled the room in search of a carriage or buggy to take her back to the plantation.

Spying Jamie on the now deserted veranda, she grasped his arm. "Come with me, Jamie, we're going back to the plantation. You're big and strong, you can handle the carriage, can't you?" Not bothering to wait for a reply, she babbled on. "Your father is bent on stopping me, but I don't have the time now to play games with him. Jamie, I promise, if you go with me, I will play the spinet for you till you fall asleep. Every day," she added at the young man's frightened look. "Every day, Jamie, I'll play whatever you want. Right now your father is angry but he'll get over it. See, all the others are going and he just wants to be stubborn. Every day, Jamie. You know how you love music."

"Jamie, stop!" the Baron shouted.

"Damn you, Jamie, get in that carriage and whip those horses. Now!" Royall ordered.

Jamie grinned suddenly. Sebastian could whip the horses and make them gallop down the drive and everyone would cheer and clap. Now he could do the same. He laughed when he saw Royall push his father away, shouting angrily at him to leave her alone. She was right, father always got angry and then he would smile and pat him on the head and forgive him for his little defiances.

As the carriage sped along, Royall slid from one

side of the leather seat to the other as she listened to Jamie laugh with glee. If she arrived at the Reino in one piece, she would be lucky. The only thing that saved her sanity was the fact that she knew Jamie would tire soon and start to whine and whimper at his disobedience to his father.

She was proved right a short while later. The carriage slowed and almost came to a halt, with Jamie wiping at his brow. "Tell me what you're going to play for me on the spinet, Royall."

"Whatever you want, Jamie. You just tell me what you want to hear and I'll play it."

"For as long as I want. That's what you said. You promised."

"Yes, I did, and I'll keep my promise," Royall replied wearily.

"Why are we going back to the plantation? Why didn't you want father to come in the carriage with us? He's very angry with both of us, I could tell."

"It might interest you to know, Jamie, that I, too, am angry, and I'm angry with your father. Didn't you hear what went on back at the house? How can you just sit there and worry about your father's anger when people will die. Have died," she corrected herself.

"Who dies, who is going to die?" Jamie asked petulantly.

"The people at the Reino. The Indians and the blacks. Don't you care? Aren't you the least bit concerned? Oh, Jamie, I didn't realize you were so much like your father. Good God, they're human beings! An epidemic could wipe out the plantation and spread to others."

"Who cares?" He didn't like this conversation. Royall seemed to be angry with him. If she was angry she might act like his father—make promises and then break them. "We'll get more if they die."

"Damn you, Jamie, stop talking like an idiot." What was the use? He didn't or couldn't comprehend what she was telling him.

"Did I tell you that Father ordered two new soldiers for me? I can't wait for them to arrive. Everyone said how handsome I looked at the masquerade ball in my uniform. Father said I outshone Sebastian Rivera, and he was quite the most handsome man at the gathering this evening. What do you think, Royall?"

"Yes, you did look handsome. Jamie, do you like Sebastian?"

"Yes. He's not mean. He's . . ." He sought for the proper word. "He's fair. Elena said he was fair."

"Elena said that?" Royall questioned in surprise.

"Elena likes Sebastian. Everyone likes Sebastian but my father. Elena says he's jealous."

Eventually the trip ended. Royall climbed from the carriage with stiff muscles crying out in pain. She had to find Elena and find out what was going on. She was nowhere to be found. The beautiful Casa looked as though no one lived in it. Everywhere she looked, mildew and dust were growing rampant. The large kitchen that was Elena's domain revealed no sign of life. A bowl of rotting fruit covered with flies rested on a stout wooden table. Royall suppressed a shudder. How ominous everything appeared. A loaf of bread with a huge knife buried in the middle lay next to the decayed fruit. It, too, was covered with the blue yellow mold.

It was serious. Until now she only imagined what it was like. Royall knew in her gut that never in all of the years that Elena was housekeeper in this house would she ever permit fruit to rot.

Royall called the housekeeper, her voice rising to a shrill crescendo. When there was no answer, fear rushed through her, making her weak in the knees. "Rosy, Bridget, Moriah," she continued to shrill. Again, there was no response.

Taking a deep breath, Royall turned to stare at Jamie. He would be of no help at all. Quickly, she gathered her skirts in her hands and raced for the stables. She didn't even bother to saddle the gray horse.

Riding the large gray, Royall began to feel the strain as the heat beat down on her. Perspiration ran down her body, and exertion caused her to gasp for breath. It was difficult to remain seated on the gray's slippery back. She held onto his mane for dear life. Royall looked around as the gray stopped. How uncanny that he knew just where to bring her. Worms of fear crawled around her stomach and up her back.

Her worst fears were realized when she looked

around the clearing that housed the blacks and Indians. Everywhere she looked there were pallets on the ground. Men and women and children moaned in agony. To her left, her eyes fought for and found the small burial ground she had noticed from her last visit. The mounds had multiplied alarmingly.

She shaded her eyes from the hot sun and tried to count. There appeared to be twenty-seven. She blinked in disbelief. To the right of the burial grounds was a mound of something with a piece of canvas over it. Royall looked at Elena, who was bent over a pallet, a cloth in her hand. Seeing the look on Royall's face, Elena nodded. "There's no one to bury them. There's no one to dig the graves. I can't do it," she said wearily. "I tried."

"How many of them are left?" Royall demanded.

Elena shrugged. "We lost as many as fifty, and those," she said, pointing a finger to the far corner of the clearing, "can never make it. They're in the last stages. There's nothing to be done for them except to give them a little water from time to time, and keep a cool cloth on their heads. These," she said pointing to several huts behind her, "are the ones who just came down with the fever a few days ago. I'm doing the best I can, Senora, but I must have some help or all of them will die."

Royall shook her head. "There's just myself and Jamie, Elena."

Elena merely nodded wearily.

"I'll help you, Elena," Royall said quietly. "If you tell me what to do, I'll be glad to do my share."

Elena looked at the American girl with the quiet golden eyes, saw the elaborately coiled blond hair, the gleaming aquamarine gown, the long slender hands with the tapered fingers and the unblemished skin. Again, she nodded wearily as she let her eyes fall to her own dirty, tattered clothing and the red, dry, cracked skin of her own hands. "Come," she said to Royall, "you can help with the children. I think there's hope for some of them."

"Is it Bridget and Rosy?" Royall asked fearfully.

Elena nodded. "Rosy I'm sure will get well. Bridget is holding her own at the moment." She led Royall into the stifling hut. Looking down into the dimness, she saw the two small figures on the straw pallets. Their eyes were bright with fever and their cheeks flushed, their lips red and cracked. Royall gathered up the train of her gown and tucked it under the gold girdle and knelt beside the two little girls. Gently, she touched their cheeks. Neither child responded.

"It's time to give them a little water, and they should be wiped down. Can you do it?"

Royall agreed and bent to the task. Elena herself rose from her knees and looked with unseeing eyes, hoping that Senora Banner was wrong and the Baron would materialize. Somehow she had thought he would return to help. Her shoulders slumped, and Royall, looking up from the children, spoke.

"Even if he was here, he would be useless. He wouldn't know the first thing to do for these people. And he'd only be in the way. I'll help you, and I feel sure that Mrs. Quince will arrive here in a few days to help us. That is, providing that there's no fever on her own plantation. I'll do all I can, Elena."

Royall was as good as her word. For four days and four nights she worked side by side with Elena as they dug fresh graves and lowered the bodies into their final resting places. Her hands were blistered and raw and bleeding. She had long since shed the satin dancing slippers she had worn. Now she walked barefoot. Her feet were cut and bleeding from the rocks and hard, baked ground. Her golden hair was tied back from her face with stout piece of cord. She resembled a bedraggled street urchin, her eyes huge dark circles in her white face.

On the morning of the fifth day, she was standing by the open fire making a weak broth when Rosalie Quince rode into the clearing. "Lord a mercy!" came the raucous shout. "Is that you, child? Yes, I can see that it is." Quickly, she dismounted and wrapped her arms around the weary Royall.

"It's a losing battle, Mrs. Quince," Royall said, waving her hand around the clearing.

"I'm here to help," Mrs. Quince said briskly.

"Remove the broth and come over here and tell me how the situation stands."

Royall sighed deeply and quickly explained. Mrs. Quince nodded mutely. "I stopped by the Casa Grande, and the Baron was noticeably absent. Jamie was stomping the floor in some kind of a temper tantrum. Do you have any strength left, child?"

Royall nodded. "I'm strong as an ox, Mrs. Quince. I can do whatever is needed. Just tell me what you want me to do."

"Now this is what we are to do. First, we must burn everything. We'll set fire to the lowlands and the marshes. I've brought along some men from my plantation. They'll set up smudge pots. They've brought their drums with them. It's the fetid air that causes the fever. It just lays there all about us, calm and still." Rosalie Quince's face froze into deep, hard lines. Her eyes took on a faraway look, and she seemed to be steeling herself to pit her strength against an ancient enemy—the yellow jack. There were graves here in the damp soil of Brazil which Rosalie had dug herself. There was a baby, dead of yellow jack, whose small bones had fed the stinking roots of some strange tree.

Rosalie Quince visibly shook herself and brought her thoughts back to the present.

"Before we do anything else we must do something about separating the sick. How many of them are vomiting blood? They're the ones beyond saving."

Royall spoke quietly. "More than a dozen, Mrs. Quince."

Within a matter of hours Royall and Elena had the sick separated to Mrs. Quince's satisfaction. All the patients were carried to the back of the clearing. Mrs. Quince herself was hacking at the stout vines and dragging them into the jungles. "We have to have enough cleared area for them when we start the fires."

Royall settled the children and tried to spoon some of the broth into Bridget. It ran down her chin and caused her to choke. Immediately, she started to vomit. Royall looked in horrified disbelief at the child. "God in heaven, not this child too. She's so small she hasn't lived yet. There must be something I can do."

Agonized, she called Mrs. Quince. The old lady took in the scene and shook her head. "I know, child. The fever does not discriminate."

"There must be something, Mrs. Quince. Something. Anything, I'll do anything," she pleaded tearfully. "I can't believe God would allow this to happen to a helpless child," she cried bitterly. "Surely, Mrs. Quince, in all of your years in the jungle, there must be something you know that could be of help."

"Child, if there was, don't you think Elena would know? Some of these are her people, you know."

Royall nodded, wiping her eyes.

"Come, child, we have work to do. We can't help little Bridget now, and perhaps we can save some of the others. I know that it's hard, but you'll find in time you'll be able to accept this."

Royall shouted vehemently, "Never!"

The two women worked side by side the remainder of the day. The heat from the roaring fires exhausted Royall and caused her to stumble and fall time after time. She was soot-blackened from head to toe. By nightfall the huts and the clothing had been burned to cinders. The marshes were still smoldering. By the light of the fire in the middle of the clearing, Royall and Mrs. Quince brushed the cinders and the rubble into a pile at the far end of the clearing.

Royall swayed on her feet.

"Come, child. We must have something to eat. We have worked long and hard. Tomorrow is another hard day of work. We both need rest and food."

"Mrs. Quince, why haven't any of the other owners offered to help?"

"They, too, have their problems. The rubber shipment has to be gotten out. Have you forgotten? They're not callous, child; they have their own sick to take care of. I came here because of you. We have but two cases on our plantation, and they're on the mend. Alonzo can see to them. The Baron has been warned time and again that the conditions under which these people are expected to live make this place a breeding center for disease. The Indians themselves are a clean people, given a chance. But they work sixteen hours a day in the rubber groves. They come here

312

to eat and sleep. The food is insufficient to keep a body going. There's no energy left in them to care about their surroundings. It's time to have some of that broth you made earlier in the day."

"First, I have to see Bridget. I'll eat later, Mrs. Quince."

The good lady merely nodded and sat down by the fire. She knew that Royall had to see to the child. She watched the tattered, golden girl wash her face and hands and walk into the hut. Royall remained inside for quite some time. Mrs. Quince looked thoughtfully around the clearing at their hard day's work and knew that the next day the work would be even harder. She knew there would be many graves to be dug. She prayed for the strength to endure and also for the slim girl who would have to work at her side. Elena possibly could help, but someone had to stay with the sick and the children. No, she and the girl would have to do it alone. She contemplated the future of the Reino with a sour feeling. How it could survive after this holocaust was beyond her tired brain. Truly, she was getting old. Every bone in her aging body ached. She was so tired. She reached for her pallet and drew it closer to the fire. She thought to rest only a moment till Royall returned.

She closed her eyes and knew no more till she woke in the morning, hearing soft sobs. She looked around the stark clearing and saw Royall carrying the small child in her arms, the tears flowing down her cheeks.

313

"I did everything I could, Mrs. Quince. Truly I did."

"I know you did, child. You know what has to be done now."

"I'll do it. I have to do it."

Royall stopped to wrap heavy green leaves around her blistered hands. Dejection was replaced by white-hot anger as the small hole began to grow larger. The dirt flew from the shovel. Mrs. Quince, spurred by the anger of her young friend, shoveled just as diligently. They lowered the small, still form into the ground. The dirt was replaced. The soft thunk of the earth on the unmoving bundle melted the tears, frozen till now within her, causing them to bubble to the surface. Rosalie Quince felt fury stir her as it had her young friend. "There must be an answer," she pleaded, looking heavenward. "There has to be an answer."

"Mrs. Quince, who is to tell the child's parents? They're on Sebastian Rivera's plantation."

"I'll do it, child. But not now. We can't leave here, as you well know. There's not a plantation in all of Brazil that would make either of us welcome at this moment."

The grim task completed, both women walked slowly back to the clearing. "I long for a bath and clean clothes," Royall said softly.

"Have you no other clothes with you, child? Can't Elena go to the Casa and fetch you clean garments?"

"I thought of that, but Jamie will not allow

either of us to go near the Casa, and he himself won't venture out of the door even to leave us something at the edge of the lawns. I fear he thinks he will be contaminated."

"Sometimes Jamie is just like his father," Rosalie Quince snorted. "How many times I've heard the other plantation owners ask the Baron and plead with him to clean up this place, especially Sebastian. This is what it has come to: all this suffering and wastefulness, all these lives lost for the selfishness of one man. I don't understand why Carl has never spoken up and at least tried to do something." She sighed at the hopelessness of the situation.

"That dress you have on reminds me suspiciously of the elegant gown you wore to your party. Is it?"

"I'm afraid so, Mrs. Quince. I think we should both eat some fruit, and then we can get on with our work. I looked in on Elena before and she was asleep. I didn't have the heart to wake her. She's just as tired as we are. I checked everyone in the early hours. I fear we'll lose three more before the day is over. There are six on the mend, and I do think Elena was right—Rosy looks as though she may pull through this too. There is one old man who is now up and around. He has been helping Elena in a small way. But he has little strength and must rest frequently."

Once again Royall checked her sick patients and joined Mrs. Quince for some fresh mangoes. She sucked the juice from the rich, tart fruit but, in truth, had not the energy to chew the meat. Neither did Mrs. Quince, it appeared.

The two women trudged wearily to the lowlands and immediately started their small fires. Royall watched as myriads of mosquitoes swirled in the air. As they slapped the voracious insects away, the smoke billowed and swirled and seemed to devour the thick swarms of pests.

"The fire won't spread, and if it should, where would it go? Only into the jungle." Royall stumbled over a low-slung vine. Gasping for breath, she lay for a minute, stunned from her sudden fall. Mrs. Quince helped her back to the clearing, fetched a small stool for her, and helped her to rest for a moment. "Let me see your feet, child. God in heaven, what have you done to yourself?" She looked at the cuts and the welts and the deep scabs that were cracked and oozing blood. "Wait here, and don't move."

She was back in minutes, Elena in tow. She pointed to Royall's feet and the housekeeper gently inspected one. Horror danced across her face. "Why didn't you tell me of this?" she asked quietly.

"We had enough problems without my feet being added to the list." Royall smiled. "They don't hurt much now. I've been so busy I haven't had time to think of the pain. Please don't worry. I'm all right. The others need your help. How are the old lady and her daughter?"

"Both gone, this past hour."

Royall rose to her feet and grasped the handle

of the shovel. "If you and Mrs. Quince can carry the bodies, I'll do the digging. You know we can't let the bodies stay in this abysmal heat."

Royall felt each shovelful of earth would be her last. But somehow, from somewhere, she garnered the strength. She thought of all the finery that money from this plantation had bought her. At each new item on the list, she felt her strength renewed. She would shovel till it killed her, and it probably would, she thought grimly. She would pay for it all. She didn't stop to think, nor did she care that the suffering was not her doing. She only knew that she had to make up for the sins of Carlyle Newsome, and this was the only way she could do it.

When the bodies were lowered into the shallow grave, Royall rested a moment before she tackled the mound of earth. She swayed and prayed for the strength to finish the task before her. As she looked at the mound of earth in front of her, it took on gigantic proportions in her eyes. She must do something. She couldn't faint now. She grasped the handle of the shovel in her bleeding hands, and muttering under her breath, she dug the shovel into the soft, rancid-smelling earth.

This is for the costly dancing lessons, and the filigree comb, and the yellow satin ballgown that I nagged father to buy me, and for the matched set of pearls—they alone would be good for many shovelsful, she thought viciously, a pearl for a shovelful of earth. It seemed a fair settlement. How many pearls were there on the strand? For the life of her she couldn't remember. The strand was quite long . . . fifty at least. She would never wear those pearls again. Shovel, don't think; shovel, shovel, pearl, pearl, shovel, pearl. Lord, she thought, she must have shoveled fifty pearls by now. She wiped the perspiration from her face with a dirty, grimy arm. Streaks of blood from her torn and battered hands appeared on her creamy skin. She looked down at the mound of earth at her feet. It had diminished slightly. Mrs. Quince was helping her and so was Elena. Just keep shoveling, remember the pearls. If you stop, you can never atone for the pearls. Just shovel.

When the last shovelful of earth was thrown, Royall tried to straighten her cramped and stooped back. She felt a million years old. She grasped the shovel in the crook of her arm and hobbled behind Elena and Mrs. Quince. Her numbed brain and eyes watched the form of Mrs. Quince falter and stagger. She couldn't have reached out to her if her life depended on it.

Back at the clearing, Elena offered a bowl of broth to the two women. Satisfied that they would drink it, she returned to her nursing. Royall tried to hold the bowl, but couldn't make her hands obey her commands. Peering at their raw flesh with interest, she marveled at the fact that she was experiencing no pain. She grasped the bowl with her wrists, which was a feat in itself, and drank thirstily. The bowl slipped. She made no effort to retrieve it. Looking down at her tattered, bedraggled gown, she saw that it was nothing more than strips of rags. It was in shreds up to her knees. She was so weary she could barely keep her eyes open, wishing she could sink into merciful oblivion and suddenly wake to find this whole thing had been nothing more than a bad dream.

"I must do something about my hands, Mrs. Quince. What do you think?" she asked, rising from the small stool she had been resting on. The bright sun beat down on her head and she swayed, sickened by the heat. She turned at the sounds of approaching horses. She tried to shade her eyes from the sun, but the effort was too great. She stood silently till the riders came into view. Mrs. Quince at her side was equally silent.

There was a hoarse shout and what seemed like a roar from a bull elephant. Royall had the impression of a dark form standing in front of her. She tried to raise her eyes, but the strong sun beat down unmercifully.

"Sebastian! Is it you? What in the world are you doing here?" Mrs. Quince gasped.

"I saw the smoke from my plantation. I knew things must be bad over here if you had resorted to fires. Tell me, what is there for me to do?"

"Nothing, I'm afraid, Sebastian. It's too late for anything more to be done. Royall and Elena have done it all. I just arrived yesterday."

Why is she babbling like that? Royall wondered wearily. Why doesn't she just be quiet and let him see for himself?

Well, he had been right. Now all he had to do was say I told you so. She waited for the stinging words. Finally, she raised exhausted eyes and looked at the tall man before her. Tired as she was, she was again struck by his dark handsomeness. She made a vain effort to squelch the stirring of her pulses. Of all the times in the whole wide world to have him see her, he had to pick today. White-hot anger spewed from her in a torrent of emotion.

"Go back where you came from; you're after the fact, Sebastian! We've done it all; look around you. Get on your horse and go back where you belong. This is all my fault and I'll make it right if it kills me. And I don't need your help, either," she rasped as she shrugged off his arm. "Just where in the hell were you when I needed you? Back in that townhouse with that sloe-eyed beauty, that's where. Go back to her, see if I care. I don't need you; Elena doesn't need you; Mrs. Quince doesn't need you." She swayed on her feet. She couldn't faint, not here, not now! She would make it on her own or not at all.

"Far be it from me to interrupt a lady, but in my own defense, I would have come if you sent for me. You know that. You're a fool, Royall. Look at you!" Christ, what was that lump in his throat, and why couldn't he breathe normally?

Again Royall swayed, only this time she didn't have the strength to right herself. Suddenly, she was enfolded in strong arms and held close to a warm, hard body. She couldn't ever remember feeling so safe and secure in her entire life. With her last ounce of strength she forced her eyes open and gazed into the jet black pools of Sebastian Rivera's eyes. I love him, she thought. I love this man. And he loves me. Wishful thinking, Royall, she sighed as her eyes closed. She couldn't ward off the badly needed sleep and rest her body now demanded. What better place to succumb than in the arms of the man she loved.

As though in a dream, she felt herself being lifted gently. From somewhere outside her consciousness she heard muttered curses of outrage. She didn't know who was doing the angry cursing, nor did she care. All she knew was that she was safe and secure. "I'm so afraid. I have to sleep, I must rest for a while. I can't dig anymore," she whispered over and over. They paid no attention to her, these nameless voices and hands ministering to her body. What had she been dreaming about? A love, that was it. A love that knew no bounds.

Chapter Seventeen

Royall tried to open her eyes to see who was speaking to her. She succeeded in opening the golden eyes to mere slits. Sebastian Rivera gazed down at her. His smile was so gentle, she was sure she must be dreaming. It had been such a long time since she had seen him smile. Not since the riverboat.

Prior to his thunderous ride into the Reino, Sebastian had paced on the tile floor of his casa. White hot anger had gripped his chest as he watched the billowing smoke rise above the trees. It enraged him: to think that one imbecile could wreak such havoc and still expect the other plantation owners to condone it.

Sebastian had looked across at the grim face of his foreman, Jesus, and again felt a pang of pity for the man. He had lived through the fever and lost everything he held dear. To ride into it on someone else's plantation and see the death and the suffering must be causing him untold sorrow. There was no excuse for it. Neglect and filth contributed to the situation.

So far they had been lucky. There were only a few cases on the other plantations. The owners had followed his advice and cleaned up the lowlands and the marshes. They had also listened to him when he explained about the sanitary conditions. And today they weren't sorry. Many of the owners had thanked him in the past few days—all, in fact, but Carlyle Newsome. A poor excuse for a man if there ever was one. His son Carl would have long before now stood on his own feet and become a man if the Baron had not pulled the purse strings.

Sebastian winced as he recalled the day he had offered Carl a job managing his affairs in Rio. The offer had been tempting; Carl admitted that he much preferred the business life to that of working on the plantation. He had thanked Sebastian for the offer, his face lighting with joyous hope and a mixture of friendliness. He also remembered the look that replaced it so quickly. Carl could not leave the Reino, his roots, his inheritance. But if the time ever came when he could leave . . . The rest had been left unsaid, an unspoken agreement between the two men that, should conditions at the Reino become intolerable, Carl would take Sebastian up on his offer. Sebastian had understood, and reminded Carl that all he had to do was ask and the position would be his.

The jungle was so silent that Sebastian felt uneasy. Gone were the raucous cries of the birds. Not a leaf stirred. It was ominous. Great black columns of smoke whirled upward. As they rode into the clearing, Sebastian took in the scene in one swift glance.

It couldn't be. That beautiful golden angel from New England was no more. In her place he saw a filthy, tattered, soot-blackened witch. Hair once golden was now dirty and gray and hung in limp, bedraggled strands, along with part of a dried vine over one bare, grimy shoulder. Rage boiled up in him once more as he watched the dirty creature raise a torn, bloody hand to shade her eyes. A sound roared from him as he leaped from his mount to catch her as she swayed. He held her soft, pliant form and felt a wave of pity engulf him. The equally grimy Rosalie Quince took matters into her own efficient hands and immediately gave him a brief description of the past days and of the accomplishments of Royall and Elena.

Sebastian looked at the soft face of the girl he held in his arms. As he inspected her bleeding hands and cut, oozing feet, Sebastian swore viciously. Quickly he issued a terse command to Jesus, and the man rode from the clearing as if the demons of hell were at his heels. Within an hour Sebastian's own housekeeper and several strong Indians appeared. Sebastian, holding Royall in his arms, issued commands like a general. All listened quietly, then sped to obey him. Royall was lowered gently into a wagon. Rosalie Quince and Elena wearily climbed in with the help of Jesus. Sebastian himself took the reins and started for his plantation. He would kill someone, he was sure of it. His mind and body held such an alien feeling that he couldn't put a name to it. He remembered his mother telling him once that when one fell in love there was no other feeling in the world like it. Sebastian would have staked his life on the fact that he had experienced every emotion there was. If so, what was this crawling, creeping feeling that threatened to engulf him? He wanted to kill, to make love, to fill his belly, but he could do none of these things. All he could do was drive the damn wagon and let his mind have its way. Helpless, that's what he was. In his entire life he had never been rendered helpless. His agile mind flitted like a bird as he risked glances behind him at the girl on the wagon floor. Again he thought of his mother and her wise sayings. He tried to force the thoughts from his mind, not wanting to think of love and its ties and bindings. He didn't want to give his soul to anyone. He wanted to own himself. What was it his mother had said? To love is to consume the other, or words to that effect. He cursed under his breath and began to drive the wagon even harder over the rutted ground, but the moans from the golden girl as she rolled from side to side made him slow down.

The moment he reined in the horses, women came. Sebastian was pushed gently out of the way while Royall was carried inside and the doors were closed to him.

"Go, Sebastian. You'll just be in the way," Rosalie Quince shrilled. "This is women's work. Go smoke a cheroot or something."

"A cheroot," Sebastian said stupidly.

"Good Lord, Sebastian. Must I tell you again, or should I draw you a picture?" she shouted briskly. "If we should find ourselves in need of your presence, we'll call you. You have my word."

Sebastian nodded briskly as he obeyed the sharp-tongued Mrs. Quince. He felt like a small boy again at his mother's knee.

The endless days crawled by on tortoise legs and slowly became weeks as Royall lay in a fever, delirious. Sebastian felt both mentally and physically exhausted. He had walked innumerable miles, pacing the wide veranda. His throat felt white-hot from the countless cheroots he had smoked during his frantic pacing. From time to time his eyes smarted—no doubt from the thick cigar smoke, he told himself. Food, he found to his disgust, would not go down past the lump in his throat.

He flung himself wearily onto one of the rattan chairs and absently stroked the silky ears of the dog that lay at his feet. His touch was gentle and soft. The animal whined in pleasure. Suddenly, Sebastian's gentle caresses ceased as he looked up and saw Rosalie Quince towering over him. In his haste to get to his feet his movements were clumsy and he stepped on the dog's paw, eliciting a yelp of pain. Rosalie Quince found it hard not to smile at this awkwardness. She had never seen the debonair Sebastian anything but graceful and completely at ease.

"The child is out of the woods, Sebastian. The fever has finally broken. I tell you now that if she had contracted yellow jack, she would no longer be with us. How she escaped it is beyond me. The poor thing was just worn out. She's on the mend, Sebastian, so you may go about your business." Shrewdly, she watched the tall, tired man fling the cheroot over the railing.

"That is good news, Mrs. Quince." Jet black eyes looked questioningly at the old woman, but no words were spoken. Mrs. Quince also remained silent. Their eyes locked in a stare. Would he ask to see the girl, she wondered, or would he be a stubborn mule and remain silent.

Should I ask to see her, Sebastian wondered. No, she was out of danger, and he'd been absent from his many duties on the plantation for too long. Sensing Mrs. Quince's thoughts, he smiled crookedly and strode from the veranda. Tonight he would leave for town; he would return by mid-morning of the following day. One couldn't fool oneself for long. And if there was one thing he prided himself on, it was not being a fool. He contemplated the tearful Aloni when he would tell her, as gently as possible, that their relationship must come to an end. He would soften the blow with a generous settlement. He wouldn't fool himself. Aloni, he knew, was more interested in the comforts he could afford to give her than she was in Sebastian.

Royall's recovery was rapid, with Mrs. Quince spoon-feeding her till she regained her strength. Within ten days she was up and about and feeling stronger by the day. She had not seen Sebastian once since her fever broke, and did not ask for him. She accepted the hospitality he extended and wished only to thank him. Something always prevented her from asking for him. Mrs. Quince herself was careful not to mention his name. Royall thought she would go mad wondering why.

It was the eve of her departure for the Reino; Sebastian's foreman, Jesus, was to drive her in the wagon and then go on, taking Mrs. Quince home.

Royall dressed carefully for dinner in the hopes that Sebastian would arrive, taking extra pains with her toilet. She still looked pale, but she felt she could pass muster if one didn't look too closely. Rosalie Quince watched her in amusement as she self-consciously patted her own springy gray curls.

As the dinner hour approached and there was no sign of Sebastian, Royall felt almost sick. Not to show up for dinner! He was making a fool of her. He was going to ignore her last evening in his house, and his absence would be all the proof she needed that he didn't care, that he was still holding her personally responsible for the conditions on the Reino. It was also painfully evident that he had been spending all of his free time in the arms of his black-eyed beauty in town.

"It appears we dine alone again, Mrs. Quince," Royall forced herself to smile brightly. She didn't want Rosalie to know how deeply hurt she was by Sebastian's action. "I'm positively ravenous. I'm looking forward to returning home to the Reino tomorrow morning. I can hardly wait to leave. I want to see how everyone is. Especially Elena, the poor woman must have been exhausted from tending the sick." On and on she rambled.

The usually articulate Mrs. Quince found she couldn't get a word in edgewise.

She merely nodded from time to time at the brightly chattering girl, but she didn't miss the fact that the supposedly ravenous Royall only pushed at the food on her plate. If she ate two bites, Mrs. Quince would have been surprised. The meal over, Royall suddenly felt deflated. As she pushed back her chair, she heard footsteps approach the dining room. A warm flush stole up her neck and stained her face. So! He arrives now!

328

Well, let him arrive now. I'm leaving! Royall looked up and felt her pulses begin to pound at the mere sight of the tall, dark man in front of her.

Royall took the initiative. She spoke first. "Good evening, Senor Rivera. I'm happy to see you this evening. I did want to thank you personally for the hospitality you've shown me during my illness. I'll always be grateful," she said, her tone cool, formal. She tilted her head in a brief nod and walked gracefully from the room.

Back in the small room that had been hers for the stay, she collapsed on the bed and let her tears flow freely. You will not, Sebastian Rivera, make a fool of me. It shall be the other way around. How dare he show up after dinner and behave as though she were some stranger who had just dropped in! It was a small wonder he didn't offer me one of those odious cheroots he smokes. She had never been so insulted in her life. Insulted and wounded to her very soul.

And Mrs. Quince, silent for the second time in her life, had stood by silently, like a wart on a frog. Suddenly, Royall laughed at the thought. There was poor Mrs. Quince with a large wart on the end of her nose, gracefully smoking one of the foul cheroots. And Sebastian, what was he doing? Why, he was just standing with his mouth hanging open and looking like a horse's ass. Royall broke into fresh laughter, doubling over on the bed.

As Mrs. Quince and Sebastian walked down the corridor, they heard the happy laughter. They

329

looked silently at each other, each busy with his own thoughts.

"Sebastian, I have only one thing to say to you. You're a fool," she said sourly.

Sebastian raised startled eyes and frowned at Mrs. Quince's sharp words.

"Spare me from foolish men in love. You're all jackasses," the good lady snarled.

"Who's in love?" Sebastian barked.

"Who? Who? You ask me who? Get on with you! If I have to tell you that, then there's no hope for the likes of you. Go! I don't want to see you again for now. I can't abide a fool, in either long or short pants."

"What have short pants to do with it?" Sebastian snapped.

"When you were a small boy in short pants, that was time enough for acting the fool. Now that you wear long pants you should behave like a man!" Turning sharply on her heel, Rosalie stepped into the bedroom and slammed the door shut.

As Sebastian stood there, a look of astonishment on his face, he looked down at his legs and wouldn't have been surprised to find them naked.

Sebastian made his nightly rounds of the house before retiring, as was his custom. He was pouring himself a last glass of brandy when he noticed a shadow in the lamplight. He waited, the glass halfway to his lips.

"Sebastian, it's me, Carl. I'm sorry to be visiting you so late, but I need to talk to someone. I just returned today. The plantation . . . My God, what happened? Have you seen my father? Sebastian, have you seen or heard from Alicia? I'm almost out of my mind. What has been going on in my absence?"

His mind raced. What was Carl Newsome doing here at this hour? His first instinct was to toss him out on his ear, but he knew he couldn't do that, for Alicia's sake. He had sworn to Alicia that he would do whatever he could for Carl, and he wouldn't go back on his word. If Alicia loved him, then there had to be good in Carl somewhere. You never kicked a dog when it was down, and Sebastian couldn't ever remember seeing a more wounded, tortured man than Carl.

Sebastian walked over to the bar in the corner of the room. He poured a generous amount of brandy into a glass and held it out. "Drink this. I have much to tell you. Sit down, relax, you can't go anywhere or do anything at this hour." Quickly, he briefed Carl on conditions at the Reino. He ended his tale with Royall's illness and her complete recovery.

"I'm glad that she's well, but I can't comprehend what you've just told me concerning my father. Are you telling me, Sebastian, that he stayed in Manaus and left Royall and Elena to fend for themselves?"

"That's exactly what I'm telling you. Now, I want you to tell me what you're going to do," he said harshly.

"Give me time to get my thoughts together,

Sebastian. I'm sorry that things have gone so sour for Reino. You were right, as usual. At the time I knew you were right, but the Baron is my father. I had to obey him or be cast out. The Reino is the only home I've ever known. Tell me about Alicia; have you seen or heard from her? She promised to write me in Belém but there wasn't one letter. Tell me, don't spare me, is she ill, has something happened to her? Please, Sebastian, I'm begging you."

"Alicia is fine. She came to me a short while ago and is now staying at my townhouse. You can go to her in the morning. She's fine, Carl, believe me. Someone told her you planned to marry Senora Banner, and she believed him. She allowed herself to become . . . ill . . . but she's fully recovered now and is waiting for you. Carl, don't make the same mistake again, for if you do, Alicia might not be so forgiving. You do recall that talk you and I had not too long ago. Where I offered you the job of managing my affairs in Rio. It would be perfect for you and Alicia. You like the city life, and so does Alicia. You can put the plantation behind you and make a new life for yourself and your wife. I'll help you in any way I can."

Carl was stunned. It was true, it would be a new life for him and Alicia. Thanks to Sebastian. He could do it; he had wanted to do it when they spoke weeks ago, but he'd been a coward. No more. Not after what he had just heard. Alicia was safe and sound, Sebastian had seen to it. The way he always saw to everything. "Sebastian, are we half brothers?"

Sebastian drew in his breath. "I don't know, Carl. Somehow, I don't think so. My mother wouldn't . . . I just don't know, Carl. Is it important for you to know?"

"Only for my own sake. I wish it were true. I know how you feel about my father, but speaking for myself, I wish you were my brother."

Sebastian's voice when he spoke was gruff, almost harsh. "I have no answer for you, Carl. Tell me, will you see your father before you leave?"

"Yes. I'll face him like the man I want to be. No more hiding. He won't like it, I know; but I won't run away like a naughty child.

"He has Jamie. He never understood me or my needs and wants. I owe him nothing. Not a thing. I know he was the one who told Alicia I was going to marry Royall. It wasn't definite; I never gave my word, and besides, he refused to believe that Royall would have a say in who she marries. You'll have to stop him, Sebastian, for when he finds out I've gone off with Alicia, he'll force Royall into a marriage that can't ever be allowed to take place. You know as well as I do that he can be quite cruel when his plans are thwarted. You'll have to handle it. Don't let Royall marry him. She loves you!"

Sebastian's heart leaped, but he said nothing. Carl was overwrought. Royall didn't love him, couldn't love him. Or could she? He grimaced when he remembered the way she had sailed out of the dining room hours ago. How could she know that it was impossible for him to sit across from her at dinner and not let her see what was in his eyes? Better to stay away and let her think he was an ill-mannered clod. Goddamn it, why did he always have all the worries of the world on his shoulders? Women were always at the root of all his problems.

"More brandy?"

"Not for me, thanks. Do you think you could bed me down for the night? I'll need a fresh horse in the morning." Sebastian nodded. They shook hands, Carl going toward a room at the end of the hall and Sebastian to his room only a door away from Royall's quarters.

Sometimes it paid to be magnanimous, like now. There were more ways than one to skin a cat. With him helping Carl and Alicia, the Baron would lose his first layer of fur. You could only hold hatred in your heart for so long before it ate away at you, making you diseased and corrupt. He had no intention of letting that happen to him. The day the Baron got his due would be Sebastian's first day of freedom.

Sebastian stood in the hall, his eyes narrowed to slits. It was his house. She was in a room in his house. He could open the door if he pleased. In fact, he could kick it down and not have to answer to anyone. Instead of thinking about it, I should do it, he muttered to himself. Why not? Who did he have to answer to, save himself. No one. On the other hand, he could knock discreetly, say

334

something inane, like he wished her a safe trip back to the Reino. But she would know it for the lie it was. Brute force. He would knock down the door and crush her in his arms. While she squirmed and fought, he would smother her with kisses and make love to her like he had done that night in Rio. He wanted to knock on the door so badly his hand itched. Some alien thing hammered in his chest, demanding release. That time in the kitchen in Manaus. His pulses pounded. Christ, what was he doing to himself? The girl had been ill. Though she didn't look ill when she sailed out of the dining room, after coolly dismissing him from her presence. Damn it to hell, she had really dismissed him as though he were some errant schoolboy, in his own house. Gall! She had more than any three women, ten women, a dozen, he told himself as he brought up his hand to knock on the door. She was a bitch too, always speaking her mind and making him a fool. After she left his house he might never see her again. What if she decided to go back to America, and then where would he be? Should he knock or kick the door down? Damnation, where in the hell was Rosalie Quince sleeping? For the life of him he couldn't remember. He shrugged. There were no locks on the doors in his house. All he had to do was open the door and walk in. Take her in his arms and do what he had been wanting to do for weeks. Make love to her till she cried in agony. He snorted. Senora Royall Banner with two L's never gave quarter in the bedroom. She gave as good as she got and was still as frisky as a kitten when he lay exhausted. Agony, my ass, he cursed as he opened the door. If she let out one peel, he'd gag her. This was his house and he could damn well do as he pleased!

Quietly, he closed the door. He listened for a moment, hardly daring to breathe. She was asleep, he could tell by the deep, even breathing beneath the light coverlet. Slowly, he advanced to the edge of the bed. She was the most beautiful woman he had ever seen. How he wanted her, needed her. But not this way, not by force. He turned to leave as quietly as he had come.

"You're late. I expected you an hour ago." A deep gurgle of laughter played around the quiet room.

"Bitch!" Sebastian laughed in delight.

"Bastard! I thought you would never get here," Royall said tossing back the coverlet. "Come here, I want to feel you next to me."

Chapter Eighteen

Shortly before dawn Carl woke. It couldn't end like this. If he was going to start a new life, then he would start it off right. A visit and a talk with his father to explain things. Time enough for the beginning of a new life after that.

Quietly, he stole down the steps, sprinted down the long dim corridor that would take him to the kitchens and from there outdoors to the courtyard and the stables. Sebastian had said he could have the pick of any horse in the stable. The sorrel looked fleet of foot. Within minutes he had her saddled. A fast, hard ride in the early dawn would remedy his pent-up emotions. Soon he would see Alicia, feel her in his arms. She would be surprised at his news, but he knew that she would welcome the chance to leave Manaus and Reino Brazilia behind. Christ, he was lucky, more lucky than any one man deserved. Thanks to Sebastian. Sebastian was a man to be counted on when the chips were down. One way or another, he always came through on top.

The sorrel sprinted over the ground as though she knew exactly where she was going and why. Once Carl dismounted and allowed the animal to drink thirstily from a stream. Another hour and he would be in Manaus. Another hour and he would be face to face with his father—and after that, the first day of his new life. He could do it, Sebastian had faith in him. Alicia would stand beside him no matter what. With two people in his corner who believed in him, how could he go wrong? It was time to stand up and act like the man he was. The man Sebastian and Alicia believed him to be. He could do it. He *would* do it.

It was early, Carl thought as he walked through the cool townhouse. Father must still be sleeping, he mused as he climbed the circular staircase leading to the bedroom. He, Carl, was in fine fettle, prepared to do and say whatever was necessary to start his new life.

Carl stood a moment next to the bed. There was nothing vulnerable about the Baron. His features were chiseled, sharp, canny, even in sleep. "Father, I would like to speak with you," Carl said loudly.

"Carl! What brings you here at this ungodly hour? Did you finish all of our business in Belém? I thought I told you to stay there till I sent for you."

"Yes, father, it is I, Carl. This ungodly hour, as you call it, is now mid-morning. The business in Benlém is finished. You lied to me, tricked me, the office manager could have done what you sent me to do. And as for my staying there till you sent for me—No. No more. I'm through being the puppet you dangle from a string. I've been to the Reino, and I want you to know that as a man, as a human being, I can never forgive you for what you've done. I spent the night at Regalo Verdad because I couldn't stand to stay in your house for even one more night. I'm leaving here. I'm leaving you, father. I'm going to marry Alicia as I told you. Sebastian offered me a position managing his affairs in Rio, and I've accepted. I just came to say good-bye." He did it, it was over now. Now he was free. Free to go to Alicia.

The Baron stared at his son as though he suddenly sprouted an extra head. All he heard was Alicia's name. An inferno of rage shot through him. "You fool," he shouted. "I say you are not going to marry that . . . slut. Haven't you heard the rumors that have been going around town? Never! I forbid it! Do you hear me?"

"Shut up! I won't hear it," Carl shouted in return. God, what was his father saying? He was lying! "Damn you, father, you can't get to me any more. You listen to me. One more word against Alicia, and you're dead to me." Angrily, he turned on his heel to leave.

"You're dismissed when I say you are and not before. You think I'm lying, well, you come with me, you young fool, and I'll prove to you what I'm saying. Your darling, pure Alicia was my mistress all the while you were in Belém. She lived here in this very house. When she found she couldn't have you, she turned to me. For a price she did whatever I wanted, and sometimes she did a little extra, if you know what I mean. She's an accomplished bedroom artisan. I was led to believe there were others in my absence. However, that's neither here nor there. She also tips the bottle quite heavily. At times she was so sotted, she made my stomach turn over. You still don't believe me. I'm going to take you down to the kitchens so you can ask the housekeeper what the name of the young slut was who stayed here in your absence."

Naked horror disfigured Carl's face. It couldn't be true. Yet, his father sounded so . . . he was lying! Alicia would never . . . not with his father . . . there had to be a reason if what he said was true. "I wouldn't believe you if God Almighty Himself was standing behind your shoulder," Carl spat. "As far as I'm concerned, I won't degrade myself or Alicia by talking to anyone. From this moment on, you're dead to me. I no longer have a father."

Trembling with anger,Carl stalked from the room. Once outside, the heat almost choked the life from his body. He needed a drink, time to get his thoughts in order. He had to get control of himself before he saw Alicia.

In a small sidewalk cafe he ordered a double brandy and a cup of strong black coffee. He sat for over an hour, his mind racing. He was his own man now, and it was time to pull up his straps and act accordingly. Even if what the Baron said was true, there was nothing he could do about it. There was no point in blaming anyone except possibly himself. Sebastian would have warned him, helped him if he thought there was something he couldn't handle. Alicia had gone to Sebastian. Sebastian had helped her, that was all he needed to know. His love for her hadn't changed. It was just as good, just as pure as it was the day he went on his fool's errand to Belém on his father's business.

In the end, with the brandy glass empty and one swallow of coffee left in the cup, Carl made his decision. He loved Alicia, had always loved her, and would love her till the day he died. They shared a love that was pure in heart. Whatever did or didn't happen wasn't important. His decision made, he felt almost light-headed with relief. All he wanted was to be with Alicia, to feel her warmth and softness in his arms. Alicia was all that mattered. And if the day ever came when the Baron's words creeped into his brain, he would drive them out by thinking of their love.

Alicia herself opened the door, thinking it was Sebastian with news of Carl. She swooned at the sight of Carl's beloved face. "Carl, I thought I would never see you again. Come in, come in." Please, please let him say the right words, Alicia prayed silently.

"I'm sorry I've been away so long, Alicia, but I'm back now and I have wonderful news. Let me look at you." His voice was husky, almost choked with emotion as he stared deeply into her eyes. He read love and compassion and a deep, hungering yearning in her steady gaze. He gathered her tenderly in his arms.

"Carl, I've missed you so. I thought you were never coming back. I didn't know what to do; I thought you had really stopped caring for me and were going to marry Mrs. Banner."

Carl stroked the soft head cradled against his chest. "Never!" he said vehemently. "It's you I love. Duty, Alicia, and my father clouded my thinking for a while, but I'm free of that now. I told you I had wonderful news and I want to share it with you. Listen to me carefully: Sebastian Rivera has offered me a job managing his affairs in Rio. I've accepted. I've just been to see my father and told him. He didn't like it, but there isn't too much he can do about it. I know that you're the only important thing in my life. You're the only one who matters. Say you'll marry me and come with me to Rio. We'll start a new life, just you and me together."

Alicia's heart fluttered madly. Carl had just been to see the Baron! Surely, he didn't . . . he wouldn't . . . not to his own son. Carl wouldn't be standing here asking her to marry him if the Baron had told him. She was safe; she didn't have to confess. Royall Banner was right; she couldn't burden Carl with her ugly secret. Not for anything in the world would she say or do anything to wipe away the happiness on Carl's face. Both of them would survive with their love; it was strong and pure. With Carl's love she would soon forget the ugly memories.

Somehow, some way, she would find a way in the years to come to thank Sebastian and Royall for giving her back her love, her life!

The days crawled by for Royall. She admitted she was bored and a little afraid of what the coming days might bring. Jamie seemed to be avoiding her, and that was odd. Since her return from the Rivera plantation he hadn't once asked her to play the spinet. Elena was still cool and polite, going about her duties, but there was a noticeable lack of spring to her step, and from time to time Royall was sure she saw her shoulders slump. Carl's absence was barely noticeable, since he was always out on the plantation doing something or other to keep busy. But that wasn't what really bothered her. It was Sebastian and the way he was ignoring her. If it hadn't been for Rosalie Quince stopping by on her way home from a neighboring plantation, she wouldn't have known if Sebastian was alive or dead. Very much alive, and in a continual black rage, according to the loquacious lady. As if she really cared what he did or didn't do. One minute he acted as though he loved her, and the next he could pretend she didn't exist.

What I should really do is pack up and go back to New England, she told herself morosely. At least people back home were predictable. The Baron could have this stinking, rotting plantation and all that went with it. So far, it had been nothing but a source of grief. But if what Mrs. Quince said was true, she couldn't do that either. The garrulous lady had said there was a rumor buzzing around Manaus that the Baron was in a constant drunken state and making a fool of himself. And she had said, her eyebrows raised heavenward, that he'd been unshaven and slovenly for the good Lord only knew how long. Then she had blessed herself repeatedly at the actions of the Baron and the awful rumors.

Why hadn't Sebastian made some comment, come to see her after that last wonderful evening they had shared? Was it just an affair to him? Was it possible that she really didn't mean anything to him? If that was true, how could she possibly stay here and be available at his whim. She couldn't, she decided firmly. Next week she would visit Victor Morrison and make arrangements to go back to New England. Her decision didn't make her feel any better; in fact, she felt worse. Damn, she wasn't going to cry. Sebastian Rivera was the last man on earth she would cry for. When something was over, it was over, finished, never to be resurrected again.

She should be doing something instead of sitting here like some ninny, she thought irritably. She should have forged ahead with the lessons for the little girls, but Bridget's death had dampened their spirits. They spent long hours quietly going about their chores, their lightheartedness a thing of the past. It would have been impossible to get them to concentrate on something so mundane as letters and numbers. She missed their happy laughter and wished they would play and giggle again. Time, they needed time. Someone else would have to teach them when she went back to New England. Perhaps if she spoke to Elena or to Mrs. Quince, they would help. Even Sebastian's housekeeper . . . No, that wouldn't work. The children should be returned, and she would see to it! Letters and numbers could wait. Sebastian would see to their education once they were on Regalo Verdad. Sebastian. Dear God, how shall I get through the next months without the sight of him. Perhaps she should stay. Seeing him once in a while would be better than never seeing him at all. She could grow old sitting in the wicker rocking chair on the veranda, waiting for him to ride by.

Days later—or was it weeks, Royall could no longer keep track of time—she decided to give up her seat on the cool veranda and stroll through the gardens. Anything was better than just sitting. The heat, while all-consuming, was better than taking root in the old wicker chairs. She watched the colorful birds as they flew overhead, and she listened to their shrill, raucous cries. She continued to watch as they swooped low as though in a convoy and nestled into the lush green foliage. Something bright caught her eye as she rounded the drive. It must be the children. Perhaps they had come out of their lethargy and were playing. Please let it be so, she murmured to herself. But she had heard Elena giving them their morning instructions. Right now they should be cleaning the bedrooms. Royall frowned. It wasn't like the little girls to be openly defiant. They couldn't have finished so quickly. Perhaps they too sensed Elena's lack of enthusiasm. Cautiously, she crept up behind the tall bush that shielded the vibrant color she had noticed.

She blinked; Jamie was tossing a ball and Nessie obediently catching it. Rosy stood on the side, her face solemn and watchful. Jamie was laughing and smiling. Royall's eyes narrowed. The two little girls looked . . . afraid. Suddenly, Jamie shouted angrily and grabbed Nessie by the arm. "I thought you liked to play ball. If you like to play ball, then play. You're acting just like one of my soldiers, stupid and wooden." He growled as he brought Nessie closer to him and ignored her efforts to free herself.

Royall was suddenly afraid for the little girls. She didn't like what she was seeing. Jamie was acting strangely. It wasn't her imagination; the little girls didn't like the change in his behavior either. Frightened, she stepped into the clearing. "Girls, girls, Elena has been calling you. Run along now, quickly, before Elena gets angry. Jamie, what are you doing out here taking the children away from their duties?" She watched as the children ran away. There was no conspiratorial wink in her direction. Her intuition had been right; they were frightened out of their wits. She sighed with relief as she stared at Jamie. He was angrily rubbing his fingers nervously together. Apprehensively, Royall watched him out of the corner of her eye as she started from the small clearing. Jamie trailed behind, his tantrum strangely abandoned.

"You must be feeling a lot better for you to be out walking in this heat, especially at this time of day," Jamie remarked as he fell into step alongside Royall.

Royall felt her stomach lurch. Would she ever forget her fright of a few moments ago. She couldn't be wrong in her thinking. She knew what she saw and what she felt. For now, she had to act as though nothing was wrong, talk to Jamie, and appear to act normally. God, what was normal? "To answer your question, Jamie, I'm bored to tears." Her tone was irritable and she felt irritable, out of sorts and, above all, angry. She lashed out. "I wish I was back in New England, away from this godforsaken, rotten jungle."

"Why?" Jamie asked bluntly.

Why? Of course he would ask a stupid question like why? "What is there for me here? Nothing," she said in annoyance. "If I'm lucky, and I use the word loosely, I may escape this jungle with my life intact. I understand from Mrs. Quince and from Elena that the plantation owners are up in arms over the Baron's actions these past weeks. For a time I was prepared to do my share and not shirk my responsibility, but with your father staying in town and not coming near the plantation, my hands are tied. I plan to see Mr. Morrison early next week and settle the matter once and for all. With or without your father present. There are so many things I don't understand about this plantation and the operation of the rubber market. All along I've wanted to know, but your father chose to keep me in the dark. The time for procrastinating is long gone. I refuse to wait any longer."

"Running the plantation is man's work, Royall. You can't ride out and do what all the men do around here. You must know that women belong in town or in the drawing room playing the spinet like you do. You're too beautiful to do a man's work." Jamie's voice was a whimper, almost a whine, as he watched her to see how she would react to the word *spinet.*

"I just want to know about the operation, I didn't say I wanted to run the plantation. I realize that there are people far more capable than myself. I must have an accounting of my shares. Your father's reluctance to do this only makes me more certain than ever that he has been less than honest concerning business. I think your father is a scoundrel and is out to bilk me of my share of this plantation and all the holdings here in Brazil." She watched covertly to see Jamie's reaction.

Jamie didn't appear to take offense at her words concerning his father. "My father has never taken either Carl or myself into his confidence. Carl would get angry and stomp out of the room. Father would just say time will take care of everything. Is that what you wanted me to say, Royall? Will that answer make you want to stay here in Brazil? I don't want you to go away. You're so pretty and your skin is so soft. You don't yell and screech at me like Elena does. Rosy shivers when I ask her to play. Once I saw Nessie stick her tongue out at me. She didn't think I saw her do it, but I did. I slapped her. When I told my father, he said she deserved to be slapped."

Oh, God, oh, God, Royall moaned softly as she shivered in the clammy heat of midday. An ominous feeling came over her. Something had to be done, and done soon.

Royall stamped up the scrubbed white steps onto the veranda. Gulping her drink, she winced at the sour taste and quickly set it down. Jamie stared at her for a moment, finally deciding her black looks would do nothing for his own temper. He settled himself in a far corner and proceeded to line up his wooden soldiers on the veranda railing. The sight irritated Royall beyond reason.

Her eyes were a storm of fury as she stalked into the kitchen in search of Elena and a cool drink. The calmness in her tone surprised Royall when she spoke to Elena. The housekeeper smiled and offered a slice of guava. Royall shook her head and requested a drink. "Elena, I want to talk to you. I need some answers from you, and I want them now."

Elena pivoted, and immediately a veil dropped over her eyes.

Royall's back stiffened. Elena was on guard as always. Why? She wanted answers and she wanted them now. "Elena, I want to know why Jamie plays with the children. Why is he permitted to spend so much time with the little girls? It isn't . . . it isn't healthy, Elena. Isn't there something he can do, some chores, something or somewhere he could be of some use? I don't want him to play with the girls any more, and I expect you to take care of the matter."

"Senora Banner, you must realize that our customs here in Brazil are quite different than those in New England."

"Elena, you're talking like a fool and we both know that you aren't a fool. We're not discussing *customs*. We're discussing an unhealthy situation; I'm concerned with the girls' safety. I saw him today and my blood ran cold. If I hadn't come along when I did he could have . . . he might have . . . he could have hurt them. Or worse."

"Worse?" The black eyes were dark pools of inscrutability.

"Yes, worse. You know exactly what I'm talking about. There's no need for either of us to hedge. If you don't tend to Jamie now, before the day ends, I'll take the children to the Rivera plantation. I mean it, Elena."

The honey-skinned hand that held out the cool drink trembled slightly. Elena inclined her head. "We understand each other perfectly, Senora. Send Jamie to me when you return to the veranda. I'm sure the drink will meet with your satisfaction."

Royall carefully placed her drink beside her wicker chair. "Jamie," she called brightly. "Elena would like you to go to the kitchen." Jamie pretended to ignore her, but he stepped off the veranda, through the French-paned doors, into the house. A moment later he was back. He slammed the door, the sound loud and angry. His fists were clenched, his shoulders hunched with fury. Jamie strode to the far end of the veranda where his soldiers lined the railing. Neither by glance nor by word did he acknowledge Royall's presence.

Royall watched in silent horror as the young man slowly and methodically snapped the heads from the brilliantly uniformed soldiers. As each small head dropped to the parquet floor, it made a soft, plunking sound. Royall found herself counting the heads as they rolled to the floor. She could sense rather than see the tautness of his muscles bulging beneath his light coat. He was being slow and careful, and that was more horrifying to Royall than if he had been violently angry.

Suddenly, an intense fury seemed to grip him. Royall held her breath. His movements were quick, almost violent as he snapped the heads. Her eyes swept to the railing. She counted the heads. There were seven. What was wrong with him? Royall spun around, knocking the drink to the floor. She stepped in the sticky, sweet drink as she raced down the wide veranda to the main door in search of Elena.

"Elena, you must come quickly. Now!" Royall pleaded as she ran pell mell into the house. "It's Jamie, something is wrong with him! He just destroyed all of his soldiers. He severed the heads. My God, Elena, did you hear me, Jamie snapped all the heads off the soldiers. Elena! Where are you?"

"I'm here, Senora. I heard you. Where is Jamie now?"

"I left him on the veranda. What's wrong with him, Elena? I've never seen him in such a state."

"I thought you were sending him to me. I've been waiting," the housekeeper snapped.

"I told him but he ignored me. Elena, can you do something for him; give him some laudanum, make him sleep off whatever it is that's bothering him."

"Senora, there is no medicine for what's bothering Jamie." Elena's voice was flat, controlled, but her chocolate eyes were wide and afraid.

"My God. We have to do something. You have to do something, Elena."

"I will, Senora."

The veranda was deserted. Only the colorful heads of the toy soldiers littered the shiny floor. Royall heard Elena's indrawn breath and shivered.

"Elena, where are the girls?"

"Moriah is upstairs doing the beds. Nessie is disposing of the trash. Rosy went to fetch water from the spring." Elena's dark eyes flashed once as Royall stared at her. Both women ran down the stairs. They ran side by side to the spring and then to the trash pile. Neither child was to be found. Jamie was not in evidence. They retraced their steps to the kitchen. There was no pail of water. The bucket that held the trash was also conspicuously absent. Royall's frightened amber eyes locked with Elena's fathomless gaze.

Chapter Nineteen

Jamie stared after Royall's retreating back. Why was she screaming for Elena? Nothing was the same anymore. Carl was still away, and so was his father. And what business was it of Royall's or Elena's what he did to his soldiers? They belonged to him and he could do whatever he wanted with them. If he stayed, Elena would give him a tongue-lashing. She never hollered at Carl the way she did at him.

He was sick of Elena always telling him what

he could and couldn't do. "Don't touch the girls, Jamie," she would always remind him. "They're here as servants, not as playmates for you. . . . Grow up, Jamie." Always telling him, "Grow up, Jamie."

Well, he didn't want to grow up. He didn't know how. He liked the girls and he liked to play with them. They felt soft and he liked it when they giggled.

Which one of the brats had told on him again? He'd warned them and warned them, but they were just like everybody else. They didn't obey him; nobody obeyed him or even cared what he said. When he found out which one of them told on him again, he'd slap her good. What was wrong with playing ball or holding one of the squirming little girls and tickling and tickling until they almost couldn't catch their breath. But Elena didn't like it; she never liked anything he did. She'd cuffed him more than once for touching the girls, but she always hugged him afterward and told him that she knew he could try harder.

Jamie bent to pick up a twig. It snapped in his hands. He didn't want to try harder. He liked playing with them; he liked touching them, and most of all he liked the way he felt inside when he was doing it. Sometimes at night he even dreamed about them . . . But he didn't want to think about that now.

It was all Nessie's fault. She needed a good slap to teach her manners. He hated it when Elena was angry with him or disappointed in him. He tried to be good, he really did . . . but he liked those little girls. What he had to do was find that mouthy little brat and teach her a lesson she wouldn't forget!

Nervously, Jamie rubbed his fingers together as he tromped across the lawn and into the grove of trees in search of the children. He called them, not bothering to hide the anger in his tone. Suddenly, he spied Nessie and Rosy heading toward the well. This was his chance. Elena was back in the kitchen and Royall must be with her. "Tattletales," he muttered over and over as he chased after the little figures. His heavy footfalls alerted the two innocents, who stopped in their tracks, their faces frightened. Jamie stared at them a moment, panting from the run, suddenly uncertain that he was placing the blame on the one who told. Maybe it had been Rosy who told on him.

"Which one of you little brats complained about me to Elena?" he demanded, his voice high and shrill. Neither girl answered, their black eyes wary and frightened as they instinctively huddled together. "If you don't tell me, I'll give you both a thrashing you won't forget." Still the children remained silent, clinging together like two little marmoset monkeys. Jamie's anger was spurred by their refusal to answer.

Furious, he reached out a long arm and grabbed Rosy, who was closest to him. "I'll teach you to tattle on me, you damn little Indian!" With one hand holding her firmly, he rendered her a stunning blow with the other. Rosy screamed, as did Nessie, who tried to grapple his long legs. He shook Nessie off with a wicked kick, sending the child sprawling into the greenery along the path.

Rosy was crying, squealing with fright, struggling wildly to free herself from his overpowering grip. The more she struggled, the more incensed Jamie became. Her frantic movements were driving him crazy with a strange, erotic need. Blinded by his emotions, he held firm to the child, whose writhing now seemed sensuously rhythmic.

Fire grew in his loins, and when he looked into the small, tear-stained face he felt his own tears spring to his eyes. What was happening to him? A small, dark hand reached up to claw his face; cursing, he felt the flesh split across his cheekbone. The fire was now approaching an inferno as he threw the child on the ground and stood looking over her. The inferno threatened to engulf him, and from somewhere in the dark recesses of his mind he remembered standing beside the Baron outside the stable's studding corral. He could almost see himself as he'd been then—a thin, shy boy of twelve. He could hear the shrieks of the mare and the whinnying snorts of the stallion as the two beasts mated. The Baron had laughed softly, remarking to one of the stable hands, "She screams like a woman, that filly. The stallion will soon teach her to act her age."

But the filly never stopped shrieking; Jamie could still hear her. Or was it Rosy?

Royall paced the kitchen, her hands shaking, voice quaking. Elena busied herself baking bread, kneading the soft, white dough with strong, capable hands. Her usual black dress was smudged with flour, and her always meticulously groomed hair fell from the knot at the back of her head and hung inn ebony strands around her face. While she wouldn't admit it, Royall could see how agitated she was with worry about the girls and Jamie.

"Elena, where can they be?"

"Don't become overexcited, Senora. There are a thousand explanations. This wouldn't be the first time that Rosy and Nessie have run off to play when they should be attending to their chores." Her fingers dug into the bread dough, punching, turning. "It's the heat. You shouldn't be in the kitchen; it's too hot." She was purposely keeping her tone on a level, her glance quickly indicating the plump cook working near the stove. "Senora, step out onto the veranda, perhaps you'll see the children coming."

Royall went to the veranda, Elena following with a cool drink. "I don't want the cook to know," she explained briefly, wiping her hands on her dress, leaving a dusting of flour. "Senora, I think we should search again. You take the path through the gardens and I'll follow the trail to the stables. At least we will be doing something."

Royall sighed with relief. "Of course, I agree. I was about to suggest something myself. I feel as though my head is going to explode. Are you sure, Elena, that Moriah didn't know anything?"

"Quite sure, Senora Banner. She was working, exactly what she was supposed to be doing. Please, you must take my word, the child knew nothing. The only thing I succeeded in doing was alarming the little one. I had no choice," she said defensively.

"I know that, Elena. It's just that I'm so worried. I feel as though I want to go in a dozen different directions. We separate here. Call out if you find them." Elena nodded.

Her eyes clouded with worry and apprehension, Royall trudged this way and that, her eyes searching the thick, jungle greenery. It was quiet, too quiet. She didn't like the stillness. A shrill, squawking bird flew overhead, making Royall gasp in fright. Time and again she called to the children. Her cries went unanswered. Faintly, she could hear Elena calling the children from the opposite direction. Apparently, she wasn't having any luck either. Royall followed the path to the spring. There was no one about. She circled back, calling the girls over and over.

A speck of color near a large, leafy bush caught her eye. It looked like Rosy's favorite hair ribbon. She called out again. This time she stood perfectly still and waited, her heart pounding furiously in her chest. Was that a sound? Tilting her head to the side, she concentrated with every fiber of her being. There it was again, the soft mewing of a cat. Dejectedly, she parted the foliage and peered

357

into the dimness, expecting to see the large tabby with a litter of newborn kittens. Two pairs of eyes stared into her startled gaze. "Rosy, Nessie! Thank God! I was so worried about you. Didn't you hear me call you? Shame on you for playing a trick on me. Now tell me, why didn't you call out when you heard me searching for you?"

Silence.

"Come along now, it's almost dinnertime and Elena needs you to help in the kitchen. She's been searching for you, too."

Neither child moved. Royall bent down to stare at the little girls. Nessie looked frightened to death. Rosy, always bright, cheerful, and inquisitive, stared straight ahead, her eyes dull and unseeing. Nessie had a protective grip around Rosy's shoulders. Royall's chest roared in panic. "Wh . . . what. . . what's wrong?" she managed finally past the lump in her throat.

Silence.

She knew.

Gently, Royall pried Nessie's stiff fingers from Rosy's shoulders. "It's all right, Nessie, I'll take care of her. You must move a little. I know you've been protecting her, but I'll take care of her. Trust me," she whispered. "Please, little one, trust me." Obediently, Nessie slid back to afford Royall leverage to pick up the blank-faced child. Her movements awkward, Royall gathered Rosy in her arms and backed from the shrubbery onto the wide path. Gently, she laid her burden down onto the well-worn trail. Brilliant sunshine made her blink after the dimness of the dense undergrowth.

Rosy appeared dazed, completely unaware of her surroundings. Royall waved a slender hand in front of Rosy's eyes. There was no response.

Her suspicions demanded an immediate response. Questioningly, she looked at Nessie. "Did Rosy fall, is that how she got hurt?" In her heart she knew that no fall would have caused the dead look on the little girl's face. "Nessie, go at once and fetch Elena. She's searching for you near the stables." The child remained still. "Nessie, you have to fetch Elena. Do it for Rosy. Now!" she commanded sternly.

"No, Senora. You take care of Rosy?" Nessie said stubbornly.

"All right. I asked you to trust me, so I want you to know that I'm doing the best I can. I have to be truthful with you. I don't know what to do for Rosy. I do have an idea, though. Go to the stable and fetch me my horse. You can do that for me, can't you? I'll take Rosy to her mother on Senor Rivera's plantation. You too, child. This place is no longer safe for either of you. Can you do it, Nessie, can you fetch the horse?"

The little shoulders set. "I can do. You wait." She scampered off and was back in an instant. "You no say about Moriah?" Again the voice was stubborn, defying Royall to give a negative answer.

"I promise to bring Moriah tomorrow to Senor Rivera's plantation. Right now, it is imperative, very important, that you two get there as quickly as possible. I promise that I'll fetch Moriah tomorrow. Please, Nessie, you must trust me." Royall wanted to scream as the child stared at her, debating what she should do.

"Not lie?"

"Not a lie! Hurry, Nessie, oh, please hurry. Don't let anyone see you. Run!"

For what seemed like hours Royall sat in the clearing stroking Rosy's head and crooning soft words of comfort. When she thought she couldn't stand it a second longer, Nessie walked down the path, leading not one but two horses.

"Two," Nessie said holding up two pudgy fingers. "We three. Need two horses. I steal."

"Can you ride, Nessie?"

Nessie grimaced. "Not so good. I bring old horse for me. He walk slow. I hold on tight."

Royall's mind raced as her mare trotted behind Nessie and the old horse. Should she go to Sebastian, or should she take Rosy directly to her mother? She firmly decided that a mother was what Rosy needed more than anything in the world, no matter how kind and compassionate Sebastian might be.

Within an hour she was in sight of the clearing that housed Sebastian's Indians. As before, the women came from all directions. They said nothing as their dark eyes watched the two riders approach. Gradually, the crowd thinned before the determined strides of a tall Indian woman who approached from the rear. She stared at Nessie and then at Rosy. Her long arms reached out to gather Rosy from Royall's tight embrace. Gently, she held the child against her breast and cradled the small dark head in her hands. Tears fell from her eyes as she rocked Rosy back and forth like a newborn babe. The jet black eyes, tear filled, looked into the face of her child. She saw. She did not believe.

A giant of a man stepped forward to take the child from her mother's arms. It must be Rosy's father, Royall thought. Suddenly, there was a babble of voices. Dark-skinned fingers pointed to Rosy's bare little leg. Royall watched in horror as the child's mother traced the dark rivulet of blood that was almost indistinguishable against the dark skin of the child. Slowly she lifted the child's skirt and then turned to look at the man holding Rosy. She nodded slightly. A deathly stillness settled over the clearing. Royall fought the urge to scream. The crowd dispersed. Rosy was safe. There was nothing she could do for the little girl now.

Royall's eyes went to Nessie, who sat patiently atop the old horse. "Now it's your turn, little one. Follow me, I'm going to take you to your new home and your mother."

"My mother?" Nessie said in awe.

"Yes, your mother. I should have done it long ago. Your mother. Some day God will forgive me for not taking matters into my own hands."

Nessie frowned. "You tell Father Juan. He forgive you. Con . . . conf . . . confession," she said triumphantly.

"That's the simple way, Nessie. First, I have to forgive myself. Come along now, and let's not keep your mother waiting another moment for the sight of your beautiful face."

The courtyard was empty. Royall frowned, not sure if she was happy or disappointed that Sebastian was nowhere about. Right now she really had no desire to see Sebastian's hard, cold, jet black eyes that looked into her soul. Better he should be absent. At the sound of the horses' hooves, Anna ran from the house. One startled glance at Nessie made her pick up her skirts and race to the old worn-out horse, her arms outstretched. Her eyes sought Royall, hardly daring to believe her good fortune. Royall nodded. "I brought her to you. She's to remain with you. She's your daughter and she belongs to you. I am truly sorry I . . . Love her, Anna, she deserves it."

"There will be much trouble when the Baron finds out you have brought my child to me, Senora."

"Yes, there will be much trouble, but I'm the one who will make it. You need have no fear, no one, I repeat, no one will ever take that child from you again. You have my word."

Royall leaned over and kissed the small, dark face. "Mind you, take as good care of your mama as you did of me," she warned the little girl. Nessie nodded soberly. With a wave of her hand, Royall rode from the clearing.

Tears scalded her eyes, making it impossible to see the horse that rode into the courtyard from the opposite side of the Casa. Nor did she see the dark eyes gaze longingly at her retreating back. She was too far away to hear the words the housekeeper spoke to Sebastian of the golden girl with tear-filled eyes and of the kiss she had given, oh so tenderly, to her little Nessie. "It would be a lucky man who could share a kiss with such a golden girl," Anna said happily as she cuddled Nessie in her arms.

Back at the Reino, Royall faced Elena. "You know, don't you? You know that Jamie raped Rosy!" At Elena's nod, Royall felt anger churn within her. "What are you going to do about it?" she demanded coldly.

"I don't know, Senora. I have to think. The Baron isn't here. I can hardly take matters into my own hands. Jamie isn't a child; he's a young man."

"A young man who just raped a small child! Don't stand there and tell me you have to wait for the Baron to come home. From what I understand, he may never come back to the plantation. I want Jamie locked in his room, and I want Moriah moved into my room immediately. She'll stay with me until tomorrow when I take her back to the Rivera plantation. Don't even contemplate telling me I can't do it. I did it and I'll do it again. If you won't do anything, I'll do it myself. Well?"

"Jamie is in his room. I'm not as uncaring or as unfeeling as you may think, Senora. Jamie is . . . has been like a son to me. I'll do what has to be done. I suggest you go to your room and let me get on with dinner. One of the servants will bring trays to your room for you and Moriah. I want your word that you will stay in your room till I tell you to come out. Your word, Senora."

"Very well,Elena, I'll do as you say, but I want you to send a messenger to Manaus to the Baron. I want him to know about this. If he chooses not to return, then I will take matters into my own hands. I want your word on that matter, Elena."

"Yes, Senora. I'll have a messenger sent out at once."

As always, Royall felt herself dismissed from the housekeeper's presence. This time she was only too glad to go to her room. Thank God, Moriah was safe. The child would be delighted when she hears that she will be going home.

How tired she was, how depressed. If only she could have gotten just one glimpse of Sebastian.

All evening long Royall cringed in the high, wide bed. The angry sound of drums beating through the jungle was setting her into a frenzy. Moriah's words did nothing to alleviate her apprehension: "The drums say there will be a death in the jungle tonight."

Elena sat down on a hard-backed chair. Her head throbbed unmercifully. How had it come to this? When had things gone wrong? The day Royall Banner arrived at the plantation, she answered herself. I knew it the moment she stepped over the threshhold that things were going to change, and not for the better. Such turmoil. Do this, do that, don't do this, don't do that, where was it going to end. Was the Baron going to come back to the plantation? She had to send a messenger as the Senora requested. She couldn't ignore the problem any longer; she would have to do as the young American woman instructed.

On lagging feet, Elena walked to the courtyard in search of one of the stable boys. Quickly and concisely, she explained exactly what he was to say to the Baron. "You are to return with the Baron and see that he . . . that he arrives safely." No need to tell the boy that the Baron might be drunk and he was needed as a chaperone on the long ride to the plantation. "You must be careful when you speak of Jamie. Just say that his presence is needed because of Jamie. Say no more. That is what you were told, and you are merely delivering the message," Elena admonished. The boy nodded and scampered off to the stables to saddle a horse.

If only she could think straight, get her thoughts together. There was something else she had to do. What was it? Dinner! Of course, even a dolt would have remembered. As if by rote, she set about preparing thick, pink slices of ham. Snowy white rice bubbled merrily as she shelled peas. The inevitable sliced fruit with sugar and cream would be dessert. There was no time for pastry, and her heart wouldn't be in preparing the flaky dough, not today.

The cook appeared at Elena's side. "Soon," Elena murmured, "and then you will take two trays to the Senora's room. I'll see to Master Jamie myself. Pour the cream and slice the fruit." The woman stared at Elena. Something was wrong. The housekeeper was acting strangely, as though she didn't care about the dinner at all. Where was the butter for the peas? Why was there no lid on the rice pot? And there were no flowers for the trays, something the housekeeper always saw to herself. Where were the pretty napkins, and where were the dishes? Something was wrong. She sniffed a moment and then hurried over to the stove. She heaved a mighty sigh as she removed the heavy skillet from the stove. Just in time or the luscious pink ham would have burned. Elena didn't even notice. She didn't notice when the cook reappeared a moment later with a handful of delicate scarlet blooms to be put in the small vases on the shelf. Perhaps the housekeeper would scold her later, but she doubted it. In plain view of Elena's unseeing gaze she arranged the trays and added the flowers and the colorful napkins. It looked just as elegant as if Elena herself had done it. Pleased with herself and what she had just accomplished, she set about ladling out the food on the plates. Gently, she touched Elena's shoulder and waited for her nod of approval. Twice she had to repeat her gentle nudge before the housekeeper could bring her eyes to focus on the tempting looking trays. She smiled wanly and said, "You did fine, Maria. Now take the trays to the Senora's room. I'll take Master Jamie's to him in a moment."

There was no choice left to her. Senora Banner was right; something had to be done, and it had to be done now before the Baron returned. She looked a moment longer at the tray. Satisfied that everything was placed exactly right, she picked up the tray and left the kitchen. Her walk was stately, her eyes straight ahead, until she reached Jamie's room. Deftly, she balanced the tray in one hand and withdrew a large key from her apron pocket.

"It's about time, Elena. I thought you were never going to bring my food to me. I don't like it when you lock me in my room. I'm going to tell father. I want you to bring my soldiers to me," Jamie said petulantly.

Elena sat the tray down on a small table. "I want you to eat your dinner, Jamie. Later, I'll get your soldiers. I don't think they can be fixed, but I can try. Why did you break the heads off the soldiers?"

"Oh, Elena, sometimes I don't know why you say the things you do; I didn't break the heads off my soldiers. I wouldn't do anything to hurt my soldiers. You should know that," Jamie scoffed as he wolfed down his food.

"I never thought you would hurt anyone, Jamie."

"Elena, why are you talking so strangely? Who did I hurt? This rice tastes funny. Change it, Elena, I don't want it."

"Eat it," Elena said firmly.

"All right, but I don't like it."

"Why did you hurt Rosy?"

Jamie stopped his voracious chewing and lowered his eyes to his plate. "I didn't hurt her. She's nothing but an Indian brat. She told on me, didn't she? That's why you gave me this rice. You're punishing me," he accused.

"You need to be punished for what you did. What you did was a bad thing, Jamie. Rosy's father and some of the other Indian men from the Rivera plantation will come here and want to punish you."

"Is that why you're punishing me with the rice, so they won't come here? That's very clever of you, Elena. Father won't let some old Indian men hurt me."

"Your father isn't here, Jamie, you know that. I've sent for him, but he won't arrive till very late." If he arrives at all, Elena added to herself.

"You can make it right, can't you, Elena? You won't let the Indians hurt me, will you?" Jamie picked at his peas and then rolled them off the plate. He watched as they rolled to the floor. "Say you won't let them hurt me, Elena," he whined.

"I'm going to make it right, Jamie. No one is ever going to hurt you. I've always taken care of you. You know I love you, like you were my own son. You trust me, don't you, Jamie?" Her voice was low, tormented, as she waited for Jamie to respond.

Jamie laughed in delight. "I'm not afraid of some old Indian men. I know you love me. I love you too. Do you love me enough to bring my soldiers to me?"

"Perhaps later, Jamie. I want you to finish your dinner now. I'll just sit here and wait till you're done." Obediently, Jamie cleaned his plate and attacked the sliced fruit with his spoon.

"Now, take your tray over to the door and set it outside."

"Now, will you get the soldiers? I ate all of the rice so you don't have to punish me anymore."

"Come with me. I want you to look out at the gardens to see how beautiful they are. I want you to remember them."

"Why? Are we going on a trip? Father didn't say anything about a trip. Can I take my soldiers with me?"

Elena swallowed hard and maneuvered Jamie to the wide double doors that looked over the garden. "A trip? In a manner of speaking, Jamie. And of course your soldiers can go with you. They're part of you. Tell me now, what do you think of the garden?"

Jamie shrugged. "Where are we going?"

Elena turned to face Jamie. "To a kind of wondrous place, Jamie. I've never been there, but there's no pain where you're going. Everything will be peaceful. You'll never be punished again."

"It sounds like a fairyland. When are we going?"

Elena stood face to face with Jamie. Lightly she cupped both her hands around his handsome head. Lightly she kissed him first on one cheek and then on the other. Her throat was like a thin rag as the words ripped from her. "I loved you as though you were my own, better than my own. I love you now. I'll always love you, remember that, Jamie." Her hands dropped to her side. Slowly, she reached into the pocket of her apron and withdrew her sharp paring knife. Her eyes locked with Jamie's as she plunged the blade into his heart. "Now, Jamie, you're leaving now."

Jamie's eyes widened in disbelief as he slumped to the floor. Elena stared down at him, tears coursing down her cheeks. "Forgive me, Jamie. I couldn't let Rosy's father take you away. He and the others would come as soon as night falls. I couldn't let them take you, I just couldn't let that happen to you."

How beautiful he looked in death. How innocent.

She had things to do. Pick up the trays, wash the dishes, clean the kitchen. Send a boy to the Rivera plantation with a message telling of Jamie's death. Only when she was finished would she allow herself the luxury of readying Jamie's body for burial. When that was finished she would wait for the Baron.

Soon the beat of the jungle drums would abate. The silence would then be thunderous. One way or another, the jungle always won. It was a fact of life that she had lived with. Only this time she couldn't let the jungle win, not with Jamie. She had been his accuser, she had judged, and it was she who found him guilty and meted out his punishment. This time she had beat the jungle by a hairbreadth.

Chapter Twenty

Royall watched in amazement as Moriah gobbled down her food. Just the thought of eating the food on her plate made her ill. She couldn't swallow if her life depended on it.

The house was quiet. Too quiet. Usually around this time of day a certain amount of bustle was going on. The stables were being readied for the night, with the young boys chattering away in the courtyard as they came to the kitchen for their dinner. The little maids were giggling and rattling dishes in the pantry. Today there was only silence. Just the sound of the jungle drums, permeating the air outside her room. The sound was loud, then muted, and always ominous. Who was going to die in the jungle tonight? Who? Royall shivered as she watched Moriah set her empty fruit dish back on the tray. The child looked inquisitively at Royall. "I'm finished, Moriah. You can place the trays outside the door. Come right back inside and I'll read you a long story until you fall asleep. Tomorrow is a big day for you. You're going home!"

Moriah's shoe button black eyes danced merrily. "I see me madre tomorrow."

"Yes, you will. Bright and early, at first light.

So, you have to go to sleep early tonight so you look especially pretty for your mother."

"I not pretty, Senora," Moriah giggled.

"Little one, beauty is in the eye of the beholder. I say you're one of the most beautiful little girls I've ever seen, and to your mother you will be the most beautiful child in all the world." And she was, with her dark eyes and honey skin. Satiny ebony hair hung down to her waist. Small pearl white teeth glistened as the little girl brought her hand to her mouth to stifle another giggle.

"You read about princess and prince? I like that much," Moriah smiled as she settled herself comfortably in the huge bed. "I like much when prince says to princess, you skin like cream." She held out one chubby mocha-colored hand for Royall's inspection. Royall laughed in delight.

Within minutes Moriah's eyes closed, and she slept. Royall scrambled from the bed and ran to the balcony. Why did she have this strange feeling? What was wrong? Why was the house so quiet? A vision of Elena's somber face rose before her. And the promise she had extracted from Royall not to leave her room till she sent for her. Now, why had she given her promise? Something was wrong. Wait. All she could do was wait for Elena to come for her.

Elena bent down and knelt beside Jamie's still form. She felt nothing, no love, no compassion, no remorse. With a strength she didn't know she possessed, she lifted Jamie's body and placed him on the bed. She didn't feel the least exertion at lifting him. She felt nothing as she began the morbid task of readying Jamie's body for its last resting place. Thoughts of what was to come clouded her reactions at hand. Call Father Juan. Notify the men that they were to dig the grave. It would be in the small clearing that she herself tended each day, that served as a cemetery. Jamie would lie beside his mother, the mother he never knew.

Tenderly, she bent to wash his face. Years of loving welled in her throat. Loving Jamie had filled her life, brought meaning to it. Not only had she ended Jamie's life, but her own as well. She continued with her methodical sponging. How beautiful he was. Carefully, she dressed him in his best suit and a snowy white shirt. Her task complete, she stood beside the bed looking down at him. In repose, his resemblance to Carlyle was astounding. Her mind spit out the name as though it were some obscene word crafted by the devil himself. Why wouldn't he admit to Jamie's disability? He had always insisted that Jamie be treated as a man, and she had tried to comply. Deep in her heart she knew she was wrong, but she was helpless to change things. She had done her best. It hadn't been enough. Nothing could change the fact that in Jamie's manlike body lived the mind of a small boy. Nothing and no one could ever change that fact.

Her duties ended, Elena gathered up the washbasin and urn and placed them outside the door.

She retraced her steps to the side of the bed. She placed a tender kiss on the cold brow. "I'll wait here with you, Jamie, till the sound of the drums stop." Primly, she settled herself on a low settee. She folded her hands and closed her eyes. She prayed.

Elena's eyes flicked open. The silence was deafening. The drums had ceased their pulsing beat. The heart of the jungle was quiet now. It was over. "Soon," she whispered softly, "soon, Jamie, I will witness the end of your father's cruel reign. His kingdom is about to fall into ashes at his very feet. His end is near. Shortly he will join you. I will revel in his death just as I once reveled in the feel of his arms about me. Soon, Jamie, my love."

Royall opened the door and placed her fingers to her lips. "Moriah is asleep. Is everything all right,Elena. Why have the drums stopped? Tell me, I know something is wrong!"

"Come with me, Senora, and you will see why the drums have stopped." Puzzled, Royall followed Elena to Jamie's room. Fear knotted in her throat as she followed the housekeeper into the lamplit room. She was more puzzled when she noticed Jamie asleep, fully clothed. "That is why the drums have ceased. Jamie is gone."

Royall felt dazed. Had Elena just said Jamie was gone? That meant he was . . . dead. "How?" she gasped.

Elena turned to face Royall. "He disobeyed me and rode into the jungle. The horse stumbled and

Jamie was thrown. His neck was broken in the fall. He was not equipped to ride the gelding."

Royall stared deeply into the housekeeper's eyes. There was no need for words. She understood. She stared at Elena for a full moment longer. "You're right, Elena, Jamie was not equipped to ride the gelding." For one brief instant Royall read relief in the housekeeper's eyes. "Both of us will carry this secret to the grave, Elena." Elena nodded.

Royall was dismissed. Elena was in another world now, a world of her own choosing. She would sit sentinel over Jamie until dawn, when he would be buried. The tightening in her breast became a strangulating knot in her constricted throat. Admiration for Elena's courage, and pity for poor Jamie, as well as outrage at his crime, became a jumble within her. She had to get out of this room before she suffocated. Moriah was safe now. She could walk outdoors in the courtyard and not have to worry about the child. She needed to clear her head of the cobwebs that were hindering her thoughts. If only Sebastian were here to help me. Her world was crumbling beneath her very feet. Soon there would be nothing left. Nothing at all.

A low, gray mist hung over the small cemetery on the hill. Heavy dew on the foliage sparkled like diamonds in the misty, humid air. Poor innocent Jamie, poor wicked Jamie. A boy locked within a man's body, outgrowing a world of toy soldiers and pretend. She was thankful he was dead by Elena's loving hand rather than the vengeance of the Indians. Killing a white man could have been the beginning of an uprising, Father Juan had said this morning when he arrived. It was just as well that Jamie had had his accident in the jungle.

All through the long, sleepless night, Royall had wrestled with her emotions. The hours before dawn had also taken their toll on Elena. How cold she looked, as though all the blood had drained from her veins. It had. Jamie had been her life, and now he was gone.

Royall expected to see the Baron riding up at any moment, demanding an explanation from Elena. He should be here; it was barbaric of him not to attend his son's funeral. It should be the Baron being laid in the wet, cold ground. His own ignorance had become his son's destruction.

". . . dust to dust," Father Juan finished his short eulogy. Elena stood still, her eyes never leaving the deep, black hole. There were no tears, no remorse, only total acceptance.

The moment Father Juan finished his short blessing, Royall turned to leave. Would Elena stay or follow her? Would Father Juan come back to the Casa for breakfast, as was the custom after a funeral? Her step slowed. Once she looked over her shoulder. Elena hadn't moved. Father Juan was walking away from the clearing toward the path that would take him to his waiting buggy. Royall debated with herself—should she wait for Elena or should she return to the house? She knew somehow that the housekeeper would consider it an intrusion if she walked back to the gravesite. Never in her life had she seen anyone look so alone as Elena looked at that moment. Nothing helped, not even Father Juan's whispered words to Elena: "Time heals all wounds. He takes care of all his children. Time, Elena, always remember what I'm telling you."

Now she had to clean Moriah up and take her back to the Rivera plantation. Some of the happiness had worn off with the death of Jamie. Still, the child, small as she was, seemed to understand.

Though the day was hot and sultry, Carlyle Newsome felt a chill run through his body as he hurried down the street to his pink bricked townhouse. It was midday, and as in the axiom, only mad dogs and Englishmen went out in the noonday sun. So it was with surprise that he saw Sebastian Rivera and Malcolm Doyle, a neighbor, deep in conversation. Eager as he was to enter his house and find some relief from the heat, Carlyle turned quickly on his heel and proceeded to stride down a side street, away from Sebastian's notice.

Ever since that day when he'd come back to the townhouse and found Alicia gone, Carlyle had lived with a growing anxiety. At first he hadn't the least idea where she had gone, or to whom, and when no news was heard of her for several days, he'd come to the conclusion that she'd drowned herself in the river or found some other tidy way of alleviating him of the increasing discontent she was causing.

And then had come the night at the opera and the party Rosalie Quince had given in Royall Banner's honor, and he'd seen her again—with Rivera. And from the menacing disgust he'd witnessed in Rivera's glance, it was evident the stupid girl had confided in him. Carlyle had expected a confrontation with his nemesis at that time, but the announcement of yellow jack had forestalled it. Now, seeing Rivera on the street, only yards away from his townhouse, the Baron knew the inevitable was upon him.

Droplets of perspiration beaded the Baron's brow. His armpits were soaking wet, as was his back. It was madness to walk in the sun this way, but it was even madder to make himself available to Rivera's tirade. His head ached, his stomach rolled, and he told himself he needed another drink. Not for anything would he admit that Rivera frightened him.

He had to keep walking and stop thinking. He had to concentrate on making it around the block, getting into his townhouse without Rivera seeing him, finding the bottle of Scotch and taking it to bed with him. Gloom plagued him as he walked; anxiety ate at his innards. Even Rivera wouldn't be bastard enough to tell anyone about Alicia. Regardless of the man's hatred for the Newsomes he would still protect Alicia's reputation, wouldn't he? Then what was Rivera doing on *his* street? And what was he talking to Malcolm Doyle about?

Once more around the block and back to the beginning of the street. Perhaps if he was careful he could meander between the buildings to see if Sebastian and old man Doyle were still deep in conversation.

The corner to be turned loomed ahead. The Baron drew on his willpower not to turn for one last look in Sebastian's direction.

Sebastian carried his end of the conversation with Doyle, but for the life of him he couldn't remember what he had said just seconds ago. The cheroot clenched between his strong white teeth tasted bitter as he transferred it from the right to the left side of his mouth. His steely gaze followed Carlyle Newsome's back as he trekked down the street in front of the long row of townhouses. He heard himself refusing, for the third time, Doyle's invitation into the house for a cool drink, and knew the conversation was drawing to a close.

Sebastian watched the old man enter his house. Christ, he had thought he was going to stand in the sun and talk the day away. His dark eyes searched the deserted street. The wily fox no doubt was going to circle the block once again. Well, two could play at that game.

Tossing the frayed tip cheroot into the gutter, he sprinted down the block and up the steep front steps of the Newsome townhouse. Forcefully, he let the knocker sound against the brass plate. The door was opened almost immediately. "I have an appointment with Baron Newsome," he said, pushing past the startled housekeeper. "I'll wait inside until he arrives. Fetch me a brandy while I wait." Authoritatively, bridging no objection, he stepped across the foyer and into the parlor. "I'll wait in here."

The housekeeper let her eyes flick over Sebastian and then to the front door. Quickly she backed away, out of his line of vision, and headed back to the kitchen.

Sebastian brought a match to a fresh cheroot and puffed deeply. A billowing cloud of fragrant smoke permeated the room. The brandy snifter found its way to his lips, and he nodded appreciatively. Carlyle certainly didn't stint himself when it came to the finer things of life like expensive cigars and good brandy.

As Sebastian's eyes traveled the perimeters of the room, he found himself admiring the tasteful decorations and furnishings. He had expected nothing less, since it was well known that the Baron liked to surround himself with beautiful things. And beautiful women. He couldn't think about Royall now, not here in this madman's house. He was only grateful for the fact that the Baron had remained here in Manaus rather than return to the plantation. From what he knew about Alicia, no woman was safe around him.

Just the thought of another man touching Royall brought Sebastian to his feet, his face convulsed in rage. The Baron! If that weasel so much as touched a hair on her head, he would kill him with bare hands. He would choke the life from his body and laugh while he was doing it! Royall Banner was his! He decreed it!

Rivera's black rage was all the Baron saw when he walked through the foyer into the parlor. At that moment Sebastian was bigger than life, meaner than a cornered rat. Carlyle knew that physically he was no match for the younger half-breed. He'd have to use his brains, his wiles, anything, but he would have to get him out of the house!

"I don't believe we had an appointment, Rivera." Cautiously, he kept his walking stick at his side, swinging it gently. "I really don't have time to see you, not that I could imagine what business you have to discuss. You should have left your card when you discovered I wasn't at home. Or have you come to spy on me?" he demanded, his voice less confident than he would have wished.

"Spy on you? What makes you think I would be interested in your affairs? I already know what you've done." His last statement had the expected results, and he saw the Baron's hand go to his brow to wipe away the perspiration.

"Are you referring to the fact that I didn't run back to the Reino when some idiot announced a breakout of yellow jack?"

"He wasn't an idiot, Carlyle, and you know it. It's a pity you never went to the Reino to see what's become of it. Shall I tell you? You've lost everything. It's all over. There was a meeting several days ago, and I'm afraid we plantation owners intend to come down hard on you, Carlyle."

Hate spewed from the Baron's eyes as he stared at the face that so closely resembled his own. He hated Sebastian Rivera, hated him and wished him dead. As long as the man was alive, he, Carlyle Newsome, would never really be safe, and neither would the Reino.

"Bah! You can't hold me responsible for yellow jack. So a few Indians and blacks came down with it. So what? The weak always die to make room for the fittest. Don't stand there and tell me it's all over. I'm a wealthy man, and I've got resources to build over again."

"No, Carlyle, you *were* a wealthy man. Senora Banner is going to have her say about the management of the Reino from now on. It's over, Carlyle. Jamie's dead, and Carl is never coming back. You're alone."

"Leave my house, Rivera. I don't want anything to do with you. I never did." A lopsided sneer marked his face. "I know what you're after. I always have. You've noticed the resemblance between us, others have. Well, it won't work. I wouldn't give you the air you breathe, and I wouldn't give you anything else, either. Not my time, my money, or *my name!*"

"You goddamned, miserable bastard!" Sebastian thundered. "I wouldn't carry your name though I be damned to hell! There are those who believe you're my father, and in truth, I don't know if you are or not! I don't want any part of you or what you stand for. And what you stand for, Carlyle, has finished you here; the planters' association will see to it! Moments ago I told you Carl is never coming back, and it was the truth. He's on his way to Rio. An opportunity arose and he took advantage of it, with my assistance. Alicia is with him," he said quietly, watching the Baron's face for his reaction. "You didn't know that, did you? You thought Carl would come whimpering back to you. You're slime, Newsome, and I should kill you, here and now. But killing is too good for you. I know what you've done; Alicia came to me and told me."

Carlyle's mind raced. Rivera said Carl was with Alicia. No, it couldn't be! Not after he'd told Carl what kind of a woman she was . . . It was a trick! "You'll say anything to try to get back at me, won't you? You've had little to complain about all these years. Old Farleigh Mallard left you his land, his house, he even educated you—but you've always had your sights set on the Reino Brazilia. All these years you've thought I was your father and you've wanted to claim what you thought was your rightful inheritance. Carl is my son. Jamie was my son. You're nothing but a bastard, born on the wrong side of the covers. Was it my fault that your mother was a whore!"

Sebastian's fist shot out and his aim was true, landing squarely on the Baron's chiseled jaw, followed with alacrity by a solid punch to his midsection. Gasping and heaving, the Baron fell backwards onto the sofa.

"I should kill you right now!" Sebastian shouted, "but I won't. You don't deserve to die an honorable death. But your day is coming, Carlyle. You're not dead yet! And when that day comes, you'll give me the pleasure of watching you suffer. I believe in divine retribution, Carlyle. Furthermore," he hissed through clenched teeth, "I've never for one moment entertained the idea that you're my father. Now stand up and pretend to be a man. I have something else to say to you and I want you on your feet to hear it!"

The Baron struggled to his feet, one finely manicured hand holding his jaw. His eyes were full of hate as he stared at Sebastian. He waited.

"Carl won't be returning to the Casa. At my suggestion and with my help, he's decided to cut his losses. He's making a new life for himself and Alicia. If I have to, I will personally spend the rest of my life making certain the two of them are free of you. Alicia is of sound mind now, no thanks to you, and I intend for her to remain so."

"She's a whore! A slut!" the Baron roared.

"Wrong! Whoremaster that you are, you would like to think so. You forced yourself on Alicia. There were no choices for her. Don't ever malign her again, or you'll have to deal with me. Go back to your precious Reino and pack your things. You're finished."

"You think so, you bastard. Not yet. Royall will marry me and things will go on as before. I proposed to her the night of the Parradays' party. You should remember the party, Sebastian; that was the night she attacked you in the middle of the dance floor. Don't tell me what to do or where to go. And as for Carl, if he wants to live with a whoring twit, let him. They deserve each other. Now get your ass out of my house before I call the authorities. Oh, one last thing, Sebastian, I give you my word that Royall and I will name *our* firstborn after you. What do you think of that?"

"You mealy-mouthed, lying bastard!" Sebastian shouted. Rage engulfed him, causing him to lose all reason. His fist lashed out, knocking the Baron to the floor. Angrily, he reached down and pulled him erect. Again his fist shot out. Again and again he drove his fist into the Baron's soft belly. Each time his fist crunched bone, he cursed the most vicious words he knew.

"Senor! Senor!" the housekeeper had come running into the room, pulling his arms back to keep him from hitting the Baron again, to keep him from killing him. "Senor, please! You're killing him!" The housekeeper threw her weight against Sebastian, pushing her way between the Baron and this wild-eyed man whose fists were clenched, tough and hard knuckled.

The Baron took advantage of the woman's interference, backing away, cowering. His glance fell on his silver-handled walking stick, and he reached for it just as Sebastian brought his booted foot down on his hand.

"Fight like a man, damn you!" Sebastian cursed.

"Get out of here! Get out of my house!" the Baron's voice rasped, his cheek twitching.

"Damn right, I'm getting out of here. You're

the slime of the earth. But I'm warning you, you'll never marry Royall. Even if I have to kill you myself. I won't wait for someone else to do it for me!"

Heaving with exertion and rage, Sebastian straightened his clothing, and without another glance in the Baron's direction, he stalked from the room, his stride angry and purposeful. Royall had accepted the Baron's proposal? And he had felt so sorry for her while she lay so sick. The man was lying; he had to be!

A bellow of rage ripped from his throat as he visualized Royall in the Baron's arms.

Chapter Twenty-One

One weary day after another passed. Royall paced the wide veranda as she wiped at her perspiring brow. What was wrong with her? By now she should have been to town to see Mr. Morrison and get her affairs on the way to being settled. The heat was becoming unbearable as she paced the wide floor. A splash of color caught her eye behind one of the wicker chairs. With an effort, Royall bent down and reached beneath the chair. Her hands closed over something round and hard. When she held out her hand to inspect her find, she recoiled in horror. It was one of the scarlet and blue heads from a toy soldier. Before she could think or reconsider, she tossed it over the railing. How hateful the innocent piece of wood was; how dirty it made her feel. It was all over now. She had to put such thoughts from her mind and think of other things.

Dejectedly, she sat down in the white wicker chair. The crimson flowers on the rattan tables made her eyes ache. Other things. Other things meant the Baron and Sebastian. It was time to put her life in order and get on with whatever it was she was going to do. Tomorrow she would go to town and talk with Mr. Morrison. She would ask his advice and then follow it. On the way back from town she would stop by Mrs. Quince's plantation and perhaps stay for dinner and spend the night. If she had the nerve, the following day, she might, just might, stop at the Rivera plantation to see how the little girls were faring, especially Rosy. And that was another thing, she thought furiously; why hadn't Sebastian Rivera come by to thank her for returning the children? While there was no love between him and Jamie, it wouldn't have hurt him to stop by. I can't blame him, she muttered to herself. I'm just being selfish, wishing he would stop by so I could see him. He had no feeling for her, that was evident. Time and time again he had made a fool of her, and she had permitted it, even enjoyed it at the time.

Idly, Royall flicked at the pages of a book. She felt drowsy, unable to concentrate on the printed words in front of her. The heavy lashes lowered, and then she was asleep.

The sound of pounding hooves startled her later in the afternoon. Quickly, she sat up and rubbed her aching shoulders. She felt cramped and irritable, her damp dress clinging to her, making her perspire all the more. Moist tendrils of hair drooped over her forehead, giving her a gamin look. The very earth seemed to be shaking in front of the wide veranda. Perhaps it was Sebastian in one of his black fits of rage. If that was so, she would have to make herself presentable for his latest tirade against her.

Struggling from the wicker chair, she was halfway across the veranda when the rider came into view. Royall's eyes widened in shock. "The Baron!" she exclaimed. Should she run and warn Elena? A shadow fell across the bright floor. No need for Royall to call Elena, she was standing inside the door watching the rider dismount.

His gait was unsteady, his appearance such that Royall shuddered. There was nothing meticulous or dandyish about the Baron now. He was slovenly and filthy. A growth of beard straggled against his neck. It was his eyes that frightened Royall most as he stormed up the steps, shouting at the top of his lungs for Elena. Royall backed off several steps as Elena appeared from the doorway. Her hands were folded, almost as though she clasped them in prayer, below her waist. "Yes," she said quietly.

"Is it true?" the Baron bellowed.

"If you're referring to Jamie's death, yes, it's true. We buried him at sunup nine days ago."

"It's your fault, Elena, and you'll have to be punished for allowing Jamie to ride in the jungle.

You were in charge of the boy. I trusted you with his well-being. You let this happen!" he spat. Suddenly, he brought up his hand and rendered a mighty blow to the side of her head. Elena gasped and fell backwards, landing with a thump against the door frame. "That's just for starters," the Baron shouted. "I should kill you. But I won't. Prepare a bath for me. Now! Fetch me clean clothes and a bottle of brandy. Where is everyone?" he asked suddenly.

"If you mean the little girls, they're gone. Everyone is gone. Only Elena and myself, along with two stable boys, are left," Royall snapped angrily. She loathed the Baron for his rough treatment of Elena, who looked dazed, not comprehending what was going on. Her hand was massaging her temple above her ear. Dear God, what if she was really hurt. Then it would just be herself and the Baron.

The Baron whirled around as though noticing Royall for the first time. "What do you mean they're gone? Where did they go?"

"They were sent back where they belong, to Regalo Verdad. The others just left in the middle of the night. Don't ask me for an accounting of your slaves, Baron. You lost that right the night we were informed of the yellow jack. You remember, the night when you said it was some small uprising. Well, that little uprising, as you call it, wiped out this plantation. I didn't try to stop any of those who wanted to leave. In fact, I gave them my blessing. It's over; there's nothing left for you here. I plan to dissolve this partnership. Now, if you'll excuse me, I want to freshen up for dinner. In my room, Elena, if you're up to it. If not, I'll eat in the kitchen with you." The housekeeper nodded, the first sign of life Royall had noticed in her since the Baron stomped his way up to the veranda.

"You'll pay for this. I know that Rivera, that bastard, is behind all of this. He's wanted my people for years, and now, thanks to you, his wishes have been granted. Elena, send the stable boys to his plantation and order my people returned to me, or I'll have the law set on him within the day." It was an idle threat, and Elena knew it as did the Baron. It was something to say to save face in front of the American woman.

"I'm afraid that it's impossible. The Senora told you, everyone is gone. If you want anything from Senor Rivera, you will have to speak with him yourself," Elena said quietly as she went through the door.

"You sicken me," Royall hissed as she swept past him to follow Elena into the house. "Don't plan on striking me, for I'll give you back exactly what you mete out. I'm not Elena; I don't have to tolerate you. Not now, not ever. And, now, at this moment, I have the advantage. You're drunk!"

"How dare you speak to me in such a manner." His hand shot out.

Royall, halfway through the doorway, neatly sidestepped and then stuck out a long leg. The

Baron sprawled headfirst into the foyer. Curses rang through the stillness as Royall picked up her skirts as though he were vermin crawling at her feet. "Your position becomes you, Baron. Crawl and grovel, that's what you've been reduced to. Tomorrow it will be all over, Baron."

Hatred spewed from the Baron's eyes as he struggled to his feet. Vile curses followed Royall and would ring in her ears for hours to come.

"Elena, are you all right?"

"There's no need for you to concern yourself about my well-being, Senora. I can and will manage."

"I'm sure that you can, Elena. Please, let me help you with the water. I'll fetch it from the spring, and you can heat it. He does need a bath; he smells worse than all the jungle and stable put together. Elena, what are you going to do?" Royall asked in a troubled tone.

"Do?" Elena asked, puzzled at the question.

"Yes, do. Are you going to stay here and continue to take the Baron's abuse? I'm not saying he would kill you, but there is that possibility. He's insane! I know for a fact that Mrs. Quince has been trying to find a suitable housekeeper for some time. I'm sure that if I spoke to her she would be more than glad to have you. I don't want anything to happen to you, Elena. I would feel responsible."

Elena's dark eyes widened. "Senora, this is my home, the only home I've ever known. I couldn't leave for any reason. You need have no fear of the

Baron killing me. Believe me when I tell you that will never happen."

"Yes, I do believe you, but it doesn't make me worry less. I'll fetch the water, and while it's heating, I can help you with dinner."

"It really is most kind of you, Senora. Tomorrow things will be better."

"In a pig's eye," Royall muttered sourly as she made her way to the spring for the pails of water. "It will never be better."

On the afternoon after the Baron returned to the Reino, Royall was increasingly aware of the man's hostility. He watched her like a hawk, and as far as she could determine, he had had nothing to drink in the way of spirits since his return. As far as either Elena or herself knew, he had still not made a visit to Jamie's gravesite.

The Baron walked out onto the veranda and seated himself opposite her. Crossing one elegantly clad leg over the other, he leaned back, making a steeple of his fingers, and stared at her with sharp gray eyes.

"It's your fault my sons aren't here, Mrs. Banner. You and only you are responsible. First Carl and then Jamie. Carl would still be here on the Reino if you'd married him as I wanted. Jamie would still be alive if you hadn't tricked him into driving you back here the night of Rosalie's party."

Royall bristled and faced him squarely. "You had no right to interfere in my life, Baron. The only reason you wanted Carl to marry me was because if I were a member of the family you wouldn't be forced to give me an accounting of my shares. As for Jamie, yes, I did trick him into bringing me back here. I'd do it again if need be. People are alive because Elena and I nursed them. You're an evil man, Carlyle. I'm not an overly religious person, but I know that God has punished you by taking your sons from you." She saw his hands clench into fists and his eyes harden.

"I wouldn't threaten me, Carlyle. Mr. Morrison and the Quinces already know about my situation. In fact, they've all warned me that I might be in danger." Her voice became stern, authoritative, something the Baron was definitely not used to coming from a woman.

"I've already sent a message to Mr. Morrison in Manaus to see about dissolving my partnership in the Reino. You'll be well rid of me, I assure you. But I'm afraid you won't have much left. Without the support of the other planters, you're ruined. You know that, don't you?"

"Go! And good riddance to you! The Reino will be mine, and that's all I've every really wanted."

"You may have your plantation and it will crumble and fall around you. You'll rot along with it. Look in your mirror, Baron. You'll find the truth there. Sooner or later even Elena will leave you, and then you'll truly be alone, and God pity you. Now, if you'll excuse me, I think I'll go for a ride."

Royall walked down the few steps onto the

lawn. As she skirted some thick foliage, her foot touched a pebble. It wasn't a pebble but the head of the toy soldier. Royall bent to pick it up. How she hated the touch. She turned and walked to stand beneath the railing at the Baron's back. "Baron, turn around, I want to give you a small memento." She thrust out the tiny head and watched the Baron as he gazed at the small circle of wood. It was a mistake, Royall knew immediately. She had to get out of here before he came after her and thrashed her to death.

Royall saddled the big gray hastily. A strong wind whipped the heavy, emerald green foliage as the sun cast dappled patterns at the scattered pebbles at her feet. The gray snorted his impatience to be on his way. Royall gave him his head and rode from the clearing into the beginnings of a storm. Her thoughts as she rode leaped about in her mind as the strong wind whipped her hair about her face. She was glad she had made the decision to go riding, even if a storm was approaching. She couldn't stand another minute of the Baron's cruel and vengeful eyes.

The horse slowed as she veered to the left, taking Royall on a path she had never explored. A sudden depression settled over her as she allowed the gray to canter along at his own pace. She would miss Rosalie Quince and Alonzo. Even Elena, at first so distant and so resentful, had become a friend.

Most of all, she would miss Sebastian, regardless of his feelings toward her. She loved the man, respected him. Never to feel his arms around her or his mouth taking possession of hers again . . . Silently she grieved for what could have been.

Her attention was caught by a sudden drop of cold rain. She glanced upwards; there were dark, ominous clouds to the west. She had lost all track of time, and her first thought was to find shelter before the storm broke. Frantically, Royall looked about. Somehow the gray had wandered off the path and they were in the middle of a wide, overgrown meadow, the jungle on all sides. Elena had warned her of the sudden, terrible storms this time of the year.

The terrain was strange, and Royall knew she was lost. Her eyes raked the sky in panic. There was nothing to do but spur the horse forward and hope for the best. Suddenly, to her right, the stark outline of a dilapidated building appeared. Quickly, she reined in the horse before the decaying remains of the building. The jungle had advanced and smothered the darkened, charred beams of the once luxurious plantation. From the lines of the building and from the way Jamie had described it, Royall knew she was looking at the original Casa. Royall frowned. For some reason she had thought the entire building had been gutted. From where she was standing it seemed like the "big fire" Jamie spoke of had just ruined the south wing of the sprawling building.

It must have been beautiful in its day, Royall thought as she dismounted. Holding the reins, she led the horse inside the building, not wanting to leave him outside in the storm. Would there be snakes and rodents inside? She shivered at the thought. Seeing a stout tree branch at her feet, she bent to pick it up. What good it would be against a coiled hissing snake she didn't know, but she did feel better with it in her hand. It was getting darker by the moment. If only she had a candle. She must find a spot and settle herself before the storm let loose its rage. A place where she wouldn't fall and kill herself. When the storm lessened, she would take stock of her situation and explore this once grand house. The thought excited her. She had heard so many tales from Mrs. Quince about the wonderful balls that were held and the magnificent chandelier that was in the center hallway. The gray wickered in fright as she continued to lead him into the main building, which still had the roof intact.

A vicious rumble of thunder rolled across the sky, followed by a slash of lightning, making her jump in fright. If there was one thing in the world that frightened her more than snakes, it was a storm such as this. In the brief illumination from the lightning she had seen something that looked like a crate in the far corner of the room. She advanced slowly, one hand holding the reins of the gray and the other stretched in front of her to ward off anything in her path. The stick tapped the crate, and Royall heaved a sigh of relief. She sat down gingerly, her back to the wall, watchful eyes straining to penetrate the gloom for signs of strange and fierce animals seeking shelter from the storm.

Carlyle Newsome stared at the small circle in his hand. It was all that remained of Jamie. That Royall Banner should be the one to give it to him was almost more than he could bear. Everything was her fault. All this was her doing. She was responsible for the straits he was in. His thin, aristocratic face darkened with rage and his eyes popped from his head. Great cords rose in his neck, almost cutting off his breathing. His heart pounded and thundered in his chest as he stomped up and down the veranda, the tiny head clutched in his hand like a lifeline. She had to pay for all of this. He couldn't let her sail back to New England after all the trouble she caused him. He was destroyed; he was no fool. There were no pieces to pick up. No place to make a new start. She had ruined it all, and she would be made to pay even if he killed her. The thought pleased him. There was nothing he would rather see than Royall Banner dead by his hand.

"Elena," he shouted shrilly, caught up in his hatred.

"Yes," the quiet, cultured voice answered.

"Fetch me a bottle of brandy, and make sure the glass is clean. God's sake, woman, don't just stand there. What are you waiting for? I thought I told you to fetch me a bottle of brandy."

"Yes, sir. May I ask where the Senora is?" she questioned softly as she turned to leave.

"I have no idea. She handed me this," the Baron said, holding out his hand for Elena to see the small soldier head, "and then she rode off on the gray."

Elena's face drained of all color. How could she have been so remiss as to forget the one little head. She should have counted the soldiers and the decapitated heads. It wouldn't matter to Jamie, but it mattered to her. Lately she couldn't seem to do anything right. She also knew that the Baron had only showed her the little head to torment her, to make her suffer still more. How insidious he was. How she hated him. She had to keep her wits about her when she was with the Baron, and right now she had to serve him his brandy.

There was no expression on her face as she watched the Baron swallow the brandy. His face was hateful as he swore and cursed between swallows. "You should have warned the Senora of the approaching storm," Elena said quietly. "She's never seen one of our storms. The gray may throw her, and she could be injured."

"I couldn't be that lucky," the Baron spat viciously.

Elena frowned with worry over Royall. Surely the Senora would seek shelter when the storm hit.

"I see that you're worried. Very well, Elena, I'll search her out. Will that make you happy?" he asked, his voice already slurred from the brandy.

"No, that will not make me happy. You're in

no condition to ride, especially with the approaching storm."

"Don't tell me what to do! Remember your place, Elena. I don't want you to take care of me; you can't be trusted. I trusted you with my son and you let him die. How do I know that you won't follow me into the jungle and try to kill me," he said craftily.

Elena was shocked. Things were worse than she even imagined. He had never spoken to her like that before. But he was right about one thing: she would follow him into the jungle if he rode out. Not for him or his safety, but for the Senora. She owed her that much. After all, she had worked alongside the American during the fever and she knew what it cost the Senora to work as she did. She had saved the lives of many of Elena's people. Yes, she would follow the Baron, but only to save the Senora. Let the Baron think what he wanted. At this point he would listen to nothing she had to say.

"Yes, Baron," Elena said dutifully as she withdrew from the veranda.

"Saddle my horse. And do it quickly!" he called to her retreating back.

The wind attacked Elena as she made her way to the stables. She was forced to walk bent over, her shoulders hunched into the shuddering gusts. The horses were nervous and restless with the approaching storm. In minutes she'd saddled the Baron's favorite gelding, then saddled the roan for herself. Leaving the roan tied to the hitching post, she led the gelding out of its stall.

This time the wind lashed her from the back, slicing into her legs as she led the beast back to the Casa. The man was insane if he thought he could ride out in this weather in his condition. And she was just as mad for planning to follow him.

She watched from beneath the kitchen shelter as the Baron climbed on the horse. The wind buffetted him, but he remained seated. He dug his heels cruelly into the flanks of the horse, who immediately bolted into a gallop down the graveled drive.

Anger and hatred churned within him as he rode with his head bent. At least he could be thankful for one thing—the strong wind was clearing his head, making it possible to hate with a clear mind. And he did hate the girl with the blond hair and strong voice. He raised his head as the first drops of rain fell on his hands. Because of the storm, it was dim, almost dark. His eyes raked his surroundings. He too needed to seek shelter. She had come this way; he could tell from the trampled vines and from the way the leaves curled back on the foliage along the trail. She couldn't be going to the old Casa. As far as he knew, she didn't even know where it was located unless Jamie or Carl had told her.

The horse reared back, and the Baron almost lost his seat as a roll of thunder ripped through the sky. He dismounted and reached for the reins.

He would have to lead the horse and hope for the best. It wasn't far now to the old plantation. If he hurried, he could reach it before the storm attacked in all its fury. Without warning, he stumbled and fell, his ankle twisted in a long, curling vine. He shook his head to clear it and looked around. The banyan tree to the left of him made him wince. In the darkness he had miscalculated. He was still a good twenty-minute ride from the old Casa. Goddamn it to hell, he cursed as he got to his feet, only to be driven to the ground again as the storm unleashed its fury with a torrential outpouring of rain. He lay still, not moving, as the rain beat at him like so many pebbles. He moaned over and over as the rain beat against him. Men had been known to drown in such storms. He prayed he wouldn't be one of them.

Royall woke as the last rumble of thunder rolled across the sky. It was getting light again as the storm moved eastward. She sat up and massaged her aching shoulders. The gray stood placidly next to the crate. She sat back again and looked about the room. She almost wished she could transport herself back in time to when the house was full of gaiety and laughter. How beautiful it must have been. Even now, with watery sunshine filtering through the broken panes, she could see the detail of the room. She was suddenly hungry. Then she remembered the papayas she had stuffed in the saddlebags as she left the stables. Always there was a basket of fruit near the door for the boys to nibble on during the day. Elena had also cautioned her early on that she should always take fruit with her when she set out for a ride. She was thankful now that she had gotten into the habit. The gray nibbled daintily from her hand as she broke off pieces of the ripe fruit.

Royall sat back down on the crate and started to eat her own piece of fruit. Bored, she looked around the room pretending she was arranging furniture. Something was wrong, out of place. She grimaced; there was barely any furniture, so what could be out of place? For that matter, there were only a few darkened beams above, with most of the walls gone. As she chewed and sucked at the soft, sweet fruit, she scanned the farthest part of the large room. It didn't have anything to do with the walls or the lack of furniture. She let her eyes go to the floor. Aside from the rotting wood, there wasn't anything out of place or wrong as far as she could see. She looked overhead at the beams. They were fire blackened, but the chandelier remained intact. The dirty, grimy glass prisms still twinkled in the pale sunshine. She wondered why it had never been removed and brought to the new Casa when it was rebuilt. That was it. That was what was wrong, what was out of place. There was something wrong with the great crystal globe that hung from the center of the ceiling. There was something odd about it. What? Royall stood up, her fruit dropping to the rotting floor in her excitement. She craned her neck, first one way and then another. Something must have caught her eye, just the way the small soldier's head had sprung into her vision. Whatever it was, it was eluding her. She walked around the room, watching where she stepped, so she could view the chandelier from different angles. She could find nothing out of the way. In her exasperation, she decided that it must have been her imagination. She was just nervous and jittery after her confrontation with the Baron and then the storm.

Shrugging, she walked back to the gray, who was waiting patiently. She should be thinking about starting back for the plantation, and she was going to have a long ride ahead of her. No, not yet. She stood up and pulled the crate over till it was beneath the chandelier. If she stood on top of it and stretched to her full length, she could just reach the monstrous globe. She arched her neck backwards and looked carefully at the dirty crystal. There it was! When the sun hit the globe, a glint of red showed. That was what it was, the pink ray had caught her attention. Anxiously, she thrust her hand into the depths of the lighting fixture and withdrew a red, calf-bound book. What was it, and why was it hidden in such a peculiar place? Excited with her treasure, Royall climbed down from her perch and opened the book. The name Carlyle Newsome, Sr., was printed in large block letters inside the cover. Carlyle Newsome, Sr., was the Baron's father. Why would he hide his journal in such a strange place? Excitement and apprehension coursed through her as she made herself comfortable. The writing was small and cramped, but she could make out the words. How in the world had it remained intact all these years?

Royall started to read. It was a dull, boring account of the records of the plantation. She flipped through the pages till she came to a page that read: "I am disappointed in my son Carlyle. I fear it was a mistake on my part to send him away. He has just now returned home no better than when he left. He is such a trial to me." There followed more mundane things of no great importance. Then a later entry:

I find with my failing health that there are a few things I must do to set matters straight before I pass on. The boy Sebastian is my son. A son much loved and wanted by both his mother and myself. It was she herself who would not let our secret marriage be announced. She was wise in the way of an Indian. She had said her marriage to me would only hamper my life. I fear I listened to her, for I loved her dearly. She made me promise that Sebastian was never to hear from my lips that he was my son. And so he shall not. On the morrow I will ride into Manaus and leave the marriage paper with my solicitor, so that on my death Reino Brazilia will go to Sebastian Rivera, the name Rivera being his mother's family name.

Carlyle has disgraced himself with me. The lack of concern for human life that is displayed by him astounds me. Even after repeated warnings from me, his treatment of the blacks and Indians did not alter. When at last he washed his hands in the blood of another human being and felt justification was ample, I could bear it no longer. That is when I disclaimed Carlyle as my son, and I am much saddened.

My hopes for the continuation of my personal ideals and, indeed, my hopes for Brazil rest with Sebastian. I trust and believe his mother will raise him with an eye well trained to recognize human suffering. My old friend Farleigh Mallard, who knows of this truth, has told me he can see qualities in my young son that bear grounds for my hopes. The speculation concerning Sebastian and his mother and their relationship to old Farleigh make my old friend mirthful. People naturally assume, since my wife acted as chatelaine at Farleigh's plantation, Regalo Verdad, that he is Sebastian's father.

My appointment with Carlyle this evening is for the purpose of informing him of these facts. Any reprisals he wishes to make I will deal with myself!

Upon my passing, should you, dear Sebastian, ever find this journal, I want you to know that I loved you as only a father can love a son. As much as I loved your mother. You are my flesh. The flesh born of my love and the love of your mother. I have watched you grow from a child to a young man. I have watched you overcome any and all obstacles that met your path. For this, my son, I am proud of you. I ached to hold you and let you know that I was your father. What is past is past. Now, it is my turn to make amends.

Startled, Royall looked up from her deep absorption in the journal. She thought she had heard a sound. Listening carefully, she decided it was probably some jungle creature. She turned to her reading again, although there was little more to read:

At last my dearest wish is to come true. Sebastian will be my heir, even though my youngest son. I think I have made my decision honestly and fairly. Upon my last visit to the doctor, he advised me that death is near at hand. I only hope the grim reaper can hold off one more day. If not, then Carlyle will inherit the Reino and Sebastian will never know the truth.

The journal ended abruptly. Frantically, Royall leafed through the rest of the dry, crackling pages. They were blank. The old Baron's intuition was right. He had died before he could make matters right. Or did someone help him into the path of the grim reaper: Hadn't Victor Morrison said he suspected the Baron had murdered his own father? And here was the reason Sebastian resembled the Baron! Not because they were father and son, but because they were brothers! There was that noise again!

Royall sat still and listened, her eyes going to

the gray's hooves. He was still standing quietly, his large soft brown eyes closed. Then she heard it again, the sound of a twig snapping. A shadow fell across her lap. The sun took that moment to come out in full force, blinding her momentarily as it drove through the broken windows. The shadow advanced. The closer the dark form came, the better Royall could see. It was the Baron, holding a revolver in his hand! Royall gasped in fright.

"You followed me!" she accused. "Why?"

"Yes, I did follow you here, and you know why. I can't let you destroy all that I've built up. I want that journal!"

"You'll have to take it from me," Royall said bravely as she slid from the crate to stand next to the gray. She clutched the journal to her breast. This was Sebastian's life, and she would do anything to protect it.

"Then I'll have to take it. It's gone too far for me to back down now. For years I've searched for that journal. I've never felt safe, knowing it could be found at any time. Now, hand it to me before my fingers get nervous."

"Only over my dead body. I'm not giving this up. Sebastian is the owner of this book. Your father wrote it for him. I'll never give it to you. Never!"

"Fine. I'll just wait till you're dead and then I'll take it from you." He brought up the revolver and pointed it straight at Royall's heart.

Royall knew the Baron wasn't making idle

threats; he meant to kill her. She raised her arm and threw the journal through the open window into the lush growth of jungle. The Baron, taken momentarily off guard, looked in the direction of the flying book.

Seeing her chance, Royall picked up the long stout stick that lay at her feet and swung out and up with all the force she could muster, knocking the revolver from his hand.

The Baron looked at her with such rage that his eyes seemed to burst from his head. His face contorted, his complexion changing from florid red to purple. He couldn't seem to get his breath as he crumbled to the floor.

Frightened at what she'd done, Royall raced for the door. God, had she killed him? Horror-stricken, she froze in her tracks, watching as he lay there, moaning. Cautiously, she inched back to the spot where he lay, holding the stick in both hands, ready to defend herself. He looked terrible, close to death. His left eye was closed shut, the other remained open, staring, spewing hatred, even now. The left side of his mouth was drawn into a ghoulish grimace as he stared at her. A stroke.

Royall brushed her hair back from her face. She had to do something, find someone, get help! Regardless of what he'd done, he was a human being, and she couldn't let him die this way. Elena. She had to bring Elena!

Only as she led the gray out of the ruined building did she remember the little red book. Only after she had it in her hand would she ride for the housekeeper.

Elena was dismounting from the roan as Royall brought the placid mare to what was originally the front of the Casa. "I was just going to get you. The Baron's inside. He tried to kill me, and I protected myself by knocking the revolver out of his hand. He was in a rage and then he just fell to the floor. I think he's had a stroke."

"I know that he meant to do you harm, Senora. I followed him. The storm delayed me, as you can see. Wait here till I see to him."

Elena returned moments later. "You're right, Senora, the Baron has suffered a stroke as his father did. Between the two of us we must get him on the horse and take him as far as the Rivera plantation. Senor Rivera will lend us a buckboard to transport him back to the Reino."

"Elena, let me ride to the Rivera plantation. I don't think it's wise to make the Baron ride a horse. Neither one of us would be able to hold him steady. Sebastian won't like it, but he can hardly refuse. Please, Elena."

Elena cautioned Royall to ride carefully.

"I'll be careful. Will you be all right?"

"There's no need for concern, Senora. The Baron can't hurt anyone anymore."

Royall shuddered as she rode off in search of Sebastian Rivera. The gray streaked ahead, finally reaching the Regalo Verdad. Royall slid from his back and screeched at the top of her lungs for

Sebastian. He came on the run, his face fearful, anticipating trouble.

She told him about the Baron, and Sebastian summoned his foreman. Together they rode from the plantation; the foreman and two men followed in the low buckboard.

Royall rode ahead. She couldn't look at Sebastian; she couldn't bear for him to see how hurt she was that he had ignored her since that last night in his house when they had loved each other. Why was it she only managed to see him when she needed help? And why did he always help her?

Royall dismounted and raced ahead to the old Casa, Sebastian following. Within minutes the men from the plantation arrived. They carried a thick, woolen blanket. It was obvious to Royall and to Elena that they didn't relish their task; they were merely doing as they were told. There was no compassion anywhere for the Baron. Sebastian's dark eyes were inscrutable as he watched the men place the Baron on the blanket. Each man picked up the two ends of the thick blanket and hefted their burden. Elena said she would ride with the Baron in the buckboard; her horse would trail behind. Royall was left standing in the dimness with Sebastian.

"I want to thank you for coming to help. Elena herself would have thanked you. You must realize that she has been under a terrible strain these past weeks."

"No thanks are necessary," Sebastian said coolly.

"Perhaps not to you, but I feel it necessary," Royall said crisply as she watched for some sign of emotion to cross the face of the man she loved. And she did love him. She had loved him from the moment she set eyes on him when he was a roué, a dashing buccaneer.

Sebastian looked at Royall and winced inwardly. Why was it she always came to him when she needed help? Would she never come to him on her own, for her own sake? For a time he had thought . . . had hoped . . . but it was not to be; he could see that now. He was the fool, and he fell in love with her. He let his dark eyes widen in shock at the revelation. He loved the golden girl. She made his blood run hot and then cold, and he wanted her for now, for tomorrow, for the next day, and for every day of his life.

Boldly, he matched her steady gaze. "Since there is no further need of my services, I'll escort you to the main trail, and you can follow the buckboard. If you ever find yourself in like circumstances, feel free to call. I don't charge for my help," he said mockingly.

"Thank you, Senor Rivera," Royall replied, matching his mocking tone. "However, I doubt if that time will ever come. I've decided to return to New England." She felt physically ill with her announcement and suddenly regretted her words. She didn't want to return to New England. She wanted to remain here in Brazil . . . even if only

411

to catch a glimpse of his face from time to time. And to perhaps feel his arms around her at carnival once a year.

Hearing her words, Sebastian's world ended.

Royall groped in her saddlebag. "This belongs to you. I came across it this afternoon when I sought shelter from the storm. I read it. It was meant for your eyes, so I must apologize. At the time I didn't realize the nature of this journal. I almost died for this little book, Senor Rivera. The Baron would have killed me for it. Now it belongs to you. I give you back the life you never had, Senor Rivera. I hope it is some small comfort to you in the years ahead."

Quickly she reined in the gray and then spurred him to a full gallop. Rivers of tears rushed down her cheeks. Damn you, oh damn you, Sebastian Rivera. Damn you to hell!

Chapter Twenty-two

Sebastian sat in his study reading the journal for what he thought was the hundredth time. Already he knew the words by heart. He wasn't a bastard. He was legitimate, a true son. His mother had married the elder Newsome. Carlyle was his brother, half brother. Sebastian Rivera, no, Newsome, was legitimate. He couldn't believe the words. They were true. It was in black and white. He closed the journal and placed it precisely in the center of his desk. His eyes were riveted on what Royall had called his life. Royall. She had said she had almost died for the journal. She said she wouldn't be troubling him again, that she was going back to New England. Goddamn it, just when his life was starting to take shape, she had to go and ruin it. Damn fool woman. Leave it up to a woman and you might as well lay down and die.

How cold and aloof she had looked sitting on the gray. How beautiful. Goddamn it, why couldn't she see how he loved her? Couldn't she tell? By God, he wouldn't get on his knees to *any* woman! Maybe she wanted him to plead with her to stay. I'll be damned if I do that either. Bitch! What did she want from him? Why was she torturing him like this? Angry at his circumstances, he slugged down a gulp of brandy. His eyes watering at the fiery liquid, he stood up and shook his leg. Damn fool thing to do, it was his throat that was burning not his leg.

He felt like a fool. Another gulp of liquor made him feel better. Royall Banner wasn't going to torment him much longer. Did she have any idea what a sacrifice it was for him to give up Aloni? Did she have any idea of what it cost him to send the China doll packing? A goddamn fortune, that's how much. By God, he should demand his money back from her lawyer. The thought amused him, and he threw back his head and roared with laughter. He should just show her the list Aloni had presented to him. Royall Banner with two L's would sing a different tune when she saw how

413

much he had paid out. Perfume, powder, lip rouge, stockings, dresses for daytime, dresses for nighttime, shoes, unmentionables. By Christ, that was a laugh. Aloni didn't have an unmentionable to her name. Shoes, lots of shoes, the list had read. Jewels, jewels. A cape for the opera and a cape for day time and a cape to walk to market. By God, he had paid through the nose. And don't forget the goddamn spinet she demanded. The brandy bottle flew to his lips and he gurgled deeply. Well, he wasn't going to let her get away with it. Where was darling, beautiful Aloni now, he wondered pitifully. Probably in some garret starving to death, all because of Royall Banner. "My ass she's starving," he thundered drunkenly when he suddenly remembered the cash deposit the tiny girl had demanded. And he had just handed it over, glad to be rid of the tiny creature who had shared his townhouse for two years. He had suffered greatly when Aloni pocketed the money and said in her best little girl voice, "It is my pension, Sebastian." It was goddamn outright thievery, was what it was!

He was drunk. If anyone had a right to get falling down drunk, it was he. He laughed again, a deep, booming sound that brought his foreman on the run. His dark eyes took in the scene, and he smirked. The boss was drunk. Jesus couldn't wait to tell the others. Something good must have happened. It had been years since he had seen the boss so pie-eyed. It was good to see.

"Jesus, come in here. Fetch me another bottle of brandy and let's have a drink. I want to make a toast, and I want you to join me." Jesus grinned as he uncorked the bottle. "No, no, a bottle for you and one for me. We won't bother with glasses, takes too long to drink that way."

"What are we drinking to, Senor Rivera?"

"To the biggest damn fool in all of Brazil. Me!" he said triumphantly as he swallowed a hearty gulp of the fiery brandy. "You must have made this rotgut yourself, Jesus. It would take the hide off a water buffalo at fifty paces. Just the stink! The real stuff would kill him."

Jesus choked on the brandy and it dribbled down his chin. He wiped at the brandy with his shirt sleeve. If he was going to get drunk with the boss, he'd better do it neatly.

"And to . . . and to . . ." Jesus waited patiently. "What was I saying?" Sebastian demanded. Jesus shrugged. "I remember, we want to toast womanhood. Those goddamn creatures who make our blood boil. Don't ever look at a woman, Jesus. They can kill you with their eyes. Do you want to hear a story? It's a sad story but I'm going to tell you anyway. Pay attention, because I don't want the same thing to happen to you."

In between sips of brandy, Sebastian unburdened himself. "I tell you, there is no justice. Tell me the truth, Jesus. Do you think I'm a good man?"

Jesus leered drunkenly. "A very good man, Senor."

"Well, as one man to another, do you think Senora Banner should pay me back for what Aloni cost me? I did it for her. Now she's going back to New England where they have to wear lots of clothes."

"For you, Senor, is big problem," Jesus said knowingly.

"I tried so hard," Sebastian said pitifully. "I gave up everything. And what does she do, she's leaving!"

"You have big problem, Senor."

Sebastian drunkenly agreed.

Sebastian nodded his head. Christ, that was his head bobbing on his shoulders, wasn't it. Jesus looked strange; he couldn't have three ears. "I know what I'm going to do, Jesus," he said slurring his words. "Soon as it's light, I'm going to the padre and tell him to get my money back. Whatever he confiscates from the . . . the . . . two L's he can have half. Isn't that fair, Jesus?"

"More than fair. The padre will then know of all your wicked ways," Jesus said toppling from the chair.

"He can pray for my soul. Father Juan loves to pray for all the souls," Sebastian said virtuously. "Jesus, get up, we have to go to bed." Loud snores ricocheted around Sebastian as he peered down at his foreman. "If there's one thing I can't stand, it's a man who can't hold his liquor," Sebastian said in disgust.

416

Elena stared down at her patient. Slurred curses and epithets rumbled from his distorted mouth. Elena's facial features remained fixed, her gaze unblinking as she listened to his vicious tirade. How terrible he looked, how ugly with his drooping eye and pulled-down lips. He was a caricature of evil, she thought as she continued to hold his gaze. His words didn't matter now. He could say whatever he wanted and it would no longer affect her. The doctor Sebastian had sent had merely shook his head and cautioned her to be tolerant. He had left a sleeping draught for the bad moments, but that was as much as he could do. It would be dawn in another hour, the beginning of a new day, a new kind of life for the Baron. Would he adjust to his disability, or would he succumb to the inevitable? She shrugged one elegant shoulder and turned to leave the room.

"Skinny old crow, you make me ill with your black dresses and your hair in a roll on top of your head. Ugly witch," he managed to sputter to her retreating back.

Elena turned abruptly, visibly shaken by the scathing words. The Baron was unrelenting. "Go down to the compound and send me some beautiful young women to grace this death room. You're old, a hag! Much too old for my tastes. But I can remember when you were young, so young and beautiful." His good eye glittered with hate and malice in a way that always made her cringe with guilt and memories best forgotten.

"There is no one left to bring. Everyone is gone. Your mind has been affected with your stroke. I'm the only person that you will ever see until the day you die. Pray, Baron, that I do not go to my maker before he is ready for you."

"Hag! Old crow! Ugly woman," he rasped in a voice that lacked its previous timbre.

Elena swept down the hall with unseeing determination.

A few moments later Elena returned to the Baron's room, a startling transformation in her appearance. She was now attired in a low-slung skirt and short bolero, common to the native Indian. Time had been her friend rather than her enemy. Her slim torso was as graceful as a young girl's, and her unbound breasts were high and softly rounded beneath the light fabric of her bolero. She paused an instant before she opened the door. With an unhurried gesture she opened the door and took two steps into the lamp-lit room. In a throaty whisper she called the Baron by a name that was known only between the two of them.

The Baron turned as though in a dream. Was he dreaming? Elena stood in the half light of the room with a secret smile on her lips, inviting him, a slim arm raised in greeting.

To his eyes she was as beautiful as she had ever been in youth. Sweet honeyed skin that tempted a man's hand to graze the velvety surface. Supple, clean unhindered lines of her figure promised passionate supplication. She was a girl again and he . . .

418

The Baron's eyes traveled beyond her to the mirror on his dressing stand. An old man, a crippled man, who would never enjoy the delights this vision of sensuousness was presenting, gazed back at him. And beneath the covers he felt a stirring, a stiffening he had thought he would never know again. The manly prowess he had considered lost, gone, regardless of what woman he was with, had returned for Elena. For the one woman who would never take pity on him.

Now he understood. At last the devious workings of Elena's hatred for him were clear. Now the tide had turned, and she would make him suffer the way he had made her suffer for the years of unrequited love. His anger moments ago had added additional fuel to her fire. There would be no forgiveness, no amount of begging would ever change things between the two of them. He understood.

Elena would remain at his side, the perfect servant, never more a friend or lover. And while she went about her duties, she would mete out the cruelest of punishments ever inflicted upon a man. She would taunt him with her loveliness, and while her attitude would be subservient, she would accept with a quiet smile all his vile words and inclinations. All the while joy would course through her blood. He would be hers. His loins would ache for the feel of her, and she would deny him. This was to be his punishment.

He read divine revenge in Elena's eyes.

Elena swayed closer to the bed, careful to stay

out of the Baron's reach. She dropped gracefully to her knees, her long satiny hair spilling down her chest. She locked eyes with the Baron. "I was fearful that you wouldn't understand," she said in a throaty whisper.

The Baron struggled for speech, and his face became contorted with the effort. "Why?"

Elena drew herself erect to her full height, a zealous light burning in her eyes. She stared at him for a long moment before she answered his question, and her reply rendered him senseless as he realized the full import of what she said.

"For Jamie."

As the Baron gasped at her words, Elena glanced through the half-open drapes. Dawn. It was fitting that the past moments had come at such a perfect time. A smile played about her lips when she noticed Sebastian Rivera ride through the gates. Her smile widened, and a spark of pleasure ignited itself within her. The pleasure that leaped in her was for Royall Banner.

Royall woke feeling sweaty and clammy. It hadn't cooled at all during the long, unbearable night. Soon it would be dawn. Perhaps if she got up and sat on the balcony outside her room she might feel a slight breeze. Hastily, she drew on the scarlet dressing gown and slipped from the bed.

She sat quietly, watching as dawn crept over the jungle to advance on the Casa. Pearl gray shadows cobwebbed the garden as the brilliant blooms woke to life. The jungle itself came to life as birds awakened to another day. Would she ever get used to this place? Perhaps if she made up her mind to stay, she told herself. But that wasn't likely. The Casa now belonged to Sebastian Rivera, and there was no way she was going to live off his bounty. No, she would go back where she belonged and make a new life for herself. This then was nothing more than an interlude. A time where she had come of age, awakened to her full potential. She had arrived in Brazil a young girl and she would be leaving a woman. She had grown here in the jungles of Brazil, and she would always be thankful for that.

Suddenly, a thunderous shout split the air. Sebastian!

"There you are. I'm calling on you!" Sebastian shouted happily as he teetered on his horse.

Oh, God, not again. He was drunk. Quickly, Royall rose from the chair and raced through the house and out to the courtyard. "You're drunk!" she shouted.

"Of course I'm drunk, do you think I don't know that? I have a right to be drunk. I'm"—his mind searched for the right word—"legitimate. That's worth drinking to, Senora Royall Banner with two L's."

"You're disgusting," Royall snapped.

"That too," Sebastian laughed. His eyes were crossing and he felt light-headed. Quickly he removed his hat and swept it in front of him with a wild flourish.

"Why are you wearing that silly hat?"

"The sun," he answered haughtily.

"It's dawn, there's no sun."

"Rain? Keeps my neck dry."

"You oaf, the rain was yesterday. Get down off that horse before you fall off and hurt yourself. You look as though you need coffee and something to eat."

"That's not what I need," Sebastian leered at her from the horse.

"Well, that's what you're going to get," Royall said, nervously checking the tiny jeweled buttons on her dressing gown, annoyed to find they were open from the hem to above her knees.

Sebastian swore in disgust as he slipped from the horse and grinned at Royall. "Why do you think I came here?"

"God only knows, but I wish you would get on that horse and go someplace else and torment someone else."

"God knows and now Father Juan knows. You're the last, but that's all right because," Sebastian enunciated clearly, "you are trespassing on my property."

"Ha!" Royall snorted. "I should have known. At first light you came to claim what's yours. Fine, you can have it. I knew it, I just knew you would come here. You want my house and my body. Well, you aren't—"

"Shhh," Sebastian said laying a finger to his lips. "Not in that order. I can take the house any time. I want . . . " he lurched for her and missed.

He righted himself and threw back his head, laughing uproariously.

"Get out of my sight. I can't bear the sight of you. You can have your plantation and the Baron. He's your responsibility now. I'm leaving."

"Not before you pay me the money you owe me," Sebastian said, wagging a finger under her nose.

"What money?" Royall screeched.

Sebastian rolled his eyes. Both hands dusted the humid air. "The money for the capes, the shoes, the dresses, the spinet, the . . . the un . . . those things Aloni . . . all that stuff you wear under the dresses—those things. Jewels," he went on undaunted, "And the cash settlement. I want it now!" Sebastian roared.

"What cash settlement?" Royall demanded hotly.

"When I leave here I'm going to Father Juan and tell him you—you reneged. Pay up!" He thundered.

"You're a contemptible bastard. I won't give you anything! Go to your Aloni, to that infant, and get it from her. Get away from me and go back to your jungle," Royall spat, as she danced away from his reaching arms.

"Damn fool woman!" Sebastian shouted. "I can't ask Aloni for the money, I gave it to her. And all those other . . . things."

"That's your problem. You gave her the money and what did you ever give me? Well, I'll tell you, Senor Sebastian Rivera, all you ever gave me was a stiff neck and a broken heart. Now, get out of here, you make me sick."

"Sick?" Sebastian was instantly contrite. "Does that mean you won't marry me till you're well. When will that be?"

"Marry you? Marry you?" Royall shrilled. "After what you've put me through, I wouldn't marry you if you were the last man on earth."

Sebastian waved his arms about wildly. "Damn fool woman, you'll be the death of me yet. Look around you, I *am* the last man. The Baron doesn't count," he said leering at Royall. "Now, what's your answer?"

"The answer is no. N-O. First, you use me, then you abuse me. You led me on, let me think you cared for me, and all the while it was that . . . that infant in your townhouse that you ran to. She . . . she even attacked me and you didn't do a thing about it. Damn you, you used me. I won't tolerate that from any man. You are a bastard and I loathe the sight of you. Go ahead, you came here to make all of us ashamed of ourselves. You're the rightful owner and you can throw us out. Who cares! I'm leaving this godforsaken place anyway, and I'm never coming back. Bastard!" she seethed.

"You're a bitch!" Sebastian spat harshly. "I came here to ask you to marry me, and you call me a bastard. Damn woman, there's no pleasing you?"

"Why didn't you try asking me when you were sober. Oh, no, you have to get drunk and make an ass of yourself. I said I won't marry you and I mean it. And as for your 'cash settlement,' you can just hold your breath. Better yet, I'll give you *my* shoes, *my* dresses, *my* capes, and *my* unmentionables! That's fair. Get the hell out of my way, you drunken lout, before I knock you over and stomp you to death."

Sebastian backed off. "You would, wouldn't you?" The thought was so appalling, he backed off another step.

"You're damn right I would." Royall gathered up her dressing gown and started around him. A long arm reached out for her and pulled her toward him. Royall screeched angrily.

"For God's love, will you shut up? You are the goddamnedest noisiest woman I've ever come across. Have you no pity for a man's ears? Shut up. I don't want to hear another word out of your mouth."

"Fine, fine, you won't hear another word from me if you just let me go."

"Ha! You think I'm so drunk I'll fall for that little trick. Well, you're wrong. I'm holding onto you till you shut that mouth of yours."

"Look, it's shut," Royall grimaced as she clamped her lips together.

"It's temporary," Sebastian grinned. "I know how to make you be quiet." Slowly he lowered his head till his lips were but a hairbreadth from hers. "See, you're all aquiver. Works every time."

With one mighty shove Royall pushed him away, unmindful of the gaping dressing gown. A long, creamy leg struck out. Momentarily caught off guard, Sebastian felt his heart hammer in his chest. He had forgotten what the sight of her satiny flesh did to him.

"Ha! You son-of-a-bitch! *That's* what works every time!" Royall said, dangling one shapely leg in front of Sebastian's eyes.

"Ladies never curse like that, especially to their intended," Sebastian said in a pained voice. "Where did you hear such a term?"

"From you," Royall hissed. "Now this is the last time I'm going to tell you to get away from me."

Sebastian sobered instantly. He didn't know whether it was her tone or the words, but he knew that she meant exactly what she said. All signs of inebriation were gone. One quick stride and he had both arms pinned at her sides. "I'm tired of this play-acting. I came here to ask you to marry me because I didn't have the nerve to do it when I was sober. I'm legitimate now. Before I couldn't ask you to bear my name. Now I can. As for this Casa, I don't want it. I never wanted it. It can rot here into the ground for all I care. Carl and Alicia can have it, makes no difference to me. The only thing that makes a difference to me is you."

Royall was stunned by his words and acted accordingly. "You miserable bastard, you . . . you . . . You tricked me! You weren't drunk at all. Curse you, why must you torment me like this?" Royall lashed out angrily.

426

"If you don't shut up, I swear to all that's holy that I'll—"

"You'll what?" Royall taunted.

Before she knew what was happening, the scarlet gown was ripped from her shoulders, exposing her full, rounded breasts. Another ripping sound, and the silky fabric slipped down to her feet. Royall gasped as she tried to cover her bosom. "Now maybe you'll shut up when you have something else to occupy your mind. I suggest you find something decent to wear. Father Juan will be arriving any second now to marry us. I hardly think a bouquet of flowers will be sufficient."

An inferno of angry fire ripped through Royall. She forgot her nakedness as she lashed out with both fists. "I'll show you you can't treat me like you do one of your whores." With lightning-like speed she brought up her knee with all the force she could muster. "How do you like that, you lecherous old tom cat. That should quiet *you* down for a spell. When Father Juan arrives, if he does, I'll ask him to pray for you."

"How could you do that to me," Sebastian gasped as he doubled over in pain.

"How? Like this," she said bringing up her other leg. This time Sebastian was too quick for her. He grabbed her leg at the ankle. Both of them went down onto the spikey emerald grass. Royall had the advantage as she rolled away from him time and again, only to be pulled back. She was suffering no pain and could make use of all her muscles as she flailed away with both fists. She was finally out of his reach and on her knees. Sebastian was rocking back and forth, his hands holding his groin. Suddenly he laughed, a great, booming sound that stunned Royall. It was probably another one of his damnable tricks. "It hurts like a son-of-a-bitch," he managed through gritted teeth.

"You deserve that and more," Royall said standing erect. "How dare you treat me like one of your whores. How dare you!"

"Shut up, Royall. Can't you let me die in peace. I am going to die. You killed me," he managed in a trembling voice.

"If you're dying, why are you talking?"

"Because you deserve to listen to someone besides yourself for a change. You may have crippled me for life. We may never be able to have children. I'll wager you never thought of that."

"What children?" Royall asked as she gathered some brilliant scarlet and yellow flowers. Demurely, she held them between her breasts. "I'm ready when you are," she said quietly.

Sebastian rolled over. His eyes widened. "Where are your clothes?"

A look of disgust washed over Royall's features. "There," she pointed, "where you ripped them off my back. You did say Father Juan was coming here to marry us. Make up your damn mind, Sebastian, before I change mine."

Sebastian grappled for words. "You aren't . . . you wouldn't . . . you can't . . . the padre will . . ."

428

"I'm not budging. You placed me in this condition and I'm staying this way. I'll leave it up to you to make a suitable explanation to Father Juan."

"Royall, if you don't shut your mouth, I swear I'll . . ."

"What will you do, Sebastian?" Royall purred, her voice throaty and inviting. "Don't tell me, show me. Before Father Juan gets here."

Epilogue

Her name was Royall. And the gifts she brought were befitting a king. She was his wife now, but always she had been his wife in spirit. Ever since that night in Rio de Janeiro when they shared the miracle of loving and giving to one another.

The sounds of the jungle outside the window were familiar songs of the night. The wind stirred the trees, and off in the distance there was a baby's cry. Their child. Born of love and bearing his father's panther's head and his mother's amber-flame eyes. A blessed child.

He listened for the sound of her footsteps padding quietly across the Persian carpet. His senses were alert and sensitively attuned, every nerve vibrating with anticipation. Soon, he told himself, she would come to him, in all her glorious, golden splendor. The sheets would rustle as she climbed into bed beside him, time would cease to have meaning, and his world would fill with the nearness of her and the love they brought to each other.

Soon, he would touch her, adore her, devouring her in a ritual of complete abandonment and adoration. The dim light in the room would somehow be brighter, and as her fingers traced those places she loved so well, he would know she surrendered herself completely and totally to him. And at the very last, when she whispered his name, they would become as one. One heart, one soul, one desire. Together they would chart the heavens and travel in worlds known only to those who truly love. And each time they rediscovered the other, tasting, touching, giving. If the world knew her as his wife, he knew her as his woman. Passionate, indomitable, courageous. Forever, his Royall Banner, possessor of the key to his life, his heart. A woman whose lusts equaled his own.

The door on the far side of the room opened, allowing a brighter shaft of light to pierce the dimness within. She stood in the doorway, knowing the backlight outlined her beautiful body, allowing it to bathe her silhouette and edge it with flame. Her dressing gown was a vibrantly red silk, bringing out the golden hair hung about her shoulders and over one breast, making her appear virginal, denying the message he read in her eyes. She had told him once that virginity was not a condition of the body but rather a state of mind.

And she was right. For all her lusty appetites, Royall was untouched, pure, fresh. The years would age all mortals, but her bloom was frozen in eternity. She held her secret of agelessness and guarded it closely. For hers was a captive innocence that defied the tick of time.